His Accidental
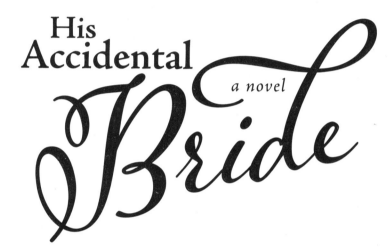
a novel

CAROLYN TWEDE FRANK

Covenant

Covenant Communications, Inc.

Cover image *Historical Woman Holding Letters in Countryside* © Ildiko Neer / Trevillion Images

Cover design copyright © 2021 by Covenant Communications, Inc.

Published by Covenant Communications, Inc.
American Fork, Utah

Printed in the United States of America
First Printing: January 2021

27 26 25 24 23 22 21   10 9 8 7 6 5 4 3 2 1

ISBN 978-1-52441-350-7

♠

Chapter 1

DOROTHY GLANCED AT THE CARDS the man in overalls held as she placed his drink on the poker table. *Two pairs: nines and sevens.* It wasn't much, but it was enough. She'd seen the other hands. With the emptied tray propped on her shoulder, and her heart just as empty, she moved around the table to relay the information to Vincent. Five years in second-rate Missouri saloons, being forced to cheat people for him, had only served to make her numb and loathe her brother.

The air she inhaled, thick with cigar smoke and the stench of cheap liquor, incited a cough. She turned her face away from the poker table and covered her mouth. The saloon bustled with customers, despite the peeling wallpaper behind the bar, the thick dust on the coal-oil chandelier, and the crack running the length of the front window. The howl of wind whistling through the swinging front doors added to the din.

She gazed across the room but barely saw her deceived employer, Walter. Gray hair, bushy mustache, and the grouchiest old bartender this side of the Mississippi, he stood behind the bar, pouring drinks like nothing was wrong. She wished she could tell him, warn him. Maybe he could even help her get away from Vincent.

Practicality once again swept away her desire to flee. She was a criminal, just like her brother. Vincent's words, words she'd heard countless times over the years, haunted her, adding to the impossibility of going: "You can't leave. You owe me. You could never make it on your own. Where would you go?" He was right. Where would she go, and how could she provide for herself? Walter couldn't help her. Neither would she want him to; then he too would be breaking the law.

She turned back to the table, needing to resume her task, or Vincent would make her pay for her distraction later. Instinct raised her hand to her eye. She could feel the thick layer of makeup and was glad it hadn't worn off. The bruise still felt sore to her touch. But her heart ached all the worse.

On Vincent's left, the man in overalls threw in a chip. "I raise."

She walked around the table, touched Vincent's left shoulder, and cleared her throat once. Hopefully he remembered this new signal for who held the winning hand. She tapped her finger twice against his rust-red jacket—the sign for two pairs. "Could I get you another drink, sir?" she said in her false, high voice. "You know the whiskey sometimes runs out by nine—at least, the good stuff." Her voice cracked from the stress. This new way of indicating the high card wouldn't always work. She glanced at the other players to see their reactions. Not a flinch, glare, or movement could be seen. She let out a pent-up breath.

"No, I'm good right now," Vincent said, telling her he had the game under control.

She surveyed the saloon to determine where next she should go. Four poker tables, one in each corner, each bustling with drunken men and cards. Vincent's table sat in the darkest corner, nearest the back of the room. So fitting. Tables one and two, by the front window, showed a variety of half-full glasses and no immediate need for her. A handful of scraggly looking men had barely sat down at table three. She walked over to it, a mere four steps away, and took drink orders as she listened in on table four's conversation. She could hear chips being thrown in and presumed they were from the three men sitting between Vincent and the man in the overalls. Vincent spoke next, tossing in two. "I meet and raise."

The man in overalls pushed two chips into the pile. Then the three other men each folded as Dorothy set her sights on the bar to fill a round of drinks.

"Call," Vincent said. "Two pairs."

Dorothy walked slowly, glancing at Vincent's game. The man in overalls spread his cards across the table. His eyes held a look of hope atypical of most men she encountered at the poker tables. For that matter, the rest of him looked out of place sitting there between a man in a fine-tailored pinstriped suit and Vincent with his expensive calfskin jacket and wicked grin. This fellow wore worn-out overalls on his large frame and a worn-out but gentle expression on his unshaven face.

Vincent took a puff on his cigar and laid down his hand. "A pair of kings and a pair of fives," he said, widening his grin, the cigar dangling from one side of his mouth. He reached across the table, ready to sweep the pile of chips his way.

"Hold on there a minute," the man in overalls said. He slapped the table in front of Vincent's cards. "Two wrongs don't make a right." He pointed to a king of hearts and queen of spades. "That ain't no pair."

Dorothy stopped cold. Had she not given the correct signals?

No, Vincent had botched things again! It was obvious he'd pulled the wrong card from his sleeve. She chewed on her lip, ready to continue to the bar, but Vincent's eyes met hers, demanding she help smooth things over. Dorothy hesitated momentarily and stepped over to Vincent's table. "Is there anything else I can get you fellows as long as I'm heading to the bar?" she asked, her voice flat.

"Not for me," Vincent said with a fake laugh. "Unless you got a pair of spectacles." He pushed the small pile of chips toward the man in overalls. "Sorry. This is yours."

"Can I get anything else for you? Maybe some pretzels?" she asked the man in overalls. Their eyes met, and she could see sadness emanating from them. Why did that surprise her so and make her stop and wonder why? Detecting such feelings only made her situation worse. Oh, it would be wonderful to have the luxury to be nice. But she didn't. She was in no position to help—not when she desperately needed help herself.

"No, thanks," he responded in a weary tone.

She steeled her nerves and looked at Vincent. "Maybe you'll have better luck with the next hand, sir," she said in her fake voice. Hopefully she'd set each of the players up so as to not be suspicious when Vince won the next hand. After making the mistake of pulling the wrong card, he'd be mad—at the world and at her. Winning soothed his anger.

She reached her hand again to her eye. With a glance around the table, she said, "Any of you other fellows care for some pretzels?"

"I'll take some," a man wearing a black cowboy hat that held not even a smudge of dust said.

"That sounds fine and dandy to me too, little lady," Vincent said, more to the other four men around the table than to her. "But please, gentlemen, allow me to step outside for a moment, to, ah, relieve myself before we start the next hand."

"Go ahead," the man in the black hat said. The other men waved Vincent onward.

When Dorothy returned with the pretzels, Vincent was still gone. She sized up three of the men with a sidelong glance: a fine-tailored, pinstriped suit, a solid gold pocket watch, an expensive jewel-studded black cowboy hat. These men could afford to play with Vincent. They sat there, talking to each other with foul language about women and money, sipping on their drinks, waiting.

The man in overalls, however, gazed off into the distance, seemingly lost in his thoughts.

She figured him to be a farmer, like her father had been, and lowered herself into the vacated chair. Vincent would be gone for at least another minute or two, trying to find a secluded place where he could readjust the hidden cards in his sleeves and in the pockets of his pricey jacket. Pushing aside her fears, she turned her attention to the man in the overalls. He drew her concern.

"What's a fellow like you doing at this table?" she asked in her normal voice. "This is high-stakes poker. You could literally lose the farm here, if you know what I mean." She motioned with a sweep of her hand to his well-worn overalls caked with mud and manure.

The man pulled his gaze away from the ceiling and focused on Dorothy. "I need lots of money and fast," he said with a faraway look in his reddened eyes.

Dorothy kept her tone light. "Problems on the farm, eh?"

"My wife died givin' birth six days ago."

"Oh." All affected mirth slipped from Dorothy's voice. She sucked in a breath through her teeth as she relived the moment ten years ago when she'd been told her mother had died giving birth. "I'm so sorry, mister."

"My neighbor's been helpin' me with the baby, but she can't do it no more." He took a long swig of his drink. "I gotta hire the baby a nursemaid or get myself one of those mail-order brides. Either of them things takes money." He mechanically set the empty glass back onto the table.

"Oh, mister, that's the saddest story I ever heard coming from one of these poker tables. Most of these sorrows come from a man's own undoing." She stood, her eyes shooting toward the door, knowing Vincent could walk back into the saloon at any moment now. She glanced over to the bartender. She needed to get back to serving drinks. "I wish I could help you." The words spilled from her mouth with sincerity. She didn't want anyone to experience what her father had gone through. What she had gone through. "But I don't know how. I *can* give you some advice though. Gambling's not the answer." *Especially not at this table.*

She scuttled to the bar to pick up a tray of mugs filled with beer, set out and waiting for her. "Sorry," she said to Walter as she approached, dreading his rebuke after work. She knew she needed to give more attention to her job as a saloon girl, but it was hard.

"Just get 'em served." Walter scowled, and she hurried to do as he said, loathing every minute.

Vincent acted like he owned her. And to a great extent, that was true. When her father had died of typhoid soon after she'd lost her mother and baby sister, Dorothy had found herself on her own at age eleven. So she'd sought out her only brother. She had hardly known Vincent at the time, being barely five when he had left home as a troublemaking fifteen-year-old. Reluctantly, he'd taken her in and immediately put her to work begging on the streets to pay for her keep. Nonetheless, he'd put a roof over her head and saved her from a possible life of an even worse hell. As her legal guardian, something he constantly reminded her of, her allegiance was to him first. He had insisted she take this job—and others in the past—to serve drinks as a cover.

Vincent strutted in, dusting the lapels of his jacket with a careful flick of his wrist. His darkened eyes met Dorothy's, telling her to prepare for another round, and he didn't intend to lose this one.

Dorothy fetched the tray and carried it over to table three, grateful he hadn't caught her talking to the man in overalls. She divvied out the drinks, beer sloshing to and fro in the mugs as she flirted with each man to look preoccupied, keeping her eyes and ears tuned to Vincent at the adjacent table. "Hey, pretty lady." Vincent raised his hand in the air. "How about you fetch me and my friends here a round of beers. On me."

At table three, Dorothy slapped a man's hand as it wrapped around her waist. "Sorry, fellow, I've got to get this other table some drinks." Jumping out of the frying pan and into the fire, she rushed to the bar.

By the time she arrived at Vincent's table with five mugs of beer on her tray, the cards had been dealt.

"I'm good." The man in the jeweled cowboy hat held up his hand toward the drink before she could set it down. She had to lean to one side to see his cards and hoped no one noticed.

The man in the pinstriped suit nodded his approval at the beer. She stole a glance at his cards as he turned toward her and gawked at her for a moment.

She brushed her fingers against the hand of the man with the watch as she served his drink. It worked; his cards opened up, and she saw all five.

The draws were made. She made sure she caught a glimpse of those cards too.

Vincent started the bidding with one chip.

Flirting wasn't necessary with the farmer. He held his cards fanned out, not pulling them in close to himself. He stared at them more than once. It was no wonder; he held a straight flush: nine, ten, jack, queen, king—all in spades. Only a royal flush could beat it. "I'm in," he said in an even voice. He tossed in a chip to meet the current bid. Then another chip. "And I raise."

"I fold," the man in the pinstriped suit said.

The man with the jewel-studded hat tossed in a single chip without a word. Dorothy walked behind him and scratched her cheek three times to indicate he had three of a kind. Then she flexed seven fingers, one of her old signals for three sevens.

Vincent glared at her, glancing at the farmer for a split second. He wanted her to give him that hand too. She walked past the man with the gold watch instead, rubbing her nose and then flicking it with a single finger: a single pair—junk. She didn't even bother giving Vincent the signal for eights. The man threw in a chip.

It was Vincent's turn. His eyes drilled into Dorothy.

Numb from seeing that dark expression day in and day out, she felt like telling him to just fold. They'd survive without winning this hand.

But she knew that look all too well. He planned on winning this hand, and he expected her response now. If he didn't get it, she would likely not be able to sleep that night. She cleared her throat, hoping he'd buy the signal for her not being able to see all the farmer's cards. The venom in Vincent's eyes told her he didn't buy it.

The man in the jewel-studded hat glared at Vincent. "Your turn." Vincent slapped down another chip. "I raise," he said in an even voice.

But Dorothy could sense his anger even from the opposite side of the table. She tried to look nonchalant despite her angst. "Can I get you fellows anything else?" she said, trying to justify her presence. Walter kept looking her way. A tray of drinks sat on the edge of the bar, waiting for her to deliver it to table one.

Vincent glared at her. It was a fleeting glance, but it communicated volumes. He would win, and she must stay and help him. Or else. And if she lost favor with Walter, they'd move on to a new town.

Emotions that had deadened by years of suppression flared to life. She loathed this. She hated ruining people's lives to put bread on the table and fancy clothes on Vincent's back. The farmer held not only a winning hand but the hand of a lifetime, dealt to him fair and square; Vincent had not been the dealer. She knew her brother could beat the farmer if she revealed the straight flush. But everything inside her screamed for her to stay silent. Her mother had taught her better than this.

"Dorothy!" Walter's deep voice boomed through the clank of glass and the din of coarse language that filled the saloon, and she jumped.

"Sorry. Coming, Walt," she said with sufficient volume to reach both him and Vincent. She weaved through the crowd, more than pleased to keep the crotchety old man behind the bar happy.

With the loaded tray now balanced on her shoulder, she padded carefully to table one, by the front window, listening in on every word coming from the neighboring poker game at Vincent's table.

"I'll meet your bid and raise," the man in overalls said to the *click* of two chips landing on the pile.

The man with the black hat cleared his throat. "I fold."

A single chip fell onto the pile. "I'll meet you," the man with the gold watch said.

Dorothy's back stiffened as she bent over to serve the last drink at the window table, knowing it was Vincent's turn.

Vincent didn't respond, except with a quick clearing of his throat; he was waiting for her.

Dorothy cringed and turned her attention to an unshaven man who reeked of tobacco, sweat, and swill. "My but that's a handsome face you've got under that scruffy beard." She set down the last drink and reached up to stroke the man's face. A split second later he pulled her onto his lap—exactly the diversion she'd hoped for. Though repulsed, she remained there, leaning as far away from his whiskey breath as possible as she tuned in to Vincent's voice.

"I meet and raise," he said.

The sound of Vincent's chips joining the growing pile worried Dorothy.

"I'll meet your bet and raise it two more," the man in overalls said.

"I fold," the man with the gold watch said.

Dorothy jumped off the drunken man's lap and playfully swatted his hands away, careful not to glance at table four; she couldn't chance meeting Vincent's eyes. She couldn't hear his chips joining the pile because of a train whistle in the distance, but she knew the chips would be there.

"I call," Vincent spoke with an edge of cockiness.

Dorothy imagined the next few minutes unfolding. She'd seen Vincent's hand, seen the only cards of value he held were a pair of kings. He'd make the best of those with the cards up his sleeves. That's how he worked. It'd be four kings now, normally a winning hand.

It was too late to fix things now. Any moment those two hands would be spread across that table, and Dorothy did not want to be there when they were. Not only would Vincent's four kings be insufficient for a victory, but they would be damning. Either the big man's king of spades would be assumed to be illegitimate, or Vincent would be exposed as a cheat. If the other men at table two insisted on patting the two other players down, the only dirt they would find on the farmer would be the dirt caked on his trousers, and then the sheriff would be called in. Vincent would not take on all the blame—not in the least. She had to get out of there.

A whistle blew in the distance, barely audible above the noise in the saloon. *The train!*

Holding on to her empty tray, Dorothy bolted toward the back. She veered off course to leave her tray at the bar. "I've got to run to the privy," she said to Walter, her hand cupped around one side of her mouth. He nodded permission, and she headed for the back door, grabbing her coat and her handbag from the hooks in the storeroom.

The moment she stepped outside she pulled on her coat to hedge against the cold spring night. She ran in the opposite direction from the outhouse, heading toward the train station.

Tears gathered in Dorothy's eyes as she ran. She'd not chosen this life; misfortune had chosen it for her. And she'd always hated it.

Maybe she should run back and talk to Walter or the sheriff and tell them the truth—tell them Vincent had forced her to partner with him in his crooked card games. No. Not a lawman alive would see or believe her side of the story. Neither would Walter.

But this was crazy, what she was doing. Where would she go? How would she survive without her brother there to take care of her? Maybe she *should* go back; maybe she should apologize to her brother for not doing her part and then face the sheriff with him.

Her lungs burned as she pulled in volumes of cold air to keep her feet moving because if she didn't, she might turn around.

At the corner where First Street met Main, she stopped momentarily to catch her breath and button her coat. The intricately laid stone of the town's bank rose two stories up from the street. She ducked behind its cover. Any moment someone would likely race out of the saloon, looking for her. She reached out and touched the sandstone. The building, cold and coarse to her touch, reminded her of the rest of this Missouri gambling town. She needed to be shed of this place, this life, and Vincent if she ever hoped to be valued as someone other than a means for her brother to continue his twisted lifestyle.

But she was not yet twenty-one and was still bound to her brother by some stupid law she didn't understand. She should really go back.

I don't want to go back.

The train whistle blew again, louder this time. The station lay a mere block or so away now. It beckoned her to choose the unknown over her known life of wretchedness—and now possible jail time.

She sprinted toward the cry of the whistle.

The shadows in the back streets grew increasingly darker the farther into the seedy part of town she ran. She felt at times as if the black would reach out and grab her, pulling her further into its depths. A slaughterhouse resided on one side of the street, emanating a stench of fetid meat. A row of warehouses and a factory sat on the other side, emptied of their workers for the day. She turned her nose toward them as she ran. A stitch in her side made its appearance, burning an ache in her. She wished the factory were still open. Scores of workers dotting the streets would provide a crowd to hide within. She'd be easy to spot in this empty street if a lawman or Vincent was indeed on her trail.

As she turned the last corner, light and happy sounds surrounded her and lifted her spirits. Union Street bustled with people headed to and from the train station.

An older gentleman looked in her direction. He removed his bowler hat as she whisked by him. "Are you all right, miss?"

"Just hurrying to catch the train," Dorothy said over her shoulder, taken aback by his concern. It felt so foreign. She clenched her coat tighter around her body, trying to ensure no glimpses of her short, red saloon dress could be seen.

As she stepped upon the platform, anxiety turned her head to the ticket booth. She'd need a ticket. A quick search in her purse revealed she had less than a dollar's worth of change—the few tips she'd been able to hide from Vincent. Added to the two bits she'd collected this evening, she hoped it would be enough.

A sheriff's badge caught her notice like a knife ripping through her chest. The man had barely rounded the corner from off Liberty Street. Panic seized her, and she froze.

The sheriff turned his head, first to one side and then the other as he searched. The same older man who'd spoken to her approached him, removing his bowler hat when they came face-to-face. They talked for a moment, and then the man pointed her way with his hat.

Dorothy bolted into the train, not bothering with the purchase of a ticket. Three short toots of the whistle announced the locomotive would move out at any moment. She squeezed through the bustle of people filing into their sleeping compartments, feeling as though the whistle had blown belatedly. She wanted the train to move now!

The floor rumbled beneath her feet, and the car crept forward. The last of the passengers slipped out of sight, leaving Dorothy feeling alone in the middle of the train with no place to go. Through the window of the door leading into the next car, she caught a glimpse of a dark-blue uniform. The conductor! He headed her way.

Clank, clank, clank.

The back of Dorothy's neck prickled at what sounded like spurs rushing up the metal steps of the train.

The sheriff!

She stared for a split second at the compartment door at her side and then tried the handle.

It opened.

With no clue as to where the train was headed or who resided on the other side of the door, she slipped inside the sleeping compartment, opting to face its occupant rather than the sheriff and, ultimately, Vincent.

Chapter 2

A HOMELY WOMAN, WHO APPEARED to be only a few years Dorothy's senior and was dressed in nightclothes, sat on the edge of a bed that appeared to have been formed by using the back cushions of the compartment's bench and sliding the facing seat cushions together to fill in space where one's legs usually went. She looked up at Dorothy's hasty entrance and gasped.

The clink of spurs resonated from down the walkway, approaching ever closer, and Dorothy quickly, carefully shut the door behind her. Its thin wood offered no sense of security. Dare she latch it? Might this woman scream out? "Please, I need your help," Dorothy petitioned in a loud whisper, surprised at her own courage. What right did she have to put such a request upon this person?

The woman remained fixed, not moving or speaking. Her close-set eyes shone with fear. A long nose accentuated the narrowness of her face, which at the moment appeared unusually pale, its only color from two prominent moles on her cheek.

The sheriff's voice boomed through the flimsy walls. "I'm looking for a woman in league with a criminal. She ran onto this train and is stowing away without a ticket."

"I'm not a criminal, I promise," Dorothy whispered in her defense. "I'm just—" She couldn't finish the part about running away from her brother as she touched the healing bruise beneath her eye. She glanced at her fingers. Very little makeup had rubbed off. Most of it had probably come off with her sweat when she was running. The one on her upper arm, where he'd grabbed her while he'd hit her, still hurt if she bumped it. Thankfully it was hidden by her coat. She still couldn't believe she'd actually left Vincent. "I'm just in trouble."

The clink of spurs moved closer. "If any of you are hiding her, you may as well throw her out right now—save yourselves the embarrassment. I'm going to ask the conductor to check everywhere. She'll be hard to hide; she's wearing a red dress that only comes down to her knees, and her dark-brown hair's piled high in the style of saloon girl."

The woman finally spoke. "Quick, latch the door." Her fear seemed to shift from Dorothy to the sheriff. "He sounds like a horrid man."

"The sheriff?" Dorothy flipped the latch into place. "I don't know him enough to say," she responded, saddened by this truth, saddened that she'd not gotten to know a soul in this town.

"I'm talking about the man who bruised your eye."

Dorothy clasped her hands together and braved a step closer to the woman. "Please, don't make me go back to him."

The pounding of a fist against wood shook the door. "This is the conductor. Sorry, but we're searching all compartments. Open up."

All in one continuous motion, the woman jumped up and motioned for Dorothy to lie down on the bed. "Coming," she hollered while covering Dorothy with a blanket. She pointed to Dorothy's hair clip. "Let down your hair," she mouthed.

The woman pulled on her dressing gown and stepped to the door as Dorothy took out her clips and ruffled her hair. She pulled the blanket up farther to hide her coat, turned her back toward the door, and whispered a prayer. "Dear God, please save me."

Dorothy heard the door open. The silence of the spurs, and then guarded footsteps, told her the sheriff remained in the hallway and only the conductor had come into the cramped compartment.

"I thought you were traveling alone, Miss Cooper." The conductor's voice rose with an air of questioning.

"Does it matter that my sister joined me at the last moment?"

"I'll need to see her ticket."

"I can show you mine." The sound of paper unfolding was followed by, "See? It says I've paid for the entire compartment. So I believe my sister's fare has more than been taken care of."

"Yes, you are correct, Miss Cooper." The conductor sounded apologetic. "But do you mind if this gentleman takes a look at your sister?"

"I most certainly do." Miss Cooper stepped next to Dorothy's bunk as if acting like a shield.

This woman didn't know Dorothy from Adam, but here she was, helping her. Trusting her. Treating her like a sister. The thought brought a tear to Dorothy's eye. Why was this woman so kind?

Miss Cooper's voice boomed stronger. "She is ill, plagued with a most painful ailment. I am sure you have awoken her already."

Dorothy let out a groan and stirred to add credence to the story.

"I promise you she is not the person who needs to be turned over to the authorities." The woman cleared her throat. "Now, if you would be so kind as to leave us alone, I would greatly appreciate it."

A long moment later, the door latch clicked, and the sheriff and conductor's uncomfortable presence left.

"All right, dear, why don't you sit up and tell me what has transpired to have left you in such a dither."

Dorothy slowly brought herself up and sat on the edge of the bed, pulling her coat around to cover her bare legs. The woman lowered herself onto the sheet-covered cushions next to Dorothy and gazed at her with compassion. The walls Dorothy had worked on for years to hide her emotions crumbled; she hadn't met with this sort of kindness before.

"I didn't think things through; I just ran away. I had to." Dorothy whimpered. "I couldn't live like that any longer." She held her hands up to cover her eyes.

The woman patted Dorothy's arm. "Tell me everything. It will do you good." She held out her hand for Dorothy to shake. "My name is Wilhelmina Cooper, by the way."

Feeling a little calmer now, Dorothy accepted her hand. "You don't say. Wilhelmina was my mother's name." She shook the woman's hand. Its softness communicated this was a lady—or, at least, a woman not subject to menial tasks. "And mine's Dorothy."

"Do you spell your name with a *y*?" Wilhelmina asked. "Or with an *a-e*?"

Dorothy pulled her hand away and rested it at her side, glad she'd at least learned to read and write her name before she was forced to quit school when her mother died. "With a *y*," she said proudly. "You sure you want to hear everything? It's a long story."

"I'm not going anywhere. At least, not tonight."

"Well . . ." Dorothy chewed on her lip to muster the strength to dredge up the memories. "My life was good until my mother died. Then my father died the following year, leaving me an orphan at age eleven." Dorothy went on to explain how she'd lived on the streets for years, begging. Then she released bits and pieces of what life was like living with her brother.

"I'm sorry," she blubbered when she'd finished her story. "I'm sure a fine lady like you won't want anything to do with the likes of me. I appreciate you covering for me. I guess I'll be going now." She stood to leave.

The woman with the same name as her ma took hold of her hand and gently pulled her back onto the bed. "I fear it is not safe yet. Stay a while longer." She patted Dorothy's hand. "I know the minds of men like your brother, and you did right to run away." She looked off into the distance. "I should have run away sooner from my fiancé."

"Your fiancé?"

Miss Cooper offered a sad nod. "He desired to marry me only for my money. I found that out almost too late. But . . . fortuitously for me, he died the day before we were to be married—died in a fistfight with one of his like-minded friends."

"Did you ever find someone else, you know, to marry?" Dorothy asked, drawn into the conversation and feeling comfortable in this woman's company.

Miss Cooper let out a short laugh, brought a hand to her face, and covered her two unsightly moles. "I am not unaware of my lack of appeal to the male population. I should have known something was amiss when my former fiancé swooned over me."

"Oh, I'm sure that's not the case." Dorothy stared into Miss Cooper's face, easily looking past the moles and appreciating the lack of judgment the woman possessed. "Any man would be privileged to have you as his wife."

Miss Cooper hesitated. "I have my doubts." She squeezed Dorothy's hand this time. "I was nigh onto retiring for the night when you burst in. It's been a long day. Perhaps we could resume this conversation in the morning."

Dorothy stood and skirted her eyes around the room, noticing a traveling trunk and various personal items tucked against the only available wall space. She glanced out the window above the bed. Darkness and an occasional black shape was all she could see through the slits in the blinds. She held back the urge to close them completely; this was not her room. She nervously brought her eyes to rest on the door. "I'm not sure where I'll be in the morning." She chewed on her lip and looked Miss Cooper in the eye and then at the tiny spot of bare floor. "Unless . . . maybe I could sleep on your floor? Just for tonight?"

Miss Cooper took in a deep breath. She stared at the door as she released her lungs. "Like I told the conductor, I've paid for the entire compartment."

She flicked her wrist above her head. "You may as well take advantage of the bunk. I had no plans for it."

"Oh, thank you!" Dorothy shook Miss Cooper's hand again. She stepped onto the bed, released what looked like a handle, and let a bunk fold out above the bed. Dorothy was ready to hoist herself up, more than relieved to have a safe place to spend the night, but Miss Cooper motioned for her to stop.

"Have you no nightclothes?" Miss Cooper answered herself with a shake of her head. "No, no, of course you don't." She stepped over to the large steamer trunk, pulled out a pale-pink nightgown, and handed it to Dorothy. She turned around, keeping her back to Dorothy. "Put it on. I'd close the blinds first though."

Dorothy gratefully closed the blinds, then let her coat drop to the floor and peeled off her red dress, kicking it to the side with a desire to kick it across the state. She never wanted to see it or another saloon again. Would she be able to truly start a new life? It sounded wonderful. It also sounded terrifying. Could she break free of her past? She had to try. Unfortunately, the dress was all she had to wear.

She removed her corset and slipped on the nightgown. It was a little large but smelled of roses and felt as soft as their petals as she pulled it over her head, and it tumbled over her weary body. "I'm done," she muttered, choking on her disbelief. "I can't tell you how grateful I—"

Miss Cooper held up a hand. "Shh. It's okay. Allow me this. I need it right now." She yawned, bringing her outstretched hand to her mouth. "And I need some sleep. I've had a lot on my mind." She crawled into the lower bed without another word.

Dorothy climbed up into her bed, snuggling under the clean bedding and positioning the sleeve of the nightgown by her nose. What a delight to breathe such a fresh scent for a change. Was the stench of whiskey, cheap cigars, and deception really behind her now?

Memories of those putrid smells made her think of Vincent. Was he all right? Had he escaped arrest? Was he home in his apartment, cursing her for leaving him in a mess? Or was he in jail? In any case, she knew he'd be angry, and it was all her fault.

The rhythmic sway of the train car lulled her to sleep and helped her remain in that blissful state all night. Then light caused Dorothy to blink several times before she managed to fully open her eyes. The sun's rays poured in through the open blinds of the window. Where was she? That same swaying brought her back to reality. Darn. Now she must face the unknown of what lay ahead. She sat up, arching her back as she stretched her arms and yawned, not wanting to think about that frightening unknown. She leaned over the side of her bunk and looked for Miss Cooper.

"Ah, finally, you've joined the ranks of the living." Miss Cooper sat on one of the seats below Dorothy, her bed having been converted back to its original purpose. With the natural sunlight streaming through the window, the moles on her cheek stood out. A tray-like table rested over her lap, its legs perched on each side of her on the seat. It held a teapot, two saucers, and a plate of scrambled eggs and biscuits. "I was afraid your breakfast would grow cold."

Cold? That was the only kind of breakfast Dorothy had ever had—if at all. "You ordered breakfast for me?" She glanced at the seat across from Miss Cooper, where a second tray holding a plate filled with scrambled eggs and biscuits had been set. Her gratitude deflated into fear. Was she expected to pay? That handful of change in her purse wouldn't last her but a day or two now that she was on her own. "Thanks, but I'm not very hungry."

Miss Cooper glanced up at her with a look of understanding warming her eyes. "Please. It's already paid for, and I much prefer eating in the company of others."

"Well"—Dorothy climbed down from the upper bunk—"I wouldn't want to disappoint you."

"Wonderful." Miss Cooper pointed to the tray across from her. "I hope you like eggs."

"I do." Dorothy sat down and placed the tray over her lap. "Though I don't get to eat them much. I usually have mush for breakfast."

Her skin crawled at the thought of her living arrangements. *Former* living arrangements. About every two to three months Vincent would set her up in an apartment in a new town and insist she get a job at the local saloon. He rented his own place. She'd make him breakfast every once in a while if he happened to wake at a decent hour and stop by. He'd complain about the mush. If she forgot to hold her tongue, she'd complain back to him about taking most of her wages for "seed money" and what else did he expect to eat? Then he'd hit her.

The only part about their guise that she liked was that Vincent insisted they appear unconnected from each other. His odious games at the poker tables could be jeopardized if the other players knew she and Vincent were related.

"I hope you don't mind tea instead of coffee." Miss Cooper poured steaming water into an empty cup, handed it to Dorothy with its saucer, and then held up two different tea bags. "There's green or Earl Grey—my personal favorites."

"Tea is just fine." Dorothy reached for the bag of Earl Grey and immersed it in the cup of hot water. "You are so kind. Here I am a stranger, one who barged into your private compartment no less, and you are treating me like your long-lost sister."

"A person in need is like family indeed." Miss Cooper spooned sugar into her tea and stirred. She took two sips and then peered at Dorothy over the rim of her cup. "I also have a favor to ask of you." She lowered her cup and saucer. "Perhaps it should be deemed more of a business proposition, for we could both benefit. I've been thinking about it since last night."

"I would love to hear it," Dorothy said around a mouthful of eggs.

"First, I believe it would be fitting for us to introduce ourselves further. I wish to give you some background, so you'll understand my request." She set down the cup and saucer. "As I told you last night, my name is Wilhelmina Cooper. I'm the daughter of Dennis and Katherine Cooper of North-side Chicago. My father is—or I should say *was*—a prominent businessman there. He was in banking."

"Was?"

"He and my mother died last year in an accident in one of those new-fangled automobiles." Wilhelmina's voice took on a timbre of sorrow. "He left the house and the greater part of his wealth to my older brother." She took a quick sip of tea. "That's understandable; my brother has a wife and three children to take care of, and I'm a spinster. But I'm doing fine with my modest allowance. And my grandaunt graciously invited me to live with her." She sliced off a bite of biscuit as if it were a fine steak and raised it to her mouth. "Your turn."

Dorothy took another bite of eggs, enjoying them too much to stop eating for polite conversation. With her mouth half-full, she said, "There's not much else to tell about me." She swallowed. "I gave you my life's story last night."

"That was more about your family. I still know little about you." Miss Cooper took a sip of her tea. "For instance, what is your last name?"

"Bednar."

"Interesting." Miss Cooper waved her spoon at Dorothy. "Maybe you know this already, but *Bednar* is the Polish name for *Cooper*. We practically share the same last name." She smiled, revealing a set of horse-like teeth. "And didn't you say your mother's name was Wilhelmina? Like I said . . . family indeed."

Dorothy nodded and then sighed. "I don't hale from any particular city. My father was a poor farmer in Iowa. When he died, he left no one anything." Except terrified. "So tell me about this business proposition."

Wilhelmina Cooper set down her cup of tea and wrung her hands. "You see, Dorothy, I've gotten myself into a pickle. A few months ago—in a moment of forlorn and thus poor judgment—I placed an ad in a magazine, soliciting for a husband. I essentially signed up to be one of those mail-order brides. By the time I regained my judgment and contacted the magazine to remove the ad, it was too late; the issue had been printed. I let it go, figuring I'd never get any response. You see, my profile was what most people would consider horribly plain, perhaps even boring, lacking anything that would attract a husband. But a week later, I received a letter from a man named Ronald Smith. I should have written back then and there and explained to Mr. Smith that I had changed my mind and no longer sought such a union. I mean, marrying someone you don't know, whom you've only met through a letter, is absolutely ludicrous. Do you not agree?"

"I suppose," Dorothy responded. She could think of things far worse.

"However, I quite enjoyed his letter. It was so well written, short and sweet and to the point. I found myself writing him back. And his next letter I relished even more than the first. He sent me a picture of himself." Wilhelmina pulled a poker-card-sized photograph from a beaded handbag at her side and handed it to Dorothy. "Isn't he quite the handsome young man?" she said with a sigh.

Dorothy examined the photograph, finding nothing about the man she would deem as handsome. But then neither was he horrid to look at. He was merely as alluring as a plank of wood—plain. He had a small, light-colored mustache that faded nearly out of sight under his average nose and unexciting eyes—which she guessed to be brown—that held only a wisp of a brow above them. If she were to have seen this man at the poker table, she'd have quickly told Vincent to expect this man to fold the moment the stakes raised. "Mm," she responded without committing an opinion.

Wilhelmina took a sip of her tea and paused for a moment before she continued. "We have been writing on a regular basis for the past three months. Every Tuesday, I receive a letter, barring poor weather, and every Wednesday, I pen a letter back to him. I must say it has been wonderful indulging in such stimulating, regular correspondence."

"I imagine it would be," Dorothy said, though she wouldn't know, never having written a letter.

Wilhelmina held her hand to her heart and sighed. "And the very idea that a fine, upstanding young man such as Ronald Smith, an attorney at law with his own practice, by the way, basically asked for my hand in marriage . . . well, it's what I have dreamed of for the past ten years of my life—ever since I turned seventeen and my father said I could marry." She clasped her hands together and rested them on her lap, her eyes meeting Dorothy's. "That's why I accepted his offer to be his mail-order bride, you see." Her focus shifted to the floor. "But now, I'm afraid, I've developed a serious case of cold feet. Having to live out West, far away from family and the comforts of life, didn't help the condition."

"So you don't want to go through it, eh?" Dorothy finished her last bite of eggs and biscuit.

Wilhelmina moved the tray to the floor as she shook her head. "No, I do not." She pulled something from her handbag and held it out for Dorothy. It appeared to be a sheet of heavy paper, folded and refolded into the size of a small envelope and tied off with a piece of red string, like a package. She lowered her chin. "I lament my lack of an envelope, but I had not foreseen the need for one when I packed. I have, however, improvised." She cleared her throat. "That is beside the point. My business proposition is that you take this letter and hand deliver it to Mr. Ronald Smith in Craig, Colorado, and give him my apologies. In exchange, I will let you have my train ticket, my paid meals, and my compartment for the next day's journey, and then the stage-coach ticket with a prepaid night at a boarding house. That way, you can get as far away as possible from that horrible man you are running from."

She glanced at Dorothy with a look of concern, and Dorothy could sense the woman's sincerity. She liked the idea so far—she certainly had none of her own—but there were holes. "What about you?"

"The train is scheduled to stop any minute now in Kansas City. I plan to get off and catch the first train back to Chicago."

"There's one big problem." Dorothy pinched the pink nightgown she wore and tugged it for Wilhelmina to see. "Though this might be more fitting to wear than my working dress when I meet Mr. Smith, it's not mine. So the low-cut, high-hemmed, red dress I had on last night is going to be what he sees. Sorry, Miss Cooper, I don't think your Mr. Smith will even let me in the door of his office, let alone listen to what I have to say." Dorothy knew that fact only too well, having experienced such treatment those few times she'd tried to reach out for help. She'd even heard from Vincent she was no good, though he'd still expected her to be a saloon girl.

"I've already thought out that angle. And please, call me Wilhelmina. Miss Cooper sounds so . . . spinsterly."

Dorothy stared at her. Wasn't spinsterhood exactly what she was choosing with her cold feet? Skepticism creeped into her thoughts for the first time since she'd met this woman.

Wilhelmina stood up and moved over to the slightly ajar trunk. "You see, I came prepared to stay for a long time. I've got more than enough dresses and corsets to share, and more back home in Chicago, so I won't miss these at all." She held up a pale-yellow dress adorned with cream-colored lace. "I admit, you are more petite than I, but I do believe with a few alterations this could work wonderfully. By chance, are you handy with a needle and thread?"

"I'm fair," Dorothy said, though she feared her sewing skills might not be up to working on fine fabric. She'd make do though.

"Come," Wilhelmina said with a sweep of the hand. "Choose three outfits you like best and keep the nightgown you have on as your own."

Dorothy went to the trunk and took the yellow dress, holding it against her body, noticing the way the fine lace laid against the finely woven pastel fabric. She'd never seen a garment of such quality close up, let alone worn one. Peering down at the hem of the dress, she loved how it reached her ankles. She glanced down the full length of its sleeves, with their puff of cream-colored satin at the shoulders. She let it fall back into the trunk.

No kind deed was done without a price. Hadn't Dorothy already learned that the hard way? How could she have fallen for Miss Cooper's kindness so easily? "What's the catch?" Dorothy asked.

"Catch?"

"No one gives away an expensive dress like this."

"There is no catch. I promise."

"This Mr. Smith—is there something you're not telling me about him?"

"No, I promise you, I simply have a crippling case of cold feet. Nothing else."

Dorothy weighed her options. They were as lopsided as loaded dice. "And you said I could pick out two more outfits?"

"Yes."

Dorothy cleared her throat. "I would need some sort of traveling bag to put them in."

"But of course." Wilhelmina pulled a black-and-burgundy brocade bag from beneath the bench. "Might I suggest the dark-blue skirt and the brown skirt for practicality's sake and the white blouse and lace-trimmed muslin blouse to go with them? Oh, and you'll want a wrap for when your coat is too hot but the air is still a tad cool." She extracted a lacy brown shawl from her trunk and placed it into the traveling bag.

"I still feel awkward for taking them without paying," Dorothy said as she took the suggested garments from the trunk.

"Oh, but you are more than earning them in my eyes." Wilhelmina placed her hand on Dorothy's arm. "Ronald is such a nice man. A telegraph, I fear, is much too impersonal for such a capricious purpose. I couldn't, in sound conscience, turn around and run back to Chicago without sending someone in person to tell him the unfortunate news."

Dorothy revisited her options. She really had no others. Except to go back to Vincent.

"I'd be glad to take you up on your offer, Miss—I mean, *Wilhelmina*."

Chapter 3

One month earlier

RONALD APPROACHED THE COUNTER OF the mercantile wondering how the Deckers could ever run their store efficiently with boxes of nails, bars of soap, and baby shoes cluttering the countertop. He looked at Sam instead of the lack of order, not wanting such a little thing to get under his skin. He really liked Sam, just as he did most everyone else in this dusty little town of Craig, Colorado.

"May I purchase a page of two-cent stamps?" Ronald asked.

"Certainly." Sam opened a drawer, pulled out a sheet of red stamps, and slid them across an open space on the counter, faceup. "The lawyering business doing good then? Lots of bills to collect?"

"Not necessarily," he said as he placed forty cents on the counter and picked up the stamps. Ronald could do better if he charged more for his services, but he lived comfortably. That was enough. "I merely have a letter to send, and regrettably, I've let myself run out of stamps."

Carefully, he tore a single one from the corner of the sheet, licked it, and placed it equidistant from each edge of the upper right-hand corner of the envelope he'd pulled from his suit pocket. After pressing the stamp securely in place, he handed the letter to Sam. "Could you make sure this goes out as soon as possible?"

Sam nodded and took the letter. "Sure thing." He made a quick glance at the address. "Wilhelmina Cooper? Chicago? A client? Or . . ." He looked straight at Ronald as a coy grin formed on his face "Is it possible our Ronald Smith has himself a lady friend back East?"

"Uh . . ." Ronald usually didn't care if the townspeople speculated about his business dealings, but the thought of others knowing what that letter contained made him uncomfortable. He was certain in many circles mail-order brides were acceptable—especially out West. But not where he came from. His neighbors in south Chicago would be appalled. Heavens, they had gossiped for weeks when he'd graduated from law school and declared his desire to move out West—either that or go on safari to Africa, which was merely a ridiculous daydream. And his mother . . . well, maybe he'd tell her he'd found his wife through this method in a year. "I'd rather not say," he responded at last.

"That's all right." Sam wagged a hand at him. "Just don't let my Lavender know you've got anything close to a gal back East, or she'll be writing the girl herself, telling her to move out here and then planning you two's wedding with bells on her toes." He winked.

Ronald wondered why people got unnecessarily excited over weddings, a mere legal union between two consensual people. It was the marriage and working together to bless each other's lives that mattered. "Don't worry. I won't say a word to her—or anyone for that matter." He turned on his heel and walked out.

A light snow fell, and he rubbed his arms through his thin jacket sleeves to keep warm. He looked forward to the end of March, the end of winter. With the promise of more warmth and color, his favorite season of the year lay around the corner. If Wilhelmina were to respond favorably to this letter in a timely fashion, spring would prove to be even more satisfying.

He turned toward home rather than returning to his office. Now that he'd finally sent that letter, he was forced to be the bearer of bad news to Logan. He treaded through the mud, slowly crossing Sixth Street before returning to the dry wooden sidewalk of Yampa Avenue for one more block. There was no easy way to communicate that his new wife might not want to share her home with an orphaned teenage boy.

As he turned the corner at Fifth Street, he could see his house two blocks away. The white picket fence encasing his corner lot added to the sense of pride he held for the two-story frame house it surrounded. He remembered the thrill he'd felt at finally moving out of Ma Hewlett's boarding house and into a place of his own. By the end of last December, having spent Christmas morning in the five-room house all by himself, the thrill had all but vanished. Come January, he'd convinced his young friend Logan to stay in the extra bedroom when the boy wasn't out at his sister's place. Though he adored the boy, a fourteen-year-old kid was no substitute for female companionship. Ronald had wanted to find a wife and settle in to a normal life ever since he'd moved out West nearly four years ago. Unfortunately, his lack of social finesse when it came to women put him at a disadvantage. There were probably five single men to every eligible female in northwest Colorado. He never stood a chance of finding a wife the conventional way. He'd discovered that after his befuddled attempts to court Doc Kate when she'd first come to town. She'd easily chosen a poor Irish immigrant over him.

The ground proved dryer on Fifth Street. He quickened his steps, anxious to put this task behind him. Concentrating on the positive, he plowed forward.

Yes, today he'd taken care of his unwanted bachelorhood, just like myriad other problems he'd solved for his clients. Researching and planning matters out was his strong point, as well as penning persuasive arguments. When he'd discovered that a man could literally order a wife out of a catalog, more or less, his problem was solved. And to top it all off, Miss Cooper was perfect, a logical choice. She came from a respectable background. Plus she was educated, and from what he gathered from her letters, she was just as methodical, conservative, and reserved as he. And today he'd asked her to come out West so that they could wed.

His only regret in this decision was it would affect Logan.

Ronald stepped through the back door of his house. The smell of hot mush filled the kitchen, and the crackle of burning wood told him the fire was freshly made.

Logan stood at the stove. He stopped stirring and looked up at Ronald. "What you doin' here right now?"

"Might I say the same thing to you?" Ronald asked, unsure now as to how to start this conversation.

Logan glanced at the pot he stirred. "I was hungry—you told me I was welcome to help myself whenever—"

"I'm not speaking of my kitchen and my pantry. My offer still stands, as it always will." Ronald didn't mind Logan staying at his place, didn't mind at all. It was nice coming home to a warm kitchen. But Logan rarely spent time at his sister's place anymore—and never at his brother, Stanley's. "It's just that I fear you spend too little time with family."

Logan grinned wide. "Heck, Ron, I think of you as family—leastwise as much as Susannah. And a whole lot more than Stanley." He broke eye contact and shrugged. "And I feel needed here."

"I *do* need you. This house is way too big for just—" Ronald broke off his words and wrung his hands together. Why hadn't he just told Miss Cooper about Logan? Maybe she would have accepted the situation.

And maybe not. There was a greater chance she would be adverse to the idea, coming from a well-to-do family as she was.

"For just what?" Logan scraped his oatmeal into a bowl. "What's wrong? It's not like you to be stumblin' over your words." He held out the pot toward Ronald. "There's a little bit of mush left if you want some."

"No, you finish it off." Ronald had to tell him, no more stalling.

Logan scraped the pot clean, carried his bowl over to the table, and sat down. He pushed the adjacent chair out from the table with his boot. "Sit down. Talk to me. Tell me why the cat just snatched your tongue."

Ronald dropped into the offered chair. "Logan, I hope I do not live to regret this but . . ." He trailed off, realizing now just how rushed his decision had been.

"But what? You can't just leave me hangin'. Spit it out."

Ronald clasped and unclasped his hands. He peered out the window at the melting snow. Then he massaged the back of his neck and cleared his throat. "I responded to an advertisement in a magazine . . . and . . . you might say I've solicited what some call a mail-order bride."

"Well, if that don't beat all!" Logan jumped to his feet and patted Ronald on the back. "Congratulations, Ron!"

"I haven't married her yet. In fact, there is a chance she will not even accept my offer of matrimony."

"I was congratulatin' you on doin' something adventuresome for a change." Logan sat back down, pushed his bowl out of the way, and stared Ronald in the face. "And why wouldn't she accept your offer? You're the best dang companion a person could ever hope to find."

Ronald pinched his eyes shut, appreciating his young friend's biased opinion, yet fully aware of his many shortcomings.

"Plus," Logan added with the zeal of youth, "if she was the one doin' the advertisin', of course she's goin' to marry you." He pushed the bowl away further and slapped his hands on the table next to Ronald. "Tell me all about her. Is she pretty?"

Ronald hesitated. "I don't rightly know."

"Why not?"

"She never sent a photograph." Ronald hung his head. He snapped it back up. "But her letters were very well written. Her handwriting was neat as a pin. Does that not speak volumes as to the type of woman she is?"

"Yeah, if you're looking to hire yourself an office assistant."

Ronald felt a frown pull down his mouth. "Her correspondence was always stimulating," he said in his defense.

"I imagine as much as tryin' to tickle your foot with a feather while wearin' your boot."

Ronald grimaced and continued. "And I found we shared similar views on many important points."

"She probably has a big mole right in the middle of her chin." Logan sported a mischievous grin. "Probably a wart smack dab on the end of her nose too. Oh, and a wooden leg. No wonder she didn't send you a photograph."

"Even if she does, it would not matter," Ronald responded with an appropriate rebuttal. "It's what's inside that counts."

"Aw, come on, I was just jokin' with you. I think it's wonderful that you gone and got yourself a mail-order bride. And you're right. It's what's inside that counts." Logan leaned back in his chair. "That's why I like you so much."

"Thanks," Ronald said, unsure if he'd just been complimented or insulted. He was not unaware of his pedestrian appearance—and personality.

"My pleasure. There's not many in these parts that would let me stay at their place for free—with my own bedroom and all."

Ronald heaved out a sigh and stared at the floor. "Unfortunately, Logan, I am unsure if Miss Cooper will be amenable to sharing her new home with you. You see, that's something I failed to mention to her in my letters."

"Oh, don't worry about me." Logan waved his hand at Ronald. "For sure your wife comes first. I know how long you've been wantin' to get hitched. Once you get married, I'm perfectly happy to bed down over at the livery stable when I'm in town. Gus lets me stay for free too. Like you did in the back room of your office. I can always go back to stayin' there."

"You won't have to sleep at the livery stable or that deplorable back room of mine. I have come up with a plan to take care of you."

Ronald surveyed his young friend. Reclined in the kitchen chair, the differing lengths of Logan's crippled legs became more obvious. His left boot held a hole in the toe, no doubt from being dragged those times the boy got lazy and didn't force his bum leg to conform. Both boots were scuffed and worn past what a good polish could restore, and the frayed hem of his trousers barely reached the tops of his boots. Logan's appearance had never stood out to Ronald like it did now. "Even if there is a chance Miss Cooper will grant permission for you to stay, I believe it is a plan we should pursue for your sake. It should have been done long before now."

"I don't need no plan." Logan flicked his wrist. "Heck, things always work out for me one way or another."

"There is a possibility I could help you come into a considerable sum of money."

"I make enough for what I need."

"But you deserve what's yours. Hear me out on this please." Ronald raked his fingers through his hair. "Just yesterday a handwritten document was discovered at the Circle J Ranch that might make it possible for us to appeal your deceased father's will. You could be set for life if we were to succeed."

"No, thank you, Ron. I want nothing to do with my pa's money."

"But Logan, the money should rightfully be yours," Ron persisted. After all, it was the perfect solution for everyone.

♠

Chapter 4

WITH BORROWED TRAVELING BAG IN hand and uncomfortable feelings in her gut, Dorothy disembarked from the train in Rawlins, Wyoming, with more anxiety than she had anticipated. She was on her own, completely on her own. As much as she despised Vincent, he'd taken care of her in his own way.

The morning before last, when she'd jumped into the opportunity Wilhelmina had presented to her, she'd failed to think things all the way through. The train ride had been wonderful: a compartment all to herself plus all the food she could eat. She'd stowed as many biscuits and dried apricots she could fit into her purse—next to her sparse collection of change. But she doubted the food would last her the remaining two days of her journey. Wilhelmina's stagecoach fare to Craig didn't include meals. And then what was she to do for food and lodging once she got there? Would she stay permanently? Or move on after delivering Wilhelmina's message? If so, to where? No, she had not thought things out very well at all.

She clenched the handle to her newly acquired carpetbag and marched off the train platform, determined to make the best of her hasty decision.

Dressed in Wilhelmina's pale-yellow dress, Dorothy soaked in the sunshine of the spring morning as she walked. She also soaked in the pleasant feeling of wearing such a fine piece of clothing. The dress hung very loose at her waist but covered her legs and made her feel like a different person. It lightened her step as she made the two-block trek to the stagecoach office, convinced this was not a bad decision.

The instructions given her by the conductor, as to the location of the stagecoach office, had sounded easy enough. At the last minute, he'd added, "You can't miss it. There's a big sign over the door with the word *stagecoach* written in red paint." She'd just look for words painted in red.

When she turned the corner that led to the street with the stagecoach office, three different buildings held signs painted in red. The letters over each door looked nearly the same to her. She studied the strokes and swishes of red of each hand-painted sign. From the numerous times she and Vincent had taken a stagecoach as they'd fled to a new place, she *was* able to recognize the word *Stagecoach*. Up until now, she'd managed okay with her poor reading skills—with Vincent's help. But who would she lean on from here on out to decipher a difficult word or read a passage that was more than a line or two long?

"I'll figure it out," she mumbled to herself and walked toward the building she'd determined to be the correct one.

The whinny of horses and the pummel of hooves sounded in the distance. A stagecoach, followed by a cloud of dust, barreled down the street and pulled to a stop in front of Dorothy's destination. Relieved, she hurried across the road.

She rounded the back of the stagecoach after the dust settled and entered the narrow building.

"Good morning, miss," said a jolly-looking man with a gray mustache and a round belly that strained the buttons of his suit vest. He looked her full in the face, smiled, and then glanced at the carpetbag in her hand. "Here to catch the ten o'clock stage, I presume?"

"Yes, I am."

"Do you need to purchase a ticket?" He scanned the tablet on the counter he stood behind. "Or would you be Wilhelmina Cooper?"

She offered him a simple nod. Not saying lies out loud had usually gotten her through the uncomfortable pinch they inflicted in her stomach. She pulled Wilhelmina's ticket from her handbag and extended it toward him.

He accepted the ticket, looked over it, made a mark in his tablet, and handed it back. "I'll holler at ole John Mills to come fetch your bags."

"That's okay. I've only got this one." Dorothy lifted the carpetbag for him to see it better. "I think I can manage just fine."

"Well then, head outside with me, and I'll help you board." He motioned for her to step through the door before him.

A husky man sporting a brown beard with no mustache leaned against the stagecoach, chewing on the end of a stalk of wheat. "Morning, Zeb," he said to the man at Dorothy's side.

"Morning, John."

The stagecoach driver glanced at her and then back to Zeb. "Just one passenger today?"

"Yep."

The man she assumed to be John Mills reached for her carpetbag. "I'll take this, miss, and put it up top while Zeb helps you aboard."

Dorothy released the bag to him. "Thank you kindly, sir," she responded, concentrating on talking like what she'd heard real ladies sound like.

When Mr. Mills took hold of the bag, he lifted it up and down several times. One eyebrow rose. "By gum, I don't ever think I've met a woman in all my days who packed so light. You're a gal after my own heart—but don't let my wife know I said that." He grinned with one half of his mouth.

"Thank you," she said again and climbed aboard with Zeb's assistance. She settled into her seat, listening to Mr. Mills secure her bag on the top of the coach. She hoped it wouldn't blow away. It was indeed rather light. She also hoped it wouldn't garner suspicion. Surely a woman traveling alone all this way across the western frontier would pack more necessities than she had. Her decision to hold onto her red dress didn't seem so ridiculous now. It helped Wilhelmina's two skirts and blouses, pink nightgown, and change of underwear fill the carpetbag and made her look that much more legitimate.

♠

The stagecoach proved much less enjoyable than the train. She swore Mr. Mills purposely hit every rut in the road, bumping and bouncing her inside the coach like rock in a polishing tumbler.

That thought made her think of Vincent, and her stomach soured. He'd spent so much money on worthless things or expensive clothes. When Dorothy had changed trains in Omaha, she'd carefully slipped out of Wilhelmina's compartment, watching her back every turn of the way as she boarded the new train. Not once had she caught a glimpse of Vincent.

Could it be she was finally free from him?

It saddened her to care so little for her only kin. She should be ashamed of herself, not sad. If only their relationship could have been different, more normal.

She opened her handbag, extracted the crumbling remains of a biscuit, and made her noon meal. Even if she only ate three of the half dozen dried apricots for supper, hunger was more than a fair trade for freedom.

As the sun set, the stagecoach pulled into a town with barely a stone's throw worth of buildings lining each side of Main Street. The coach slowed considerably and then came to a stop. Dorothy could hear Mr. Mills slide her bag from off the roof of the coach and hop down. The door opened, and he stuck his head in.

"We've made it to Baggs." He offered his hand and helped Dorothy climb out. "We'll be stayin' the night here. I'll walk you over to the boardin' house. Ole Mrs. Stewart charges four bits a night. You might want to dig it out and have it handy. She's not the most personable woman I know." He nodded at her handbag as he slung her carpetbag over his shoulder like it was filled with air.

"The boarding house was paid for with my stagecoach ticket. Leastwise, it was supposed to be." Dorothy's gut tightened. Had she heard Wilhelmina incorrectly?

"Well, get out your ticket and look at the back. That'll tell you." Mr. Mills started walking down the dusty street.

Dorothy pulled her ticket from her handbag and turned it over. It held scribblings of unfamiliar words. She hurried to fall in step with him, ready to rely on some old tricks to get him to read it for her. Walking at a brisk pace, she held out the ticket so he could see its backside. "Is this what you're talking about?"

He glanced at it. "Yep."

Relieved, Dorothy opened her handbag and tucked it inside. Mr. Mills slowed his pace. They approached a whitewashed clapboard house at the end of the Main Street shops. It held a faded sign set on a post in a dirty weed patch of a front yard.

"Here you are." Mr. Mills handed her the traveling bag. "I'll see you bright and early in the mornin'," he said over his shoulder as he walked away.

"Thank you so kindly for your help." Dorothy's response sprung from her heart. Though she liked her freedom, she didn't like being on her own. For one thing, she'd have never suspected this rundown place to be the boarding house.

She stepped onto the small covered porch and knocked on the door. After a long minute that felt like ten, a sour-faced woman with numerous wisps of hair escaping a bun at her nape opened the door.

"Can't you read?" the woman barked. "Let yourself in!"

"Sorry." Dorothy hadn't seen anything that could have held such instructions. She stared at her feet. There to the left of her foot, covered with dried leaves, sat a thin piece of wood with writing on one side and a small hole at the top. She picked it up. "Is this what you're talking about?"

"I suppose." The woman snatched it from Dorothy's hand and hung it from a nail protruding from the clapboard. "Come in." She walked inside and, with her back to Dorothy, muttered, "I take it you're Miss Cooper."

"Uh . . . yes, ma'am." Dorothy followed her.

"Ain't there any more coming?" The woman looked out the window. "You know, from the stagecoach? You the only one?"

"Sorry, it's only me, Mrs. Stewart. I presume you're Mrs. Stewart?" Dorothy said this to make conversation and lighten the mood. She felt the woman wasn't ornery by nature—she was just hurting for some reason. At least that's why Dorothy got ornery.

"Yeah."

"What about Mr. Stewart?" Dorothy hadn't recalled Mr. Mills mention the woman's husband. "Does he help you run this boarding house?"

"He's dead." She turned her back to Dorothy and lit a lamp sitting on a high table by the door. "So are my two children. Typhoid . . . four years ago. I run this place myself." She opened a ledger of sorts that lay beside the lamp. "Sign here first. Your room is the first on the right." She pointed down the hall that led away from the living room. "I'm sure you can find it just fine. Supper's at six sharp in the dining room."

"The meal's included with my room?" Dorothy's eyebrows rose slightly with disbelief and relief.

"Course it is," Mrs. Stewart grumbled. "Gotta get customers somehow."

Dorothy wished she dared to give the woman a hug, understanding fully the woman's pain of loneliness. Instead she merely said, "Thank you," and signed her name. She gave her signature a quick glance, proud it was something she'd learned quite well. Then she caught her breath.

She'd signed it Dorothy Bednar. Quickly, she put the pen back to the paper and began slowly scrolling the name Cooper at the end. She envisioned the letters as she'd seen them on Wilhelmina's train ticket, hoping she was spelling it correctly. As for a middle name of Bednar, and Dorothy in the place of Wilhelmina, her brain scrambled to come up with a viable story to gloss things over.

Mrs. Stewart's brow wrinkled as she read the ledger, but she said nothing. Dorothy breathed a sigh of relief and hurried to her room.

At six, Dorothy made her way to the dining room off the kitchen. Eight chairs were squeezed around a rectangular table that practically filled the room. A soup bowl, cup, and spoon had been placed at the head of the table as well as in front of the seat to the right. A small plate holding two slices of bread sat somewhat in the center of the table.

With mitted hands, Mrs. Stewart stepped in from the kitchen carrying a pot and set it on the table.

"Is there only two of us for supper then?" Dorothy asked.

"Yep." Mrs. Stewart sat down and bid Dorothy to do the same. She ladled a serving of watery soup into Dorothy's bowl, pointed to the bread, and said, "Eat up."

Dorothy complied. The apricots and biscuits she'd rationed hadn't made for much of a dinner earlier that day. Though thin, the soup had a nice flavor. "The soup is good," she said, feeling she should say more. The fear of the woman questioning the inconsistency of her name held Dorothy back. She would be glad when this journey to Craig was over and she'd no longer have to be traveling as Wilhelmina Cooper.

"Hmph." Mrs. Stewart twisted her mouth to one side. "Thank you. I don't get near enough compliments." Her face relaxed, and she took a sip of soup. "I wish I got more customers the likes of you." With another sip, she continued, "So, what are your plans once you get to Craig?"

Dorothy froze, her spoon halfway to her mouth. She had no plans. Not really. Only to get to Craig and live as far away from Vincent as possible. Wilhelmina's original plan would make for better conversation. "I'm meeting someone there, a man I've been corresponding with," she responded, wondering how much longer she'd have to carry on this charade—she'd had her fill of acting the part of someone she wasn't.

"Well, I hope all goes well for you and this fellow, and you two can . . . you know, get hitched 'cause out West here is no place to be a woman living alone."

"Thank you for your well-wishes." Dorothy nodded.

After the two of them finished their supper and a conversation about the difficulties of running a boarding house in Baggs, Wyoming, Dorothy bid Mrs. Stewart good night and retired to her room.

Dorothy climbed under the stale sheets and listened to the scurry of rats in the attic. The scratchy sound lulled her toward sleep; the rodents running across the ceiling were less threatening than the rat she used to live with—they didn't expect the impossible. She took comfort in the fact that she was going to a place in the middle of nowhere. Craig, Colorado, was a new town. Very few people she'd talked to in the last two days had ever heard of it. That likely meant Vincent wouldn't have either. She would deliver Wilhelmina's letter to

Mr. Smith then settle herself into a secluded corner of that frontier town and start a new life. Surely there was some sort of employment a gal who wasn't afraid to work long hours could find to pay the rent.

Yes, that's what she'd do.

And hopefully, it would take Vincent the good part of a week to talk his way, and pay his way, out of jail. If only she could have run away from her brother without getting him in trouble or at least fixed things before she left for good.

She suppressed her guilt and tried to dwell on the positive. Her trail would surely be cold by the time Vincent got out. And he would never find her.

Chapter 5

MR. MILLS'S VOICE BOOMED OVER the grind of the stagecoach wheels on the rocky road. "Craig, Colorado, is comin' up just over this next rise."

Dorothy lifted the flap of the window and peered outside to see the endless expanse of sage brush that had filled her view ever since she'd left Baggs. A wave of dust rushed in and invoked a cough. Letting go of the window covering, she leaned back in her seat inside the empty coach. She'd had no company yet again for this last leg of her trip. Though she was used to being alone, she was never really alone. Whether in the shadows of the saloon or the shadows of her fears, Vincent was always there. But now was different. Some companionship would have been preferred—a little light conversation and perhaps a chance to obtain some information about Craig. Anything to quell these feelings of loneliness that seemed to have come out of nowhere.

She felt the coach climb and then descend. She lifted the flap again and looked out. Neatly laid-out blocks of a small town stretched out in front of the stagecoach. The road ahead was lined with shops of varying shapes and heights. It cut down the center of town, while whitewashed houses, surrounded by picket fences, dotted the streets laid out in lattice fashion on each side of the main street.

She continued to stare at the town, analyzing her current emotions. It wasn't really fear that she felt—she'd been in much scarier situations before. Neither was it excitement—after she completed her commitment to deliver Wilhelmina's letter, she had nowhere to go. No, the emotion building inside her was that nagging loneliness again.

She pulled from her handbag the photograph that Wilhelmina had given her of Mr. Smith. Making note once again of his indistinctive face and wishing photographs contained color, she scanned the faces of the men walking down the street to see if any of them looked like him. According to Wilhelmina, in

Mr. Smith's last letter, he'd said he would pick her up at the stagecoach stop in front of the town hall. If this Mr. Smith was not true to his word, Dorothy had no clue what to do. Wilhelmina had been so kind to her; Dorothy couldn't let the woman down.

Why all this fretting? From Wilhelmina's letters, it sounded like Mr. Smith was a man of his word.

The stagecoach rolled to a stop in front of a drab brown building that held two doors and two different signs. She could read one: Town Hall. That was enough.

"We're here," Mr. Mills hollered.

A minute later, he opened the door to the coach and helped Dorothy down onto the damp road. She gathered her skirt with one hand and cinched it back up on her hips with the other hand. Once the loose-fitting garment rested somewhat in place, she reached out to take her bag from Mr. Mills and hurried onto the wooden sidewalk so as to protect her new blue skirt. Once securely on the wooden planks, she scanned the sidewalk first to her left, then to her right, both times down the length of the street.

"Is this the usual place to stop the stagecoach?" she asked Mr. Mills as he climbed back up onto his driver's seat.

"Yes 'm." Mr. Mills gathered the reins into his hands. "Is someone supposed to be picking you up, miss?"

"Well, yes, they are." Dorothy swallowed hard, forcing down her anxiety. "A man named Ronald Smith. I believe he is an attorney here in town."

"Ronald Smith, eh?" Mr. Mills smiled as he scratched his head.

"You know the man?"

"That I do."

"Is he the reliable sort? Or should I expect to wait here a good spell before he comes?"

"He's reliable as they come." Mr. Mills wrinkled his brow and then scratched it. "If he said he'd pick you up, then . . ." He pulled a watch from his pocket. "Hmm, I'm not more than a minute or two late. I'm guessing something must have happened. You might want to walk down to his office. It's on the north side of the road between Sixth and Seventh Street. You can't miss it; it says, 'attorney at law' right above the door—he's the only one in town." He pointed down the street.

"Oh." She couldn't keep the angst from her voice.

"I don't mean to pry, miss, but do you know Mr. Smith? Is he an acquaintance, or are you client of his?"

"Well, neither, I guess." Dorothy stared at her shoes. That was a mistake. They looked too much like ones belonging to a saloon girl with their shiny black leather and pointed toes. "I . . . I've been corresponding with him," she said as if she were Wilhelmina.

Mr. Mills's smile spread from the edge of one cheek to the other beneath his bushy gray mustache. "Ah, well, I'll be! Are you the mail-order bride I heard rumor ole Ronald was thinking of sending for?"

His statement unsettled her. It must be her nerves; they'd been frayed beyond anything she'd faced as part of Vincent's con games. Her mind wasn't numb like usual. Dorothy felt her cheeks flush, and she stammered, "I—I suppose—"

A horse galloped toward them, startling Dorothy and causing her to step backward toward the building. "Maybe that's Mr. Smith," she said. "A tad late, that's all. I'll be fine."

Mr. Mills let out a deep-belly laugh. "That ain't Mr. Smith," he said as the horse and its rider pulled to an abrupt stop several feet in front of the stagecoach's team. "That there is Logan. Maybe he can help you find Mr. Smith. From what I understand as of late, the two of them have become good friends."

"Howdy, miss," the young man said atop a gray-and-white horse. His mount nuzzled the snout of one of the horses hitched to the coach. When he lifted his hat and the sun shone full on his face, Dorothy could see he was more of a boy than a man. Perhaps fifteen years old or so would be her guess. "Are you Miss Wilhelmina?"

Dorothy nodded. "That's what my ticket says at least." She held up the stub of paper as she sported a crooked grin.

"Great. Ronald asked me to come fetch you for him. He's kind of busy at the moment." The boy climbed down from his horse. "I'll walk you over to the hotel where he'd like you to wait until he gets back from the business he's tendin' to." He looped his reins over the hitching post and then pointed to her bag. "I hope you're as excited to meet Ronald as I am for you and him to meet up. Can I carry your bag for you, Miss Cooper?"

She bit her lip as she handed it to him, unaccustomed to deceiving a child. She'd never stooped this low before, and she didn't care for it. But now didn't feel the right time and place to explain her real purpose for being here. She needed to meet Mr. Smith first—explain the situation *to him*. After she delivered Wilhelmina's message, she hoped he could point her to a cheap place to stay and maybe even help her find employment.

Logan joined her on the sidewalk, looping her bag over his shoulder. As he walked beside her, a definite but endearing limp became apparent. The smile he wore seemed to soften his mismatched steps to where they were barely noticeable. "You must be a special lady." He looked at her, his face radiating from within. "Willin' to leave your family behind and come all the way out here to marry my friend when you don't hardly know him. But I know him. And I promise you won't be sorry."

Dorothy offered another nod, no words coming to her in the way of response.

"You sure is pretty, Miss Wilhelmina Cooper. I know Ronald is goin' to like you just fine." His smile remained but seemed to shift purpose. Whereas a minute ago it appeared born of delight to serve her, now she sensed it was one of gladness for his friend.

"Well, I uh . . ." The awkward nature of this conversation tied her tongue. "Thank you, uh . . ."

"The name's Logan, Logan Jones." He held out his hand for her to shake.

Dorothy accepted his hand and shook it. "Dorothy, Dorothy Bednar." *Oops.*

Logan's forehead scrunched up above a raised eyebrow. "But you just answered to Wilhelmina Cooper."

Dorothy averted her gaze and spilled the excuse she came up with for Mrs. Stewart but never used. "Uh, well, Wilhelmina is my mother's name too. To avoid confusion, and honestly because I don't care for the name, I prefer to go by the nickname Dorothy. And Cooper is the English the version of the Polish name of Bednar." She grimaced—it wasn't all a lie. "I guess I'm not quite used to the change." That *was* a lie.

"Ah, so you're tryin' to sound American, are you?" Logan bobbed his head as his eyes concentrated straight ahead. "I understand. But to be truthful, miss, I don't think Ronald will care if you're Polish, Portuguese, or Pennsylvanian. He just wants a good woman to help him not be so lonely out here." He looked at Dorothy, and that pleasant smile of his returned. "And I get the feelin' that you are good."

"Thank you, Logan. You are too kind," she said, feeling undeserving of his praise. "Well, unfortunately, I'm not exactly who . . ." She paused, unsure how to word it, having hoped not to even need to delve into this.

"No, you're just what he needs," Logan finished for her. "I can feel it in my bones." He opened the door for her to step into the two-story, red-brick hotel.

"But—"

Logan held out his hand toward her mouth in a silencing gesture and turned toward a man with a pencil-thin mustache standing behind the counter. "Campbell, this here is Miss Cooper. Ronald said he'd reserved a room and everything already for her. Is that right?" He turned to Dorothy and handed her the bag. "This here is Mr. Campbell Tucker. He'll take good care of you."

Mr. Tucker looked down at a ledger book and then raised his eyes to meet hers. "Yep, that's right. Mr. Smith has got you a room reserved clear through this month and into the next. Paid for it in advance."

"But—" Dorothy chewed on her lip. What would it hurt to take advantage of Mr. Smith's hospitality for one night? She'd been traveling for three days, and her hair still reeked of saloon cigar smoke. She needed a bath and a place of safety where she could regroup and "hang her hat" while she looked for a job. "Would it be possible for you to refund Mr. Smith's money if I chose to stay but one night?"

"No!" Logan tugged on her sleeve. "Miss Cooper, you can't say that. Please don't give up so easily. It'll work between you and Ronald. I just know it. I told him that too."

Dorothy took in a good breath, ready to set things straight. "But—"

"He was afraid you'd not like him once you met him," Logan cut in, "but I gotta tell you, 'cause I think it's right grand of him; he doesn't want to force marriage on you if you don't cotton to it. That's why he set you up here at the hotel for over a month so he could court you all proper-like before you two actually got married. So you gotta give him a chance."

"I'm agreein' with the boy here." Mr. Tucker stroked his chin. "Give Mr. Smith a chance. He's a good man. But if you do change your mind, don't fear; I'll be more than glad to refund his money."

"You're so very kind, Logan. And I'm sure Ronald Smith is a good man." Dorothy sensed that already, and she hadn't even met the fellow. "But it's not like that at all. You don't understand. I—"

"There's nothin' I need to understand, miss. Just trust me. Give him a chance." Logan tipped his hat. "I gotta be goin'. Ronald'll be by in about an hour or so to meet you." Logan handed Dorothy her bag and slipped out the door.

"Would you like me to carry your things up to your room for you, miss?" Mr. Tucker held out his hand for her single bag.

Dorothy had the urge to laugh, knowing the sparsity of her belongings and how easily she could carry the bag by herself. "Thank you," she said, to be as ladylike as possible, and followed him up the stairs, glad for a bit of something to make her smile.

"I'll be putting you in room three. I hope you will enjoy it. It has a right nice view of Yampa Avenue." His boot clapped a rhythm up the thin, carpeted steps. "There's a bathhouse across the street—you can see that from your window too." At the top of the stairs, he turned to the first door on the right, motioned to it, and handed her the key. He quickly scanned her from head to foot. "Sorry, I wasn't thinkin'—most of our customers are menfolk. I'll ask my Mary to draw you a bath in the bathroom at the end of the hall. It might take a little longer than across the street, but I'm sure you'll like it better. Mary got upset with me last time I recommended Porter's Bathhouse to a lady, so don't say nothin' to her about it."

"Don't worry. I won't." Dorothy chuckled silently.

"Thank you kindly."

"You're most welcome, Mr. Tucker." Dorothy took the key, fearing she must smell of saloon, else why would the man ramble on like he had? "And yes, I would appreciate it very much if you could ask your wife to draw me a bath as soon as she is able. It's been a long trip, and I've had to stay at some places that were—how do I say this?—a little less than perfect," she said, keeping up the image of a well-bred woman the best she could. She smiled at him and unlocked the door.

"I'll tell her right now."

"Lovely. I would like to clean up before I meet with Mr. Smith if possible."

Mr. Tucker grinned. "Right."

"It's not like—" *That*, she was about to say. She saved her breath, opened the door, and stepped inside her room. "Tell your wife I'll be ready shortly." She turned and offered him a nod before shutting the door. "Thank you very much."

Dorothy set her bag on the wing-backed chair by the window and plopped onto the bed covered in a fluffy, peach-colored spread. It felt heavenly. She'd never felt such a soft mattress before. Straw poking through holes and scratching her legs as she slept was more what she'd been accustomed to. And the room smelled of flowers—not of cheap cigars. She breathed in a hint of lavender wafting her way from the sachets by the basin and one on her pillow. The aroma made her smile inside.

She lay there but for a minute and then jumped up. None of this was for her; it was intended for Wilhelmina. She paced from one end of the room to the other, wondering how much all of this cost. How much would she have to repay Mr. Smith if he wasn't gracious enough to pay for this one night? She wouldn't blame him if he didn't—she was nothing but a messenger to him—one bearing bad news.

The warmth, softness, and pleasant scents of the room lured her to the armchair by the window, and she allowed herself to sit down. Everything in her life up to now seemed to be cold, hard, and smelly.

"But those things are behind me now," she muttered to the bowl and pitcher made of fine porcelain and imprinted with orange and pink flowers. She stood and walked over to where they rested upon the finely crafted table next to the chair. Running her fingers over their smooth surfaces, she asked herself, "Can't they be behind me now?"

She walked back and sat down on the edge of the bed to run through her plan of action, determined to put her past behind her.

After delivering Wilhelmina's letter and message to Mr. Smith, she would beg him to let her stay the night in this lovely room, insisting that she would pay him back as soon as she could for his graciousness. Tomorrow she'd find employment and a cheaper place to stay. Perhaps she could work as a housekeeper or in a shop measuring out yards of fabric for the womenfolk in the town. Maybe there was a tailor in town who she could hire on with to do all the hemstitching. With a little practice, she was sure she could become proficient. She'd be willing to do pretty much anything. Except work in a saloon. Right now, however, she needed a bath.

She grabbed her bag and headed down the hall, hoping Mr. Tucker's wife had started on the tub.

The bathroom was empty when she walked inside, except for the oblong tin tub that sat against one wall, a cupboard attached to the opposite wall, and an old kitchen chair under that cupboard. Light streamed in through the lace curtains of a window of the wall opposite the door. She placed her things on the chair and hurried downstairs.

Mr. Tucker looked up from his ledger as Dorothy reached the bottom of the stairs. "Mary's in the kitchen. It's through the dining room. You can't miss it." He pointed to an adjoining room with a dozen chairs encircling a dark cherry wood table. "Follow the smell of baking bread."

"Thank you." Dorothy gave him a nod and hurried to the dining room, wondering and hoping that fresh bread was included in her night's stay. Once through the dining room, she pushed the swinging door and discovered that it indeed led to the kitchen—the source of the intoxicating aroma of fresh bread. Dorothy felt her mouth water.

A woman stood to the side of the stove scooping water from the reservoir with a saucepan into a bucket sitting on the floor. Numerous strands of dark blonde hair escaped the bun at the nape of her neck, and the remnants of breadmaking spilled over from her apron onto her blue dress.

The woman looked away from her task and to Dorothy. "Howdy." A young child with straw-colored braids emerged from the shadow of her mother and wrapped arms around her mother's leg. The woman set the pan on the stove, hugged the child, and then moved her to one side slightly. She held out her hand to Dorothy. "I'm Mary, and you must be Miss Cooper."

Dorothy shook her hand. "Uh, yeah, but call me Dorothy, please."

"Dorothy," Mary said with a nod. "I'll take your first load of bathwater up in just a min—"

Another girl, a tad older than the one wrapped around Mary's leg, bolted into the kitchen. "Ma, Nyda's teasing me again."

A taller girl shot in. "Don't listen to her, Ma. I was just tellin' her things the way they were." She pointed to the middle girl's blond, tangled hair. "Her hair's a mess and needs a good combin'. That's all."

"Bethany's hair is fine. Now come take little Caroline so I can prepare this nice lady's bath, and then the three of you make yourselves scarce. I'm sure Miss Cooper is not used to a passel of young'uns running around." Mary looked to Dorothy. "I promise I'll keep my brood clear of you once your bath is ready upstairs. The last thing I'm sure you want is a half dozen little eyes peeping in on you." She let out a soft laugh as she shooed her children through the swinging door into the dining room.

That did little to reassure Dorothy that her bath would be uninterrupted. She'd hoped for one that would relax her—and wash away years of filth along with the dust of the road. But those little girls and their mother offered her a sense of peace in a different way. She felt love permeating this kitchen. It filled her with a sweet feeling she hadn't experienced for years.

Mary was right; Dorothy wasn't used to it. She felt a pang of sorrow emerge inside her. She'd missed out on what these little girls had. The sorrow grew and threatened to transform into anger. She did not want to let that happen, and so she focused her eyes and thoughts on Mary.

"I'm not worried," Dorothy said, though she sensed Mary was. "So neither should you be. I'm just grateful for this bath. The thought of going across the street to that bathhouse didn't appeal much to me. Thank you."

Mary grinned and out of one side of her mouth muttered, "That place *is* rather awful. I'm glad my husband didn't forget and send you over there. We just got this bathroom fit to be used a few months ago." She scooped steaming water into a second bucket. With a potholder in each hand, she picked up the buckets and walked toward the door.

Dorothy rushed to Mary's side and attempted to relieve her of one bucket and potholder. "Here, let me help you with those."

Mary resisted. "Oh, no. You're a guest here. And a lady."

"I'm going upstairs right now. My hands may as well be doing something." Dorothy tugged at the bucket, and Mary released her grasp. "And I really don't mind helping. Honest." She wondered if she dare ask Mary if they were in need of an extra set of hands around the hotel. No, surely they wouldn't need anyone, leastwise not someone like her.

"That's really kind of you to offer," Mary said as she began her assent up the staircase. "I suppose we really should hire a housemaid for such tasks."

"You don't have one already?" Dorothy bounced on her toes as she climbed up behind Mary, her load seemed light.

Mary laughed. "Heavens no. Me and Campbell could never afford to pay for hired help."

"Oh." Dorothy's bucket went back to feeling heavy. She emerged onto the landing and followed Mary to the bathroom. The *swoosh* of water in her bucket filled the silence of their abandoned conversation.

Once in the bathroom, Mary put in the cork, dumped her bucket of hot water in the tub, and motioned for Dorothy to do the same. Then she worked the pump at the head of the tub, adding several inches to the water level. The oldest daughter hauled in another bucket of hot water. Mary dumped that in, handed the girl the empty buckets, then immersed her hand in the bathwater.

"Feels tolerable." She glanced at Dorothy. "You tell me what you think."

"I'm not picky." Dorothy stuck her hand into the water. It felt cool. "It's not bad."

"We want good!" Mary stepped toward the door. "A lady like you is sure to be accustomed to a good, warm bath. I'll go fetch another bucket or two," she said as she hurried out the door.

Dorothy picked up her things and sat on the chair, staring through the door but not really looking at anything in particular. She only thought about the soft mattress in her room, the smell of fresh bread wafting up the stairs, and being treated like a lady—things she *wasn't* accustomed to.

A few minutes later, Mary emerged at the top of the stairs with two full buckets in hand. As she poured the hot water into the tub, she asked, "What brings you out West? It's not like Craig, Colorado, is the most desirable place on earth." She rolled her eyes.

"You make it sound like you don't care for this place," Dorothy observed, purposely avoiding answering the woman's question.

"First of all, it's no place to raise four little girls."

"I only counted three," Dorothy said to keep the conversation going down this lane.

"The fourth one's—well, gracious be, I don't know where she is. But I'm sure she's around." Mary brushed away the hair in her face with the back of her forearm. "Helping my husband run this place and raise a family isn't a job for the faint at heart—or in body." She rested her hand briefly on her stomach, which Dorothy noticed for the first time was round and pushed out at her apron. "I just hope I have the strength to take on yet another one." Mary motioned for Dorothy to feel the bathwater. "Here, try it now."

Warmth enveloped Dorothy's fingers the moment she submerged her hand. "Feels good," she responded, thinking about how so many other things about this place felt good. "Oh, before you go, I was just wondering, what kinds of jobs might a young single woman be able to find around here?"

One of Mary's eyebrows rose. "What, you came to Craig looking for employment? Heaven forbid. Why?" By the look on Mary's face, it was obvious her husband hadn't confided in her as to his knowledge of Wilhelmina Cooper being Mr. Smith's mail-order bride.

"Not necessarily," Dorothy said quickly, realizing she didn't want to go down this lane either. Most assuredly it would lead them back to topics she wanted to avoid. "Like I said, I was just *wondering*, for curiosity's sake."

"I could certainly think of a passel of better topics to be curious about." Mary pulled a towel from the cupboard on the far wall, draped it on the back of the chair, and pulled the chair next to the tub. "But since you asked, I'll tell you. 'Cause it's been a sore spot with me in the past."

Dorothy felt her own eyebrows rise. "You were a single woman seeking a means to take care of yourself before you met Mr. Tucker?"

"Heavens no. The only place a single woman could find employment around here would be at Rosy's Brothel on the edge of town." Mary brought her hand to her mouth. "Heaven forbid. No, Mr. Tucker dragged me and my three oldest girls here to Craig five years ago to manage this here hotel for his uncle. My sore spot is the lack of things for women to do in this town, besides bearing and raising young'uns. Which ain't a bad thing. But I'm just saying it's not the place I would have picked to live—if I'd had my choice back then." Mary glanced away momentarily. "But I'm doing good now. I've taken to decorating each of the guest rooms up right nice. I've found it quite delightful, so I'm content." Her gaze returned to Dorothy. "But as for some young gal coming into town looking for a means to take care of herself, that just ain't done out here."

Dorothy shook her head ever so slightly. That was not what she cared to hear. "There must be something a single gal could do. Besides working at a saloon or a," she cleared her throat, "um, you know—" She bit on her lip. Why had she brought up being a saloon girl? Especially when Mary hadn't even mentioned that. And then for Dorothy to lump her previous profession together with working in a brothel? She should bite her lip 'til it bled! In the past, she'd always been downright angered by folks when they'd assumed they were one in the same. And she'd given it her all to maintain that difference.

Mary wagged a hand at her. "Nope. It's not like a gal could get paid to decorate up nice hotel rooms or the like." She blew a wisp of hair out of her eyes. "My suggestion for some gal who was looking for a way to be taken care of is to find a husband. Lord knows there's plenty to choose from. The men outnumber the women five to one."

Mary stuck her finger in the bathwater. "Enough of my yakking. You'd better get to this bath before it gets cold." She pulled her fingers out and wiped them on her floured apron. Shaking her head, she added, "I don't know what's gotten into me. A year or so ago, you'd never have gotten a word out of me. It must be Kate's fault."

"Kate?" Dorothy *wanted* to get to her bath before it got cold. But then again, she kind of enjoyed Mary's rambling. The woman seemed sincerely delighted with Dorothy's company.

"She's the new woman doctor in town. Though she's not that new anymore. Been here over two years now. She helped me get over my blasted shyness." Mary stepped toward the door. "I guess I was wrong. Kate came here all on her own, looking to work at a job so as to take care of herself. But then she'd been to college to be a doctor. Even she had a hard time at it—you know, taking care of herself."

"Oh." Dorothy let out a sigh. She barely read a handful of words, let alone had gone to college.

"Miss Kate, she got married." Mary's face lit up. "To a right nice young fellow that owns a sheep ranch outside of town."

"Well, thanks for everything. And it was nice making your acquaintance, Mary." Dorothy prompted the woman farther toward the door. "I'd best hurry into this tub before it gets cold."

The door clicked shut behind Mary. Dorothy immediately peeled off her dress, wanting to get to her bath, sink down into the warm water, and rethink things. Perhaps she should hightail it out of Craig as soon as she delivered Wilhelmina's message to Mr. Smith and found a more suitable place to start over with her life.

Where would she go? How would she get there? She had but a few coins to her name—and she needed to spend a few of those pennies immediately on a needle and some thread to fix her clothes. As soon as she took her bath and before Mr. Smith arrived would be preferable. She needed desperately to take a tuck in one of her skirts so she wouldn't have to constantly pull it up.

She dipped her toe into the clear water. Its warmth lured her feet into the tub. The need to wash away the sweat and dust of the road pulled her the rest of the way in.

As she immersed her tired body in the water, she imagined it washing away not just days of grime but years.

Chapter 6

RONALD MOUNTED HIS HORSE, MEHITABLE, kicked his heels into her flanks, and sped through the archway of logs, anxious to put this official visit to the Circle J Ranch behind him. He pulled out his watch once he was on the main trail back to town. He flipped open its cover and saw the hands read 4:00. *Drat.* It would be another hour before he made it back to Craig. What kind of impression was that going to leave with Miss Cooper? Any person that couldn't keep to a schedule as promised deserved serious scrutiny—at least in his book. Miss Cooper's too, he was sure. From her letters, he could tell she was punctual and organized.

He thought back to two weeks ago when he'd worked out a plan as exactly how to take care of both Miss Cooper's and Logan's needs. He'd finally gotten hold of the documents discovered in an old suitcase at the Circle J Ranch and discovered for himself that they were indeed a will penned by the hand of Benedict Jones shortly before his death. That same day, he'd received Miss Cooper's reply. A niggle of excitement rose inside him. She'd actually said yes to his proposal of marriage. He'd wired her the funds to make the trip out West, and now she was here.

Unfortunately, his visit to Logan's brother, Stanley, had not gone as smoothly as Miss Cooper's acceptance of his offer. But no matter; he'd keep working at getting Logan a rightful share of his inheritance—or at least a portion of it. No son of Benedict Jones should have to bed down at night in a livery stable. Nor in the borrowed room of a friend who was getting married. One sixth of old Benedict Jones's wealth still wasn't fair, but it could easily buy Logan a house of his own and all the comfort the boy could ever imagine.

"Enough thinking about that bullheaded Stanley Jones," Ronald muttered to Mehitable. He'd just needed a signature on that simple affidavit declaring that Stanley recognized the handwriting on those documents as that of his deceased father. But Stanley wouldn't sign it while he waited. The man said he had to think on it for a while. Even though two weeks earlier he had admitted aloud, when the documents were first discovered, that they were, in fact, Benedict's. "He must have gotten wind of what those documents actually were," Ronald continued, "and the threat they pose to his ridiculous share of the Circle J Ranch." He patted Mehitable's neck. "But I've said *enough* about Stanley Jones. I am headed to meet my future wife." A smile lifted the corners of his mouth as he remembered her exact words.

Yes, I accept your offer, and I will make plans to come to Craig, Colorado, immediately. And I think your idea of courting for two months before we commit to matrimony is wise. I look forward to spending the rest of my days with a man who appreciates the quiet simplicity that good planning brings to one's life.

He looked forward to that too. To be shed of this bothersome loneliness *plus* have a likeminded woman with whom to accomplish said task, he'd say he had met in with a bit of luck if luck wasn't such a specious concept.

He just hoped Miss Cooper would be understanding of his late arrival. And he couldn't begrudge Ma Hewlett for throwing off his schedule. When his old landlady stopped by his office first thing in the morning and asked for his help to fix a hole in her roof, what else could he do? He had to help her—the shingles wouldn't survive another storm. He just had not expected the shingles to take as long as they hand. Nor his visit to the Circle J.

He prompted Mehitable to go faster. The less Miss Cooper had to wait in the hotel all alone in a new town without a familiar face to console her, the better. To a fine woman like her, this venture must surely be taking its toll on her nerves already.

A quick glance up at the gray clouds rolling in confirmed his decision to move his appointment with Stanley Jones to the afternoon was the correct one. If only he'd been able to get Stanley to sign that affidavit. A drop of rain fell in his eye. One dripped on his nose . . . and another on his cheek.

Then a bucket's worth showered him and Mehitable.

♠

The rain thankfully tapered off to a drop here and there by the time he reached town. Mehitable slogged through the mud on Yampa Avenue, flipping some up onto Ronald's pant legs. He contemplated heading over to the hotel directly, but his coat smelled unsuitable to meet a woman—something akin to a wet dog. It would be best if he stopped home first and cleaned up.

Fifth Street proved to be less muddy—or at least less stirred into a mess by traffic and rain. He hurried to his home on the corner of Fifth and Breeze Street, trying not to worry about the mud it would add to his pant legs, telling himself it didn't matter because he was going to change his clothes anyway. He guided Mehitable around to the small stable at the back of his property. There he promptly unsaddled her and gave her a quick rub down before walking briskly to the house.

He had to admit his yard looked quite lovely after that drink of spring rain. Green shoots of native grass poked through the brown remnants of winter's dead blades. The tulips he'd planted last November, when he'd purchased the place, showed vibrant red blooms.

Ronald went around to the back door, not wanting to track mud on the front door rug—he'd proven himself relatively inept when it came to housekeeping. He looked forward to having a woman's touch in his home. Once inside, he undid his tie and top button as he eyed the staircase that led off from the kitchen.

"Good, you made it home." Logan stepped away from the sink with a glass of water in hand. "I'd suggest you take off them shoes before you go upstairs."

"Oh!" Ronald stopped, having barely noticed Logan—and remembering his muddy shoes. This wasn't like him at all. He slipped them off and placed them neatly by the back door. "Did everything go all right?"

"Of course." Logan smiled. "I done fetched her already and got her all set up in the hotel right nicely."

"Thank you, Logan. I do appreciate that. After all—" Ronald cut his words short. Logan need not be reminded that the trip out to the Circle J had been primarily for Logan's sake—baffling how the boy didn't seem to hold much interest in the will.

"I done told her that you'd be by in an hour or so—that was an hour ago. So you'd better hurry and," he glanced at Ronald's soiled pant legs, "clean up."

"Yes, that is for certain." Ronald blew out a breath. He would be late yet again. He headed for the stairs.

"She sure is pretty," Logan said.

Ronald stopped with one foot on the first step. "She is?" Had he heard Logan correctly?

"Yep." Logan gulped down his water, then grinned again. "I know you're goin' to like her." He set down his glass. "'Cause I like her; I like her a lot. She's not all stuffy like some ladies can be."

"Well, I do hope, like you say, that I'm 'going to like her' and that 'she is pretty.' Although, those are not prerequisites."

"Pre what?"

"Never mind." Ronald lifted his other foot onto the first step. "Both Miss Cooper and I know this will be more of a plutonic relationship than anything— at least at first. And we are both fine with that arrangement."

"Plutonic relationship? That sounds as invitin' as sittin' on an old board racked with slivers."

"Don't worry." Ronald held up his palm toward Logan. "I have taken measures to ensure, to the best of my ability, that our union can have a good margin of success. Procuring a room for her in the hotel while we become acquainted with each other is part of that plan. Also I have envisioned some outings and purchased her numerous gifts so as to win her affections. I have even drafted a few," he cleared his throat, "love letters to move the process along at a reasonable pace."

"And you're hopin' to make her fall in love with you—all in two months?" Logan raised both eyebrows.

"That is the plan." He took one more step up. Then Logan's words registered, and he swung around. "Who told you my goal was to marry her by June tenth?"

"It was Campbell who said you done reserved the hotel room for two months, starting today, April tenth. And I put two and two together." Logan dropped into a chair at the table. "What I don't understand is why you just don't have me go fetch Reverend Brown right now—at least as soon as you change your britches—and marry her tonight." He wagged a spoon at Ronald that had been left on the table. "Save yourself all that money. Ain't that what men usually do when they get themselves one of those brides out of a catalog?"

"First of all, you make it sound like I ordered Miss Cooper from back East like I would a new law book."

"Why else would they call 'em mail-order brides?"

Choosing not to answer that, Ronald continued. "Second of all, how does a fourteen-year-old come to be an expert in such matters?" He gave Logan a mock glare. "I only found out about this opt—curiosity less than four months ago."

Logan wagged a hand at him. "Heck, loads of fellows around here got themselves a wife that way. Good ole Joe at the blacksmith shop and Ned over at the telegraph office, to name a few. 'Cept they didn't put Sally and Constance up in the hotel for no month or so; they married them right away." He scratched his head. "I suppose most fellows around here couldn't afford that."

"Well, I can." Ronald continued up the steps. "And I want to make sure Miss Cooper has no regrets in marrying me." *And I have no regrets marrying her.*

Ronald had completely unbuttoned his shirt by the time he reached the top of the stairs. He hurried into his bedroom and tossed the garment over the armchair in the bay window—there was no time to fold it. A minute later, he added his muddy pants to the pile. As he pulled on a clean shirt, he had to stop. Those two pieces of clothing couldn't remain as such, not if he chanced seeing them again as he dressed. He stepped over to the chair and folded the shirt so he could place it neatly in the basket where he kept his soiled laundry until Mrs. Stedman picked it up on Thursdays to wash. Then he hung his pants on a hanger so they could dry before he folded and added them to the basket.

He freshened up, rinsing his face in the basin and dabbing a damp cloth in less accessible spots where perspiration had gathered from his ride. After his hair and well-trimmed mustache were combed and he'd donned a fresh shirt, suit, and clean pair of shoes, he hurried down the stairs. He waved to Logan as he uttered a quick goodbye and stepped outside. A cluster of tulips caught his eye as he leaped off the shallow porch. The foundation of the house contrasted the red blooms, which appeared extra vibrant against the gray stone.

"Flowers. But of course," he uttered to the spring breeze. He'd read that bouquets of flowers were one of the recommended ways to court a young lady in the proper way. He pulled out his pocketknife and cut a dozen of the stems from their bases, each at exactly the same length, forming a cluster of blooms that fanned out like an umbrella. Grasping them all in one hand, he walked briskly toward the hotel two blocks away, grateful the evening air was neither too cold nor too warm and neither humid nor dry.

He took extra care to avoid puddles from the storm. Miss Cooper must not see even a skiff of mud on his pants. That could add one more variable of difficulty to his task of courting.

He took long strides as he crossed a somewhat dry spot on Yampa Avenue, all the while focusing on the two-story, red-brick hotel. What a magnificent building, rising from the muddy streets of this coarse western town. He wished his office was so stately. Would Miss Cooper deem him unworthy because he worked out of a plain wooden building with a solitary window looking out onto the main street of this community? And his house—would she find it too small, too simple? He knew she came from a well-to-do family in Chicago. Unfortunately, that was about all he knew about her—except that they shared the common goal of wanting to find a compatible companion. Most of their correspondence dealt with current events, positive features of Craig, Colorado, and being a lawyer in the "Wild West." But her letters were neatly penned, and her prose showed organization. Those things *had* seemed enough for him.

Was she actually pretty? And "not stuffy" as Logan had said? Ronald stared at the sky momentarily.

Ronald brought his thoughts down from the sky and focused on reality. He was not unaware of his boorish, plain looks. She might be suitable for him, but were his qualities sufficient for Miss Cooper? His stride lessened into short, quick steps as his heart pounded faster. Had this all been a mistake? At least living his lonely life as it was had been a known. He had full control of that life. Having a wife could change that. Had he planned for that adequately? He stepped slowly onto the wooden sidewalk in front of the hotel, took a deep breath, and slunk into the hotel.

"Good afternoon, Mr. Tucker," he said to the hotel manager standing behind the counter examining a ledger. "Or should I say, good evening? Perhaps that would be more accurate."

Mr. Tucker looked up. "Ah, Ronald, you're here. Would you like that I go fetch you your gal? I believe she is up in her room waiting for you."

"There's no need—well, perhaps it would be best if you did." Ronald cleared the nervousness from his throat. "I don't know if it would be proper for me to knock on her hotel room door. Or would it? Gracious me. Help me out here, Mr. Tucker. I don't know what is proper and what is not when it comes to courting."

"Come on, none of this 'Mister Tucker' stuff; it's Campbell to you. Heck, Ronald, you've known me for nigh onto three years now." He gave Ronald a friendly slap on the back. "And if'n you don't knock on her door, then I'll have to. Either way, it's still a knock on the door. It's not like either of us are entering her room."

"I think I'd prefer if you would knock on her door. And then tell—I mean ask her if she would like to come down and join me for dinner over at Sunny's Place." He cleared his throat. "If you'd oblige me so, uh . . . Campbell."

"Sure enough." Mr. Tucker took the stairs two at a time. A knock sounded at the top of the stairs, then an exchange of voices in low tones. He barreled back down the stairs with a grin spreading past the edges of his thin mustache. "She'll be down in a minute. Have a seat." He motioned with his eyes to the red-orange sofa in the corner of the tiny lobby.

Ronald stepped to the sofa, started to lower onto it, but stood back up and paced.

The sound of dainty footsteps descending the stairs pulled Ronald's eyes away from the floor and toward the staircase. The woman walking down the stairs had perfect posture, held her head high, and bent her elbow precisely at ninety degrees so as to safely carry the coat draped over her arm. She flowed down each step with grace. Truly, a fine lady stood before him. He'd figured such was the case with Miss Cooper but . . . He swallowed a wad of saliva that had somehow lodged itself in his throat as if it were solid. He'd never expected her to be so striking. She had piled her dark-brown hair onto her head in a pleasing fashion. Wisps of four tiny curls framed her face, a face reminiscent of a child's, yet gracefully mature with its rosy soft lips, high cheeks, and small, round nose.

Why had she not sent him a portrait of herself? It was the first thing he wanted to ask as she stepped from the last stair and glided toward him. He moved his lips to talk, but his tongue seemed to lie dead in his mouth. Words refused to come.

"You must be Ronald. Am I correct?" She held out her hand rather awkwardly at first and then extended it fully, palm facing the floor.

Was he supposed to take it? Oh, bother. All that reading he'd done flew out the window—along with his wits. "Uh . . . uh, yes, that would be me." Instinct caused him to grip her hand and give it a firm shake.

She grinned.

He detected a hint of amusement in her alluring smile, and he feared embarrassment would flush his cheeks to where they'd be rosier than hers. He released her hand, shoved his into his pocket, and with his other hand thrust out the flowers. "And you, I presume, are Miss Wilhelmina Cooper."

Still smiling, she took the flowers from him. "Um . . . well . . ." She sounded somewhat hesitant.

Had she taken a good look at him and decided against this whole mail-order marriage? Though spirits dampened, Ronald determined to convince her to give it a try, even though they'd signed no formal contract, and they had only a "gentleman's agreement" to wed. He'd already invested a considerable sum of money into this venture, what with her train fare and hotel room. Money well spent as far as he was concerned. Staring at her, standing before him in a simple white blouse and dark-blue skirt looking the model of loveliness and practicality, his heart wanted to continue down this path. Remembering his etiquette, he extended his elbow. "Would you care to accompany me to the nearby restaurant for supper, Miss Cooper?"

She looped an arm around his elbow. "I would love that," she said with a sincerity that boosted his confidence. She turned to Campbell. "Would you put these in water for me? Oh, and take them to my room? Thank you."

Campbell nodded and relieved her of the tulips.

As Ronald and Miss Cooper moved out onto the sidewalk, she said, "Before we proceed any further, there's a matter I need to discuss with you."

"Oh." Ronald slowed his steps. Just like he had feared, she'd taken one look at him and now had cold feet. "Could we possibly eat our supper first?" He wanted to postpone the inevitable. Perhaps he could say something during their meal to convince her otherwise.

His heart sunk. Without a pen and paper at his disposal, he'd be hard pressed to express his feelings to any woman, let alone this one—who was obviously above and beyond his station.

♠

Chapter 7

DOROTHY'S STOMACH GROWLED AS SHE strolled down the sidewalk arm in arm with Mr. Smith. Surely it wouldn't hurt to wait until after supper to tell him she wasn't Wilhelmina—she might not be able to afford a decent meal for days. She patted the letter tucked safely in the pocket of one of the few things that was actually hers—her coat. Bless Wilhelmina Cooper's heart for every other piece of respectable clothing she had. Memory of the dear woman's kindness rekindled that good feeling in her chest. She wished more people were like Wilhelmina. And Mary Tucker, who'd just given her a needle *and* a spool of thread this afternoon. Dorothy wished *she* was more like those ladies. Being nice to others shouldn't have to be a luxury that only the rich could afford.

"So, Mr. Smith," Dorothy spoke up to break the silence between them. Their shoes, however, tapped out a cheerful rhythm against the planks of the sidewalk. "What does one do for diversion in the town of Craig?"

"Diversion?" He said the word like it was a foreign concept to him.

"You know . . . fun? What do you do in your leisure time?"

"I don't know that I have any leisure time." His eyes took on a look of panic, as if he'd said something wrong.

"Really?"

"I do take time off, mind you. I help Ma Hewett out now and again—she's a widow who doesn't know the right end of a hammer," he said with a sheepish grin Dorothy found quite endearing. "I promise, I am not a complete bore."

"I'm sure you're not." Dorothy wagged a hand at him, wondering why this fellow was so hard on himself. His kindness already surpassed that of any man she'd previously known—all men Vincent had insisted she pretend to court for the purpose of getting them to the poker table or loosening up their pocketbooks.

He blushed and kicked a pebble off the sidewalk. His elbow stiffened as she clutched it further to assist her descent from the sidewalk onto the damp road.

The firming of his arm for her support threw her off balance for a second, and she stumbled. "I'm sorry," she said as she gripped his arm tighter, unfamiliar with such chivalry. Some gal would really win the jackpot were they able to snag such a gentleman as this. Dorothy thought about the men who had courted her, and her stomach soured. What did she expect? She was a saloon girl. And worse—a swindler. And she was showing her lack of breeding already by her clumsiness.

Mr. Smith's eyes widened in noticeable fear. "No, it is I who should be sorry."

She took a deep breath to steel her nerves like so many times before when acting her part. "Not at all. I am quite fine," she responded and patted his arm. Luckily, this façade need only last until after she had her fill of supper.

She surveyed the main street of the town as she and Mr. Smith strolled in silence down the sidewalk, now on the other side of the street. They walked past a butcher shop, a gunsmith, and then a telegraph office. Dorothy hoped one would possibly, maybe hire her on. They approached a whitewashed wooden building bearing a large sign. She didn't need to read it to know it was a saloon. The swinging double doors and the smell of alcohol was enough.

"Is this where we're going to eat, in a saloon?" she asked, realizing her voice had risen higher than she'd expected.

"Uh, oh no, sorry. Let me explain." His face flushed again. The touch of pink added a measure of spice to his otherwise dull face—so dull she found it rather charming. "There is a restaurant on the other side of the building. This side is The Sunny Saloon." He prompted her past the swinging doors that did little to hold back the drunken noise. "Around the corner is Sunny's Place. It's a whole different room—a restaurant fitting a woman of your caliber. I hope."

Dorothy squirmed. If she wasn't so hungry, she'd tell him right here and now the caliber of woman she really was. She'd pull him inside that saloon without batting an eye, give him the letter, and be done with this task. She calmed her steps and walked around the corner, still arm in arm with Mr. Smith.

The entrance to Sunny's Place had a regular door with yellow glass set into four small windows that formed a square near the top. Mr. Smith opened the door and motioned for her to step inside before him. "Thank you," she bid, nodding at him. A smile formed on her face without effort, and it felt good.

He nodded in response and then stood there like a statue just inside the door, waiting to be seated she assumed.

"You don't say much, do you?" she blurted like the saloon girl she was and then brought her hand to her mouth. "Sorry."

"That is quite all right. It is true."

A curvy woman in a red dress similar to Dorothy's old one approached with a paper and pencil in hand. "Land's sake, Ronald, is this who I think she is?" She looked straight at Dorothy.

"And who *do* you think I am, exactly?" Dorothy responded as Ron's blush grew pinker.

"His new mail-order bride, of course."

"Who—" Mr. Smith swallowed hard "—told you I had plans to acquire a," he cleared his throat, "'mail-order bride,' as you call it? I have mentioned my intentions to very few."

"Ah, word gets around." The woman in red smiled as she gave Mr. Smith a wink. She turned to Dorothy. "My name's Sunny."

"Excuse my lack of manners, Sunny." Ronald cleared his throat and held his hand out toward Dorothy. "May I introduce to you Miss Wilhelmina Cooper?"

"A pleasure to meet you," Sunny said. "Welcome to Craig. We're sure glad to have you, Wilhelmina—for Ronald here. And for us. More womanfolk here in town is always a good thing." She motioned for them to follow her. "I'm giving you the best seat in the house, which ain't much different than any of the other spots—it just sounds good," she said out of the corner of her mouth. She sat them at a table in the far end of the room. "And the dessert's on me tonight. One of Lavender's famous sweet rolls, okay?" She winked at Ronald again, and Dorothy found herself feeling comfortable around this woman.

Ronald blushed. "I am fully able to pay for Miss Cooper's sweet roll if she so chooses to have one."

"Heavens, I know that—that's not why I offered it." Sunny flapped her hand at him. "It's my way of congratulating your courage to take the bull by the horns and do something about the lack of young ladies in this here town." Sunny's eyes moved their focus to Dorothy. "Miss Cooper, you say? So you two aren't married yet?"

"Oh no," Dorothy said, holding her hand out in Mr. Smith's direction. "No, it's not what you think. We're just—"

"What I believe Miss Cooper is trying to say . . ." Mr. Smith cut in. By the wrinkles forming on his forehead, Dorothy gathered that action appeared to take effort. ". . . is that we are merely in the courting stage of our relationship. I have . . ." He swallowed. ". . . rather, we have decided together to do things properly . . . and get to know each other first before we commit to marriage."

"So where are you staying in the meantime?" Sunny looked at Dorothy.

"The hotel." Dorothy chewed on her lip. The sooner they ate supper and she delivered that letter, the better. "At least for tonight. But who knows after Mr. Smith gets to know who I really am," she said with a nervous laugh.

"Aw, nonsense." Sunny waved her pencil at Dorothy. "Ronald here likes everyone, so don't you worry." She raised the piece of paper closer to her pencil. "What would you like, honey?"

"What'da ya got?" Dorothy hurriedly cleared her throat, hoping to dispel her barroom response. "I mean, what is it I have to choose from?"

"Tonight we got our roast beef platter, a piled-high ham sandwich, or beef stew and a wedge of bread." Sunny glanced at Mr. Smith and shrugged. "Nothing new tonight."

Dorothy turned to him. "Apparently you've eaten here before. What do you suggest?"

"It all tastes good," he stated.

Sunny leaned toward Dorothy. "The roast beef is my favorite. It comes fresh every day from the Circle J Ranch just outside town."

"That sounds good. Yes, I'll take the roast beef. Thank you," Dorothy sincerely added.

"I will take the ham sandwich," Ronald said. He then folded his hands in his lap and stared at Dorothy's hair as Sunny headed to the kitchen.

Dorothy wondered if she'd not combed it well or if a strand or two had worked their way out of the clips. "Is there something wrong with my hair?" She reached up to surmise the problem.

"No." Mr. Smith's eyes didn't move an inch. Nor did his body.

Dorothy swore even his lip didn't move. Could he see right through her? See her past? She felt her hair, looking at Mr. Smith for more than just a "no." Her fingers found nothing amiss. She had to say something, get him to talk, move, anything. "Then why are you looking at it like you've seen a rat's nest up there?" she asked, though her insides felt the more appropriate question was "like you've seen the life I've led the last five years?"

"It's striking."

She laughed to hide her embarrassment. Most men who showered her with compliments were after something more than sharing supper together. Yet she sensed that was not the case with Mr. Smith. He now stared at her face. She wished he'd say something; his silence unsettled her more than the noise of an erupting fistfight in the saloon around the corner in the connecting room.

"So, how's the law business? Do you keep busy in this Wild West town?" It was the first thing that came to mind. She doubted those men who were in the saloon would come to Mr. Smith for assistance. She knew their type all too well.

"Sometimes." He sank back into silence. A second later, he piped up with an edge of nerves to his voice. "But that does not mean I don't keep busy enough to pay my bills."

"I'm sure you do fine." Dorothy smiled. He didn't want her—or rather Wilhelmina Cooper—to think he couldn't provide for her. *How sweet.*

"Take today, for example. I worked on a case that promises a sizable income. Not that I'm taking on the case for monetary reasons. It's for a good friend of mine, for his future welfare actually."

Dorothy liked that the man was finally talking—not just staring at her. She wanted to keep it that way. "Tell me about it," she urged.

"Where do I start?" Mr. Smith ran a hand through his mud-brown hair.

She had all night. "How about the beginning?"

"Well, I'll start with the death of Benedict Jones. He died a year ago when his ranch house caught on fire."

"This Benedict Jones, was he someone important?"

"I suppose some might have considered him as such."

"What about you?" Dorothy sensed Mr. Smith didn't consider him all that important.

"I didn't know the man very well, so I have no room to judge." Mr. Smith moved his fork out of the way and rested his clasped hands on the table. "Let's just say he owned one of the largest ranches in northwestern Colorado."

Dorothy thought this Mr. Jones sounded like a perfect victim for one of Vincent's poker games. Grateful those days were behind her, she let out a sigh.

Ronald stopped talking and stared at her. "Are you all right, Miss Cooper?"

"Yes, quite. Please continue," she urged.

"If you insist," Ronald said. "A few days before Benedict's death, he came into my office and paid me to rewrite his will. I obliged him and set right to work. I had the will all drawn up, ready for his signature by the end of the day. Unfortunately, he never got the opportunity to sign it before he died."

"What was wrong with his first will?"

"He had removed his daughter from the will about five years prior, and now he wanted to put her back in."

"Why would a father do such a thing? Taking her out in the first place, I mean." Not that Dorothy would know, but she couldn't imagine a father doing something like that.

"He had been afraid her suitors only wanted to marry his daughter, Susannah, for her inheritance."

"So what happened to change his mind and have his daughter put back into his will?"

"I'm not sure." Mr. Smith shrugged. "Maybe he was finally having a change of heart. Let's hope so." He gazed away for a moment. "Yes, that must be it because he added his youngest son into his new will as well. The boy was never in the will from the very beginning, unlike his older sister."

"What kind of man leaves out one of his sons? A young boy by the sound of it?"

"A distraught man."

Dorothy looked Mr. Smith in the eyes, wanting more explanation.

"His wife died in childbirth, and he blamed poor little Logan."

"Logan? The young man that picked me up and brought me to the hotel?"

"Yes."

"He's the friend you referred to then?" Dorothy appreciated Mr. Smith referring to this teenage boy as a friend, the same as he might a colleague.

Mr. Smith nodded as a proud smile formed. "Yes, and a better friend would be hard to find."

"So you're helping Logan do something about his father's will? Is that what you were doing when he came to pick me up from the stage?" Dorothy couldn't think of a better reason for a man to miss picking up his future bride from the stagecoach, though she had a hard time believing this was the case. No man she ever knew did things to help others.

"Not exactly." Mr. Smith let out a breath of obvious frustration. "The boy doesn't seem to care that he inherits anything from his father's legacy. He says he likes earning his own keep. He is employed at the livery stable—and now by me."

"He works for you?"

"It's more like he does odd jobs for me in exchange for a room at my house. He still works at the livery stable for his spending money." Mr. Smith wrung his hands together, and she sensed his worry once again. "But he assures me he will find another place to bed down by the time we marry—if I don't get his inheritance to him in time. So you will not have to share your home with a teenage boy—if you don't want to."

His last line transmitted a strong feeling of hope. It touched Dorothy. This man wanted to continue to help Logan, yet he wanted a wife too—and he feared both could not coexist. But from what she'd come to know about Wilhelmina, she figured that dear woman would have welcomed Logan into their home.

Heck, if Dorothy were in Wilhelmina's shoes, she'd welcome Logan to stay too. But she was not Wilhelmina. And now Mr. Smith was without the woman he'd planned to marry. And no matter how delightful Logan was, he was no substitute for a wife. Dorothy moved her gaze from Mr. Smith's hands up to his face. She didn't know how to respond. "Uh . . ."

The rattle of teetering dishes pulled Dorothy's attention to the tray Sunny carried their way. "Okay, Ronald, you had the sandwich." Sunny set a plate in front of Mr. Smith heaped with a thick ham sandwich, a dollop of mashed potatoes, and a pickle. "And Miss Cooper, you had the roast beef. Right?"

"Yes." Dorothy eyed the thick gravy-covered slice of beef resting atop a mound of mashed potatoes and cooked carrots placed before her. "And please, call me Dorothy." The moment Dorothy said her name, she wished she hadn't.

"O—kay," Sunny said with a wink. "Dorothy it is." Sunny stepped back. "Holler if you need anything else." Then she headed into the saloon.

"I thought your name was Wilhelmina?" Mr. Smith's voice wobbled as it came out barely above a whisper.

Dorothy swallowed her bite of mashed potatoes, eyeing her plate, hoping to have finished more of the meal before she ventured toward this subject. "I guess now is as good a time as any to tell you." She let out a sigh as she set her fork to the side of her plate.

"Tell me what?"

The panic in Mr. Smith's eyes startled Dorothy. "Don't look so afraid. It's just that I'm not, um . . . how do I say this . . ." she said, trying to reassure the fear flowing from the man at full force.

She could tell he was lonely. She could easily visualize his story: logically, he knew a wife was the answer, but his social awkwardness served as a dead weight pulling down his ability to find one. It had probably taken great courage to answer that ad in the magazine Wilhelmina had placed. And most likely, he doubted he could do it again.

Dorothy doubted he could do it again too. Embarrassment surely would add fuel to the fire and would consume his courage. How would such a timid man ever dare look for another mail-order wife, especially if the first one got cold feet and up and left him before she ever got to Craig?

She gazed at Mr. Smith, at those worried brown eyes, wanting to soothe the hurt that the letter inside her coat would assuredly bring. His eyes exuded kindness despite their gloss of fear. In fact, everything about him spoke of goodness. She'd never met a man like him—never knew such a man existed.

She couldn't tell him the truth about Wilhelmina right now. Later, she'd do it later. When the moment felt better.

"Well, I'm not . . ." Dorothy pulled again from years of weaving tales to cover for Vincent. ". . . as organized and prim and proper as you probably gathered from my letters."

"That . . . I guess is okay." Mr. Smith took a deep breath. "Yes, yes, that is okay. Some people say I need to learn to tolerate a bit of chaos, so, um, this could be good."

Dorothy smiled. She found this man's quirks as charming as his plain face—with other men, she'd found their quirks alarming. "You see," she spun her explanation further, "I've always thought the name Wilhelmina was a mouthful to say and a little too formal for my personality—even though it was my mother's name. So I go by my middle name, Dorothy, when I'm with friends."

"Oh." Mr. Smith's face relaxed.

"So I hope you'll call me Dorothy."

His eyes widened. "Most certainly, Miss Cooper," he said with a definite note of relief in his voice. "And please, now that we are officially courting as agreed in our correspondence, do call me Ronald."

"Only if you call me Dorothy." She'd figure out how to get past the Cooper part later.

Then it hit her. Hard. She had wanted so much to leave her old life of deceit behind her with Vincent, to start anew. But here she was, conning a vulnerable man into carrying on a phony courtship. What was she doing?

I'm protecting his feelings at the moment. She couldn't tell him the truth right now, not with those brown eyes of his staring at her, expressing such sadness one moment and such hope the next. *I'm also keeping a roof over my head until I can get on my feet—that's what I'm doing.*

"Dorothy it is." His delighted smile tore at her heart. "And allow me to say, Dorothy, I am most grateful to have the pleasure of getting to know you better." He reached across the table and squeezed her hand.

Instinct made her want to pull her hand away, but her acting skills kept it in place. "Likewise," she responded. Curiously, her skin didn't crawl at his touch. In fact, she found the sensation of his fingers upon her hand rather soothing.

"I am so glad you came to Craig. Please allow me the pleasure of inviting you to a picnic lunch tomorrow down by Yampa River. What do you say?"

"Yes, I'd love that." Her response flew from her mouth before she had time to contain it. She turned away and mustered a cough to hide the surprise of her unnecessary forwardness.

Chapter 8

RONALD STROLLED DOWN THE STREET toward his house. Springtime always seemed to make the moon shine brighter. Or was it bright because he'd enjoyed this evening more than any other he remembered? Now, he was definitely glad he'd responded to that ad in that magazine. Miss Cooper—Dorothy—had proved to be delightful company. She always kept the conversation going. Quite a pleasant surprise given that her letters lacked much in the way of conversation. Perhaps writing was not her strong suit. Not to worry. That was his strength.

He opened the gate and walked toward his new house with lightness in his step. A few months ago, when he'd acquired the place, he'd feared it was an extravagant purchase. But now he was glad to own it. With its three bedrooms, two stories, white picket fence, and garden, it could easily fulfill its original purpose: to house a family.

Taking the front steps two at a time, he leaped onto the wide, covered porch and opened the front door. A warm glow of yellow filtered down the stairwell from above.

"Is that you, Logan?" he called out.

"Who else?" Footsteps shuffled across the floor above, and Logan appeared at the top of the stairs. "How'd it go with Miss Cooper?"

"Fine," Ronald said, making sure he contained his inner feelings and maintained his usual businesslike exterior—even if this was Logan. He needed that consistency to keep things functioning comfortably.

"Are you goin' to see her tomorrow?" Logan asked in a voice as excited as Ronald felt.

"Yes." Ronald began his ascent up the stairwell, careful to keep his words as steady and methodical as each step he took on the darkened stairwell. "I have invited her to join me on a picnic down by the river."

"That's wonderful!" The lamp in Logan's hand flickered from his jerking movements. "Did she agree to go with you?"

"Yes."

"I knew it! I knew you two were goin' to hit it off."

"We have not 'hit it off' as you put it. We have, however, agreed to continue the courtship we decided upon in our correspondence. We shall see—"

"You goin' to make the picnic lunch yourself?" Logan's interrupted.

Panic seized Ronald's gut. "I—I hadn't planned on it. I am rather helpless in the kitchen. Drat!"

"What you goin' do then?"

"Uh . . ." What was happening to him? This was not like him at all. He liked to have his days planned out at least a day ahead and written down. To have come up with this idea on the fly should have sent him into a panic the moment he uttered the ill-planned outing to Dorothy. Yet it hadn't; it had sent a refreshing burst of energy clear down to his toes.

However, it appeared he was paying for it now. He swallowed hard. "I don't know. I have never been on a picnic, let alone prepared one."

"I'll help you!" Logan held out his lamp so Ronald could see the top steps. "I've been on my fair share of them with my sister and townsfolk who invited me along. I've also seen plenty at a distance, ones involving a fellow courtin' his gal."

"Perfect! Tell me what I need."

"Get yourself an old quilt for sittin' on. You'll spread that out on a flat, dry spot by the river. Lucky for you, the weather looks to be good tomorrow. The only other thing you'll need is a basket full of tasty food." He handed Ronald the lamp and rubbed his hands together as if imagining the picnic lunch himself. "You want I should do that for you?"

"Are you going to make it?" Ronald sent Logan a fearful glance.

"Heck no." Logan laughed. "I'll ask Sunny to put a basket together for you. It might cost you a little extra. Is that okay?" He winced. "But I'll do all the arrangin'. And I'll get your buggy hooked up right nice to Mehitable and set the basket in the back so you and Miss Cooper have plenty of space up front to sit." A mischievous grin curved his lips. "Or maybe I'll just set the basket on the far side of the seat so she'll be forced to sit right next to you."

"Let's go with your first plan," Ronald said, though he smiled inside at the idea of sitting close to her. "Miss Dorothy Cooper is a fine lady and must be treated as such."

"Of course, Ron." Logan raised an eyebrow as he titled his head to one side. "Dorothy is it, ay? I see you're callin' her by her nickname already. This is good."

"She prefers her friends call her Dorothy," Ronald explained, grateful that was all there was to that uncomfortable moment early on. "Okay, once Miss Cooper and I arrive at the river bottom with the basket of food and I spread out the blanket, what do we do next?"

"You have your picnic, of course."

"Please, Logan, I know this must seem intuitive to you, but I need some specific details on what one does at a picnic. I want to put my best foot forward on this first excursion in our courtship."

"Hmm, what does one do on a picnic?" Logan stared at the ceiling in obvious thought. "Well, for one thing, you get to eat your food with your fingers."

"Your fingers?" The very idea made Ronald's insides quiver. "Isn't that rather messy?"

"Naw. It's fun. It's my favorite part."

"What else does one do?" Ronald hoped there was more, something less unnerving.

"Well, you talk about how nice the weather is, and you keep brushin' your trousers to make the ants stay away from your plate of food. Leastwise, that's what I do."

"What about the couples you've seen picnicking? Is that what they did?"

"Heck if I know if they talked about the weather. Probably not. Probably talked about each other. And I'm sure they had ants—that's part of a picnic. But I don't think they cared about them. They were too interested in kissin' each other." Logan's mouth curled up in that same mischievous grin. "They sure looked like they were enjoyin' themselves."

Ronald cleared his throat as he cleared the image of himself and Dorothy enjoying such a picnic. "I think it would be best if Miss Cooper and I started out with the picnic you first described. Weather is always a safe topic. And I'm glad it will be good tomorrow."

"Aw, shucks." Logan offered a halfhearted pout. "Suit yourself," he said and limped off to his room.

With lamp in hand, Ronald hurried into his room to plan what he would wear tomorrow and make a list of possible conversation topics. He would go one step further than weather and make this picnic memorable for Dorothy.

♠

Dorothy took in a big breath, the smell of springtime, and listened to the river splashing over the rocks in its bed. "This is so beautiful, Ronald. I never got to enjoy nature like this back East."

"Nonsense, they have rivers back in Chicago—maybe not right where you lived but close."

Dorothy scrambled to steer the conversation in a different direction. "I didn't get much chance to visit the outskirts." *Or anything outside a saloon or the apartments Vincent set me up in.* She wasted no time in spreading out the quilt Ronald had handed to her back at the buggy. "This is beautiful. It looks almost antique," she said as she smoothed out its wrinkles and knelt down. It felt too nice to be using on the ground. "Where did you get it?"

"My great-grandmother made it for my grandmother when she got married. My mother passed it to me when I moved out West." Ronald set his neatly packed basket of food in the middle of the quilt. "My mother and father still live in Chicago along with my younger brother, William . . . in the Hyde Park district. Did you ever get to the south side of the city much?"

"No," Dorothy responded, probably quicker than she should have.

"I had an older sister. But she died when she was eight. I was five." He sat down on the other side of the quilt, never looking at Dorothy. "Do you have any siblings?"

She peeked inside the basket, again determined to keep the conversation elsewhere. "What a scrumptious-looking picnic lunch. Did you make it?" she asked, skepticism raising her pitch slightly.

"No. I had Sunny's Place prepare it for me. You would not like my cooking."

Dorothy laughed. When he didn't crack a smile, she realized he was dead serious.

"My brother and I might look alike, but we are actually quite a bit different," he said as if he didn't want to drop the subject, yet his stiff posture told her he didn't necessarily feel comfortable continuing on.

She supposed talking about *his* family would be safe enough. "That's too bad—for him." She rushed her hand to her mouth. "I'm sorry. Did I say that?"

"Yes, you did." He appeared to suppress the smile that formed along with an obvious flicker in his eyes.

"I'm sorry. I don't know what possessed me. I meant it's too bad his personality is not like yours—I wasn't speaking of appearance at all. It's just that you are such a gentleman," she rambled, rolling her eyes secretly to herself. She was making quite the mess of this. "And if your brother is that different from you, he must not be a gentleman."

He smiled again. "I say he is different because he is five years my junior, active in myriad social circles, and loves the family business. As we speak, at twenty-one, William is stepping into my father's shoes—a role my mother had always hoped I'd assume. But I could never manage a factory, oversee all those employees, and wine and dine the buyers of products so unimportant to humanity."

"What is your family business?" Dorothy's interest was piqued. She'd never seen him so passionate in his speech.

"They manufacture crystal stemware," Ronald said as if it were something he was ashamed of. "And to think my brother had the gall to offer me a job on the production line last time I was home."

It was Dorothy's turn to smile. "He was probably just teasing you. Maybe he was in need of new employees, it was on his mind, and he offered you that job in jest."

Ronald looked at her. "You very well might be correct." His forehead wrinkled. "Why is it that people twist things? Why can they not talk straight, tell it like it is?"

"Because," Dorothy sucked in breath, "we—he's human." She quickly pulled the cloth from the top of the basket. "My heavens, you have surely gone to more detail than you should have. A simple sandwich would have been fine."

Ronald smiled at her. "Practicality is such an admirable quality." He pulled a cold, roasted chicken from the basket and set it with its accompanying plate in front of Dorothy. "But there is a time to be practical and a time to dismiss it," he said, pulling out a loaf of bread. "Now is such a time. I am courting you. And I want to do it properly. A lady of your quality deserves to be made a fuss over."

A pang of heartburn brought her fist to her chest. Not only were his words too kind, they were completely, utterly false. She was no lady. The fact that she continued in this masquerade proved that.

Ronald took hold of the bread with both hands, tore off a fist-sized piece, and placed it on her plate. He then did the same for himself.

Dorothy thought it a bit odd for a man who, up until now, came across as very orderly and proper. She thought it even more out of character for him when he tore both legs from the chicken, placed one on her plate and one on his, then he wiped his hands on a napkin like he'd performed a most disgusting task. He then placed a pickled cucumber on each plate.

"Shall we eat?" He slowly lifted his chicken leg to his mouth with his fingers barely grasping each end. He took a sizeable bite as Dorothy nibbled on her chicken leg, then he set his down, wiped his hands, and brushed an ant off his trousers and several times more after the poor ant was gone.

Ready to take a bite of her bread, Dorothy asked, "By chance, is there butter to go with this?"

"But of course." He retrieved a lidded butter dish from the basket and handed it to Dorothy.

Dorothy removed the lid, set the dish next to her, and waited for him to hand her a knife. When he resumed eating his chicken, she cleared her throat. That produced no response from him, so she reached for the basket. "Is there no silverware in there?"

"I believe there is. Though I am not sure why."

At the moment, Dorothy was glad this courtship was a phony. This man was a little too odd for her taste. "Well, would you give me a knife please?" she asked in a soft voice that did not reflect her irritation. "I do not wish to butter bread with my fingers."

"This is a picnic, is it not?"

"Yes, at least I thought so," Dorothy responded with a touch of her annoyance hardening her voice. She cleared her throat, reminding herself to stay in character.

"I was told at picnics one eats with their hands." The color drained from Ronald's face. "Oh, dear me. Is that not correct?"

"To a certain extent, yes," Dorothy said, realizing he was the one acting out of character. "I fear you've taken someone's advice much too literal." She wondered who gave him such advice and why. "Have you never been on a picnic before now?"

"No. My mother did not care for them. When Logan told me what one does on a picnic—shooing away ants and eating with one's hands—I finally understood why Mother never took us on one." He hung his head. "I wanted to make this outing special. I fear I have done quite the opposite."

"Oh, that's not true." She lifted his chin with her finger and made him look her in the eye. "I've never had such a . . . unique picnic before. In fact, now that I understand what you were doing, I find it rather . . . humorous." She removed her hand from his chin and covered her mouth as she laughed quietly. "Don't you?"

His eyes lit up. "So I have not offended you?"

Dorothy shook her head. "Not in the least."

His eyes appeared deep in thought and then lit up further. "Yes, this is quite humorous," he said with a hint of laughter in his voice.

"It's about time I butter my bread." She tore off a small piece from her bread and ran it over the top of the butter. Holding up the butter-slathered morsel she said, "This is much more fun than using a boring old knife," and popped it into her mouth.

Ronald appeared hesitant at first as he tore his bread in similar fashion and ran it across the butter. When he placed it in his mouth and chewed, his body noticeably relaxed. "I have always had a taste for lots of butter but never dared indulge." He did the same with another piece of bread. This time he laughed.

Dorothy found the pitch of his laughter delightful. It sounded nothing like the raucous noise of men seated around a poker table but more like that of a child's in a grown man's voice. "What else do you have in that basket?" she asked, not caring if this picnic continued all day now.

Ronald peered under what remained of the checkered cloth. "There are some sweet rolls in there, so save room. Oh, and a bottle of something."

"To drink?" Dorothy's mouth was rather dry. "Wine, perhaps?"

"I doubt it is wine. Sunny caters to a cow town palate." He extracted a narrow-necked, corked bottle that held a burgundy liquid. "No, I do believe it is."

"May I?" Dorothy held out her hand. She accepted the bottle from Ronald, uncorked it, and sniffed. "Smells like decent stuff." She lowered the bottle to her mouth and took a sip. "It is." When she noticed his jaw drop, she added, "Aw, come now, I'd thought we'd already thrown our manners out the window." She handed him the bottle.

Ronald hesitated momentarily and then raised the bottle to his mouth. He took a deep breath, as if to steady his nerves, pushed the bottle against his lips, and took a sip. "Quite tasty, if I say so myself," he said as if he'd accomplished a feat. He handed the bottle back to her.

"You seem to be enjoying yourself, Mr. Ronald Smith," Dorothy said and took another sip.

"That I am." He accepted the bottle from her. "There is this odd sense of thrill doing something against one's better judgment—that is harmless of course." He took another sip. "I'm sure it's safe to assume that you as well have never engaged in such activity?"

"Safe as anything," Dorothy said in her hearty, actress voice. *Safe as meeting head-on with a stampede of cattle.* She was doing something that was against any decent person's better judgment, something that wasn't necessarily harmless. She held up her hand to refuse his offer of more. The action accidentally knocked the bottle from his hand.

Ronald's eyes followed hers down to the pool of burgundy on the blanket. His face paled to its worst yet.

Dorothy gasped. "I didn't mean to—this quilt, it's probably very special to you."

"Yes, it is."

"I am *so* sorry." Dorothy shook her head. "Why on earth were you using it for a picnic?"

"Logan told me I needed an old quilt to sit on." Ronald pounded his palm to his head. "I was merely trying to ensure that I did everything to the utmost detail." His hand fell to his side, and his shoulders slumped.

"Don't you worry." Dorothy sopped up as much wine as she could with the checkered cloth. "I can try to wash this spot out if you'd like me to." She looked at him and awaited an answer. His long face made her heart ache. He'd tried so very hard to impress his mail-order bride, even to the point of losing his common sense, which, for this man, must have been a big sacrifice. It was too bad Wilhelmina Cooper didn't realize what she was giving up when she got that case of cold feet.

"I would love for you to try," Ronald said. "My laundering skills are worse than my culinary skills." He offered a feeble smile that convinced Dorothy further that Wilhelmina had made the biggest mistake of her life.

Chapter 9

DOROTHY ENJOYED THE SUNSHINE ON her face as the buggy jostled them down the rutted road. Ronald had been the one to suggest they take a ride before heading back to town, but he hadn't said much the whole time. She didn't really mind. The cottonwoods along the river bottom adorned in budding leaves held her attention just fine. She finally turned to him. "I'm enjoying this ride almost as much as our meal."

"So you enjoyed the picnic?" Ronald kept his eyes on the road, but it appeared as though they lit up with surprise. Or was it hope?

"Yes, I did." Dorothy realized she had enjoyed it a lot—much more than she should have. That picnic had been intended for Wilhelmina, not her. She jerked her gaze away from his profile and stared at the road ahead.

A horse trotted toward them. Its rider caught Dorothy's notice and sent a shiver of fear down her back. He had dark hair and wore an expensive hat and a rust-colored calf-skin jacket. *Vincent?* She stiffened. The urge to jump out and run overwhelmed her.

The rider stopped, holding up a hand for them to do the same. That intensified her urge to run.

Ronald reached out his arm and bid her to relax. "I know this man. It's okay."

Did Ronald know Vincent? Impossible! The rider's face was now in view. Her stomach twisted. He sported a larger mustache, and his steely eyes sat too close together in his narrow face to be Vincent's. Still, her intuition blared a warning about this man.

"Howdy, ma'am." The man lifted his hat and nodded at Dorothy. His eyes focused on her much too long for her comfort. "You must be—"

"This is Miss Dorothy Cooper," Ronald interrupted him. "If you could state your business and move on, Mr. Jones, I would appreciate it greatly. Miss Cooper and I have a tight schedule to keep."

Mr. Jones? She glanced to Ronald for confirmation. "As in Logan's brother, Stanley?"

Ronald nodded to her and turned his attention back to Mr. Jones. "Or do you just happen to be passing by and you've decided to be hospitable?"

"A little of both, you might say." Mr. Jones set his cowboy hat back on his head. "I'm passing this way on my way into town. Catching the two o'clock stage to Baggs. Tomorrow I'm headed back East on business. But when I caught sight of you, I thought this would be a good chance to tell you some bothersome news."

"Oh?" Ronald said with a hint of skepticism in his voice.

"You see, that paper you brought out yesterday for me to sign and I told you I had to think on it first? I'm afraid my housekeeper mistook it for garbage and used it to start the stove this morning."

Ronald's jaw jutted forward and blew out a breath. "That would not have happened if you had merely signed it while I was there."

"Don't worry. I'll dock her pay a fittin' amount for that." Mr. Jones scratched his abundant mustache. "But unfortunately, now I won't be able to sign your paper 'til I get back. Unless you got another one on you." He smiled, but it didn't reach his eyes.

Ronald clenched his hands into fists but kept them to his sides. "I told you yesterday I needed to pick that up by this afternoon and have it to Judge McConnell by tomorrow or your sister will have to start the appeal process all over again."

"I'm powerful sorry, Mr. Smith, but it was out of my hands." Mr. Jones held out his arms, palms up, while that same empty smile hung on his face. "Maybe I'll stop by your office when I get back. For now, I'd better be off if I don't want to miss that stage." He tipped his hat and sunk his spurs into his horse.

Dorothy breathed a sigh of relief when Mr. Jones's figure disappeared in the distance. "I'm sorry, but I don't much care for that man," she said, reeling inside from the way the man had looked at her, as if he was seeing her in her red dress, liked what he saw, and wanted more. She brought her hand to her mouth. "I apologize; that was uncalled for."

Ronald's face relaxed. "I share your sentiment. I admit, if you were not present, I fear I would not have expressed my feelings nearly as politely as you. You are both lovely and kind, such admirable traits."

Dorothy ducked her head to hide her blush—and her shame. "I take it you are not pleased with Stanley Jones?" she said to divert her pain.

"You would be correct." Ronald clenched his jaw. "If I was a betting man—but I'm not," he glanced at Dorothy as if to assure her, "I'd wager that that paper was not accidently placed in the stove but shoved in there by none other than Stanley Jones himself."

"You think so?" Dorothy smiled at this naive side of Ronald. Intrigued, she probed further. "What was it that he was supposed to sign, if you don't mind me asking?"

"No, I don't mind." He flicked the reins, and the horse pulled the buggy forward. "You know that case of the unsigned will I was telling you about last night? A few weeks ago some handwritten documents were discovered on the Circle J Ranch. It was believed they were penned by none other than Benedict Jones himself. No one knew old Ben's handwriting better than Stanley, so they were taken to him. He didn't read through them all, but at that time, Stanley wholeheartedly assured me the documents were written by Benedict. That was before he knew they were the pages of a handwritten will."

"Ah." Dorothy gasped, enjoying this story. She could see where this might be going. "Who found them—if it wasn't Stanley Jones?"

"Actually, it was Logan."

"Where did he find them? And how? I thought he was living with you?"

"Logan discovered them in a suitcase of his father's that for some reason had been left down at the ranch hand bunkhouse." A tender smile flitted across Ronald's face as he said, "The boy still visits there, even though he's not really welcomed by his brother."

"I like that kid."

Ronald's smile returned. "So do I." He cleared his throat and continued. "Logan took the suitcase to his sister, Susannah, knowing Stanley cared little about mementoes. When Susannah sorted through the items in the suitcase, she noticed a pocket in the lining of the case. In there, she found three sheets of paper that I now believe was the rough draft of the will Benedict gave to me to have written up as his official new will—the one he never had a chance to sign. But that rough draft *was* signed."

"Where does Stanley Jones fit into this?"

"Susannah wants to use this newly discovered will to appeal Benedict's old one. In order to do that, we need to verify that it was indeed written and, more importantly, *signed* by Benedict Jones. Everything I have read states that it requires three different parties to verify if the handwriting is indeed that of Benedict Jones." Ronald pulled up on the reins as they approached a curve in the road. The buggy slowed, and he continued. "Susannah signed an affidavit, swearing to the best of her knowledge that the signature was her father's. I signed one as well, being familiar with his handwriting as his attorney. We just need one more signature. The only other person that would be familiar enough with Benedict's signature, sufficiently to satisfy a judge, would be Stanley Jones."

"It's obvious," Dorothy said, "that Stanley doesn't want to sign that afa-David." Dorothy stumbled over the unfamiliar word. "But why? If that's his father's will, surely he would want the inheritance due him."

"That's the problem—at least in Stanley's eyes," Ronald said. "The new will gives him the inheritance *due him*. The current one in place gives him *everything*."

"Oh," Dorothy murmured, feeling further justified in her low opinion of Stanley Jones. "So in this new will, Logan gets his share?"

"Not quite his share." Ronald clenched his jaw. "But at least something. Enough to live on."

"Don't worry; I'm sure you'll get the rightful will put into place. You seem a very capable lawyer," she said with sincerity.

"I do appreciate your optimism, Dorothy, and your high opinion—which I'm not so sure I deserve." He cleared his throat. He then reached out with a trembling hand. "I would like to hold your hand. Would you allow me to do so as we continue home?"

"Uh . . . yes." She was taken aback momentarily by his direct honesty. She slipped her hand in his, wanting to play her part well. Buried memories of disgusting hands she'd been forced to hold—and pretend to enjoy holding—surfaced as his warm skin touched hers.

"Thank you, Dorothy." He held her hand firmly in his left. With his right hand he pulled the reins to guide the horse into an open meadow and turned the buggy around.

Their ride home continued without much conversation either, only an occasional, "this is a lovely day" or "hold on around this corner." The longer his hand remained intertwined with hers, the less upsetting it became. By the time they made it to town, his hand felt somewhat comforting. Crazy as it sounded to her, it almost created a sense of belonging. Not belonging as she did to Vincent but like a child belongs to a parent, a good feeling she'd long forgotten.

Without forethought, she gave his hand a squeeze.

Chapter 10

"SHE SQUEEZED MY HAND," RONALD told Logan, careful to hold his voice steady. Even Logan couldn't know the true extent of his feelings.

"That means she likes you." Logan settled into the overstuffed chair while Ronald added a log to the fireplace in the parlor.

"You really believe that is the case?"

"Of course." Logan propped his feet on the ottoman. "And I can tell you're sweet on her too. Look at you, pacin' the room like it's eight in the mornin' instead of eight at night."

"I guess I should let you get to bed. I too should retire," he said, but he chose to sit down on the sofa a little longer. "Thank you for listening to me ramble on like a schoolboy. I had to tell someone."

"Of course you did. And I was honored." Logan pulled the last piece of bread from the picnic basket that sat on the end table and took a big bite. "Thanks for bringin' me your leftovers of leftovers. Makin' two meals out of Sunny's fixin's was a grand idea. I'm sure Dorothy didn't mind. Did she?"

"No. She appeared delighted when I showed up with them at the hotel this evening, then profusely thanked me again when I left."

"She's got a good heart, Ronald. I can feel it."

"I can too."

"And she's not one of those ladies who needs you to spend a heap of money on her either."

"No, she is not."

"Not that I'm an expert on such matters," Logan said with a crook to his grin. "But I'd think that's a good quality to have in a wife."

"I think so too." Ronald's insides warmed.

"So are you goin' to keep goin'?"

"Come again?" Ronald raised an eyebrow.

"Are you goin' to keep courtin' Miss Cooper?"

"But of course." He looked in earnest at Logan. In the light of the single lamp they'd lit, Logan probably couldn't read his face or see his sincerity. Even if he hadn't found Dorothy as much to his liking as he had, he was committed to make this courtship succeed and marry her in two months' time. He had promised as much in his last letter, feeling a sense of duty to help ease her loneliness, and in return, she would help ease his. A symbiotic relationship. He liked the logic of it all.

"So what you goin' do next?" Logan ate the remainder of his bread with one bite. "You're goin' see her tomorrow, ain't you?" he said with his mouth full.

"I want to." Ronald smoothed his hair with his fingers. "But I have not yet decided on an activity." He picked up the red leather-bound book he'd left sitting on the end table. He'd purchased it from back East the moment he began correspondence with Wilhelmina—or rather Dorothy as he liked to think of her now. "In here it says I should wait a good number of days before I again call on Miss Cooper. You see, we've just barely begun to court."

"But you yourself said you're plannin' on marryin' her in two months. You gotta pick one or the other, Ron—what you want or what that blasted book wants." Logan shook his head. "I say use the book for kindlin'. Go with your gut instincts when it comes to courtin' Miss Dorothy. I like her. I like you even more. So I wanna see you two tie the knot in early June—it's such a pretty time of year, what with the Yampa Valley all green."

Logan's advice sounded logical and even touched Ronald in way that made him feel good. But the thought of proceeding without a well-orchestrated plan made his stomach sour. "We'll see." He quietly tucked the red book at his side and out of Logan's sight.

Logan swallowed the last remnants of his bread and yawned. "I guess I should head on up to bed. I got an early shift over at the livery stable tomorrow." He stood and headed for the stairs. "Thanks again, Ron, for lettin' me stay at your house. And I promise I'll be outta your way once Miss Dorothy marries you and moves in here."

"Please, do not worry yourself about that." Ronald nodded at Logan and then watched as he climbed the stairs. He pulled out the red book, ready to plan his and Dorothy's next excursion.

As Ronald opened to the page where he'd left the bookmark, his mind wandered to Logan. His gut tightened at the thought of letting the time period allotted by the judge to lapse. It would take time to begin the process all over again. But it had to be done. Logan needed that inheritance as meager as it was, to have a place and the means to live respectably on his own. Ronald bristled at the inequity of it all.

♠

Sunlight peeked through the curtains and shined in Dorothy's face. She rolled over, wanting to sleep longer—there was little else to do. She'd finished altering all of Wilhelmina's clothing yesterday. The smell of fresh linen filled her nose with a pleasant scent of lye and lavender rather than an accumulation of sweat and grime. She buried herself in the hotel's soft sheets while her back relished the comfort of a cotton-filled mattress and bedsprings. She lay in bed, enjoying herself until her stomach rumbled in hunger. Darn it all, she'd forgotten to go down for breakfast. She still wasn't used to such luxuries. Unfortunately, she'd need to scrounge up something to eat by noon.

"Get up," she said to herself and swung her bare feet over the side of the bed and stood. Stretching her arms above her head without any new bruises felt good. Thankfully, the two old ones were healing nicely. She doubted she'd even need to hide the one on her eye with makeup after today. A full night's sleep after the leftover chicken Ronald brought over had felt good too. She could definitely get used to this.

After a sponge bath using the fancy porcelain bowl and pitcher of fresh water Mary Tucker had brought up last night, Dorothy patted makeup on her eye and put on her brown skirt. Yesterday she'd spilt butter on her blue skirt, and she'd need to wash it out today. She thought it best to wear her brown skirt with her white blouse anyway, to mix things up. Her spirits sank. Surely Ronald would notice sooner or later that she only had two skirts and two blouses to her name—and the pale yellow dress she would keep for special occasions. Wilhelmina was supposed to have come from a well-to-do family.

How long could she keep up this charade?

At least until she got on her feet.

Then she'd give Ronald Wilhelmina's letter and move on.

Her handbag caught her eye. She grabbed it, opened it up, and counted her money once again. Eighty-five cents. Hardly enough to buy a new outfit. And she didn't even know if this town had a store that sold anything besides horse feed. Her stomach rumbled again. There was also the matter of feeding herself. She couldn't very well depend on Ronald to provide her every meal, now could she? Up until now, he'd done a fair job of doing so, but he'd mentioned nothing about today. Would she even see him?

Melancholy touched her heart with the thought that she might not.

Strange. This was a "business arrangement," the same as it had been for Wilhelmina—only with a different twist.

Well, she couldn't sit around waiting, hoping he would come by and buy her breakfast. She donned the shawl Wilhelmina had given her and headed down the stairs to see what this town offered in the way of breakfast for a nickel or two.

Once out on the street, a light spring breeze kissed her nose with its scent of pine. It was a shame she hadn't come out of her hotel room before now and enjoyed the new scenery on her own. She'd not been that observant of Craig's buildings, streets, and shops when she'd been with Ronald yesterday. It didn't look like a bad place to live—a lot prettier than the town in Missouri she'd run away from. Whitewashed shops lined both sides of the main street, each with a colorfully painted sign above the door. And there appeared cheery-looking people on the sidewalks too.

She stepped from the wooden sidewalk at a corner, then decided to venture down a cross street and take a stroll through a neighborhood. Charming houses lined both sides of the dirt road, each with a fresh coat of whitewash applied to its clapboards. Highlights of color set off many a gable bracket or porch rail. Her favorite was the blue trim on a particularly striking two-story home on the corner. Its wraparound porch had its posts and rails and even a swing painted in a lighter shade of blue. Strolling past it, she touched the top of each picket of its fresh-white fence, imagining chatting to the people of the house as they sat outside in the evening on that swing or picking the cherries from the tree that was budding with pink blossoms.

The thought of moving on to yet another city wearied her. This town was filled with lovely houses—and lovely people from what she'd seen so far. Maybe she *should* stay here. She definitely liked the idea.

Unfortunately, Ronald would want nothing to do with her once he learned who she was and that she'd been using him to survive for the past two days. There'd be no hotel room or meals from him when that day came. She'd best keep her eye out for places to work right here and now.

She spotted a shop bearing the words R. H. Hughes Mercantile. A sense of satisfaction swelled in her chest from reading that sign with no problem. Perhaps she could purchase a box of crackers and maybe even some raisins on which she could snack. Carefully stepping in and out of the ruts of hardening mud, she continued across the street. As she stepped onto the sidewalk, an elegant woman in a black dress emerged from the mercantile. Her blonde hair seemed to tumble from her head down to her shoulders.

The woman inclined her head at Dorothy. "Good morning. How are you doing today?" she asked in a friendly voice.

"Uh . . . fine, thanks," Dorothy responded. She felt as though she and this woman had met before, but that surely couldn't be the case. She'd arrived in Craig only the afternoon before last.

The woman extended her hand. "I'm Sunny, owner of the Sunny Saloon and Sunny's Place. Ronald brought you there the other night, and I served you your supper."

"Oh, yes. Sorry, I didn't recognize you." Dorothy shook her hand. "The roast beef I had was delicious by the way."

"Thank you. I appreciate that." Sunny released Dorothy's hand and wagged hers at Dorothy. "And don't feel bad; a lot of folks don't recognize me when I'm out of uniform."

Confused, Dorothy wrinkled her brow.

"I wouldn't wear that tight red dress—or my blue one—to do my shopping for love nor money. I only wear 'em at night because that's what folks expect to see in my saloon."

Dorothy knew that feeling only too well. She wondered why she even kept her red dress, even if it was still tucked away in the traveling bag. She wondered something else. "What about in your restaurant?"

"Well, now, that has been a problem from time to time with some of my customers." Sunny's eyes closed slightly. "But there's not much I can do about it. Right now the saloon business is the one paying the bills—so I dress for it."

"I understand," Dorothy said.

"I appreciate that, Miss Cooper, more than you can know. Good day now." Sunny nodded and continued on her way.

"Good day," Dorothy responded, thinking it hadn't bothered her seeing Sunny wearing a knee-length red satin dress to serve roast beef to her the other night. But what about the churchgoing womenfolk of this town that might go in there with their husbands? That's probably who Sunny had been referring to but politely had not pointed any fingers.

Dorothy bid her farewell with a wave and then stepped into the mercantile.

The store proved to be a tad smaller than the ones she'd frequented back in Missouri, but the necessities seemed to be there. Everything from flour to crackers to horse feed filled the left-hand wall. A large counter filled most of the right wall with three rows of shelves behind it brimming with bottles of medicine, baking supplies, and boxes of whatnots. Stacked crates filled the center, each loaded with various sundries and farm supplies. Dry goods covered the far wall. In front of bolts of fabric, made of every shade of the rainbow, was a small counter. A large woman worked behind it, straightening spools of thread. She appeared to be the only person left in the store.

Dorothy approached the woman. "Good morning, ma'am. Do you by chance have any need for an extra clerk?" she said, thinking she may as well ask while she was here.

"Nope," the woman said with a smile. "We're doin' fine runnin' this place by ourselves. Why do you ask?"

"Just curious," Dorothy said. The truth wouldn't have hurt anything here, but she couldn't seem to spit it out. "Inquiring for a friend, that's all." She pushed aside the gnawing guilt of the lie—it had rarely bothered her before. At least not for years. "Do you by chance have any raisins then?"

"Sure thing." The woman stepped out from behind the counter and bid Dorothy to follow her. "You're not from around here, are you?"

"No."

"What brings you to Craig on this fine Wednesday mornin'?" The woman wore a cheery smile that welcomed Dorothy like she was family.

Dorothy chewed on her lip, not wanting to answer. Why hadn't she just found the raisins herself? A lie, truth, or Ronald's perceived truth were her options. None of those appealed to her. "The stagecoach," she responded and grinned at her own joke.

"Lands, girl, ain't you the clever one." The woman wagged a hand at her. "I'm Lavender Decker. Me and my husband, Sam, run this place. He's out makin' a delivery right now."

"I'm Dorothy." She hoped this woman named Lavender wouldn't push for her last name. She was tired of lying. Unfortunately, she'd woven herself a web of lies the past couple of days, and she felt trapped.

"Where you stayin'?"

"The hotel for now," Dorothy said, savoring this spot of truth.

Lavender's eyes lit up. "Ah! You're Ronald's mail-order bride, ain't you?" She shook her head from side to side, smiling. "He's puttin' you up in the hotel while he courts you right proper now, isn't he?"

Dorothy nodded. Her heart sunk, realizing she was being sucked in by her own lies.

"Not many men would go to such lengths. They wouldn't give a lick about what would make you the most comfortable about marryin' a complete stranger. All men aren't that considerate."

"No, they are not," Dorothy said firmly.

"That young man is surely a catch worth hangin' on to, mark my words."

"He is." Dorothy's spontaneous response surprised herself. All the more reason she should come clean, deliver Wilhelmina's letter, and let Ronald move on.

Lavender pulled a box of raisins from the shelf and handed it to Dorothy. "Should I put this on Ronald's account?"

"No, no, I'll pay for them myself." Dorothy opened her handbag and looked at the handful of coins at the bottom.

"An independent soul, I see." Lavender nodded her approval. "I did hear you came from a well-to-do family. That set my mind—and other friends' of Ronald's—at ease, knowin' you weren't after him for his money. Just two lonely folks with like minds wantin' to hitch up." She grasped her hands together and smiled. "I think that's right down sweet if you're askin' me."

"Yeah, I suppose." That's what Dorothy had always dreamed of being: an independent soul. But the truth was, she was a lying, cheating soul. She cringed inside. "How much for the raisins?" She picked up a box of crackers from of a nearby display. "Oh, and a box of crackers?"

"Ten cents."

As Dorothy placed a dime on the counter, Logan stepped inside the store.

"Miss Dorothy! You're just the person I was lookin' for." He hobbled toward her. "I was just over at the hotel, and Campbell said you'd left."

"What can I do for you?" Dorothy gathered her purchases and met Logan halfway between the counter and the door.

"I got something for you."

"Oh, really?" Dorothy half hoped it would be loaf of bread—anything to help her crackers and raisins last a little longer. "What is it?"

Logan pulled an envelope from his pocket. "It's a letter."

"A letter?" Dorothy hoped she kept the angst out of her voice and remembered Ronald's mention of how Logan loved to deliver mail. "From whom?" From Vincent possibly? Buy why? He knew she couldn't read all that well. Still, she dreaded the answer.

Logan handed it to her. "From Ronald of course."

"Oh." Dorothy let out a sigh. "Why would he need to send me a letter when he lives right here in the same town?" She took the letter, worried Logan would expect her to read it right then and there. "Why can't he just come and talk to me if he has something to say?" She feared her embarrassment came across as annoyance. What was wrong with her? Where was her poker face—and voice?

"Ron ain't much good with talkin' to people face-to-face."

She had a hard time understanding that, him being an attorney and all. "That makes about as much sense as a handful of one-eyed Jacks."

Logan cocked his head and stared at her.

"What I mean is . . ." She scrambled to hide her natural choice of words. Wilhelmina would faint if she knew Ronald thought Wilhelmina knew how to play poker. Actually, the poor woman would do more than faint if she knew Dorothy was pretending to be her instead of just delivering her letter. She gulped and continued. ". . . is that Ronald couldn't possibly struggle with such things. I'm sure he's good at talking to judges and his clients and—"

"He's not too practiced in talkin' to women."

"But he and I talked together quite well last evening."

"Really?" Logan's eyes widened—as did his smile. "That's great." He motioned for her to open the envelope. "Open it, why don't ya? I think he's going to ask you join him again for supper."

"Uh . . ." She opened the letter, hoping the little she remembered from school would somehow make those words make sense. A small piece of paper, about the size of a large poker card, fell from the folds of a letter and fluttered to the ground. She picked it up as she glanced over the larger page, and her heart sank. His fancy handwriting looked beautiful, but it wasn't the same as those simple printed words she'd learned years ago from her primer. Frustration watered her eyes. Not so much for her inability to read it but for what she was doing to Mr. Smith. He'd obviously spent a lot of time penning this letter. And why would he send her a letter to ask her to dine with him again? A more likely reason would be that he wanted to take their relationship further.

"What is it, Miss Dorothy?" Logan reached out. "Did Ronald say something wrong? That don't sound like him. He'd never want to do anything to hurt you."

Yet she was doing something that could hurt him. Dorothy felt full tears come on. What was going on? She'd played roles a lot worse than this plenty of times—she'd gotten through them without a lick of emotion. "No, *he* hasn't done anything wrong." She wiped her eyes, and though dreading it, she needed to know what the letter said. Second nature caused her to reach for a lie to fix her problem. "In fact, *he's* doing everything right, and it's making me cry. I can't see from the tears. Could you read them for me?" She held out the letter and the small paper for Logan.

"Sure." He took them both. As he held up the small one to read, a crooked grin appeared on his face. "Ah, one of them 'love letters,' I'm guessin'. I'm goin' to read this one first, okay?"

Dorothy nodded, unsure of what Logan meant by that.

Logan cleared his throat. "Tulips are red, the sky is blue, honey is sweet, and so are you."

Dorothy stifled a laugh. "That was—" Was Ronald trying to be awful with the pen? *No.* She hadn't seen any hint of such a sense of humor before this. Or . . . was he trying to be original? "Ronald is the one who is sweet," she found herself saying. She dabbed her eye—to stay in character of course. "Please, read the next one for me too."

"Dear Miss Dorothy," Logan began, "I, Ronald T. Smith, do hereby request the pleasure of your most wonderful company tomorrow night, the first of April 1897, for a sunset stroll along the bank of the Yampa River. After the stroll, we shall dine at Sunny's Place. I do apologize for the repetitive nature of our evening activities, but unfortunately, the town of Craig lacks in suitable entertainment for a lady of your caliber. And I, too, lack the creativity necessary to offer you the courtship you deserve. Still, I do hope you will accept my invitation. You are a fine lady, and I very much look forward to spending Thursday evening getting to know you better. I would hope that you desire to better acquaint yourself with me as well. I shall call on you at the Craig Hotel at 5:00 p.m. You may send your response via letter through Logan Jones. Or if it suits you, respond in person at my office at 564 Yampa Avenue."

"Oh, ain't that lovely," a female voice said.

Dorothy turned her head the same time Logan did in response to the voice.

Lavender Decker rested her elbows on the counter with her chin cradled in her hands. Her eyes blinked dreamily as she sighed. "Oh, to be young."

Logan folded the letter back into threes as he stared at Dorothy. "So, you gonna send him a letter or tell him in person?"

Dorothy stood there, unable to think, let alone speak. Logan left out a third option: go away and not take advantage of this man any further.

"I'm sure Lavender's got a piece of paper and a pencil if you want to write a letter."

Lavender sorted through a drawer in the counter. "That I do. You want one with lines? Or some of this pretty stuff?" She held up a white sheet of paper with red roses printed in one corner.

"I'm going to walk over to his office right now and talk to him." Dorothy heaved a sigh. Even if she could write, the matters she needed to discuss would be best done in person.

Chapter 11

Ronald looked up from his work and glanced out the window of his office. No longer did he need to daydream of traveling to Africa to convince himself that his life wasn't platitudinous. Daydreaming of a stroll along the river side by side with Dorothy was much more enjoyable. He envisioned taking her hand in his. The very thought sent a most enjoyable shiver down his arm—like it had the other night when he'd held her hand. He had mustered the courage to ask her permission to do so and had no clue where it had come from. He only hoped he could find it again tomorrow night. Never had he imagined enjoying the companionship of a young lady so fully. Conversation actually came, unbidden at times, when he was with her.

Then, in a most prodigious coincidence, the object of his musings appeared in the window. His heart leaped a beat forward. She waved to him, and his heart leaped further. He scooted his chair back, toppling it to the floor, and rushed around the partition that separated his "office" from the waiting area. They met at the door.

"Dorothy." The mere pronouncement of her name generated the most delightful of feelings inside him. He reached for her hand, shook it, taking longer than was acceptable for a proper handshake. What did he care? At the moment, his heart felt like throwing caution to the wind. "Come in, come in. You are here to give a response to my letter, I presume?" He motioned for her to come around the partition and into his office.

She settled into the chair in front of his desk and stared out the window. "Yes and no," she said.

Ronald sat down at his desk, befuddled by the illogic of her answer. "It can be either or, but not both." A pang of discomfort tore through his chest at the possibility that she would choose not to accept his invitation.

"I really do enjoy your company, Mr. Smith," she said, continuing to stare out the window while she folded her hands in her lap. "But I'm afraid I've deceived—" She stopped as her body tensed, and silent sobs appeared to fight for release.

"Are you all right?" He reached out, wanting so much to pull her into his arms and comfort her. Instead, he clasped his hands together and rested them on his desk.

She squared her back, her demeanor calmed, and she turned to the left, her eyes scanning the side wall. "What are all these books for?" she asked as if she wanted to change the subject.

Ronald turned and glanced at his meager collection of law books on the shelves. "For the most part, they contain reports of cases published in sets according to court, subject, or geographic area. I use these cases in building arguments to sway a judge or jury or bring a criminal to justice, depending on the case. Unfortunately, so far I have found nothing in them that can help me concerning multiple wills—I don't have that big of a collection. It would be nice if I could solve the matter of Benedict Jones's will without Stanley. Now if I could travel to a bigger city, I would have access to more," he said, realizing he had not comforted her one bit, only exposed the worries on his mind. "I apologize for my selfishness. Is something amiss? Can I render assistance?"

"No, I am fine." She swallowed hard. "What are you working on?"

Perhaps if he shared the prosaic details of securing Logan's inheritance, she could relax about one worry, and that might help her. "Drawing up another document for Stanley Jones to sign. As I recall, I you told you about the situation with his father's will the other day."

"Yes, I remember that." A slight smile tugged at her lovely lips. "You are a good attorney—going the extra mile for your clients. And a good man." Her eyes met his as she declared this with seeming sincerity.

"I am only doing what any civil-minded attorney would do when an injustice has been served. It isn't right that Stanley Jones gets the entire Circle J Ranch *and* all of his father's money while his siblings get nothing, especially when a signed will exists to prove that's not how Benedict intended it to be."

"You'd think if he's got so much, Stanley would be willing to share with his own brother and sister," Dorothy said with passion.

Ronald was glad to see her melancholy fade—and that she shared his feelings on the matter. "Ah, yes, Mr. Stanley Jones is certainly a man I have little desire with which to associate."

"That's putting it rather nicely." Dorothy rested her hand briefly on top of his, igniting a tingle. "Like I said, you're a good man." She gulped. "And you deserve a good woman. I'm afraid in my book, Mr. Stanley Jones would garner a tongue lashing of unladylike words." She jerked her hand away and shuddered.

"What's wrong, Dorothy?"

"Nothing." She shook her head. "Nothing you need to worry yourself about. Mr. Jones just reminds me of someone." She shuddered again, then her face shone of turmoil. "Someone I never care to share the same room with ever again."

"A past suitor, I presume?"

"I'd rather not talk about him," she said, pinching her eyes shut as if to rid her mind of painful memories.

Ronald's heart ached for her. It appeared she had been emotionally hurt by this unspoken man. He remembered now the bruising around her eye he'd noticed when he'd first seen her. Had that been from him too? His back bristled. He wanted to help her heal from her pain. "Do not give that old suitor another thought. I will do all that is within my power to make sure he never bothers you again. If that is the problem. I mean, if he is still trying to be part of your life, that is. If it is merely a matter of you forgetting him . . . well, then, I could try my best to help you forget him . . . but I'm afraid my abilities might fall short there. That kind of thing was never taught in law school, and I realize—"

She pressed her fingers to his mouth. "Shh," she said softly with a tenderness that matched the sensation of her fingertips on his lips. "I trust your ability, and I appreciate your offer." She leaned across the desk and brushed her lips across his cheek with a hint of a kiss as she stood. "And I look forward to your company tomorrow night. I'll be ready and waiting for your arrival at 5:00 sharp."

Ronald sunk down in his chair as she left, his emotions spinning in a most enjoyable sensation. He doubted his brain would function properly the remainder of the day.

♠

Dorothy left Ronald's office and walked back to the hotel, all the while chiding herself for kissing his cheek. What was she thinking? From the moment she stepped into his office, it had been her intent to tell him the truth and then pack her bag and find a cheaper place to stay—a much cheaper place. Maybe even the livery stable. But when painful memories of Vincent had pushed their way into her thoughts, she panicked. She couldn't go back to Vincent. She just couldn't. And the fear that he'd find her somehow rested like a steel weight upon her heart.

If anyone could help free her from Vincent's "guardianship" claim upon her, if need be, it would be Ronald. He offered safety—at least until she turned twenty-one in November.

Could she keep this charade up until then?

Yes, she had to.

Why couldn't she just forget about delivering Wilhelmina's letter and become Ronald's mail-order bride-to-be? It wouldn't be a hard part to play. Not at all.

If she were to keep running, Vincent might find her, and then she'd be defenseless. The town of Craig offered her safety in the way of Ronald. If by some twist of bad luck Vincent traced her here, he'd be unable to touch her as a betrothed woman. Ronald's knowledge of the law would surely see to that. But this would only work as long as Ronald still thought he wanted her. She couldn't blow her cover now.

But that gave her no cause to kiss his cheek like she had—and enjoy it like she had. She'd better be careful. The more she was with Ronald, the more she actually enjoyed his uniquely dull company. If she were to actually marry him after his and "Wilhelmina's" two-month courtship was finished—she smiled at Ronald's scheduled approach to matters that rarely conform to such logic—it wouldn't be fair to him. He deserved someone better, someone marrying him for the right reason. She'd just have to find ways to keep putting off the wedding. On her twenty-first birthday, she'd skip town.

Dorothy went back to the hotel. Inside her room, she found the bed made without a wrinkle in the covers and with a sachet of lavender on the pillow. "Such a shame to undo Mary's hard work," she said to no one in particular as she removed her coat and sat on the corner of the bed. While unbuttoning her shoes, she noticed worn spots in the leather. No amount of black polish could fix those. She'd need a new pair soon. "You gotta last for seven more months, you hear me?" she muttered to her shoes.

She scooted farther onto the bed, propping a pillow behind her back and stretching her legs out on the mattress. She opened the boxes of crackers and raisins and nibbled as she thought about running into Sunny this morning and how much she had enjoyed talking to the woman. It was like talking to one of her kind—but a lady at the same time.

The box of crackers slid off her lap as she sat upright, a brilliant idea having spawned in her mind. Sunny needed help, and Dorothy needed a job. She'd need to convince the lady that she needed Dorothy and not as a saloon girl. She just hoped her people skills were up to the task.

She stuffed spilled crackers back into their box, brushed the crumbs from the bed, and stood, coming up with what she'd say to Sunny. She needed this job, needed to cut her dependence on Ronald, and needed to fill her time with things unrelated to him.

Wrapping Wilhelmina's shawl around her shoulders, she headed down the stairs. Determined to find employment, she headed to Sunny's Place. She wanted to talk to Sunny before the evening customers wandered in.

She strolled down the sidewalk on the south side of Yampa Avenue, listening to her shoes clap against the wooden planks. She found the warmth of sunshine on her face pleasant. Rarely had she been able to enjoy daytime; she'd usually slept until late in the afternoon to compensate for her late hours at the saloons. The few times she had arisen early, she hadn't dared to stroll through town in her bright satin dresses, showing her legs to the townsfolk and her obvious belligerence to Vincent. He'd demanded that she keep to her apartment except for work and the barest of necessities. But she didn't have to answer to him any longer. She was her own person now and would survive on her own. It didn't matter what he'd always told her.

When Dorothy reached the Sunny Saloon, she kept on walking around the corner and to the side entrance to Sunny's Place. She took a deep breath and entered.

Sunny, still dressed in her black dress, stood at the cash register counting a stack of dollar bills. She looked up as Dorothy closed the door. "Ah, Miss Cooper. To what do I owe this visit so soon after our delightful conversation this morning?"

Dorothy took another cleansing breath, not nearly so deep this time. "I have a proposal. I would hope you would hear me out, for I think it would benefit us both."

"Well, then certainly." Sunny motioned to the nearest table. "Sit down; tell me more."

Dorothy sat down across from Sunny. "I've been doing some thinking about your place ever since we talked this morning. The restaurant part, that is. I imagine you get a few womenfolk in here that come with their husbands. Correct?"

"Yes, quite a few in fact."

Dorothy was about to ask if those women ever stared at Sunny's saloon dress with looks that could kill, but old memories tightened her throat. Scorn-filled eyes flooded her inner vision—all from women she'd met on the street while wearing *her* red dress. Had Sunny ever experienced such venom as well? Perhaps a different, less painful angle might be best to convince Sunny to hire her on.

"Now that I think about it, yes, more and more womenfolk have been coming in," Sunny continued.

Dorothy nodded. "Your business is obviously doing good then?"

"Yes, yes it is."

"Have you ever considered hiring a waitress for your restaurant?" Dorothy asked, letting the important part of the idea tumble from her mouth. "She serves the food while you serve the drinks in the saloon." She looked Sunny straight in the eye. "I think you'd have more happy customers all the way around, and I even know who you could hire to wait tables in your restaurant."

Sunny's face lit up. "I think you are absolutely correct." She chewed on her fingernail for a second as the light faded from her eyes. "Unfortunately, I'd rather work in the restaurant. Would this person you know be willing to work the saloon instead?"

Dorothy let out a sigh. "The person I was talking about is me—and I would rather not work in a saloon if possible."

"Of course you wouldn't." Sunny moved a saltshaker out of the way and touched Dorothy's hand. "And I never would think such a thing with you being Ronald's gal and all. I'd just assumed you were speaking of someone else. Of course you wouldn't be in need of employment because," she held her hand to her mouth and quieted her voice, "practically the whole town knows you two are getting married in June."

"They do?" Dorothy felt her face flush.

"They do." Sunny smiled and nodded. "My guess is Logan is to blame. He adores Ronald and has always wanted him to find happiness out here in the West, so he'll stay. Logan talked up a streak yesterday afternoon when he stopped by—that was after your picnic—telling me about you. He thinks you are perfect for Ronald."

"That can't be—" *right*. Dorothy caught herself. Of course she wasn't perfect for Ronald. She was a saloon girl, a con artist, an imposter. He deserved an upstanding woman, someone to be a pillar in the community.

"Of course it can be." Sunny smiled at her. "I personally feel the same way. In the three years I've known Ronald Smith, I've never seen him happier than

I did yesterday. And—" She hesitated and scratched her head. "Wait a minute. You're looking for employment?" Another pause. "Why?" Her eyes narrowed. "Oh, please, honey, don't tell me you aren't planning on marrying Ronald after all. Just tell me you're looking for something to make the next month or so move along faster until you two are wed."

"Uh . . . yeah, that's what I meant," Dorothy said, the cords of her deception wrapping tighter, squeezing her chest with sharp claws. "Something part-time to help fill my time would be nice and to help me buy crackers and raisins." Her mind raced to the half-empty boxes in her hotel room. "I can't expect Mr. Smith to feed me night and day," she said, glad for a spot of truth to dilute the lies.

"Well, if you are interested, Miss Cooper, stop back here in about an hour, and I can start training you. By Saturday's suppertime, I think we can have you ready to wait tables. Heaven knows my restaurant business is booming, and I should have done this long ago."

"I *am* interested." Dorothy nodded.

With a slight incline of her head, Sunny said, "Okay then, honey, we'll see you later this afternoon."

Chapter 12

DOROTHY CROSSED TO THE OTHER side of the street at the edge of town. The mud on Yampa Avenue had dried a little more since the morning, and she didn't have to worry so much about soiling the hem of her dress. As she stepped onto the sidewalk on the other side of the road, a cowboy atop a gray-and-white horse approached. He looked to be heading her way. As he neared, she recognized him as Logan.

He pulled his horse alongside her and dismounted. "Mornin' again, Miss Dorothy." He hobbled down the road at her side, matching his pace to hers as he looked up at the sun. "Or should I say afternoon?"

"Afternoon," Dorothy said both as a greeting and as a correction.

"Did you go visit Ron?" he asked, excitement obvious in his voice and in the smile on his face.

"Yes, I did."

"And?"

"I accepted his invitation for tomorrow evening." Dorothy figured she'd just convince Ronald to take her home shortly after they ate to keep their phony courtship to a minimum.

"Great!" Logan relaxed his shoulders. "Where you headed, Miss Dorothy? Sure is a pretty day, ain't it?"

"Nowhere really. I just need to head to Sunny's Place in an hour."

"For a spot of dinner?"

"No, I've eaten," Dorothy responded, referring to her raisins and crackers. "I'm . . . I'm helping her with something." She chewed on her lip. Telling Logan would be like telling Ronald. Then again, maybe she could recruit Logan to help shield Ronald from knowing about her new job.

"Help her with what?"

"Uh . . . serving folks supper in her restaurant."

Logan's smile faded. "How can you be with Ron in the evenings if you're waitin' tables at Sunny's?"

"Oh, I hadn't thought about that." Dorothy's gut twisted at not having thought this all the way through. "Only that I need the job." The idea of having no time to see Ronald did not sound appealing. Plus the appearance of their pretend courtship needed to be maintained. "I'm sure I'll have a night or two here and there that I won't have to work. I'll figure something out." She inclined her head. "Besides, I think it'd be best that I don't see him every night anyway. Absence makes the heart grow fonder," she said, putting on an actress smile.

"But, Miss Dorothy, you don't got to get a job. Ron'll take care of you. He's got money."

"I don't feel comfortable putting on him for my support. It's bad enough that I'm letting him pay for my hotel room."

"He don't mind one bit. In fact, if you told him, he'd give you an allowance. I'm thinking he figures you've got some of your own money; that's why he hasn't pushed this idea on you. If you're hurtin' for money, Miss Dorothy, you should tell Ron. I'd be glad to do it for you if you want."

"No, no, don't do that." Dorothy couldn't bear owing even more to Ronald than she already did. She just wanted his safety and a little food and a roof over her head until she could pay for it herself. "I-I need this job at Sunny's so I can fill my time. Ronald is a busy man; he can't spend all day with me."

"I bet he'd like to," Logan said with a teasing smile.

"Well, that's not practical, now is it?"

Logan scratched his forehead. "No, it's not, Miss Dorothy. And I think that's part of the reason Ron likes you; you have a good head on your shoulders. And you're always thinking of others. Leastwise, that's why I like you. I'm sure Ron feels the same on that."

Dorothy's stomach twisted again. She would have liked to believe that was true. But it wasn't. She was thinking of nothing but her own hide. After all, she was planning on doing all in her power to distance herself from Ronald while remaining his fiancée. That was low, just plain low. "Well, thank you, Logan," Dorothy said in a flat voice.

"You're welcome." Logan lifted his hat.

"Oh, and Logan, please, don't say anything to Ronald about me working at Sunny's. I feel it would be best if I told him myself. In fact, if you could help me keep this secret from Ronald—until I'm ready to tell him—I think it would be best for him. Okay?"

"If that's what you wish." Logan stuffed his hat back on his head. He climbed back on the horse and rode away.

Dorothy continued down the north side of Yampa Avenue, peeking into the shops as she walked.

A woman with a child in tow smiled as Dorothy approached from the opposite direction. "Good afternoon," the woman said in a friendly voice.

"Good afternoon," Dorothy responded as she passed. She offered a somewhat delayed smile, knowing she needed to blend in, act like she was Wilhelmina and would soon be part of this community.

Several other people passed her on the sidewalk, each giving their version of a "good afternoon."

An older man wearing an apron stepped out of the gunsmith shop with a broom in hand. "Howdy, miss," he said as he put the broom to work.

"Good afternoon," Dorothy said.

"Lovely day, ain't it?"

"It is." She enjoyed the simple conversation and figured she should continue it. "How's business?" she asked, glancing down at her brown skirt. Funny how Wilhelmina's clothes lent her a feeling of legitimacy.

"Just fine. Say, you're new around here."

"Yes, I am. My name's Dorothy, and I'm quite enjoying Craig," she added with an incline of her head.

"Dorothy, you say?" The man's eyebrow rose. "Are you by chance Ronald's new gal?"

How many people had Ronald told about her? Or was it Logan who'd done the telling? She'd place her bets on the latter. She turned away from the gunsmith momentarily and cringed. Craig would have been the perfect place for her to start a new life. But she'd never stuck around a town long enough to see the consequences of their cons, so why start now?

"Ronald and I are merely friends at this time," she responded. "I don't think calling me 'his' is an accurate statement." The desire to stay in this town nudged at her heart. So did a wisp of a desire to be "his."

How could she possibly stay after the truth came out? Maybe the consequences could be weathered. *Yeah, like picking up the pieces after a tornado.*

"Sorry, miss, I didn't mean nothing by it." The man's face reddened.

"I know you didn't." She hadn't meant to make him feel bad. "And I didn't take it as such to be sure. Don't give it another thought." She waved him on and continued down the sidewalk, wishing she wouldn't have to give leaving Craig, or Ron, another thought.

She found herself at Sunny's Place a little early but ventured inside anyway.

"Ah, Dorothy." Sunny approached her with open arms. She gave Dorothy a quick hug. "You're a smidgeon early, but that's fine; there's no customers right now. There's lots to learn if you're going to be serving tables Saturday night."

"Where do I start?" Dorothy put on the apron Sunny handed to her.

"We'll begin with learning how to carry a tray on your shoulder." Sunny pointed to a large, round tray sitting on a nearby empty table.

Dorothy stepped over to the table and loaded the tray with some empty dishes, and then lifted it and spun it into place on her shoulder in one fluid motion without disturbing a cup. She carried it back over to where Sunny stood with her jaw hanging slightly agape. "Will this work for you?"

"Uh, yeah." Sunny pinched her mouth together in a curious grin. "Now carry it all the way back into the kitchen, load the dishes in the sink, and come back—without the tray." Dorothy made it halfway to the kitchen when Sunny added, "There's a little black notebook on the cupboard. Bring that back in, and I'll teach you how to take orders. I'll give you some tips on how to abbreviate the dishes so you won't have to write every blasted thing down."

Dorothy's steps slowed. Once in the kitchen, she made fast work of clearing the trays like she'd always done when working in the saloons. Hesitation, however, slowed her movements to that of cold tar when she spotted the black notebook. She was tempted to slip silently out the back door and never return. Where would that get her? She at least owed Sunny the decency to tell her why she had to back out of this job. She picked up the black notebook, pushed through the swinging doors, and trudged out into the dining area.

Sunny looked up from the table she cleared. "Honey, what in tarnation's gotten into you? One minute you dance around this dining room, balancing trays on your shoulder like you're a juggler from a circus, now you look like someone's gone and run over your favorite cat with their wagon." She stepped away from the cluttered table and motioned for Dorothy to come. "What's wrong? You can tell me. There's very little that will surprise this gal's ears."

Dorothy hesitated yet longed to tell someone. This charade needed to end. "I'd just as well start now," she mumbled.

"What was that?" Sunny urged her closer.

Dorothy hung her head. "I'm sorry, Sunny. For your sake, I'm afraid I won't be able to take this job."

"But you were the one who gave me the whole idea. Why're you backing out now?"

"Because I won't be able to do it properly." Dorothy glanced up and forced herself to look Sunny in the eye. "I can't read or write."

"At all?"

"I can sign my name and read a few words, but that's all." *Oh, and read numbers on poker cards.* Dorothy glanced around the room at the tables soon to fill with customers and the familiar din of people out for an evening of enjoyment. She really needed this job.

Determination stirred inside her. She'd never needed a notebook to take drink orders. "But I got a real good memory," she blurted. "I could memorize the menu. Folks could tell me what they want, and I could tell the cook without missing a beat."

"So are you backing out of the job or saying you want to give it a try?"

"I'd like to give it a try." Dorothy chewed on her lip. "But that'd be up to you. I thought you ought to know so you can decide though."

Sunny tilted her head to the side. "I do appreciate that," she said. Her eyes then appeared as if they were off in thought somewhere else.

"I know I can do it 'cause I—" Dorothy caught her tongue before it blabbed on about her years of serving drinks in saloons. "Never mind." She set the black notebook on the table and turned to leave.

Sunny grabbed her by the elbow and spun her around so they were face to face. "Hold on. I didn't say no. Heck, I don't use this blasted thing all that often myself." She pointed to the notebook. "And if I can remember people's orders, I'm sure you can. Probably be a whole lot better at it than me because my memory ain't all that good. I just thought I'd help you out by giving it to you."

"Are you saying you'll give me a chance?" Dorothy's chest swelled.

"Yep, I am. But, honey, I've got one big question I need you to answer first." Sunny sat down at the table with the notebook and swept her hand toward the other chair. "Sit down. You tell me what I'm itching to know, and I'll help you memorize the menu—it ain't all that long, so you'll have no problem."

Dorothy lowered herself into the chair slowly as her heart beat rapidly. She winced inside. "All right. What can I tell you?" she responded. Though she'd opened up about the reading and writing, she wasn't quite ready to tell Sunny everything. She barely knew this woman. What if Sunny had connections with saloon owners back in Missouri? Dorothy didn't want to take any chances, no matter how small, for word to get back to Vincent or to the sheriffs of some of those towns as to where she was.

"Why are you so all-fired anxious to get a job when in a month or so you'll be marrying Ronald Smith?"

"That's your only question?" Dorothy measured what to say next. Was Sunny on to her or merely fishing for gossip?

"Yep."

"I already told you it's because I need to keep busy." Dorothy chewed on her lip.

"There's got to be more. You're courting a young man who is determined to court you, so that doesn't make sense to me." Sunny patted Dorothy's hand. "And no worrying here; it don't bother me that you'll quit in June. It kind of gives me a chance to try out hiring myself a waitress. If I decide I don't need one, it saves me the pain of letting someone go." She gave a smile that reached into her eyes. "I just want to know the whole truth."

"The truth?" Dorothy's stomach twisted—she wondered how that load of bricks would go over. Then it dawned on her: the truth was the truth and she could give Sunny just a piece of it. She let out the breath she held. "There is always the chance that we'll need longer than two months to figure out if we're right for each other—or if things won't work out at all between me and Mr. Smith. Then where would that leave me? I don't really care to move away from Craig." Images took form in her mind: the Yampa River bottom, wide swaths of grasslands hemmed in by snowcapped mountains in the distance, and friendly smiles on the townsfolk of Craig.

Sunny smiled. "I can see some wisdom in that."

Dorothy merely chewed on her lip in way of response.

♠

For the next hour, Sunny showed Dorothy around the restaurant, explaining how best to seat people and make them feel welcome. Then she introduced Dorothy to the cook, George. He told her how to serve the dishes so they looked good and how to clear the tables—and even help with the dishes if she had time. After that, Sunny ran over the menu with Dorothy, helping her memorize every dish and their every detail.

In between the roast beef and the corned beef sandwich, Sunny muttered, "You know that Mr. Smith of yours is an exceptional character. I've been around lots of years and lots of places, and I ain't once heard of a man spending the time and money to court his mail-order bride before he married her."

"Yes, he is exceptional," Dorothy said, trying to concentrate on the components of the corned beef sandwich. It was no use. Thoughts of Ronald easily pushed away thoughts of sauerkraut.

Chapter 13

RONALD PUT A BIT OF a skip to his step as he walked across Yampa Avenue to the hotel. He'd never experienced the desire to skip before. He was about to temper the urge—it being illogical—but he doubted Dorothy would temper such an action. That was one of the reasons he liked her. He found her spontaneity intriguing.

"Good evening, Ronald." Campbell Tucker greeted him as he stepped inside the hotel. "Comin' to see Miss Cooper are you?"

"Yes, that I am. Would you be so kind as to go up, knock on her door, and tell her I'm here?"

"I'm a might busy. You can go up there and knock on the door yourself. I've got no rules against it."

"But—" Ronald swallowed the wad of uncomfortableness lodged in his throat. "I feel I would be invading her privacy. Wouldn't I?"

"No, you wouldn't. Just go up there and pretend it's the front door of her house. Loosen up a bit, Ronald. You'll be fine. She's in room three."

Ronald gave him a hesitant nod and proceeded up the stairs. He paused in front of her door, ran a hand over his hair to make sure it was still combed in place, and reached out to knock. He pulled his hand back in and stood there. Like a bump on a log. His darn shyness was so bothersome. It was not logical. Dorothy had, on her own accord, paid him a visit yesterday morning, in person no less, to accept his invitation for tonight. And she'd left a kiss on his cheek. How could he forget that? He lifted his hand back up and touched the spot on his cheek before he knocked on the door.

It opened and Dorothy's face appeared in the doorway. His heart pumped faster. My, but she was lovely in yellow. It complimented her golden, dark-brown hair and the pink blush of her cheeks. "Good evening, Dorothy," he said in an even tone, masking how uneven he felt inside with his heart thumping one speed and his excitement ricocheting around at another. "I have come to call on you for our appointed dinner engagement. Are you ready to go?"

"Give me just a minute." She opened the door wider and swept her hand toward a wingback chair by the window. "Would you care to come in and wait?"

"Oh, no, I'll just wait here, thank you." He thought it odd that a woman of her breeding would ask such a thing.

Dorothy's eyes darted around the room. "Oh, yes, that would probably be best." Dorothy quickly shut the wardrobe and lowered herself onto the chair. She sat on the very edge of one side and twisted to where it was difficult to see what she was doing.

Ronald caught a glimpse of black leather—she was putting on her shoes. Why did she do it in such a fashion? As she buttoned them up, he noticed how worn they appeared. Was that her only pair? He glanced around the room to see if another pair might be tucked away, perhaps awaiting a good cleaning. After all, it was spring, and the mud could be quite annoying this time of year. He saw no shoes. They must be in the wardrobe. Oh dear. Dirty shoes in the wardrobe. The thought made his stomach tense up. He quickly channeled his thoughts elsewhere and gazed at Dorothy. He noticed a couple of blouses draped over the back of the chair where she sat. They appeared to be drying from being laundered. She could have sent her laundry out, but no, she was doing it herself. That would make for a good wife.

"Okay, I'm ready." Dorothy rose from the chair. "Shall we go?" She walked toward him, blocking his view of the wardrobe and filling his mind with more pleasant things, like her smile.

"Yes." He extended his elbow, she latched on, and he escorted her down the stairs.

"I apologize for taking you to Sunny's Place yet again to dine," he said as they stepped outside. "Unfortunately, most people around here cook their own suppers, so I doubt a second restaurant could make a go of it in this town."

"Who usually eats there then?" she asked, curiosity apparent in her voice.

"Couples going out for a special occasion or people like me."

"Single men who don't like to cook and have the money to have someone do it for them?"

"Yes, that would be accurate," Ronald said, thinking how confident her voice seemed when she'd described him. Had he told her about his aversion to cooking? He must have because she barely knew him. But she did know he was financially secure. He'd told her so in his letters. It was a logical declaration; after all, she was a woman used to finery and would need to be assured she could continue her way of life after they were married. But unfortunately, it wasn't that accurate—he wasn't what one might consider wealthy. Folks around here often paid him however they could: doing his laundry, credit at the mercantile, or like the widow, Nettie Harris, who was still paying him with fresh eggs for probate expenses on her late husband's will. Was she trying to ascertain just how well-to-do he was?

A wave of panic hit him. Had he led her to believe that he had more money to offer than he really possessed? His back stiffened with the thought.

"Is everything all right?" Dorothy grasped his elbow tightly and steadied him as he stumbled off the sidewalk onto the street.

Ronald regained his footing. "I'm fine, thank you."

"Beautiful evening, isn't it?" She let go, looping her arm through his instead.

"Yes." He glanced down at her arm on his and smiled.

"Look at that sunset, why don't you." She let go of him entirely and pointed with both hands to the pinks and oranges glowing through a silhouette of poplar trees at the west end of Yampa Avenue. "It's gorgeous!"

"Did you not ever see sunsets like this in Chicago?"

"Chicago?" Her voice lost its light tone. "No. No, I never saw sunsets. At least, not like the ones I see here," she quickly added, looping her arm back in his. "But I'm here now, with you and beautiful sunsets. And I'm happier."

Ronald wanted to stop right there in the middle of Yampa Avenue and have her expound. No one had ever said he made them happy—not even his own mother. In fact, he'd disappointed her greatly by moving out West. "I am glad." He wished he could say more.

Dorothy let go of his arm, rubbed her palms together like she was excited, and then looked at him with eyes wide open. "Do you ever just sit out on your front porch and watch the sunset at night?" She winced. "That is, if your house has a porch."

"Yes, it does have a front porch. And no, I have not sat on it and watched the sunset," he admitted. "I have only been living there a few months, and it's been winter." He'd come back with a just reason. But he did agree it would be a perfect place to do so, facing west like it did.

"Where'd you live before that?" she asked as they stepped onto the sidewalk on the other side of the road.

"The attic room at Ma Hewlett's boarding house."

"Oooh, it doesn't sound good."

"It really was not that bad," he said, probably a little too quickly.

"I'm glad you bought your house. You deserve a nice place to live." Her eyes lit up. "I know! After we eat, we could take a stroll over there. I'd really like to see it. We could sit on the front porch and look at the . . . the stars—oh, never mind. I shouldn't be—" She clamped a hand over her mouth.

"I like that idea." He more than liked it. He hadn't planned anything past supper at Sunny's. Except for the kiss. The book he'd read suggested a kiss on their third outing if expediting the courtship was one's intent. He did hope he wouldn't lose courage by the end of the evening and leave that goal unfulfilled. "We shall indulge as per your suggestion."

Dorothy chewed on her bottom lip ever so slightly in a manner he found rather charming.

Sunny's Place bustled with people as they walked inside. Ronald spotted Sunny right away in her bright-blue dress this time. With notebook in hand, she ran in from the saloon, took orders at one table, and immediately moved to the next to jot more orders in her notebook. He found himself tapping his foot against the floorboards to calm his impatience.

"Sunny'll seat us as soon as she gets a chance," Dorothy said in a soothing tone.

"You are correct."

She placed her hand on his arm. "And please, don't be nervous on my behalf. Someone else's lack of good help is no reflection on you. I would never think less of you because you brought me to a place where we had to wait an extra minute or five to be seated."

"Thank you." My, how he wanted to take her into his arms at that moment and show his gratitude for her logical thinking with more than mere words. *Hold on a minute, Ronald, that is so ungentlemanly.*

"Besides," Dorothy said, "we should be happy for Sunny that business is good, not upset with her."

"Right you are." Gentlemanly or not, he still wanted to take her into his arms and tell her he approved of her thinking.

"She is doing something about it though."

"She who? And about what?" He had better start listening better and not be so distracted.

"Sunny. I convinced her this morning to hire some more help."

"Wonderful," Ron said, glad she was making friends already and influencing people for the good.

"Ah, here she comes." Dorothy inclined her head toward the approach of Sunny.

"A table for two?" Sunny asked boldly over the noise before she made it all the way to them.

Ronald nodded. "Business is good, I presume?" He took Dorothy by the elbow and followed Sunny.

"Yes. In fact, thanks to this young lady," Sunny pointed to Dorothy as she showed them to their table, "I am convinced I need to hire a waitress to help me out."

"I think that's an apt idea." He glanced at Dorothy and then back at Sunny. "She just told me about that." He pulled the chair out for Dorothy to sit in and then sat down across the table. Sunny handed him a menu. He glanced to one side and then the other, noticing their good fortune; it had provided them the last empty table in the place. "Too bad your new waitress couldn't have started tonight. It appears you could use her."

"Now that wouldn't have worked out too well for you tonight, would it?" Sunny licked her pencil and readied her notebook. "What'll you have? The pork cutlet is new. You might want to try that."

"Okay, I will take that," Ronald said. "And what do you mean it wouldn't have worked out for me?"

Sunny stared at Dorothy. "You haven't told him?"

"Told me what?" Ronald didn't like the sound of that.

"I was going to do that tonight," Dorothy said to Sunny. "After dinner." She turned to Ronald. "But I suppose now might be good." She looked at him with apology glistening in her eyes. "I'm going to be Sunny's new waitress."

"What?" Ronald surprised himself with the volume of his voice. It rose above the clink of silverware against dishes and dinner conversations of twenty or so people.

"She said she's going to be my new waitress," Sunny said. Her eyes commanded him to calm down. "The girl's got to do something to fill her time while you take your *time* to court her."

Dorothy noticeably stared at the adjacent table, as if trying to avoid the conversation.

"But—" Ronald had thought taking time to court her properly was a gentlemanly thing to do. Dorothy waiting tables was not only unfitting but would complicate their efforts. He glanced around again at all the people dining on their meals, and his biggest fear surfaced. "Don't you need her mostly at suppertime?"

Sunny nodded. "That would be correct."

"But—but it's not proper. And I'm in my office during the day. Night is when I—" His pleasant evening felt to be slipping away.

Dorothy turned toward him and placed her hand atop his. "We could spend an occasional noon meal together. And once or twice a week I'd have an evening off." She looked to Sunny as if for approval.

"That's right." Sunny licked her pencil again. "Now, Dorothy, what would you like to order?"

"I'll have the roast beef again. That was so tasty. No wonder your place is doing so good, Sunny. You've created some great dishes."

"Well, thank you, honey." Sunny jotted down Dorothy's order. "I'd love to stay and chat but—" She motioned around the crowded dining room with her jutted chin and then headed for the kitchen.

♠

With her elbow hooked into Ronald's, Dorothy strolled down Yampa Avenue, enjoying the warm breeze on her face and the meal of roast beef in her stomach. "So, how big is your new house?" She liked it when he talked about things close to him.

"It has six rooms," he said like he was stating the number of eggs in a half dozen.

"That's a good size."

"It is practical." His face showed a hint of satisfaction. "A kitchen, dining room, and parlor on the main level. Upstairs there's three bedrooms: one for the girls, one for the boys, and one for—" He abruptly turned his head away from her.

Dorothy couldn't hold back a grin. Then, out of the corner of her eye, one block down, she spotted the darling two-story house she'd been drawn to the other day when she'd taken a stroll. A yellow glow spilled over from the streetlamp on Yampa Avenue, lighting the house just enough for her to see the picket fence and tell for sure it was the one with the blue gable trim. She pointed to it as a touch of disbelief reached her voice. "Is that your place?"

"It is. Do you like it?"

"Yes, I do." Not only had it caught her eye the other day, it had been the kind of home she'd daydreamed about those many times when her life with Vincent became unbearable and she had to escape somewhere.

"I am so glad," Ronald said.

They walked without a word between them until they reached the picket fence. Ronald swung the gate open for her. "Welcome to my house."

"Thank you." She stepped inside the yard and past a ten-foot tree that grew in the middle of the lawn. There was another one just like it on the other side of the sidewalk. She envisioned the trees growing to a grand size in time with young boys building a treehouse in their branches and little girls with dolls beneath their shade. The trees standing there like sentinels, the cherry tree at the side looking so pretty in pink, and the white pickets surrounding the house lent immense safety to this yard.

"In a short time, this could be your house as well. To this end is why I purchased it, not for myself. The boarding house was sufficient for me, but I knew if I was to find a wife, she deserved a place where she could feel at home, feel like she belonged, feel happy, feel safe." He glanced at her, his eyes lit by the glow of the streetlamp. "I do so hope this will be the case."

"I am sure I could be safe and happy here." Her words spilled out. Aching inside, she tried to gather them back. She had to because she couldn't stay.

"Wonderful." Ronald took her hand in his and led her up the sidewalk.

Dorothy tightened her grip on his hand, feeling his warm fingers against hers and not shying away.

They stepped onto the porch and then into the house. Lamplight poured into the entry from what looked like a living room because of the clawfoot table and sofa leg she could see through the doorway.

"It appears Logan is still up, waiting for me." Ronald motioned for her to follow him into the lit room.

Logan looked up from a book. "Howdy, Ron." His voice perked up further. "Oh, howdy, Miss Dorothy." He jumped up from the sofa and motioned for them to sit there. "I'll sit over here." He pointed to an overstuffed chair and hobbled toward it.

Ronald lit another lamp. The room brightened to where she could see the dark blue of the upholstery and the floral carving in the woodwork in the sofa's arms. The rest of the room looked as impressive with another chair to match Logan's. It too was upholstered in rich blue fabric, and a second clawfoot table sat between the two chairs. A piano sat against the inside wall.

"Do you play the piano?" she asked. She lowered herself onto the sofa, hugging its carved wooden arm.

Ronald sat on the sofa nearer its other arm than Dorothy. "No, I do not."

Logan spoke up. "He told me he got it 'cause he wants his kids to learn how to play it."

Ronald blushed.

Dorothy smiled. Ronald could be so blatantly honest sometimes as to matters of marriage and having a family and so dreadfully bashful about it at others. She found that endearing and let go of the sofa's arm to inch across the cushion, closer to Ronald. Reaching the rest of the way across the cushion between them, she touched his arm. "I think that's a wonderful thing to want. I wish I'd learned how to play the piano in my early years."

Ronald turned to her. A puzzled look filled his face. "But I thought you knew how to play. At least, that's what I gathered from your letters."

Dorothy stiffened. Here it was, the moment she feared would come sooner or later. How did she seriously think she could avoid Wilhelmina's past? She hadn't—and she hadn't planned this part out at all. She needed to tell Ronald the truth once and for all. If she had to leave town first thing in the morning, so be it. She glanced at Logan in the chair with his legs draped over one arm. A smile lit his face like always. She couldn't speak of these matters in front of the boy. It would be hard enough with an audience of one. Hopefully, Logan would retire to bed soon.

"I can play a little," Dorothy said, trying to gloss over the situation. And it was true. But she could only play by ear. She'd taught herself while at a saloon that had a piano. A grand upright had sat in the corner next to the bar, collecting dust for the most part, until one slow day she'd plunked out a familiar tune with a single finger. The bartender insisted on more. By the time she and Vincent had to flee that place, she was playing the piano with both hands and had at least five tunes she could play all the way through. Out of all the places she'd had to work, that saloon proved to be her favorite. But she feared all of those songs would be inappropriate for this setting. She rubbed the back of her neck. Would she be goaded into playing?

"I'm sure you are just being modest." Ronald looked at her and inched a little closer.

"No, I'm being truthful." *For once.* "I can't read a note of music. What little I play, I've learned to do so by ear. So I fear I would be a very poor piano teacher."

"That is a most admirable skill, to play an instrument by ear." Ronald's eyes remained fixed on her. He scooted onto the center cushion. "A skill I fear I shall never possess."

"Oh, but dear Ronald, you have so many other skills and admirable traits," Dorothy said, paving the way for her declaration of truth—as soon as Logan left. "Mine are but a drop in the bucket compared to yours."

"Not true." Ronald slid squarely onto the middle cushion, just inches from Dorothy now.

"I would beg to differ." Her eyes connected with his, and their playful banter ignited delightful sparks of energy in her chest. She moved away from the arm of the sofa and closer to him, intensifying those sparks.

"Oh, you would, would you?" Ronald smiled.

"Yes, I would."

"I graduated top of my class. Debate was my best subject."

"I didn't need a school to teach me. I learned to argue on my own." Dorothy could feel a smile spread across her lips. "I'll take you on."

"Are you challenging me?" His smile was more charming than Dorothy had ever recalled.

"Maybe." She chewed on her lip but could not shield the merriment from her eyes.

The sound of shoes clapping against floorboards tore Dorothy's gaze from Ronald's and toward the opposite end of the room.

Logan was on his feet. "Ah, I've had enough of this mush. I'm heading up to bed." He limped across the braided rug in the middle of the floor. As he approached the doorway, he wagged his hand at Ronald and Dorothy. A knowing grin formed on his lips and filled his eyes. "You two continue on."

Dorothy stared straight ahead as Logan clomped up the steps.

Ronald did the same. When the footsteps faded into silence, he turned to Dorothy. He seemed hesitant, and fear touched his eyes.

She sensed he wanted to say something but was struggling. *No.* She didn't want him to slip back into his old self, not now. She reached out and took hold of his hand to lend him support. "What's wrong?" Then her heart sunk. Logan was gone. She couldn't put off telling him any longer. "Before you tell me, I, uh . . . need—"

"Nothing is wrong," he cut in and squeezed her hand. "I would merely like to ask you something."

"Uh, okay." She should allow him to say what was on his mind first before she told him.

He took a deep breath. "May I kiss you?"

"Oh," she said as a near whisper. His bluntness caught her off guard, and she couldn't help but smile inside. Did she actually find that charming? "Yes," she muttered to herself out loud.

Before she realized what she'd said, he closed his eyes and leaned toward her. *Is he going for my lips or cheek?* He seemed at such a loss. Instinct kicked in, and she took control to help him out. She let go of one of his hands, reached up, laced her fingers through his hair, and guided his mouth to hers.

Ronald's lips met hers in quick fashion. But . . . they felt tender and sweet, like rose petals brushing across her lips on a cheery, summer's day. Never before had a kiss made her feel more cherished.

Unfortunately, it was too short; she wanted another. Not necessarily tonight but tomorrow. And the next day. Maybe she should quit fighting it and just become Ronald's mail-order bride, not just his fiancée, until she turned twenty-one when she'd skip out of town.

Heavens, he deserved someone to take Wilhelmina's place, and he'd been more than willing to marry Wilhelmina without knowing *her* at all. Why couldn't she just fill Wilhelmina's shoes, and he would get to know her rather than Wilhelmina? He need not know *everything* about her.

Chapter 14

RONALD FELT LIKE PUTTING HIS feet up on his desk and not caring one whit that they might leave a spot of dirt or that someone might view his careless behavior through the window. But reliving last night through his thoughts was indulgence enough. The way Dorothy had run her fingers through his hair and then pulled his head to align his lips with hers . . . he would have sworn she'd truly *wanted* to kiss him.

When he had tried to court Doc Kate when she first moved to Craig, he'd ascertained her disinterest right away. Back in Chicago, the few women he'd attempted to court had responded similarly to Kate. He knew his personality, like his appearance, lacked excitement. But Dorothy seemed different. He sensed she liked him. And never before had a woman turned his head like she did—literally when she kissed him and figuratively when she walked by him. And distracted him from work. And made him want to throw caution to the wind and marry her immediately instead of waiting the entire two months as he had planned. His heart skipped a beat at the thought of her. He'd never felt such illogical yet delightful feelings.

Unfortunately, he had documents to file and letters to draft. He ceased leaning back in his chair, lowered his feet to the ground, and examined his list of tasks for the day.

As he filed the paperwork for the Peterson divorce case, he thought about how sad it was that these two people, who must have loved each other at one time, couldn't work things out and stay together. They had little children for goodness' sake. Now she was taking them with her, moving back East to live with her mother, and leaving poor Mr. Peterson a lone man back here in Craig.

This strengthened his determination to stick to his guns and wait his fully allotted time to marry Dorothy. It was imperative to make sure they were compatible, despite what his heart was telling him.

With that task done, he glanced at his list to see what was next. *Redraft the affidavit for the Benedict Jones case.* He could do that easily enough—getting Stanley to sign them was another matter. The door opened, and he looked up from his desk to await whomever walked around the partition.

Dressed in a blue skirt and white blouse, Dorothy appeared. He rushed to his feet. "Good morning," he said with more excitement than he'd intended. Keeping his emotions under control was a must. Gracious be, what happened to his skills as an attorney?

"Good morning, Ronald." Dorothy breezed in and motioned for him to sit down as she took the chair in front of his desk. "Or perhaps I should say, 'Good afternoon'?" She glanced at the clock on the wall. "It's a minute past noon."

"That it is."

She set a basket on top of his desk. A red-checkered cloth covered its contents. He hadn't taken notice of it until now. "Since this evening's my first night at Sunny's and I have no idea how long I'll be there, I thought I'd bring you something at noon, and we could eat dinner together."

"That is very thoughtful. Thank you." He then got to thinking. "You couldn't have possibly made this yourself staying in the hotel like you are," he quickly added, not wanting to insinuate that she couldn't cook a chicken. Not that it was important.

"No, I'm afraid I turned to Sunny for help." She peeled back the checkered cloth, pulled out a cold chicken drumstick, and handed it to him. "Actually, she offered. Sunny said she felt bad for taking me away from you in the evenings." She reached in the basket and pulled out a piece for herself. Before taking a bite, she said in a quiet voice, "Believe it or not, I'm going to miss seeing you tonight."

Ronald smiled. "You are?"

"Yes, I am." She peered at him over her chicken leg. "I don't know how to tell you sufficiently how much I enjoy being with you. You make me feel safe."

"You just did, very sufficiently in fact. Thank you." Warmth flushed his face. "Why do you have to do it?"

"Do what?" Dorothy dabbed her mouth with a napkin.

"Work at Sunny's. It's such a short time, so why even start? You will barely get the knack of things, and then you'll have to quit."

"Why would I have to quit?"

Ronald bristled slightly. "Because we'll be married." How could she not see this? "I won't have my wife working as a waitress. There's no need. I have plenty of life's means to take care of us both—and our forthcoming family," he added, wincing past his embarrassment. If they were to be married, it was high time they discussed such delicate matters.

She set down her chicken, biting on her lip instead. She appeared to be thinking. "What if we don't end up getting married?"

"Why do you say that?" he asked. Was his boring demeanor more bothersome than she let on? Or was there something even more dislikeable about him that she could not tolerate?

"Because there are a lot of things you don't know about me, things that might not sit well with you."

"Then tell me about them and let me decide for myself if that is the case. That is what this courting period is all about."

"What if two months is not long enough for you to get to know me? I fear it might not be—for your sake." Her cheerful countenance faded. "I'm sorry I've continued on as I have. Though I admit I couldn't help myself," she said and stood. "I've never felt so happy as when I'm with you. I really want to marry you, but unfortunately, that's one of the few things I've led you to believe that is true." Tears gathered in her eyes. She brushed them away and turned her face toward the partition. "I had not intended to tell you this when I came here. I had intended on going through with everything, but perhaps it is a good thing the subject arose." She cleared her throat. "You're a good man, Ronald Smith, and you deserve better than me." Turning away from the partition, her eyes, glistening, met his. "I have led you on to think I am someone I am not. For your sake, it wouldn't be fair for me to marry you." She took a noticeable breath. "It would be less embarrassing for both of us if I didn't go into detail. Just trust me; our marriage would never work—because of me. I guess this means goodbye. Goodbye, Ronald. Thank you for everything. And I promise to pay you back for the hotel room as soon as I get paid." She raised her hands to her face and ran around the partition.

When the door clicked shut behind her, Ronald slumped in his chair, dumbfounded.

♠

Dorothy darted out of Ronald's office and headed toward the solace of her hotel room, the only place she could call home.

"But it's not my home." Her throat tightened as she ran. Halfway up the block, she did an about-face and turned tail to the west end of town. She had no place to call her own. That tiny room at the top of the Craig Hotel stairs was not even hers—Ronald was paying for it. And it would be at least a week before she would have the means to pay the bill. As soon as she had a few paychecks to tide her over, she'd leave town. It would be for the best. Vincent was relentless. Why she ever hoped he'd give up looking for her, she didn't know. Pure foolishness was what it was. She knew, somehow, he could very well be on his way to Craig.

She kept running down the street, unsure of her destination, knowing only that it was somewhere far away from Ronald's office and the hotel room he'd provided for her.

Once at the edge of town, she noticed wisps of green on the branches of the willows growing along the riverbed. "The river," she muttered as her steps slowed to a brisk pace. No one owned the river. God made it for everyone. That meant it was part hers. She wouldn't be putting anyone out if she could find a place to hole up for a few days amongst the fallen branches.

As she neared the river, she scanned for any nooks or crannies in the undergrowth with a sufficient roof to shield her from the weather. She and Vincent had slept outside before. An awning of bramble caught her eye as did the growing clouds in the sky. Could she survive the night? Maybe she could "borrow" a quilt from the hotel. The thought made her shudder. That part of her life was behind her, regardless of what faced her now.

She sat down upon a boulder and stifled the urge to cry. Alternatives were what she needed, not tears. Okay, so she had nowhere to stay and little to her name, a name that was partially borrowed no less—just like her clothing and traveling bag. The only thing that was hers was a worn-out coat, a pair of shoes, and a red satin dress she could do nothing with. But she could figure out something. Maybe Sunny would let her bed down in the storage room behind the kitchen.

Though blurry-eyed, she recognized the spot along the river at which she sat. It was where Ronald had brought her. Tears flowed. There'd be no more picnics with him.

A twig snapped. Dorothy twisted to see who approached.

Ronald stood a few yards away. His brow creased. "Dorothy." He spoke with such tenderness that her throat tightened, and she nearly choked.

"Ronald," she whispered, feeling a drop of rain on her cheek.

"Come." He held out his hand as he approached. "A storm is brewing. We need to get back to town."

"We?" She liked the sound of that, but she didn't dare cling to it. "You didn't need to come out here. You have no need to feel responsible for me any longer."

He took hold of her hand. It seemed to her a bold move for him. She liked it. If only that sense of belonging was truly hers to enjoy . . .

"You may say I have no need," Ronald said, but his eyes didn't meet hers. They looked at her feet. "Nonetheless, I feel the need. It was I who asked you to come out West. You have every right to decide against marrying me, but that doesn't change my responsibility concerning you. It is apparent you do not have the funds to take care of yourself sufficiently. When your wages become sufficient, I will back away, and if you'd rather not have to look at me anymore, I will give money to Mary Tucker every week to leave on your bed stand."

"Oh, I can't allow that." Dorothy clung momentarily to his hand. "I don't deserve your help." She relinquished her grasp, ready to let go of his hand.

He held on tighter and pulled her away from the boulder. "What kind of man would I be if I were to withhold my resources from one who is in need?"

"But I have deceived you," she said, yet spitting out the words did little to relieve the pain.

"I have yet to understand how you have deceived me, but it does not matter." He walked toward town, pulling her with him.

Dorothy scurried to keep up with him. Raindrops moistened her face. She considered pulling her hand free from his, but where would she run? Back to the river to wait out the oncoming storm under a leafless tree? "I'm not who you think I am," she continued, trying to free her conscience further.

"How do you know who I think you are?"

She'd not expected such a response. "My name is Dorothy Bednar, not Wilhelmina Cooper." The words tumbled from her mouth.

"Logan has mentioned your last names. It is not uncommon for immigrants to change them to their English counterparts."

"You don't understand. I'm not an immigrant. Maybe my father was—I don't know. He never spoke of his parents and neither did my mother." She sensed she was rambling. "Then my mother died when I was ten and my father when I was eleven, and I never heard nothing more from either of them." Dorothy swallowed a lump that had risen in her throat. Why was it there? She didn't know—she thought she was past such grieving.

Ronald didn't respond. He only slowed his pace to a normal one and grasped her hand tighter.

They walked in silence for some distance. His quiet unsettled her. Surely he was piecing together the lies she'd heaped upon him and drawing a mental picture of who she really was. She may as well give him more fodder. It was his happiness that mattered now.

"Dorothy is not my middle name; it's my first name. And I'm not even sure if my name is spelled with a *y* or an *ea*. My parents never told me. My mother could neither read nor write. I myself just barely learned how to read and write in school—I missed a lot because Mother was often sick—and I've since forgotten most of what I'd learned. I'm not from Chicago, and I didn't write those letters to you. I was just pretending to be Wilhelmina Cooper." Dorothy braved a look at Ronald to see his reaction.

He kept his eyes forward, as unmoving as his mouth, which pinched tight in a straight line.

That was enough of a reaction for her. There was no doubt now that he was dismayed, and he'd be shed of her as soon as his good nature allowed him to do so. "Don't worry," she said as they stepped upon the wooden sidewalk on the west end of town. She felt a shower of raindrops on the top of her head. "Sunny said she'd pay me once a week, so I'll be able to start paying you back for the hotel room real soon. In the meantime, I'm hoping she'll let me bed down in the storage room at her place for a while—'til I get on my feet. Then I'll leave town so you won't have to see me and be reminded of how I deceived you."

Their feet clapped upon the sidewalk for a distance, creating a disjointed rhythm.

"Thank you for coming down to the river and bringing me back. I fear I would have stayed otherwise." She looked up at the gray sky as more raindrops pelted her face.

Ronald continued to stare forward, his hand still clasped around hers. His steps slowed. "I could never allow you to do such an unwise thing."

Without realizing it, she found they were on the sidewalk in front of the hotel. Her heart swelled with conflicting feelings: gratitude, regret, affection, sadness, and a thousand more. She stopped him before they reached the main door and turned to face him, wishing he would say something about her lies. Was he mad? Was he sad? Was he totally disgusted with her? He let go of her hand, and instinctively she reached up and cupped his chin in her fingers. She pulled his face toward her and brushed a kiss across his cheek before she realized what she was doing. It was too late; the corners of their mouths touched. He did not respond. She stepped away, her heart racing from the pain she had obviously inflicted upon him—and the pain of him not responding to her kiss. "Goodbye, Ronald. Thanks for being so kind to me. I am truly sorry for all the trouble I have caused you." She walked into the hotel, certain he'd never speak to her again.

Chapter 15

Ronald stood in the middle of the sidewalk for a good minute or two before he could muster the wherewithal to quit staring at the hotel door. Dorothy brushing the edge of his lips with a kiss lingered in his thoughts, as did the illogical nature of this woman. One minute she was telling him he makes her happy and wants to marry him; the next she was telling him goodbye. Then she ran away, ridiculously willing to live amongst the deer down by the river. Then she willingly took his hand and let him bring her back to town. Lastly, and most unreasonable of all, she tried to tell him how to think. He, and only he, determined what he thought. Why she should think he'd think less of her because she lacked money or was illiterate was beyond him. True, there was a measure of deceit, but obviously it was motivated by fear. Fear of what? Discovering her true identity? He certainly did not want her to be afraid of him.

"Hey, Ron, what ya doin' just standin' there like a hitchin' post in the middle of the sidewalk?" Logan sat atop his horse next to the hotel's hitching post, adjusting his hat against the rain.

"I was just deep in thought. That's all," Ronald muttered, not even bothering to meet Logan's eyes.

"Thinkin' about Miss Dorothy, are you? You just said goodbye to her, did you?"

"Something like that." Ronald stepped off the sidewalk. "I best head back to my office. By the way, do you know when your brother will be back in town?"

"Stanley?" Logan scratched the back of his head, tipping his hat into his eyes. "You know we don't talk much."

"I meant, have you heard anything around town, you know, as to when Stanley might be back?"

"Nope. Just that he was going to Missouri on business. Sometimes he gets to gamblin' when he's out of town, you know, poker, so he might take his time. Or not." Logan straightened his hat back into place. "Why do you want to see my brother anyway? Most folks steer clear of him."

Ronald cleared his throat, gathering his words. He needed to tell Logan this sooner or later. "I need him to sign a document. I need you to sign one too, a different one. This was Susannah's idea—mine too. The two of you need to appeal your father's will now that a more recent one has been discovered."

"Ah, the old one's fine."

"But your father left you absolutely nothing."

"I know. My pa didn't seem to need me." Logan pinched his lips together, and his eyes lost their spark. "That's okay 'cause I don't seem to need his money either. I'm doin' fine on my own—like always."

After a long pause, Ronald said, "Well, neither did he leave anything to your sister."

"Oh, yeah." Logan looked off into the distance, and his face contorted as if trying to understand something. "She and Joseph are doin' fine though, what with that coal they found on their land. What does she want more money for?"

"She is not concerned about herself. That's not why she is appealing the old will. It is for you, Logan."

"Don't you two do it on my behalf." Logan straightened his hat.

"I'm sorry, but I agree with your sister. You deserve something of your father's estate. And I'm going to see that you get it."

"Well, if it makes you happy, Ron, go right ahead. But like I said, don't do it on my behalf. And good luck gettin' Stanley to go along with it." Logan lifted his hat. He prompted his horse away from the hitching post and rode away.

Ronald dragged himself toward his office. "Why are some people so resistant to help?" he muttered to the wind. He hoped Dorothy wouldn't be as bullheaded as Logan. Like it or not, he was determined to help her too, even though it appeared she wanted to end their courtship. Her mention of a past suitor, who had obviously caused her much distress, came to mind. That very well could be the impetus for her deceit. Could that also be the reason for her inconsistent behavior?

Once inside his office, he dropped into his chair and set to work preparing a new document for Stanley. His brain churned, thinking of ways he could gain some leverage over Stanley to get him to sign that affidavit. Nothing came to mind. Maybe he would set that aside for a while so he could start helping Dorothy.

The first thing he did was pull out all of her letters—rather, the letters he once thought were hers. Regardless of whether she wrote them or not, they held a return address. Maybe whoever still lived there could shed some light on this whole ordeal. Had he or had he not responded to an ad for a mail-order bride? Yes, he had. And he was certain the magazine and the ad were legitimate. But he was still unsure if there ever was an actual Wilhelmina Cooper.

Chapter 16

DOROTHY LOWERED THE TRAY FROM off her shoulder, set it on the table, and served the party of four identical roast beef meals. "Is there anything else I can get for you?" she asked, making sure she kept her grin wide. She'd been working as a waitress for over a week now, and her cheeks were tired of all those fake smiles she had to muster. The people shook their heads, so she headed to a booth at the back of the restaurant. A lone man sat at the table, waiting. The back of his booth was toward her so she couldn't see most of him, just the top of his head. He'd been there for some time. Sunny had seated him while Dorothy was back in the kitchen. It was a wonder he hadn't turned around and whistled for some help—or complained. She opened her notebook as she scurried.

As she approached his table, she tucked the empty tray under her arm and pulled out her pencil, ready to jot down the letters Sunny had taught her to help remind her of people's orders—she'd also been teaching her all the letters of the alphabet and giving her several reading lessons. *RB* for roast beef and *CB* for corned beef sandwich were the hardest to keep straight. But she was getting the hang of it.

Licking her pencil, she moved into place at the foot of the table. "What can I get for you, sir?" She peered over the top of the notebook to make eye contact as she took his order.

"Ronald?" The pencil fell from her grasp. She stooped to retrieve the pencil from the floorboards.

Ronald leaned down and beat her to it. He picked up the pencil. His face moved within inches of hers.

They jerked away from each other at the same time.

Dorothy grabbed the table to regain her balance, all the while staring anywhere but at him. "Thank you," she said, her voice hoarse. Regaining her composure, she stood, avoiding his eyes. "What are you doing here?"

"Uh . . . uh . . ." His voice sounded more unsteady than her own nerves. She felt sorry for him and braved a glance. Their eyes met.

He cleared his throat. "A man's got to eat. It's not like I can go anywhere else—except my own kitchen. And that could prove dangerous."

She couldn't hold back a grin. Had he made an attempt at humor? It was so unlike him. "Yes, it could be dangerous."

"I should know; I've been eating my own cooking for the past week and . . . well, I couldn't stay home any longer. Sorry you have to wait on me, but . . . I hope you understand."

"You hope *I* understand?" Had she heard him right? "I tell you I've been lying to you and end our rela—" She glanced from side to side to see who might be listening. The last thing she wanted was for more gossip to spread concerning poor Ronald's mail-order mishap. As it was, the rumor around town supported the notion that Ronald merely wanted to take things slower than the fast pace with which they had started their courtship. "I mean . . . this here is Sunny's Place. You are welcome to come anytime you want," she said in low tones.

"And bid you a good evening?"

"If you would like, sure."

"Do you really mean that?" His voice squeaked.

"Of course I do." She kept her eyes on her notebook.

He cleared his throat. "May I continue courting you?"

"Why would you want to?" Dorothy blurted out, caught off guard.

"Because you have not presented me sufficient reason to discontinue."

Wordlessly, Dorothy stared at him.

"Plus, a person in need is like family indeed."

"Where have I heard that before?" Dorothy scratched her head, trying to remember.

"It was one of your sayings that I quite liked. Or rather, Wilhelmina Cooper's saying—whoever she might be." Ronald wrinkled his brow.

"Wilhelmina?" Dorothy sucked in a breath. Why had he brought up her? If only she had Wilhelmina's letter on her she could deliver the darn thing and get at least that off her conscience. After deciding to "become his mail-order bride," she'd decided to keep some things hidden so it could work—including that letter. But she'd never be his bride now. It was time to talk about it. Unfortunately, the letter was tucked away in the bottom of her traveling bag beneath her red dress. "Let me explain about her." Her eyes skirted around the room, hoping everyone was more interested in their beef than her conversation. No heads turned in their direction. *Good.*

Ronald held up his fingers toward her mouth. "Not here. And not until you are ready." He lowered his hand, folded it in with his other, and rested them in his lap. "Also when you are ready . . . and only then, will we continue our courtship. Right now I am ready to order. I am famished."

She readied her notebook and pencil and steadied her hands. "So what will you have? The corned beef sandwich? Or do you want to try something new?"

"The corned beef will be fine."

"Oh, come on. Be daring; try something new for a change," she said, trying to lighten the mood so her hands would stop shaking. Gracious be, he was waiting for her to give the word to continue their courtship! "Sunny's got some new chicken and dumplings that are really good. Might I suggest those?"

Ronald stared at the menu, grimacing. He let out a sigh. "What can it hurt; it is only food."

"Exactly." She tapped his wrist with her pencil in a daring move—she so wanted to touch him and make the awkwardness go away, to make things go back to the old awkwardness. "And for dessert, you've got to try an oatmeal-raisin cookie. They're new too. I talked Sunny into trying them out."

"You?"

"It's my mother's recipe. Only she called them oat cakes. She and I would make them all the time." Dorothy pointed to her head with the pencil. "I memorized the recipe. It's been locked in here for over ten years, doing nothing. Sunny was a peach to let me dig it back out and use it."

"Then definitely. Yes, I would like to order one of those cookies for my dessert."

Dorothy scribed a big *C* at the bottom of the page. "Done."

Ronald placed his hand on hers and pulled the notebook into his view. "I thought you struggled with . . . um . . ."

Dorothy let him see the notebook, enjoying his gentle touch. "Sunny's been teaching me. It isn't much, but I've relearned my letters already, and I've worked out a code to take orders."

"That is wonderful." Ronald smiled. He looked somewhat handsome in that moment. Even more so as his hand remained on hers.

Dorothy stared at him, amazed. He should be looking down his nose at her, not praising her. "I'd better hurry and get your order back to the cook," she said quickly. She needed to get away before he saw her eyes tear up.

She hurried into the kitchen, pushing the door open with her hip. "Hey, George," she hollered over the sizzle of steak and clang of pots. "Another chicken and dumplings."

"Okay. Got it." George wiped the sweat from his brow with the back of his hand and pointed to two full plates sitting on the counter. "There's your other two chicken and dumplings. Better get them out there before they get cold."

Dorothy nodded in agreement and hurried out into the dining room with a plate in each hand. She delivered them to the booth next to Ronald's, stealing a glance at the side of his head.

After serving the two plates of chicken and dumplings, Dorothy took another order and then went back to the kitchen to see if Ronald's dish was ready. The moment George pushed Ronald's order across the counter, she scooped it up and delivered it to him, looking forward to serving it. "Here you go, sir," she said, keeping her emotions in check as she placed the plate in front of Ronald.

He offered her a simple nod. "Thank you," he said as he unfolded his napkin and placed it on his lap.

Dorothy smiled. His manner reminded her of their first night together. It was hard to believe that was over two weeks ago. "You are most welcome." She turned to leave.

"Are you working tomorrow evening?" His voice rang of hope and made Dorothy stop.

"Yes, I am."

"Maybe I'll try the pork tomorrow. What do you think?"

"I think you'll like it," she said, finding herself anxious to come to work tomorrow.

She then grabbed a tray from the stash by the wall and walked over to the other end of the dining room. As she cleared off a table, a man staggered into the restaurant from the saloon side of the building.

"Whoa there," Sunny said, blockading the man's further entrance. "The bar's in there. If you've had more than one drink, that's where we'd like you to stay." She turned him around to face the saloon.

He turned back around, and Dorothy got a look at his face. *Stanley Jones.* Her skin crawled once again at his resemblance to Vincent.

"This is where I intend to be," Stanley growled, "and I want to be seated now!" His eyes scanned the dining room and came to rest upon Dorothy. Then his finger pointed. "And I want her to wait on me."

Sunny sent Dorothy a worry-filled glance.

"It's okay, Sunny." Dorothy abandoned the half-filled tray on the table. She sucked in a deep breath and plowed toward Stanley, eyeing a single empty table as she moved through the dining room. "This way, Mr. Jones." She showed him the table and handed him a menu as he sat down. "Would you like a minute to decide?"

"Naw, just give me some pretzels." He pushed the menu away.

Dorothy bristled. "You could have asked for those in the saloon if that's all you want."

"It's not all I want."

"But you just said—"

"I didn't come here for no watered-down beef steak. I got my own beef— and a cook I pay good money for back at my place."

"So . . ."

"I came here specifically to talk to you, little lady."

"You don't even know me."

"I know enough." A snide grin uglied his face. "In fact, maybe you and I should go back over to the saloon side. I know you'd feel right at home over there."

"What are you talking about?" Dorothy's arms prickled.

"Sit down."

"I can't. I got customers to tend to."

"Sit down!" Stanley slapped the table next to an empty chair. "Unless of course you want everyone to hear what I got to say—and I don't think you do."

Dorothy lowered herself into the chair. "What do you want?" she asked with sharpness. She knew this kind of man all too well.

"First, let me tell you what I know, then I'm sure you'll be a little more willin' to help me."

"I'm sure 'willing' will never be the case."

"You think so, ay?" Stanley wrinkled the eyebrow that ran over both eyes and smiled with one side of his mouth. "Well, let me tell you a story. I think that'll change your mind." He scooted his chair back a bit, as if to make himself more comfortable. "Last week I went to St. Louis on business. While there, I went to my favorite saloon on the west side and played a few games of high-stakes poker—'cause I can." A sense of cocky pride lit his eyes. "While I was there, I ran into a fellow by the name of Vincent Bednar."

Dorothy stifled a gasp.

"Name ring a bell?"

Dorothy's back stiffened. She kept quiet.

"It should because apparently he is a friend of yours."

The desire to yell, "He's no friend of mine!" consumed her. She struggled to maintain her poker face as her entire body wanted to run out of Sunny's Place and away from Craig.

Stanley stared at her as if he'd expected more of a response and then continued. "Back to my story 'cause I think this Vincent fellow is more than just a friend to you. Let me explain." He laced his fingers together and then pushed his palms outward, cracking a knuckle or two. "He was walkin' around the saloon, showin' everyone who'd give him the time of day a photograph of his wife. Said he was tryin' to find her. She up and left him and ran away, and he was hurtin'. I said the gal looked vaguely familiar. Then me and him played a few games of poker together. Did some talkin'. He lost to me, then I lost a lot more to him. He kept talkin' about his wife, said she boarded a train headed out West about three weeks ago, and he hasn't heard from her since. He wants her back awful bad."

"So," Dorothy responded, boiling inside at Vincent's lies while her outsides shivered in fear. "What does that have to do with me?"

"A lot. You see, he said her name was Dorothy. The train she got on in Missouri could have got connected with the one that brought you to Rawlins."

"Dorothy is a common name. And how do you know what train I took to come here? You know nothing about me."

"I know plenty, as does everyone else in this town. You're Dorothy Cooper, Ron Smith's mail-order bride—or rather, you're his bride-to-be." He rolled his eyes. "Ole Ron is the craziest man I know. Shellin' out all that money to *court* his mail-order bride," he mumbled under his breath and then laughed.

"You yourself said the woman that Mr. Bednar was looking for was his wife. Thus, she would be Dorothy Bednar, not Dorothy Cooper," Dorothy said, trying to talk her way out of this mess.

"Of course you'd change your name. He said you were good at connin' people. You cheated people out of their money all the time. That's why he wanted you back—he's worried about your soul." His grin held a twisted sort of admiration. "How you ever managed to con Mr. Smith into payin' for your trip out here—so quickly and underneath your husband's nose no less—is beyond me. But hey, you're good."

"I am not a criminal," Dorothy blurted out with more volume than she'd intended. "I-I . . ." Faces turned in her direction. "I am not this woman you speak of, and that man is certainly *not* my husband," she said in a quiet but determined voice. She was about to tell him Vincent was her brother, to add to her defense, but tying herself to Vincent in any form could be damning.

"Oh, I beg to differ. Remember, he showed me a photograph. It caught my attention right off, though I didn't let him know that. You see, I never forget the face of a pretty woman."

Dorothy found no words to refute him. Her shoulders slumped. "What do you want from me?"

"You do a favor for me, and I'll not say a word to my new friend, Mr. Bednar, about your whereabouts. How about it?"

"What could I ever do for you? Even if I could get you all the free meals you want," Dorothy said, flicking her wrist at the chicken and dumplings on a nearby table, "it's not like that would be a favor to you."

"When I first saw that photograph of you, it gave me an idea." Stanley's smile made Dorothy's skin crawl. "I want you to turn on your charm and convince Ron Smith to abandon his efforts to get my father's old will thrown out."

Dorothy froze. "No! I can't. I won't."

"Oh, I say you can. And you will . . . if you don't want not only ole Ron but also everyone else in this town to know what kind of person you are. And I don't mean *just* a saloon girl. And if you're thinkin' of runnin' instead of doin' what I ask, think again. I know how to contact your husband, and he'll be out here in two shakes of a stick. You'll not get far."

Chapter 17

RONALD GAZED UP AT DOROTHY as she set his pork chop dinner on the table before him. "Thank you so much," he said, hoping she'd stay a minute or two to talk.

"You're welcome," she said without looking at him and hurried off.

Ronald forked a bite of pork into his mouth and chewed slowly as he watched Dorothy take orders at the table on the far side of the restaurant. She seemed perfectly at ease with the customers. And yesterday, when he'd been daring and tried the chicken and dumplings, it had been such a relief when she had finally warmed up to him. Why then had she fidgeted so much when she'd taken his order ten minutes ago? He tried to catch her eye. It was as if she was purposely avoiding him.

He took a bite of potatoes and then sliced into his pork chop again, racking his brain as to what he might have done to cause Dorothy to be so skittish.

As he finished up his last bite of pork and dabbed his mouth with a napkin, his eyes caught sight of Stanley Jones walking into the restaurant side from the saloon. He found it odd that Stanley would choose to eat at Sunny's two nights in a row. As he recalled, last night Stanley hadn't even eaten much of meal as it was. The only thing he recalled seeing Dorothy deliver to Stanley's table, as Ronald himself had finished his supper and stood to leave, was pretzels.

Dorothy had stood stiff as a board when she'd served Stanley his pretzels. And when Ronald had walked past Dorothy on his way to the door after that, she'd stiffened again and said not a single word to him.

It made no sense. Was there some connection between Dorothy and Stanley Jones? Now that Stanley was back, it was about time Ronald paid him a visit. This time, he had two reasons to do so.

♠

Dorothy pushed the kitchen's swinging door open slightly with her hip, stopping to get a better grip on the three plates she balanced on her arm. Her gut twisted as she peered out into the dining room through the narrow opening. Stanley Jones strolled into the restaurant. Wasn't last night enough? His eyes skirted from table to table, and she knew he must be looking for her. She stepped back in and set the plates onto the counter.

"Hey, what's going on?" George pointed his huge spoon at the plates.

"Nothing. I'll be back in a sec." Dorothy crept into the dining room.

Stanley's big eyebrow furrowed at the sight of her. "You," he said, motioning for her to come with the whipping of his head.

Dorothy scurried toward him, hoping Ronald would be fully engaged with his pork chop and pay no notice of her walking toward Stanley. "What do you need? Would you like me to seat you?" she said, knowing full well that wasn't what he wanted.

"We need to talk."

"I don't get paid to talk, only to take orders and serve."

"Fine by me." His mouth curled up on one side.

"That in no way means—oh, never mind," she said under breath. She motioned for him to step back into the saloon.

"Like I thought, you're at home over here," Stanley said as he followed her.

"Shush," Dorothy whispered. When they'd moved out of sight and ear-shot of the restaurant, she asked, "Okay, what do you need now?" *You snake,* she felt like adding.

Stanley leaned his back against the wall to the side of the bar, lifting his foot and resting his boot against the floor molding to support his relaxed stance. He took out a pouch of tobacco from his jacket and rolled a cigarette. "I was wonderin' if you had a chance to bat those pretty eyes of yours at ole Ron to get him to give up on his foolhardy efforts." He lit the end of the cigarette and took a puff. "You know, to appeal my pa's will." He blew a ring of smoke into her face. "The original one, the real one, the one my father intended to be in place."

Dorothy held her breath and then turned her face away and blew out as much bad air as she could, wishing she could rid herself of the mounting pressure inside her as easily. "No, I have not."

"Funny, I thought maybe you had."

"What do you mean?"

"You see, I'd almost expected to see ole Ron on my door with his paper to sign today 'cause I just got back yesterday. But he never showed up. I figured you must be smarter than you look and done what I asked the first time. I guess I was wrong." He blew another puff of smoke her way.

She coughed. "Maybe he changed his mind on his own," she said, hoping that was the case.

"Not on your life and not on his own. So you see, pretty lady, I'm glad I came in here tonight and got things straightened out in my mind and reminded you of what you need to do. I got some big purchases I plan to make down the road, and I want to make sure I'm going to have the money to do so. I'd hate to have to tell ole Ron some things that would break his heart. So just take my orders and serve me up right, if you know what I mean." He winked.

Dorothy clenched her fists. "You—you are as low as a snake's belly, Mr. Jones."

"Not any lower than how far you've sunk, little sister. You see, you and me ain't too different." He laughed. Thankfully the sickening sound got swallowed up by the ruckus of the saloon. "I know ole Lavender Decker over at the mercantile will be powerful disappointed to hear of your past. This mornin' when I was in there, I heard her talk up a streak to Mary Tucker about how wonderful Ronald Smith's bride-to-be was."

The elation over Lavender's opinion of her lifted Dorothy momentarily. Then reality rushed back in. Vincent would find her if she didn't do something. "I'll see what I can do," she said through gritted teeth.

"That's what I like to hear." Stanley tipped his hat and stepped to the bar.

Dorothy hurried back into the restaurant and went straight to the kitchen.

After she served the three lukewarm plates of food to their rightful customers, she treaded over to Ronald's table.

His plate had been slicked clean, and he sat there at the table seat as still as a tree on a breezeless summer evening. She wished she could be so calm. "Are you finished?" she said, suddenly self-conscious of her obvious remark. She'd never found it difficult to speak to Ronald before. Now she felt as if she'd need a crowbar to extract words from her mouth.

"Yes, thank you." Ronald motioned to his plate and gazed into her eyes.

The light coming from his brown eyes emanated a new sort of warmth she'd not detected before. How could she ask this kind man to go against the very fiber he was made of? She forced the words out. "How are things at the office? Are you keeping busy?"

He seemed to light up further at her attempt at conversation. "Yes, busy." He swished his hand in the direction of his office. "But I am never too busy for you," he said with the most darling hint of a smile.

"I worry you might overdo it. Perhaps you should cut back on your case load," she said, struggling to keep her voice from shaking. Her gut tightened, and she continued. "Cut out any unnecessary work. For example, trying to appeal Benedict Jones's will. From what you've told me, his daughter doesn't need an inheritance, and Logan doesn't care one whit about the money."

Ronald's smile disappeared. His eyes filled with something Dorothy had yet to see within them. Was it rage? Anger? Or something else? "I am not persuing this new will for my sake or for Logan's income alone. I'm doing it for fairness' sake; and for Benedict Jones, God rest his soul. In his old age, he finally sought to be equitable, at least somewhat, with all three of his children. I merely desire to bring to pass his wishes and a bit of justice."

Dorothy, unsettled by his passionate response, ripped his receipt out of her notebook, slapped it on the table, and stepped back. "Here's your bill. You can pay Sam over at the cash register. And sorry I said anything about your work." She darted into the kitchen.

George looked up from the stove as she ran through the kitchen toward the back door. "Hey, where are you going? I got two roast beefs ready to go out."

"To the privy," she lied and slipped outside into the alley.

The glow from Sunny's side window reached around the back of the building, adding barely enough light to the dusk sky to see. She plopped down onto a pile of crates and let the tears come. Her frustration soon converged into anger, drying her tears.

"Lies," she muttered to darkness surrounding her. "It's all I ever do." She hated lying. Yet here she continued that path of deceit even though she was a thousand miles away from Vincent. "It's because of him." She continued her ranting. "I can't go back. I'll never go back." Yet she was living a similar life here: one of deceit. It had to stop if she was ever to be free from Vincent.

♠

Ronald patted Mehitable affectionately on the neck as he settled into the saddle. "Don't worry, girl, we won't be gone any longer than we have to be." He gazed at the dark clouds gathering in the sky west of town, fearing them much less than the task of talking to Stanley Jones. He'd put this off for several days. Procrastination did his stomach a disservice.

Serving Stanley with another affidavit to sign would be the easy part. Getting him to sign it could prove difficult. Confronting him about Dorothy would be even more difficult. He had no hard evidence that Stanley was manipulating her, only her untypical nervous behavior and the man's unscrupulous nature—all circumstantial evidence at best. But this wouldn't be the courtroom. The law was not necessarily on his side.

Ronald wiped his sweaty palms on his pants, one hand at a time, and rode out of town rehearsing his preplanned discourse aimed at Stanley.

An hour later, he spotted smoke billowing above a stand of poplar trees on the edge of the Circle J Ranch and hoped that meant Stanley was at home. It was not in his plans to ride out on the range to confront Stanley and be even more out of his element. He needed a controlled set of variables to have a chance at success.

He guided Mehitable around the trees and emerged onto the vast grassland belonging to the Joneses. A single-story ranch house spread out almost as immense as the grassland behind it compared to the small patch of lawn that resided in the old homestead's place. It was with sadness that Ronald reminisced over the blue-and-white two-story place that used to house the Joneses before it burned to the ground, killing Benedict and starting this mess with multiple wills.

He dismounted, tied Mehitable to the rail fence of the adjacent corral, and pulled the correct paper from the folder in his saddlebag. His feet felt like boulders as he lumbered toward the front porch. He put on his attorney face, shook off his apprehension, and knocked on the door. A minute or two later, he knocked again. The housekeeper opened the door.

"Yes?" She scowled at him.

Ronald removed his hat. "I wish to speak with Mr. Stanley Jones. Is he by chance at home?"

"Naw, he's out and about." She held on to the door, fighting a gust of wind.

Ronald peered into the great room behind the woman. Numerous deer and elk heads hung from the walls, but not a single glimpse of Stanley could be seen. "Do you have someone that could send him a message that he has a caller?"

"What do you think this place is, one of those highfalutin estates from back East with a passel of servants?"

"I, well—no ma'am, I—"

"Well, it's not." She scrunched her lips together.

Ronald wiped a bead of sweat from his brow with the back of his hand holding his hat. "I am sorry, ma'am. Could you perhaps take a message for Mr. Jo—"

The slap of a screen door diverted their attention to the back of the house.

A moment later, Stanley strutted into the great room. Surprise filled his expression. He then glared at Ronald. "What's he doin' here?" He glanced at his housekeeper. "I've told you a thousand times to keep that front door closed. You never know what the wind'll blow in."

"Come in so I can shut the darn door." The housekeeper motioned Ronald inside, then huffed and walked away.

"If you must voice your frustrations, Stanley, do it to me." Ronald steadied his nerves. "And by your reaction, I take it you already know why I am here."

"I dooo?" Stanley stretched out his words like a belligerent five-year-old.

Ronald handed the document to Stanley. "This is a copy of the paperwork you misplaced. I beseech you to sign it right now so it will not become lost once again. I am willing to wait."

"What if I don't want to sign it? What if I don't think that dang will they found down at the bunkhouse is real? I think it's a fake."

"You have every right to think what you want. And what you would be signing here does not declare that you believe the handwritten will is authentic. It merely gives your sworn statement that you believe the handwriting is Benedict's, which you already stated when I first showed it to you. It is up to a judge to decide the will's authenticity." Ronald held out a pen. "So, Mr. Jones, it might very well be in your best interest to sign this document in case you are right. Do you not agree that it will be best to have the matter of your father's legal will decided officially and not by me or your sister so that your father, God bless his soul, may rest in peace?"

Stanley wrinkled his forehead. "So you're sayin' there's a good chance that new will could be deemed a fake?"

"Not necessarily fake but invalid," Ronald responded, knowing very well it could be the case but nonetheless hoping it wouldn't be. Either way, he had to try.

"You should have put it to me like this the first time." Stanley accepted the pen and scanned the document. "It would have saved me a good bit of hassle." He stepped over to an end table and placed the paper upon it.

"By hassle, do you mean having to pull others into your scheming? And by others, I mean innocent victims."

Stanley laughed. "Innocent is hardly the correct label." He stared at the affidavit.

As Ronald motioned for him to sign, he wondered if they were speaking of the same person. He took a chance and asked, "So you do not deny coercing Miss Dorothy Cooper into attempting to talk me out of this?"

"Hey, I didn't coerce her. She done chose on her own to talk you out of it."

"On her own, you say?"

"Yep, otherwise I would have had no choice but to tell you the truth about her." Stanley twirled the end of his mustache and mumbled. "She did a pretty lousy job at it too."

"That is coercion."

"No, it ain't." Stanley brought his hand to the side of his mouth as if to shield his words. "By the way, her name is not Dorothy Cooper; it's Dorothy Bednar."

Ronald fumed inside. "I am aware of that."

Stanley let go of his mustache, and his eyebrow rose. "You are?"

"Yes, and I believe it is time for me to go." Ronald's idea of probing into the relationship between Dorothy and Stanley had been a bad idea. "Could you hurry your signature along?"

"No, I don't believe I care to right now." Stanley handed the document back unsigned. "I've changed my mind."

Ronald's jaw sagged, and he reluctantly accepted it. "Very well then. Good day, Mr. Jones."

"Are you aware that she used to be a saloon girl and ran crooked poker games and she's already married?" Stanley asked as Ronald turned to leave. "My guess is she's playing you like a fiddle. But then what do you expect when you order a wife out of a catalog? Me, I don't even order trousers from a catalog. I have everything custom made for me."

Ronald opened the door himself. "I said, 'good day,'" he uttered through gritted teeth. With his back firmly set toward Stanley, he walked as calmly as he could out the door and shut it behind himself. If he were a gambling man and this were a game of poker, he'd be awfully tempted to fold.

♠

Chapter 18

RONALD RODE MEHITABLE AT A brisk pace home from the Circle J. His mind raced at a similar speed.

The June tenth date he had set for his wedding approached, being a little over four weeks away. His stomach twisted like it always did when goals got disrupted. But even more bothersome was the empty, painful pit he felt in his heart. He never dreamed Dorothy could have captured his affections so quickly, but her mounting deceit was becoming too much to bear. Logic screamed for him to let go of her and run away as fast as he could.

Was she, in fact, after his money? Even worse, was she already married? He shook his head as if that could dislodge those possibilities from his mind. But why else would a girl as pretty as Dorothy be interested in him? He should be ashamed, letting his heart get in the way. His reputation in the courtroom for seeing through people's lies was most certainly unwarranted now.

His sadness deepened. Had she never cared for him? And it all had been an act? He swore he had felt sincerity in her words and actions.

If only he knew the truth, the whole truth. Who was he to pass judgment without having all the facts? But he certainly wasn't getting them from Dorothy. What about Stanley Jones? Could Ronald trust him? The only thing that was for certain was that he needed more evidence, more witnesses.

The only new source that came to mind was the person who'd penned those letters as Wilhelmina Cooper.

He had a return address.

Sending an inquiry would take too long . . .

He could get to Chicago in three or four days—if he left immediately and rode Mehitable hard the entire way to Rawlins and then caught the express train to Chicago.

When he stepped into his house, the place felt empty. He noticed a basket with a half dozen eggs on the cupboard with a note.

Widow Harris dropped these off. I hope you don't mind if I scrambled myself up a half dozen of them before I left for the livery stable.
Logan

"It's good someone has an appetite so Mrs. Harris's payment won't go to waste." He supposed he could force himself to cook one or two of them before he left. No, he didn't have time. He ran upstairs to pack his saddlebags.

He neatly folded two shirts, two pairs of pants, and two sets of undergarments and tucked them carefully, but quickly as possible, into one side of the saddlebags. Realizing he still had some room, he placed another set of clothes in the one side, thinking it would be good to spend an extra day or so in Chicago to visit his parents while he was so close. Then it dawned on him: he could visit the library at the law school while he was there. He'd be killing three birds with one stone: Wilhelmina Cooper, parents, library. The very idea made this unplanned trip more palatable.

Maybe he should take the easiest course—stay put and place another ad to solicit yet another mail-order bride. Or maybe he should consider the widow, Ms. Harris. He had no attraction to her whatsoever, but perhaps they could ease each other's loneliness through a marriage of convenience. *No, that wouldn't be proper.* Her husband barely passed away in March. He honestly should place an ad for a mail-order bride first thing when he got to the office.

No, he wouldn't. He could not face the humiliation yet again.

He put on his traveling jacket, grabbed the saddle bags, and hurried down the stairs.

Logan walked in the back door while Ron packed a variety of dried fruits and jerky into his saddle bag. "Ron, what's got you so all fired in a hurry and packin' your saddlebags no less?"

"Logan, I am glad you're here. I need your help." Ron grasped him by the shoulders.

"Things were slow over at the livery stable, so I hurried home for something to eat. Sorry, I can't help you much at the moment."

"No, this does not need to be done immediately," Ronald said between breaths. "Just by tomorrow afternoon. That's when my appointment with Mr. Hoy is scheduled. I need you to ride out to his place and tell him I had to cancel. I also need you to go through the schedule book on my desk and cancel all my other appointments for the next two weeks. Can you do that for me?"

"Sure." Logan nodded but looked confused. "But where in tarnation are you off to?"

"Chicago. I don't have time to explain now. Just know it is something I have got to do. Oh, and if you see Dorothy . . ." Ronald paused. "Oh drat. I don't know what I want you to tell her." He patted Logan on the back and headed out the door.

♠

Dorothy buttoned the top of her coat against the morning breeze and headed toward Ronald's office. He hadn't stopped in to eat at Sunny's for the last three nights, and she'd wanted to tell him she was ready to talk about Wilhelmina and everything else—including her desire to continue their courtship. Was he having second thoughts about her though? With each labored step, she rehearsed in her mind how she'd spill the entire truth about her past. Wilhelmina's letter, tucked securely in her skirt pocket, wouldn't help a bit when it came to explaining why she'd cheated all those men out of their money—it might even hinder her explanation.

Her stomach felt as though it had been beaten and wrung out like dirty laundry by the time she stepped onto the sidewalk that ran in front of his office. She hadn't felt like looking into the shops along the way, only like keeping her energy focused straight ahead. A lump formed in the base of her throat. She seriously doubted that once she revealed the entirety of her past, Ronald would choose to continue their courtship.

She stopped and grabbed hold of the doorknob to his office. It remained immovable when she tried to turn it. She hurried around to the front window and peered inside. Perhaps he'd forgotten to unlock the door. She craned her neck this way and that, trying to gain a view of every nook and cranny of his office. Nothing.

With courage waning, she headed for his house. Hopefully, he'd be at home. If she didn't unload her burden now, she'd never muster the courage again to face Ronald. The other night's pain refused to leave. Stanley's threats still burned hot after three days, fueling her determination. She'd thought it through, again and again. She cared too much for Ronald to make a hasty decision on this matter. It would be painful, but she'd decided it best to tell Ronald the truth rather than stoop to Stanley's demands.

She ran down Yampa Avenue to Fifth Street, not stopping until she turned the corner and the two-story house, with its white picket fence and cherry tree loaded with blossoms, came into view. Her pace slowed.

A woman dressed in black stepped out of Ronald's house and down the porch. She had a dark-gray shawl wrapped around her hair like a scarf, and she carried a small basket half-full of eggs. As she walked away from the porch, she turned, and her eyes followed the roof line with the same longing Dorothy's had when she first saw the house. The woman finally noticed Dorothy when their paths nearly collided.

"Oh dear, excuse me," the woman said as she came to an abrupt stop three feet from Dorothy. "I was just admiring the woodwork on Mr. Smith's house and not watching where I was going."

"Yes, it is rather pleasing to look at," Dorothy said.

"Is Mr. Smith doing legal work for you?" the woman asked.

"No, we're . . ." Dorothy was about to say *friends* but wasn't even sure about that anymore. "No, just paying him a visit." She tilted her head and studied the woman, wondering if Ronald always had his eggs delivered and by such a handsome woman, around the same age as Ronald. Dorothy guessed that age to be about twenty-five by the woman's smooth face and shiny, dark hair. Was she jealous?

I have no right to be.

"Oh, excuse me, I'm Nettie Harris." The woman extended her hand to shake. "My husband died a few months ago, and Ronald Smith is helping me procure my late husband's assets. They're tied up in what's called probate—at least that's what Ronald, I mean *Mr. Smith*, says. He's such a nice man, helping me when all I have to pay him with is eggs." She lifted her basket momentarily.

"Yes, he is such a nice man." Dorothy repeated the woman's words, each one digging a reminder into her heart like they came with barbs. She nodded her goodbye to Ms. Harris and broke into a brisk pace up the sidewalk to the house, wondering if this woman would be so cordial if she knew the truth about Dorothy's past.

Once on the porch, she gave the door a timid knock. Shuffling footsteps sounded through the door. Her heart sank, realizing she'd forgotten about Logan. She liked Logan and valued his friendship, but she wasn't ready to tell anyone but Ronald yet.

The door opened. Logan stood in the entry wearing a smile. "Howdy, Miss Dorothy. What can I do for you?"

"Is Ronald at home?"

"Nope."

"Do you know where he is?" Why had she said that? She didn't want to confront him anywhere else.

"He should be in Chicago right about now." Logan rubbed his chin. "He left in rather a hurry three days ago."

"Chicago?" Dorothy felt like the wind had been knocked out of her. "Did he say why?"

"Nope, just that it was something he had to do. Oh, and that he'd be gone for two weeks." Logan pointed toward the kitchen. "I just got a delivery of eggs though. You're welcome to come in. I can cook you some up. There's way more than I can eat myself."

"Thanks for the offer, but I'll wait to talk to Mr. Smith another time."

"Mr. Smith?" Logan raised his eyebrows as if she'd spoken something obscene. "Now don't you be callin' him that. You two got to be on a first-name basis right off. I liked that. Don't be revertin' back to being strangers to each other. Ron and you belong together like potatoes and gravy. I can feel it in my bones."

"That's very sweet, Logan." She backed away from the door. "But there are things at play here that you don't understand—and I'd never expect you to." She turned away. Over her shoulder, she muttered, "Good day," and hurried down the steps before she had to say any more and take the chance that her voice would crack.

"You'll meet up with him when he gets back, won't you?" he hollered to her back.

"Yes, I'll do that. Thank you." It took all her strength to say that in an even tone. Moisture gathered in her eyes. Here she was, lying yet again. She'd never meet up with Ronald again—he'd obviously talked with Stanley. But why go to Chicago? To run home to his mother because he was so upset? No, that didn't seem likely.

Dorothy gasped. *Wilhelmina!* This could only lead to more trouble.

Chapter 19

RONALD PAID FOR THE CAB and climbed out as the driver held the horse steady. He waved the cab on and stood for a moment, staring at the family home. The intricate pattern of the brickwork stood out on the three-story house even though it was well past eight at night. The gas streetlight on the corner hadn't been there the last time Ron was here and neither was the paved street he stood on. He wondered what other changes had occurred in his absence.

A light shone through the window from the formal living room on the main floor. Bill was most likely down there reading in the good light like Ron's brother often did. A basement window was also lit but harder to see, being at ground level and tucked behind a bit of shrubbery as it was. Ron knew that to be the maid's quarters. All other windows were dark. He wished he'd had time to send a telegram to tell his parents he was coming. His gut tightened. Such lack of planning surely would lead to disaster. Whatever had he been thinking?

At least Bill is up.

His effort to look at the good things of the moment were feeble at best. He lumbered up the sidewalk, then the front steps of the main porch, and turned the doorknob. It was locked. *What else could I expect?* He lifted the ring in the lion's mouth of the doorknocker and let it fall with a *clap*.

After a minute, the door swung in to reveal Bill wearing a satin-collared robe, standing before him. Folks often commented on how Ron's brother looked like a carbon copy of him, only younger. It had been nearly four years since he'd seen Bill last. With his brother now twenty-one and Ronald twenty-six, they looked even more alike. "Ronald?"

"Yes, Bill, it is your prodigal brother from out West."

"What in the world are you doing here at this hour looking like you've slept in that same shirt and trousers for the past three days?"

Ronald held up a hand to curtail further questions and pushed his way in. "I don't wish to talk about it here and now. I just want to go to bed. Is my old room still available?" He headed for the main staircase.

Bill followed a step behind. "I presume it is. We've got a new maid; Hattie's her name. Would you like me to go ask her?"

"No, please don't bother her. Whatever state it is in, I'm sure it is better than my sleeping arrangements of the last three nights." Ronald peered into the lit formal living room, then skirted his eyes down the hall then to the darkened staircase and even darker upper floor where he was headed. He'd wait to greet his parents in the morning. "Could you fetch me a lamp?"

"'Fetch me a lamp'?" Bill mimicked. "You sound like someone from the West. Oh, wait a minute, you are that brother who up and left for a dusty cow town to practice law, not giving an ounce of consideration that it might break your mother's heart."

"You make it sound like I didn't plan my move at all." Ronald bristled as he placed a foot on the first stair.

"Well, of course *you* planned everything out. You just left your family out of your planning."

"I said I didn't want to talk tonight." Ronald proceeded up the stairs.

Bill followed. "Sorry, I didn't mean to rile you. I really am glad to see you. How long do you plan to stay? Will this be a short visit, or have you perhaps decided to move back indefinitely?"

"At the moment, I can't rightly say."

♠

Ronald awoke with the sun. After taking a quick bath and putting on a fresh set of clothing, he headed downstairs to the breakfast nook for some of the eggs and bacon he smelled cooking.

The new maid smiled at him when he stepped in the kitchen. "If you bring me your traveling clothes, I can wash them for you after breakfast."

"How did you know—"

"I told her." Bill's voice pulled Ronald's eyes to the table nestled into a sunny nook of the kitchen's far corner. Light streamed in the numerous tall windows and lit his brother's face.

Ronald sat down at the table, opposite his brother, and poured himself a cup of coffee. Hattie set a small platter filled with eggs, bacon, and biscuits in the middle of the table. "Thank you," he said, thinking of how nice it was to be home: running water, someone to do his laundry, a hot breakfast every morning. He could definitely get used to this again. Easily.

Reaching across the table, he scooped some eggs onto his plate. He hesitated to take all he'd like. There only seemed to be enough for him and Bill. "What about Mother and Father? Will they not be down soon?"

"Sorry, brother-who-didn't-send-word-before-he-came," Bill said, wearing a teasing half grin. "You just missed them. They left for New York on vacation yesterday morning. They're going to visit Niagra Falls, then head up into Canada. They'll be gone for a month." He chuckled. "Mother will be livid when she finds out she missed you."

"So you will be running the factory on your own then for the month?"

"That's correct." Bill's half grin returned. "Hey, there's still a position on the assembly line if you want the job. You know, if you're coming back home because things didn't work out for you in Colorado."

"Thank you, no. Things are working out just fi—" Ronald couldn't finish the word. Things were not fine. "I don't find that humorous in the least."

"Oh, come on, Ron. Don't be so stiff. You haven't changed a bit." Bill shook his head, took a bite of eggs, and then swallowed. "Seriously though, if you are coming back for good and you need a job, there's plenty of room at the top for you. Father wants to retire, you know."

"No, thank you. And I am not moving back to Chicago, I think."

"You mean you don't know?" Bill's brow wrinkled. "My big brother wrought with indecision?" He set his fork down and stared across the table at Ronald. "What's going on?"

Ronald shrugged.

"Let's start with what brought you to Chicago and away from that dusty little town you love so much."

Ronald turned his head and stared out a window, noticing the honeysuckle was in bloom. There was no way he could tell his brother the real reason. His acrimony toward Dorothy's deceptions were not something he cared to share.

"Wait a minute! This doesn't have anything to do with that mail-order bride business you jumped into, does it? When you mentioned it in the letter you sent six weeks ago, I almost fainted. I'm positive Mother would have—but I didn't tell her, promise. Just like you asked. Personally, I thought it a bold move on your part. I applauded you, in private of course, for doing something so out of character and daring." Bill looked him in the eye. "So does your being here have to do with a woman?"

"I would rather not say." Ronald returned to eating. "I do, however, have two pressing matters of business I need to attend to while I am here. How they turn out may affect whether or not I return to Chicago at a later date to stay." When he'd set out for Chicago, he'd not intended for this to be a possibility, but the more he thought about it, the more it appealed to him. He doubted life could be the same for him back in Craig if he were to discover Dorothy's deceit was real and intended. To share the same town with her would be too painful.

"Can you, or rather, will you tell me about these 'matters of business'?"

"Only that they have to do with a case I am working on." Ronald took the last bite of his breakfast and chewed thoroughly. "Now, if you will excuse me, I have a full day ahead of me."

"Do you want me to send Miles to hire you a cab?"

Ronald was glad to hear the family's gardener, who also filled in roles wherever else they needed him, was still here. He had fond memories of the dear fellow, a quiet, shy individual who Ronald had often shared his fears with while growing up. "No, I'd rather keep my extra change in my pocketbook. The train to Chicago cost me more than I'd expected. Besides, I don't mind taking the streetcars."

"If you're hurting for funds, I'd be glad to pay for your cab."

"I'm fine." Ronald dabbed his mouth with his napkin and stood. "I will be back for supper."

♠

Ronald reread the return address on the envelope he held and rechecked it with the street sign and the number on the house. The tree-lined street of modestly nice houses and the green gable trims of the Victorian home that stood before him also told him he was in the correct place; it was just as Wilhelmina had described. He was unsure if he was relieved or further confused. He took a deep breath, rehearsed in his mind what he was going to say, and proceeded up the porch steps.

He cleared his throat and knocked on the door.

The door opened, and an elderly lady stood behind the screen door. "Yes, may I help you?"

"Are you by chance Mrs. Fields?" Ronald asked, remembering the name of the grandaunt Wilhelmina's letters had mentioned she'd lived with.

"Yes."

Ronald squared his back. So far this was going as planned or, rather, hoped. "Do you by chance have a grandniece by the name of Wilhelmina Cooper?"

"Yes." The elderly lady stretched out the word. "Why do you ask?"

The sound of footsteps pulled Ronald's attention to the staircase directly behind Mrs. Fields. A somewhat young lady descended. "Who is it, Aunt Cynthia?" The drab shades of brown she wore matched the hair pulled severely back into a tight bun at the nape of her neck. She leaned so as to look around her aunt, and Ronald noticed two large moles on her cheek. Her eyes widened as if she recognized him. "Ronald Smith?" she uttered in a shaky voice.

How could she know? *The photograph I sent her.* "Wilhelmina?" Ronald replied.

"You two know each other?" Mrs. Fields stepped aside, allowing Wilhelmina the spot in front of the screen door.

"Sort of." Wilhelmina wrung the handkerchief she was holding. Her eyes met Ronald's briefly, then she looked away. "What are you doing here?"

"We need to talk." Ronald glanced inside, looking for a suitable place where they could be alone. "May I come in?"

"But of course." Mrs. Fields pushed the screen door open. "I was just about to have tea in the sitting room. Would you and Wilhelmina care to join me?"

Wilhelmina's face twitched. Her eyes then skirted around the entryway, up the stairs, and then came to rest on a parlor of sorts furnished with an antique sofa and wingback chairs upholstered in burgundy velvet. The room sat on the opposite side of the entry from the sitting room where a tea kettle, cup, and saucer awaited on a silver tray. Pale green curtains allowed the morning sun to stream in at will, lending the room a homey feel.

He wished Wilhelmina would have spoken up and invited him to sit in the burgundy room with her, but she remained silent as if the cat had her tongue. He pulled his mouth into a straight line and then forced himself to take the lead in the conversation with these ladies. "I need to speak with your niece in private if that is permissible. Might we step into your formal sitting room?" He pointed to the burgundy chairs separated by a clawfoot table.

"Come." Wilhelmina motioned for Ronald to head into the room with a jut of her pointy chin. Her face appeared slightly more relaxed. "Aunt Cynthia, thank you for the offer, but we won't be joining you."

Ronald followed her into the room and sat in one of the wingback chairs. Wilhelmina took the other chair. The moment Mrs. Fields settled into her chair in the other room and lifted her teacup to her lips, Wilhelmina turned to Ronald. "Why are you here? Did I not make it clear in the letter that I'd had second thoughts and no longer desired to be a," she cleared her throat with an *ahem*, "'mail-order bride,' as some call it?"

"I am afraid I am at a loss here." Ronald stiffened his back. "The last letter I received from you distinctly stated that you were planning on coming to Craig. It stated you would be leaving in two days' time and that you were nervous but anxious to meet me."

"Oh dear." Wilhelmina placed a hand on her chest and heaved a sigh. After a moment or two of awkward silence, she said, "Our meeting this morning has been . . . how do I say this without offense?" She paused again. "So sudden. I would be better prepared to speak with you if you were to return this evening after supper. Would seven o'clock work into your schedule?"

"Yes, seven o'clock will be fine." Ronald reluctantly rose from the chair. He could certainly understand the lady's need for planning. He was grateful he'd planned to visit the law library at the university. The way things were going, he feared he'd glean little else from this trip to Chicago.

Chapter 20

After leaving Ronald's house and running into Widow Harris, Dorothy didn't slow down until she reached Yampa Avenue. A block up, she passed the swinging doors of the Sunny Saloon. She looked inside as a cowboy walked out, smelling of the familiar stench of whiskey and tobacco even at this time of the early afternoon. Sunny had often expressed her preference for working the restaurant over the saloon. Dorothy didn't blame her.

An idea grew. It was a chance to do her friend a favor—perhaps the only friend she'd still have after this was over. She'd expose herself to all of Craig as a saloon girl so Ronald wouldn't have to deal with that unpleasant task when he returned. It was for sure he wouldn't be marrying her now. But with this, Stanley would have nothing to hang over her head, for the truth would be out. At least she would still have the means to take care of herself and hopefully stay put in Craig with Sunny as her friend. And if for some reason that snake, Stanley, saw fit to tell Vincent of her whereabouts, she'd cross that bridge of confronting her brother when she came to it. Facing him might even be a good thing. She'd show him she *could* survive on her own without him because she was already doing that. Almost.

She made her way back to the hotel. Campbell Tucker stood behind the counter when she walked inside. "Afternoon, Mr. Tucker."

"Afternoon, Miss Dorothy." He gave her a nod.

"You'll be glad to know," she said as she headed for the stairs, "that'll I'll be getting my first paycheck tomorrow, so I'll be able to pay for my room from now on." If Sunny agreed to let her work in the saloon, she'd more than be able to pay for herself. Alcohol always seemed to embellish men's tips more than a good beef steak. Perhaps this was a good thing after all. She didn't need a passel of friends as much as she needed a roof over her head.

"There's no need for you to pay. Ronald's got your room paid in full for the next month."

Dorothy stopped before placing her foot on the first stair and turned to face him. "That was his original plan—when he thought we'd be married in June. I'm sorry to say things have changed between us."

Mr. Tucker lifted an eyebrow. "Oh."

Dorothy held her breath. "And you might be kicking me out of your hotel too as soon as you find out, so I may as well just tell you right now to get it over with."

"Tell me what?" Mr. Tucker's eyes shone with concern.

"I'm a saloon girl. Been one for nearly five years now."

"That can't be right."

"Yes, it is, and I'm not the kind of girl you maybe thought I was."

"No, I mean it can't be right you've been doing that for five years." Mr. Tucker looked at the ceiling as if calculating. "I daresay you can't be more than twenty, and that would put you at fifteen when you started."

"That's right." No one needed to know about Vincent forcing her to cheat people. She'd reveal her past slowly. It might be easier that way—on her. "So do you prefer that I pack my bags right now and move out? Or could I beg a little favor of you to allow me until tomorrow so that I might find another place?"

"Move out?" Mr. Tucker jerked his head back. Then he smiled and wagged his hand at her. "Nonsense. Your money—or should I say Mr. Smith's—is as good as anyone's. I'm in the hotel business, and as such, I don't make it my *business* to know any of my customers' *business* or else I'd go broke. Besides, I like you, Miss Dorothy. You got a good streak runnin' through ya."

"Uh . . ." Dorothy sucked in a quick breath. "Thank you, Mr. Tucker." With her knees a bit wobbly, she turned and headed up the stairs.

Once in her room, she brushed out her hair, twisted it, and pinned it into place on the top of her head. She stepped over to the wardrobe and pulled its door open. Her red saloon dress lay at the bottom of the piece of furniture, still tucked inside the borrowed traveling bag where it'd been hiding for the past few weeks from possible prying eyes. She very well might regret this later. That was often the case when she decided on things without much forethought. Right now she didn't care. Her feelings were numb. Ronald was probably talking to Wilhelmina Cooper right now. Things couldn't get much worse, so why not go out in style?

She removed her skirt and blouse, stepped into the red satin dress, and looked into the mirror above the porcelain pitcher and bowl. She certainly looked the part—and why not? She had years of experience. Yes, she'd go out in style. She'd be one of the most well-known saloon girls Craig would ever have. She buttoned up the side of her dress and then ran her hand down the smooth surface of the satin. Yes, she was a saloon girl, and she'd probably always be a saloon girl now that Ronald was finally learning the truth. So why should she worry about her past catching up with her? Everyone knew that women like her were no good, so why should they be shocked to learn she had a seedy past?

After applying some bright red lipstick that, luckily, she'd had in her purse when she fled Missouri, she put a dab on her cheeks, rubbed it in, and glanced once more in the mirror. Then she put on her coat, covering her dress. Except for her red lips, she looked normal again. Mr. Tucker's words rang in her thoughts.

You got a good streak runnin' through ya.

Was it true? Was there actually something good about her?

She opened her coat for another glimpse of her dress. Was this a mistake?

"Too late," she said to her reflection. "I've made the decision."

She walked out of her room and headed toward Sunny's.

♠

"What in tarnation?" Sunny exclaimed.

Dorothy dropped her coat all the way as Sunny walked completely around her. She was grateful the early afternoon hour left the restaurant empty. "I used to be a saloon girl."

"So why wait until now to tell me? Not that it matters."

"I guess I was hoping to put it behind me; start a new life."

"And you've changed your mind?"

"Not really. It's just that I knew I had to quit living a lie. I've been doing it for almost as long as I can remember."

"What, working in a saloon or living a lie?" Sunny smiled.

"Both," Dorothy said without emotion. "A saloon girl is who I am. I'd just as well face it and get on with life." She dropped into a chair and moved an emptied glass out of the way so she could rest her arm on the table.

"Technically, I'm a saloon girl." Sunny lowered herself into the chair at Dorothy's side. "Does that make me bad?"

"Oh no, no, that's not what I meant at all." Dorothy felt her face flush. "I adore you, Sunny. You're the most kindhearted woman alive."

"And I feel the same about you, honey." Sunny placed a hand on Dorothy's bare arm and touched the short sleeve of Dorothy's dress. "This doesn't define who you are no more than it does me." She swept her hand down the front of a blue satin dress that had a row of ruffles at her knees. Sunny patted the ruffles at her chest. "In here, that's who I am, and it should be the same with you. Don't let anything—or any person—let you believe otherwise."

Dorothy gazed at her friend. "Good fortune surely shined upon me the day I met you, Sunny." Her throat tightened, and she barely managed to add, "I'll try to do that."

Sunny moved a wisp of hair out of her face and re-pinned it in place amongst the pile of blonde hair atop her head. "Okay, so you decided to open up to me and tell me a bit more about you. I appreciate that. But why wear this red dress? I'm afraid I'm going to have to ask you to go back to the hotel and change before you start your shift. Folks have gotten used to my waitress being dressed in more, um . . . conservative attire. Funny thing, these people are. This restaurant is connected to the saloon by an open doorway, yet they pretend it's completely separate."

"I figured I'd give you a break. I'll work the saloon tonight. You wait tables in the restaurant—I know how much you enjoy that."

"Honey, that's very kind of you." Sunny stood. "But are you sure? I don't blame you for trying to start a new life. So why undo the progress you've made?" She patted her chest again. "Remember, in here, that's what you are. So follow that. Be true to yourself."

Dorothy rose from her chair. "What about you? Are you being true to yourself?"

Sunny looked off into the distance. "At first I suppose I wasn't. I didn't want to run a saloon. But my late husband sank all our savings into this place. And when he died, God rest his soul, I was stuck here. Nobody wanted to buy me out. I realized I could carry on hating my situation and be miserable or carry on and make the best of this opportunity and be happy. Dressing up in satin and showing my ankles never defined who I was after I decided to do the latter."

"That's wonderful advice, but I'm afraid it doesn't apply to me."

"And what makes you so special?" Sunny grabbed a tray and cleared the glasses from the table.

Dorothy took a deep breath. She had to tell Sunny. As her employer, Sunny deserved to know. "I've got more things sullying my past than wearing skimpy dresses and serving whiskey to drunken men."

"Really now?" Sunny continued to clear the table with not even so much as a glance toward Dorothy.

"I helped cheat men out of their money."

"Um-huh." Sunny wiped the table with a cloth.

"Me and this man worked as a team. He got high-stakes poker games started. I distracted the men by serving them drinks, and I looked at their cards. Then, through a variety of ways, I let him know what their hands were. He always made a killing."

"What about you?" Sunny stopped cleaning and looked Dorothy square in the face. "How much did you make off each of those poker games?"

Dorothy couldn't meet her eyes. She looked off to the side. "Nothing."

"I thought so."

"But he gave me a living allowance."

Sunny glanced down at Dorothy's feet. "A really hefty one, I'm guessing, by the looks of your shoes."

Dorothy stepped behind the table to hide her feet.

Sunny carried the tray toward the bar. "I'm getting a clear picture here. You're in no way, shape, or form the 'bad girl' you're trying to paint for me. What you are, honey, is a victim. My suggestion would be to do exactly what you started out to do—start a new life." She wagged her hand at Dorothy. "Now hurry home and go change."

That sounded tempting to Dorothy. She grabbed her coat from off the floor, ready to head for the door and then hesitated. "No. No, I can't do that. I don't want to hide anymore. If people can't accept me for who I am, shady past and all, then that's okay. It'll only serve to weed out who my true friends are." She looked at Sunny, and her heart swelled. "I know I can carry on because I have at least one of them: you."

Maybe it wasn't the best idea, and maybe she should have thought it out a little better, but she wanted to do it. "Please, allow me to work in the saloon."

Sunny nodded. "Sure, honey, if you're positive that's what you want to do. It could backfire on you."

"I'm positive." Dorothy hid her trembling hands behind her back.

♠

Chapter 21

RONALD LOOKED AT THE CLOCK above the library's reference desk: shortly after five. He closed the law book with reluctance, having found one case he could possibly use in Logan's favor, but he would need more than just one. *Tomorrow.* He'd best leave now if he was to have something to eat and clean up before meeting with Wilhelmina tonight.

Hattie had a meal of pork cutlet, roasted potatoes, and fresh asparagus set out when Ronald arrived home. He ate it faster than good manners allowed and chided himself silently for it, and for putting off talking to his brother for yet another day. But showing up at Miss Cooper's house after 7:00 p.m. would churn his stomach even more.

When he finally stepped onto her porch, he had a mind to turn around and go home. Speaking to a woman would be difficult enough, but speaking to her about matters that made little sense would be excruciating. Tonight he had little more than a "hello" planned out as to what to say.

He slowly raised his knuckles to the door and knocked.

Miss Cooper answered the door. Her outward appearance had changed very little from this morning, but she did appear more composed. "Mr. Smith," she said with a nod. "Do come in." She showed him into the sitting room with the green curtains. They appeared mossy gray now in a mixture of light from the gas lamp in the center of the ceiling and twilight from the window. She motioned for him to sit down, which he did, and she proceeded to pour two cups of steaming tea.

"Do you prefer sugar or honey with your tea? Or lemon? Or perhaps nothing?"

"Honey would be nice, I presume." Ronald swallowed.

She drizzled honey into his cup, handed it to him, and then stirred her own, silently staring at it for at least a minute.

"It has been a while since I've had tea," Ronald said to break the silence. "In Colorado, we mostly drink coffee."

"Oh yes, out West." She took a sip of her tea but didn't look up from her cup. "I hear things are quite different out there, devoid of most creature comforts."

"It is not all that bad."

Miss Cooper took another sip of tea but said nothing.

Ronald uncrossed his legs, recrossed them, and then cleared his throat. "As I mentioned this morning, the last letter I received from you distinctly stated you were planning on coming to Craig, that you would be leaving in two days' time, and that you were nervous but anxious to meet me." He uncrossed his legs and scooted to the edge of his seat, hoping to get the woman to look at him rather than that blasted cup of tea. "Yet you claim you made it clear in a letter that you'd had second thoughts about being a 'mail-order bride.' I'm afraid, Miss Cooper, I never received such a letter. Are you positive that you placed it in the outgoing post?"

Miss Cooper finally looked up from her cup of tea. "I didn't send it by post."

Ronald waited for her to continue. After a length of silence he asked, "Then how did you send it?"

"I asked someone to deliver the letter personally to you. I thought the mail would be much too impersonal for such a dubious message."

"Who was it you asked to deliver said letter?" Ronald scooted even farther to the edge of his seat.

"A friend. At least I thought she was a friend." Miss Cooper set down her cup and rubbed her temples with her forefingers. "I'd barely met her, but in that short time, I grew to like her very much and trust her. Apparently, that was a mistake. I'm so very sorry, Mr. Smith, for any distress this might have caused you."

"Did this friend—as you referred to her—happen to be a beautiful young woman with sable-brown hair, green eyes, and high, rosy cheeks? And did she go by the name of Dorothy?" Ronald could see pieces of the puzzle fall into place. Yet, he hoped he was mistaken.

"Why, yes. Dorothy Bednar was her name. At least, that's what she told me." Miss Cooper's mouth opened into an O, stretching the moles on her cheek so as to look even larger. "Oh, dear me! You don't mean she . . ."

Ronald nodded, sensing what this woman was thinking. He continued for her. "She came to Craig posing as you, my wife-to-be." His back stiffened as a wave of disbelief washed through him. Or was it anger? In either case, it consumed his chest.

"Why on earth would a pretty, young woman do such a thing?" With her hand on her cheek, covering her moles, Miss Cooper shook her head.

Because Stanley was right. She is a con artist, and she is married. Ronald's heart felt as though a knife had slashed through it. "Tell me everything that transpired between you and Dorothy. Did you say something to her so as to unwittingly convince her to take your place?"

"Oh no, no, no. I never intended for her to take my place, only to deliver my letter to you. In return, I offered her the remainder of my train fare and stage-coach ticket to Craig so she could continue to run away from the man that had beaten her. I got off in St. Louis." Miss Cooper winced. "I admit I had a bad case of cold feet. The idea of living out West scared me. I am sorry to have reneged on our agreement. It was a poor decision that has pained me ever since I returned." She hurriedly picked up her cup of tea and took an extra-large sip.

"What do you mean by, and I quote, 'the man who had beaten her'?" Ronald's newfound resolve to forget Dorothy softened. He wondered if this could be that man who had once courted Dorothy, the one who had instilled such fear in her.

No, don't be duped. That could have been an act too.

Or could it be her husband, the one Stanley spoke of?

That scenario didn't help him feel any better. Only worse.

He listened intently as Miss Cooper told how Dorothy broke into her private compartment on the train, acting the part of a saloon girl who was running away from the law, and told her about the man who had inflicted the realistic-looking bruise by her eye. Miss Cooper convinced the sheriff Dorothy was not the girl they were looking for, took her in, fed her, gave her some clothes, and then gave her the means to continue on to Craig.

"All that time, I was thinking I was helping a person in need," Miss Cooper said. "That's why I treated her like family. But I have to wonder if all that time she was playing me like a fiddle, planning all along to take my money and yours." She shook her head back and forth several times. "It's not like she took that much from me. Please tell me she wasn't able to rob you of much, Mr. Smith."

"No." Ronald realized that Dorothy, in fact, had not. "At least not in the way of money," he added, trying his best to keep his emotions from showing.

"Where is this woman now?" Miss Cooper asked.

"Still back in Craig, Colorado, as far as I know."

"Oh dear. I do have a rough draft of the letter I gave her to deliver to you—if that will help in some way, perhaps to have her prosecuted. Do you plan on returning to Colorado anytime soon?"

Ronald swallowed a lump that had risen in his throat. "I am not sure any-more." And he wasn't sure he wanted to turn Dorothy in to the authorities.

"Now that we've met . . . face to face, I mean," Miss Cooper said in a voice that was a mere whisper to a minute ago when she'd spoken about Dorothy, "we could perhaps pick up where we left off."

"By that, you mean what?"

"Engage in a normal courtship here in Chicago, where there's running water and we're close to family. This setting would be much more conducive to getting to know each other."

"You make a good point." Ronald had always admired Miss Cooper's—the real Miss Cooper's—sound logic. His desire to return to Craig waned. For certain, he'd gather the evidence he needed from the university library to help Logan. He'd return to Colorado long enough to make that happen, but then he'd move back to Chicago. He'd given life out West a chance, but there was nothing but pain for him there now. It was time to come home.

He stood to leave. "Miss Cooper, I appreciate you giving me your time this evening. If it would be amenable to you, I would very much like to call on you tomorrow evening." He couldn't believe he'd just said that. He scrambled for a plan. Fortunately, he had a small measure of experience with courting. "We could dine at a restaurant of your choice and afterward come back here, sit on your porch swing, and . . . chat—or rather, discuss a plan for our continued courtship."

"That would be most acceptable, Mr. Smith."

♠

"Are you seeing Miss Cooper again tonight?" Bill said to Ronald but eyed the mashed potatoes Hattie had set on the table.

"Yes, I am. But don't worry. I shall eat supper with you this time. She and I have not planned to dine together this evening. We are merely attending a play tonight." Ronald pulled out a chair and sat down at the dining room table. Hattie had set the table with linen napkins, their best silver, and crystal stemware from their family's factory. She had insisted on the finery when she'd discovered Ronald was finally going to dine at home. A bit of guilt gnawed at him for being gone so much, but drat it all, he'd been busy at the library all day and with Miss Cooper every evening.

"Seven days in a row you've been with her. Now I know why you came for a visit." Bill grinned out of one side of his mouth as he unfolded his napkin.

"I still say if you can afford to take the time off work to come all the way to Chicago to court this woman, you can take two months off to travel to Africa with me—I know it's a secret dream of yours. Besides, the animals you meet on safari can't be any scarier up close than Miss Cooper."

"That was uncalled for," Ronald said in Miss Cooper's defense. It saddened him that his brother viewed her as homely.

"Sorry, you are right." Bill slumped his shoulders. "I'll stick to the topic. I have a question—actually, I have several, but this one I must know. How on earth did you get to know Miss Cooper when you live all the way in Colorado and she lives here?" His brow wrinkled. "You must have known her from before."

Ronald filled his plate and shook his head. "No."

"Then how?"

"It is complicated." Ronald took a bite of potatoes.

"I've got time. Most plays don't start until eight at the theatres. You owe me some time, big brother." Bill looked Ronald in the eye and wagged a fork at him. "Especially when it comes to my future sister-in-law. Mother has fretted for years that you'd never marry. I, myself, wondered if there was a woman in existence capable of putting up with my eccentric brother and his fetish for organization. So, yes, I insist you tell me more about Miss Cooper. She must be one special lady to have captured your heart."

"Well, actually . . . she has not yet captured my heart. I don't even know if that will be possible . . . anymore," he added under his breath. "But she is logical in her thinking, very organized, and comes from a good family. Being in love is not a prerequisite for marriage. I am simply ready to settle down, Bill. Miss Cooper is a logical choice, so I am pursuing that possibility. That is all."

"You still have yet to tell me how you met her." Bill finally took a bite of his supper.

"I found her through an advertisement in a magazine," Ronald responded without forethought. He took in a quick breath at his mistake.

Perhaps it was for the best he told his brother the truth sooner than later, when it would inevitably come out. But he hadn't had a chance to plan out exactly how he wanted the story to unfold. He took a long drink of water to try to settle his stomach.

"Ah, the mail-order bride!" Bill's brow and forehead wrinkled. "Wait, wasn't she supposed to go out to Colorado and marry you there?"

"Yes. Here is where it gets complicated." Ronald proceeded to tell his brother about his and Miss Cooper's correspondence, then about their decision to court for two months to see if they were compatible before they went to the justice of the peace to perform the marriage. "But even with those safeguards in place, Miss Cooper changed her mind on the train before she got to St. Louis. A case of cold feet."

"So you came running to Chicago to beg her to reconsider then?"

"No."

"No? Then why are you here?"

"I have yet to come to the most complicated part." Ronald breathed deeply. Did he really want to harrow up those memories, ones that not only made him appear foolish and gullible but were also so very painful to his heart? "Miss Cooper arranged for a messenger to deliver a letter stating her decision to renege on our 'mail-order marriage,' as you might call it."

"What did you do when you got the letter?" Bill had set his knife and fork down and leaned across his plate toward Ronald.

"I never received the letter. The messenger, whom Miss Cooper gave her train and stage tickets to so as to complete the trip, never gave the letter to me."

"Why on earth would he do that? What did he have to gain from withholding it?" Bill leaned back in his chair and sported a teasing smile. "Heck, you should have just pulled out your gun and shot the fellow. Isn't that what you do out there in the Wild West?"

"Don't say that!" Ronald snapped. "I do not find that humorous in the least."

"Whoa, calm down, I was just joking."

"It was not a fellow. She was a she. I mean, the person Miss Cooper sent was a young woman." Ronald rubbed the back of his neck and pinched his eyes shut. "Her name was Dorothy and—never mind."

"Soooo, you met this so-called messenger?" Bill didn't wait for an answer. "Obviously, because you appear to know her name and are noticeably bothered by the mention of said name. But let me get this straight; she still did not deliver Miss Cooper's letter to you?"

"Correct." Ronald balled his hands into a fist.

"Whoa, this Dorothy woman has really upset you. Calm yourself. It was just a letter. Though I still don't understand why she didn't deliver it to you."

"Because she pretended to be Miss Cooper. She conned me into believing she was the woman I had arranged to court and eventually marry." Ronald held his voice steady.

"And you fell in love with her!" Bill smiled. He clasped his hands behind his head and leaned back in his chair. "Then what happened? She stole all your money and skipped town like a true con artist?"

"No." Ronald's hands relaxed. "She never took any of my money. I paid for her hotel room and for her meal each time we went out, but that was it," he said with a fraction of the volume he'd been using.

"That doesn't sound like much of a con to me," Bill said without a trace of humor.

"No, it does not." Ronald bowed his head. "More like a woman who is down on her luck and needs a place to stay and a free meal or two. I hope I have not made a big mistake." *And made an erroneous error in judgment.* He also hoped he was not pursuing the wrong woman. He stared at Bill as if his brother could convince him otherwise.

♠

Ronald straightened his tie as he stood on Miss Cooper's porch, waiting for his knock to be answered.

"Ah, Mr. Smith, you are right on time," Miss Cooper said as she opened the door. She motioned him inside and then to the formal sitting room. "Would you like to sit down and chat for a moment until the cab arrives?"

Ronald nodded his approval, though he found Miss Cooper's use of words rather inaccurate. Very little chatting would take place unless he instigated the conversation, like usual. He didn't feel up to it this evening. Except for the discussion they'd had on their first evening together, the one about Dorothy, all of their conversations seemed to require excruciating effort from both parties—hence his decision to take her to a play tonight. They wouldn't have to converse while there.

"Nice weather we've had today," he said after a moment or so. He'd taken his usual seat on the burgundy chair farthest from the sofa where Miss Cooper sat.

"Yes," Miss Cooper said with a nod. Her hands lay clasped tightly together in her lap, and her back appeared uncomfortably straight as she sat there on the edge of the sofa cushion.

"This play should be enjoyable. I've heard good things about it." Ronald had heard *one* good thing about it, and he highly doubted he would enjoy his time with Miss Cooper tonight. What was happening to him? Resorting to untruths simply to make conversation. He didn't care for it. He'd never had to resort to such measures when he'd been with Dorothy. *But she'd resorted to untruths.* Was it possible that she'd merely been in an uncomfortable situation, and that's how she dealt with it?

An image of Dorothy formed in his mind—her striking brown hair, soft pink cheeks and lips, and captivating smile. He glanced at Miss Cooper. *No, that is not fair.* He couldn't hold Miss Cooper to such an expectation of beauty. That was not what was important in a woman or in a man, thank heavens. A good marriage was based on other things.

"The honeysuckle is very fragrant. I am referring to the vines you have growing up your front porch," Ronald clarified.

"Yes, it is."

Ronald stared at her. She'd been eloquent in her letters. As had he. Would theirs be a marriage where communication would be best accomplished through letters? *Heaven forbid.*

"How is your Aunt Cynthia? She hasn't joined us for a while."

"She says she desires not to horn in on our conversations. Otherwise, she is doing fine."

"That is good to hear." Ronald let out a sigh. If only Miss Cooper could generate the conversations Dorothy had. His eyes gravitated to the two unsightly moles on her cheek. Those moles would be easy to bear if only she could talk to him and make him feel as valued as Dorothy had.

Why had Dorothy made him feel so valued? Was that part of her act? That hardly made sense. Her beauty alone was sufficient to reel a man in to open his wallet. There it was again; he hadn't really opened his wallet to her. In fact, she'd insisted on working at Sunny's to earn her own money until they "wed."

Miss Cooper leaned toward the window and peered out. "Our cab is here."

"Shall we go?" Ronald stood and offered her his elbow, grateful for a distraction from his thoughts. He couldn't afford his resolve to soften. Miss Cooper would make a suitable wife. Dorothy would not. He also couldn't forget the fact that Dorothy was already married.

Or *was* it a fact?

"I need to inform you that I shall be returning to Colorado tomorrow," Ronald told her as they stepped outside.

"That is so sudden." Miss Cooper gasped. "Why did you not tell me of your plans before now?"

"It is a last-minute decision, I fear." *Very last minute.*

Miss Cooper raised a bushy eyebrow. "Mr. Smith, this seems so out of character for you, at least what I have come to know and like about you."

"Yes, it is a bit out of character, but the situation demands I step beyond what is comfortable."

"What on earth could make you do so?" Miss Cooper's hand grasped his elbow tighter than usual as they walked down the sidewalk of her house.

"I need to make an investigation."

"For that case you've been working on for your friend back in Craig?"

"No, this is for a new case, one that should have been investigated long before now." Ronald climbed into the cab, wishing he was climbing onto the train to Rawlins.

Chapter 22

WITH THE MONEY FROM HER second paycheck in hand, Dorothy made a quick glance in the mirror before she headed for the mercantile. A loose thread dangled from the sleeve of her white blouse. She bit it off with her teeth, hoping the seam would remain intact—new clothing was not in her budget.

She'd been clinging to a thread of hope, as thin as the one she'd pulled from her blouse, that by some miracle, when Ronald returned from Chicago, he would be willing to give her a chance to explain everything and make amends. But two weeks had come and gone. She feared he had chosen to say in Chicago. It made sense, especially if he had indeed met up with Wilhelmina. He'd once said he had always planned to return home if he was unable to find a wife to settle down with him in Craig.

"Let go of it, Dorothy," she spoke firmly to her reflection. "Even if he comes back, he is far above you. Just because he never acted like it, he is. He deserves better. Someone like that widow, Mrs. Harris."

She smoothed one last hair into place and walked out the door to her room, the room she was proud to say she'd be able to pay for as of today. At the bottom of the stairs, she rang the bell on the hotel's desk.

Mr. Tucker walked in from the kitchen. "Yes, Miss Dorothy?"

"I'd like to pay for my room starting today."

"May's not over. It's paid in full for another four days."

"I know, but it's what I want." Dorothy pulled some paper money from her handbag and laid it on the counter. "That should cover through June. I hope to have a place by the end of next month."

"You and Ronald planning on gettin' hitched after all?" Mr. Tucker's smile looked hopeful.

That made her next words that much more painful. "No, I plan on getting myself set up in my own apartment."

"Oh," Mr. Tucker said without any hint of emotion. "I wish you well. It has been a pleasure having you stay at our hotel, Miss Dorothy."

"Thank you." Dorothy offered him a sincere smile before stepping outside. At least the Tuckers didn't seem to care that she was a saloon girl. They hadn't treated her any differently since she'd donned her red dress and started working Sunny's saloon almost every day. As for other members of the community . . . some smiled and said hello the same as usual. Others . . . she couldn't say they were rude, but they weren't necessarily friendly either. But she'd take living in Craig without many friendships—including Ronald's—over her life with Vincent any day.

She walked across Yampa Avenue and headed for the mercantile with a touch of sadness weighing on her heart. Of all the people to remain friends, she had hoped Lavender would be one of them.

"Good morning, Lavender," Dorothy said when she first walked into the store.

"Mornin'." Lavender nodded curtly and turned her attention back to the customer she was helping.

Dorothy gathered a box of crackers, some more raisins, and some jerky this time and carried the items toward the counter. She grabbed a spool of yellow thread on her way, determined to at least attempt to mend her yellow dress. Once at the counter, she spied the peppermint sticks on the shelf. She would have liked to indulge in one, but she thought it wise to save her money for essentials right now. Plus, she didn't want to bother Lavender.

Dorothy paid for her items. Lavender didn't say so much as a goodbye. Dorothy hurried outside and across the street, telling herself she didn't feel like chatting anyway. She had to launder her two skirts before she went to work this evening. It was a good thing she would be wearing her red dress.

♠

Ronald patted Mehitable's neck as they rode into Craig. "We're home. Thanks for putting up with my last-minute change of plans. Spending two and a half weeks in a livery stable and me riding you from Rawlins to here . . . I promise I'll never do that again."

As soon as Ronald reached his house, he removed Mehitable's saddle, brushed her down, and gave her some fresh hay to eat. Now it was his turn.

He walked inside his house, hoping Logan would be there to help him pump and heat some water for his bath while he hurried and shaved. The place was empty, and with no lamps yet lit, the gray of twilight made the house feel almost eerie. Thankfully, the extra kitchen lamp and box of matches were sitting on the cupboard nearest the back door, just where they were supposed to be. He lit the lamp and immediately set to the task of building a fire to warm some water. The stove was stone cold. Logan must be visiting his sister—he certainly hadn't been here all day. Even though it was late in May, during the day it'd been cool, and the evening air was bordering on chilly.

As he filled a bucket from the pump in the kitchen sink, he contemplated skipping his bath and going over to Sunny's Place immediately. For the last three days on the train and the trail, his thoughts had continually gravitated to discovering the truth, the whole truth, and nothing but the truth about Dorothy. Pieces of her "con" didn't fit, and he was determined to either make them fit or totally obliterate them. And the best witness to call to the stand would be none other than Dorothy Bednar herself. Even if that wasn't her real name. He caught a whiff of himself as he lifted the bucket from the sink and decided against leaving immediately.

He shaved while the water heated and kept his bath short, which wasn't hard given the temperature of the water in the tub. After dressing in his best suit and combing his wet hair, he hurried off to Sunny's Place. Halfway down his sidewalk, he came to a stop. He had no idea if Dorothy would even be working tonight. He had no idea if she was even still in town—he'd been gone for nearly three weeks.

Well, if anyone would know where to find Dorothy, Sunny would, and Ronald needed something to eat. He leaned into the evening breeze and hurried off to Sunny's Place.

He walked around the saloon to the restaurant side of the building and slipped inside. The number of empty tables told him it was a weeknight, and most people that had money enough to eat out had already come and gone. He looked around for Dorothy only to find it was Sunny who was waiting on the few customers who remained. She glanced over at him, and her eyes lit up. "Ronald!"

"By chance is Dorothy here?" he asked in a subdued voice.

Sunny nodded toward the saloon.

Ronald shuffled toward the doorway to the saloon, realizing for the first time since he entered that piano music accompanied the background noise of the bar. It wasn't symphony quality, but still, it was pleasant to listen to, somewhat catchy. The bar was not crowded either. His ears drew his eyes to the piano in the corner of the room. A woman in a red satin dress sat on the stool, her back to Ronald, running her fingers across the keys like she was enjoying herself. With her brown hair piled fashionably upon her head and the softness of her shoulders flowing like cream from the tiny sleeves of her dress, even from behind, she caused Ronald's heart to skip a beat. The music, her beauty. He felt drawn to her and then he realized why. *Dorothy?* No, it couldn't be.

He wove around the poker tables and headed toward the piano, determined to disprove his erroneous conclusion. Halfway to her, his eyes caught hold of the pianist's hands. He'd recognize those slender fingers anywhere, remembering with perfect detail how they'd pulled his face toward hers in their first kiss.

"Dorothy?" He spoke her name with reverence. She was obviously not hiding her past from him now. Or from anyone else. More pieces to the puzzle. The need to figure things out lured him closer. He uttered her name once again, only as a statement this time. "Dorothy."

Her head turned, and her eyes met his. "Ronald?" She appeared surprised. Her fingers continued plinking out a melody upon the keyboard. "W-what are you doing here?"

The saloon exploded with noise. Ronald glanced at the bar. Men elbowed themselves a spot up to the crowded bar as the swinging doors were kept open with the influx of what he thought must be every ranchhand from the Hoy place.

Payday. No, not right now!

He focused back on Dorothy, determined not to shy away from this. "We need to talk."

"What?"

"We need to talk," he said in a near yell.

Dorothy turned toward him, removing her hands from the keyboard and placing them on his arm. "Yes, Ronald, I would really like that."

Her touch sent tingles up his arm. Desperation poured from her eyes and ignited his insides. She sincerely needed him. He could see it in her eyes and feel it in the heated air between them as she leaned closer. The very thought filled him with desire. "Dorothy, I need you to tell me the tru—"

Her beautiful face slipped from his view. "What in tarnation—" Ronald turned to see a dirty-shirt cowboy pulling Dorothy toward a nearby poker table.

"It's my turn," the cowboy said as he dropped onto a chair and pulled Dorothy onto his lap. "How about you spend a little time with me, pretty lady?"

Every muscle in Ronald's body tensed and screamed to take action. He stormed toward the unmannerly cowboy, fists clenched.

Dorothy reached out, cupped his fist in her hand, and squeezed. "It's okay, Ronald. It's part of the job. I know; I've been a saloon girl for close to five years now."

The cowboy knocked their hands apart with fist. "I said it's my turn. What da ya say, pretty lady? How about you do your job and get me a beer?"

Dorothy hopped out of the cowboy's lap with obvious relief. She brushed by Ronald on her way to the bar, her lips moving so close to his ear that he could feel her warm breath on his neck. "Sorry, but I've got to get back to work. Tomorrow's my night off though."

In an instant, she was gone, gliding like an angel in the midst of hell. She didn't belong here. Ronald didn't care what she said or what Stanley had said—he could feel it in his bones. More than anything, he wanted to stay. He'd hole himself up in the far corner and wait for her to get off work. Then they'd talk. Then he'd get to the bottom this.

Ronald stood where she'd left him, his feet rooted to the floor like a tree, when she returned with a beer in hand.

Dorothy gestured to the swinging doors with her chin. Leaning close to him, she whispered, "Call on me tomorrow evening at five. We'll talk then. Okay?" She turned her back to Ronald and placed the beer on the table in front of the dirty-shirt cowboy.

Chapter 23

SITTING ON THE PORCH SWING at Ronald's house, Dorothy pinched her lips together to gather courage. "Where do I start?"

"How about telling me what you know about the real Wilhelmina Cooper?"

"The real Wilhelmina Cooper?" Dorothy chewed on her lip. She knew it would come to this, but still, she wasn't looking forward to it. Thankfully it was warmer than last night or she'd have even more chills. "I'm afraid I don't know very much."

He reached into his jacket and pulled out an envelope. "This is a copy of a letter she claims she gave you to deliver to me. Does it look familiar?" He handed her what looked like the letter stashed in her pocket, only not quite as neatly written nor folded as small. Still, it held the same flourishing handwriting.

Dorothy took it and turned it over in her hands as she quelled her pain. She handed it back. "I can't read that well. I thought I'd already told you that."

"Yes, that you did. I apologize." He took the letter. "I had forgotten. But with the way you manage so well, can you blame me?"

"I've learned a little, thanks to Sunny, but not enough to read fancy hand-writing." She pointed to the letter that Ronald now pulled from its envelope. "Not the way I feel right now."

"And how is that? The way you feel?" He said it not as a dig but as if he sincerely wanted to know.

"Scared. It's hard to talk about my past. Especially to one I care deeply for. I'm the first to admit that my past is nothing at all to be proud of."

"You . . . care for me?"

His words caught her off guard. She'd expected him to ask about her past. "Yes, immensely," she replied with sincerity, then bit hard on her lip to keep it from quivering. "No one has ever made me feel so valued as you do."

"You promise, under oa—" He cleared his throat. "You promise you are telling the truth on this?"

"Absolutely."

Ronald leaned back, causing the swing to rock slightly. He closed his eyes momentarily as he breathed deeply. "That changes a lot of things, things I had wrong."

She touched his arm again, longing to wrap hers around it. "Who wouldn't love you, Ronald? There is not a more kindhearted, wonderful man in the world."

His eyes showed a hint of surprise.

Why? She figured he surely knew that. Everything about him shouted "wonderful."

"So, you swear you are not married?"

"What?" She jerked away from him and folded her arms. "Haven't I told you enough lies? Even if I were to add another to the list, it certainly wouldn't be that." She looked him in the eye. "Where'd you get that one?"

He ducked his head. "Stanley."

"And you believe him over me?" The minute those words flew from her mouth, she wished she could take them back.

"Well, under the circumstances . . ."

"I know. I know." She swallowed hard. "But Stanley?"

"My turn to say, 'I know.'" He slapped the seat of the swing between them, and his hand remained there. "Out of everything he said and what I've learned about you, that hurt the worse."

What did he mean? She stared at him. No, no, he couldn't possibly still have thoughts of marriage. "You have no need to apologize to me." She placed her hand on his. "It is me who owes an apology to you, one so big I fear I shall never fully be able to convey it. I have lied to you. It's obvious you know that now. Exactly how much of the truth you know, I'm unsure. But I can bet my last dollar, which unfortunately doesn't account for much," he smiled and melted her resolve, "that you don't know it all."

"That's why we are here." Ronald kept his hand under hers. "So, Dorothy, please tell me everything. I feel there are missing pieces and evidence you are withholding from me that will vindicate you from all the lies told me by others and created for my sake by you." He stared off at the cherry tree. "At least I hope that is the case."

She kept her hand securely attached to his. "I will do my best." She pointed to the letter that lay in his lap now, loosely gripped by his other hand.

"I have one just like it." She pulled it from her pocket, still tied up neatly in its red string, and handed it to him. "I know I should have given this to you the first time we met, but I couldn't bring myself to do it."

"Given what Miss Cooper told me, this is beginning to make a little sense now." Ronald turned away. "That's where I've been for the past few weeks."

"Yes, I know."

"How? Logan?" He returned his gaze to her. "Surely not, for I told him only that I was going to Chicago, nothing else."

"That was enough. I figured the rest out on my own." Dorothy chewed on her lip again. "Please tell me how this makes sense. I feared I'd never hear those words from you."

"What kind of woman goes to all the trouble of moving out West to marry a complete stranger and then decides she just wants to work for pennies, eking out a living for herself? I had a hard time believing you were the con artist Stanley painted you to be. It didn't make sense, unless you were truly married and you were running away from your husband. Then when I got Miss Cooper's side of the story, I was tempted to believe maybe you were indeed a con artist. But I remember her mention of the bruise on your face." Ronald rubbed his eyes like they hurt. "He would have had to be a most horrible man to make you run like you did," he said out of the corner of his mouth. "But you are not married, and I believe you on this point."

"Thank you," she murmured.

"The only thing that made sense to me as to why you were so hesitant about our arranged marriage was because of me. I did understand that." He looked away from her. "Until I heard about this other marriage."

Dorothy couldn't believe he could ever consider he was less than desirable. No words would come.

With his eyes still averted, he said, "Did you really mean what you said a minute ago? That you care deeply for me?"

The truth pummeled her heart to near bursting. "Yes, it's true."

He turned to face her, his eyes brimmed with emotions she dared not decipher for surely she had read them wrong. He smiled, scooted closer, and took her hand in his. "So who gave you that bruise?"

"Let me finish my story. Or perhaps it would be accurate to say *begin*."

He nodded. "Please. I hope you include the name of the man who hit you, and why you withheld Wilhelmina Cooper's letter from me."

Dorothy's heart sank. Here was yet another deception. This would be the nail in her coffin. She never imagined Ronald would go to the trouble to contact

Wilhelmina. She'd hoped to brush that part of the story partly under the rug and say that Wilhelmina had *asked* her to take her place, but that would have been yet another lie. She needed to be completely through with such means of self-preservation or, rather, self-destruction.

"Like I said, I was running away." Dorothy shuddered at the memory.

"From what?"

"Not what—who."

"Well, then from whom?"

"Vincent," she said through gritted teeth.

"Okay, so you've established that he's not your husband. Was he a man you courted, a fiancé by chance? Who exactly is this Vincent you speak of? Your voice betrays you. There is fear in it. Did he harm you before this?" It was Ronald's tone that now betrayed *him*. Never before had she heard such distain in his voice.

"Plenty of times." She flicked her wrist. "But they were nothing. This time, though, I was certain he wouldn't be so nice. He was angrier than usual."

Ronald tilted his head. "What could you have possibly done to make him so angry?"

"I refused to help him cheat this poor fellow who had just lost his wife." She could see the confusion in his eyes. "Here's where the real explaining comes in."

"Okay, I'm ready." Ronald released her hand, folded his arms, and gazed at her with anxious eyes.

"Ronald, I'm no good, no good at all. For the last five years, I've been working as a saloon girl."

"I knew that."

"But what you don't know is that for five years I've been cheating men out of their money in crooked poker games."

"You actually sit at the table and play the game?"

"No," Dorothy said, thinking how Ronald's question sounded so similar to Sunny's. "I would walk behind them, serve them drinks, and peek at their cards."

"And that cheats them out of money how?" Ronald's voice stretched on that last word.

"I gave signals to Vincent. He placed the bets and pulled cards from his sleeves."

"Um, I see."

"Yes, you see what a wretched soul I am." Dorothy closed her eyes as she let out a breath.

"Whose idea were these card games? Did you come up with this plan together?"

Her eyes flashed open. "No, I wanted nothing to do with his wicked scheme!"

"Then why did you participate?"

She couldn't believe how calm his voice was and how devoid of accusation. "I had no choice," she said, rounding her back, shying from the memories.

"Everyone has a choice. You should have left him a lot earlier." His eyes narrowed. "He must have had some kind of hold over you. What kind of fiancé, boyfriend, whatever, treats their girl like that? Why didn't you terminate your relationship the first time he asked you to be partners in crime?"

"Oh, how I wished I could have. I wished it every day—for nine years. But I owed him that much."

"You owed him nothing!" Ronald clenched the rope that supported the bench and made it swing.

"I owed him my life." Why did she raise her voice? It wasn't as though she wanted to defend Vincent.

"What did he do, save you from drowning? Pull you from a burning building? He sounds much too selfish of a man to do something so valiant."

"He's my brother, the one who took me in and saved me from living on the street after both our parents died. He's my legal guardian. I owe my life to him. I shouldn't have left him." She buried her face in her hands. "But I did, and I left him in a mess. I couldn't take it anymore. He could have been thrown in jail because of me." Under her breath, she added, "But he wasn't. Probably out looking for me now."

The swing stopped dead. Ronald's silence made her lower her hands and brave a glance his way. His eyes clenched shut and quivered. "Vincent is your own brother?" he said through gritted teeth.

"Yes."

"And he did this to you?" Ronald fisted his hands.

"Did what?"

"Took an innocent child and made her into his partner in crime." He glanced at her. "What about your grandparents? Could they have not taken you in?"

"I have none—that I remember. Ma said they were immigrants but spoke little more where family was concerned. I was all alone when Pa died, until I found Vincent and he took me in." She was amazed at how the words fell from her mouth, releasing locked-away horrors. They flowed now like the filthy water of a newly dug well. "He was nice to me for a week or two. Then he made me beg on the street, or he would beat me. I was lucky I matured early because he was able to pass me off as much older and got me a job in a saloon at age fifteen. That got me off the street."

"Out of the frying pan and into the fire," Ronald mumbled. He took a deep breath as if to calm himself. "How old were you when your mother died?" he asked in a slow, deliberate tone.

"Ten."

He winced. "And when Vincent got hold of you, how old were you?"

"Eleven."

He winced again. "And now?"

"I'm twenty." She swallowed, doubting Vincent would have simply let her go when she turned twenty-one. "Oh, Ronald, it was terrible living with my brother. I pray you won't require me to go into any more detail than that. I know he's my legal guardian, but I don't want to go back—I can't, not after what I did to him. That's why, when I ran into Wilhelmina on the train and she offered to let me take her ticket to Craig because she had cold feet—oh, I'm sorry. I forgot to tell you that little detail—I jumped on the chance. I wanted what Miss Cooper was giving up. It was so tempting. I had nothing and nowhere to go. That's when the lies came. I was just supposed to come and deliver this letter to you. But when I got here and met you and discovered that there was such a thing as a kindhearted, wonderful man, I wanted that dream, the dream I'd always had to be loved by a good man, like my ma was by my pa. At first I tried to do what Wilhelmina asked, but no one would let me get the truth out—they assumed I was her. So I just took Wilhelmina's place." She stared at the ground. "Thinking things out before I leap into something is not my strong suit."

Ronald reached out and gently pulled her close. "Dorothy, just because Vincent is your guardian, he has no right to treat you like he has. His actions could easily be used in court to void his guardianship. You need never go back to him if you so wish." His hand slipped around her back. "And if he does come looking for you, I will protect you."

His arm felt like an angel's, his closeness like heaven. "So you are not upset with me?"

"Upset with you?" His voice rose slightly. "Quite the opposite. And I promise nothing like this will ever happen to you again." He pulled her closer. "I think it would be wise if we were to resume our original plan of marriage. I can easily take care of the guardianship issues. And if you have even the slightest fear that Vincent," he cringed as he said the name, "will attempt to find you, it would be safer if you were my wife. Do you not agree?"

"Is this a proposal?" Dorothy reigned in her emotions and tried to be more Ronald-like. "I ask this . . . because you and I never officially agreed on marrying each other—that was you and Wilhelmina Cooper."

"Yes, Miss Dorothy Bednar, that is precisely what it is—a proposal of marriage."

Chapter 24

RONALD LAID ON HIS BED, staring up, watching the flicker of the lamp dance its light upon the ceiling. His mind wouldn't shut off. This evening with Dorothy had been bittersweet to say the least. The unspeakable ordeals Dorothy had suffered continued to make his head ache. When he'd wanted to uncover the mystery behind this woman, he could have never imagined a story so full of injustice. That for a moment he had doubted her character and thought perhaps she was a shyster out for his money made him ashamed of himself. Condemnation was the last thing this dear woman needed.

One thing was for sure; he would never allow something like this to happen to her ever again. If only Dorothy had been more willing to speak of Vincent. She'd avoided any mention of her brother past the essentials to tell her story, and Ronald hadn't pushed the matter. He had heard of cases where the abused still cares for their abuser despite all they've experienced. The only description he got concerning Vincent was that he looked somewhat like Stanley Jones. That in itself was enough to send shivers up Ronald's back.

The lamp burned into the wee hours of the morning before his mind succumbed to drowsiness. It didn't help that in between visions of locking Vincent up and throwing away the key were visions of Dorothy's lovely face nodding her permission for Ronald to pull her into his arms and protect her for the rest of her life.

♠

Dorothy walked down the staircase of the hotel, putting a little extra speed to her steps. She would be late for work if she didn't hurry. Tonight was her turn to wait tables in the restaurant. She much preferred that to the saloon.

Ronald stood by the counter, talking to Campbell Tucker when she reached the bottom of the stairs. He turned and smiled when he saw her, warming her heart.

"Ronald, what are you doing here?" Dorothy hurried to his side. "It's the middle of the afternoon, for goodness' sake. Shouldn't you be at work?"

"I just happened to be in the neighborhood." Ronald wore the worst poker face ever. "So I thought I'd see if I could escort you over to Sunny's Place. I believe you are due to be at work in ten minutes, am I right?"

"Yes, you are," she responded. "And you are so very kind to do this for me. I'm not used to such thoughtfulness."

Ronald held out his arm for her to take. "It is time for a change."

They stepped outside. The afternoon sun shined through fluffy white clouds, warming Dorothy's face as Ronald's presence warmed her heart. "Thank you, Ronald." The words spilled from her mouth.

"Thank you for what?"

Their feet clapped along the sidewalk in sync for a moment or two before she could rally the correct words. There were so many reasons to be thankful for Ronald. "For just being you." She moved her hand from his elbow, slid it down his arm, intertwined her fingers with his, and squeezed. "Tell me again that you are actually going to marry me, that you'll not back out—it's too hard for me to believe," she said in jest, but the fear was real.

His hand returned the squeeze. "I would never back out, Miss Bednar, and I swear on a stack of Bibles that I will always be there for you."

"Like you were at the hotel," she said with a timid smile, "waiting to escort me to work."

"That is correct. And I shall be there every day at the same time, waiting at Sunny's door at night when you've completed your shift."

"You really don't need to do this, Ronald. I am quite capable of walking back and forth to and from Sunny's on my own."

"I insist. If anything were to happen to you, Miss Bednar, I would be devastated."

This all felt so foreign, yet wonderful. "Fine, Mr. Smith," she teased. She was going to have to soften him back up to return their relationship to a first-name basis. "I would be delighted to have your company to and from my place of work."

"Speaking of that," Ronald said, reverting to his old, stoic voice. "Work, that is. Must you continue your employment with Sunny if we are soon to be wed?"

"I owe that much to Sunny—at least until she finds a replacement. She says she can't get along without help now. Besides, I need something to keep me busy until I become Mrs. Ronald Smith." She let go of his hand and clutched his arm with both her hands. "Oh, I like the sound of that."

Ronald smiled wide. "I do too."

♠

That night, after the customers in the restaurant dwindled down to one couple, Sunny placed a hand on Dorothy's back as she cleared the last of the dirty tables. "Why don't you go home early. I can take it from here."

"But it's an hour before I usually quit." Dorothy wiped a spill of mashed potatoes from the table with her rag.

Sunny pointed over her shoulder. "I don't think Ronald's too comfortable there by that spittoon. He's been sitting there for the past hour—hasn't taken his eyes off you. Quite romantic if you ask an old softie like me. But he looks exhausted. Take him home, why don't you."

Dorothy glanced at Ronald. Her heart warmed. "Yeah, he does look tired. He's such a gentleman, insisting he walk me home every night now. I don't deserve such attention."

"Honey, yes, you do."

"Thanks, Sunny," Dorothy responded, appreciating their friendship. Earlier that day, she'd opened up to Sunny, telling her most everything she had told Ronald last night. Sunny had taken it as well as he had. Dorothy felt fortunate indeed.

Dorothy slipped into the kitchen, removed her apron, and hung it on the hook by the back door. She stepped over to the sink next to George and washed the frosting from her hands from the last plate of oatmeal cookies she'd served.

"Hey, George, see you tomorrow."

"Where ya going?" George wrinkled his brow.

"Sunny said I could leave early. My fiancé," the word felt like music to her tongue, "is waiting for me. He wants to walk me home."

"Good man that Ronald is."

"Yes, I know." Dorothy rushed out of the kitchen, anxious to see Ronald. As she walked toward him, his stoic expression melted into a smile. He appeared extremely handsome in that moment.

He held out his hand for her to take. "Miss Bednar, are you ready to go?"

"Yes, *Mister* Smith," she said with emphasis. The moment they stepped out-side, she hugged his arm. "Really now, if we are to be married in less than two weeks, don't you think it's time to drop the *mister* and *miss?* When you thought I was Wilhelmina, you called me by my first name or, rather, what I told you was my nickname. What's changed?"

"I have discovered how truly precious you are, and you deserve to be treated with nothing but respect."

Dorothy was touched but . . . "That doesn't make sense," she blurted.

"It is perfectly logical to me," Ronald said in a flat voice.

She ran out in front of him and, with her hands held out to each side, stopped him. "How about we don't be logical on this point? I loved it when you used to call me Dorothy and I called you Ronald. It made me feel connected to you. It made me feel safe and warm and cozy. What do you say? Let's try it again."

Ronald leaned into her hand. "Your point is well taken." Something sparked in his eyes. "I say yes. Dorothy it is."

She turned around, and they strolled arm in arm down a section of covered sidewalk. A warm breeze kissed her face as they approached the hotel. It prompted thoughts of other forms of kisses. When would Ronald kiss her? She'd had to help make the one full kiss they'd shared happen. Was he not fond of such affection?

It didn't matter. She had more than she'd ever dreamed of already.

"Here we are," Ronald said when they reached the front door of the hotel.

"Yes, here we are."

The bark of a dog in the distance and the slam of a shutting window next door sounded especially loud as their conversation lagged.

"Thursday is my day off," Dorothy said to keep things going. "That's the day after tomorrow."

"I am fully aware of when Thursday is."

Gosh, she loved his dry humor. "I was thinking maybe we could plan something for that evening, something fun to do together."

"I'm afraid I'm not much good at having fun."

Dorothy laughed. "Oh, Ronald, you are such a delight." She couldn't stand it. It'd take forever if she had to wait for *him* to kiss her. She stood on tiptoe and kissed his cheek. Maybe that would plant a seed. "I'll see you tomorrow, I presume?"

"Most certainly." He cleared his throat. "Dorothy. I will see you tomorrow, same time, same place." He tipped his hat and turned to leave. "I look forward to it."

Dorothy hurried into the hotel and ran up the stairs. She had an idea.

The next morning, Dorothy arose earlier than usual and went downstairs to find Mary Tucker. In the dining room, she pushed the swinging door open and peered inside the kitchen. The four young Tucker girls sat at a small table in the corner, gobbling down pancakes. Mary was nowhere to be seen. Dorothy walked in and stepped over to the table.

"Where is your ma?" she asked the oldest girl, Nyda.

All four girls looked up at Dorothy. She'd seen each of these girls several times before, but for some reason, they looked especially darling this morning. Maybe it was the way their mother had neatly brushed their blonde hair and worked it into french braids, each girl with two plaits running down her back.

"She had to run to Deckers' for some flour," Nyda said.

"But she'll be back as quick as a whistle," the next-to-oldest girl said. "Leastwise, that's what she said."

The littlest girl looked at her sister. "I thought you blow whistles—I didn't know they were quick."

"It's just a saying, silly Caroline." The next-to-youngest girl tugged on little Caroline's braid. She turned to Dorothy as she poked her fork into a stack of pancakes in the middle of the table. "You wanna have a pancake with us?"

Dorothy had never really noticed children much until now. She'd either viewed them with jealousy—enjoying a life she never had—or as poor unfortunate souls she ached for because they might very well grow up to be like her. But right now, at this moment, she saw these girls differently. She saw them as being children like the ones that would soon join her and Ronald in that white frame house with the blue trim and picket fence.

"I would love to join you." She scooted onto the bench next to little Caroline.

A swoosh of air turned everyone's attention to the back door. Mary entered, arms burdened with a big bag of flour, her round belly making it difficult to hold. She set it down on the cupboard and seemed to notice Dorothy for the first time. "Oh, mornin', Dorothy. What brings you downstairs so early?"

"I need to ask a favor."

"Ask away." Mary put on her apron.

"Could I borrow your kitchen? I want to bake something special for my fiancé."

"So it's official?" Mary's eyes lit up. "Of course you can."

"Oh, and could I have some of that flour and raisins you just bought? I got money now. Sunny paid me yesterday. I'll be glad to pay you."

"Now, you're not goin' to pay me a red cent. If you got something special you want to bake up for Ronald Smith, it'd be my honor to donate the flour . . .

and the eggs and everything else I'm sure you don't have stuffed in those pockets of yours."

An hour or so later, Dorothy carried her giant heart-shaped cookie up to her room on a plate, taking small steps, careful not to drop it. As she set it on the end table next to the bed, it looked a little blah, even though she'd gone the extra mile and put a thin layer of sugar glaze on top. The desire to spruce it up a bit pulled her over to the wardrobe. She grabbed her purse and headed to mercantile.

The store bustled with customers when Dorothy arrived. Two men stood at the front counter in a heated discussion with Mr. Decker while another one wandered the store. Lavender Decker measured out blue fabric at the back of the store—most likely for the woman holding a toddler in one arm and fingering the fabric with her free hand. And a young girl, parked in front of the end of the front counter by the candy, stood with eyes wide, staring at the row of confection-filled jars on the shelves. Dorothy set her sights on the candy as well, feeling braver now that Ronald had asked to marry her. Word must have spread because numerous townsfolk had actually approached her and given their congratulations. Lavender had even warmed up a bit. Today Dorothy would assert herself a little more and ask Lavender to help her with the candy—after she got what she came for.

Lavender looked up from the fabric as Dorothy approached. "Howdy, Dorothy," she said and set her scissors down. She looked to the woman with the toddler. "Kate, this here is Dorothy, Ronald's soon-to-be bride."

"Ronald is getting married?" Kate asked with a tone of reverence in her voice. She turned toward Dorothy. "Nice to meet you. I am absolutely delighted to hear of this." She extended her hand.

"Well, thank you." Dorothy shook Kate's hand. "So I take it you know Ronald?"

"Know him!" Lavender piped up. "Why, she and Ronald courted up a storm at one time."

Kate pinched her lips into a faint smile. "I wouldn't exactly call it a storm. He merely asked me to dine with him from time to time."

"Oh, he was awful sweet on you though." Lavender brought her hand to her mouth and shot Dorothy an apologetic glance. "Oops. Maybe that wasn't the best thing to say."

"It's okay," Dorothy said, yet inside it made her wonder why Ronald sent away for a mail-order bride when he had someone like Kate to choose. The woman was friendly, pretty, and had an intelligent look in her eyes. "Why, may I ask, did it not work out between you two? Ronald certainly is a fine catch. I keep having to pinch myself to tell me this isn't a dream and I'm going to wake up and he'll be gone."

Kate shifted the toddler onto her other hip. "I agree. Mr. Smith is a very fine catch. He just wasn't right for me." She cleared her throat in what sounded like embarrassment. "I'm afraid he was a little too dry, um . . . how do I say this? Boring, too by the book, so to say. But obviously you see a side of him I missed. I think that's wonderful."

"Or . . ." Lavender leaned over the counter with her finger wagging at Kate. "This is a case of opposites attract. You ever thought about that? That's the case with me and Sam." She jutted her chin toward the front counter.

Dorothy turned and surveyed Lavender's rail-thin husband as he continued to argue with the two men, then glanced at the roly-poly figure of Lavender who almost always wore a smile.

Lavender reached out and grabbed hold of Dorothy's hand. "Okay, so when's the big date? And where you goin' to get hitched? In the new church? Or outside with Mother Nature doin' the decorating? And of course you're goin' to invite me and Sam, ain't you?"

Startled, Dorothy managed only an "Uh . . ."

"My husband and I would like to come too," Kate said. "If that's okay?"

"Goodness," Dorothy said with a sinking feeling. "I haven't thought about such details. The only one I can answer is the date: June tenth."

"So soon?" Kate asked. "Have you thought about moving it to July or August so you'll have time to prepare?"

"That's the date Ronald's planned on all along." Dorothy smiled inside at this little quirk of his. "And he hates to have plans disrupted."

"But that's just two weeks away and ten days before Rosie and Hank's wedding—that's my daughter, by the way. You oughta meet her sometime." Lavender's eyes lit with pride. "She's marrying Hank Walker, the marshal. And it's about time. I've had nearly seven months to make her dress—way too long if'n you ask me." She rubbed her chin. "Say, do you even have your wedding dress made?"

"No. I figured I'd mend this nice yellow dress I have, and we'd just go to the town hall and the justice of the peace would marry us. It's practical. I think that's what Ronald would want."

"Oh, but, honey, that just won't do. Don't you agree, Kate?"

"I'm not the one to say—"

"Well, I'll say it then." Lavender put her hands on her hips. "No bride should be wed at town hall—leastwise not our town hall. You ever seen the place?"

Kate touched Dorothy's hand. "You are welcome to borrow my wedding dress if you'd like. I believe you and I are about the same size. If not, I'm sure Mary could make the alterations within a week's time."

"Mary Tucker, Campbell's wife?"

"Yes, she's the one who made the dress for me two years ago."

Dorothy found her tongue a bit tied.

"Now, I suppose you came in here for something other than to chew the fat with me and Kate," Lavender said. "Is there something I can get for you?"

"Oh yes, I totally forgot. I'd like to buy some walnuts and a peppermint stick. I didn't want to bother Mr. Decker. He appears rather busy."

Lavender sent a frown in Mr. Decker's direction and returned her attention to Dorothy. "I'll be happy to help you. Just let me finish up with Kate, then I'll be right over."

A few minutes later, Dorothy walked out of the mercantile sucking on a peppermint stick with a small bag of walnuts in her hand, a fun decorating idea in her head, and a lightness to her step. She couldn't get over how genuine Lavender's and Kate's concern felt. Perhaps everything was back to normal. And perhaps it would be best to talk to Ronald about moving their wedding day into July.

When she got to her room, she pulled the walnuts from the bag and a teacup-size rock she'd picked up off the street and placed them on the table between her heart-shaped cookie and the porcelain water bowl—which she quickly moved out of the way. After cracking the walnuts with the rock, she sprinkled them onto the cookie, smoothing them evenly across the glaze. She stepped back and scrutinized her creation. It didn't have the desired effect she'd hoped for; it needed a touch of color.

She glanced at the new clock Mary had put in her room just yesterday. It was almost noon. Ronald, she guessed, would be taking his dinner break any time now. She'd really hoped to get this to him for his dessert. Maybe she should have thought this silly little idea of hers out a little better.

As she picked up the plate holding the cookie, she had a wave of brilliance. She set it back down, fetched her lipstick from her purse, and rolled a generous portion onto her lips. Bending over the cookie, she brushed a portion of the nuts away and planted a big kiss on the upper right-hand portion of the heart.

"Yeah, that looks much better," she said and picked it up. The main purpose of this little surprise was to soften Ronald up and somehow get him to kiss her again. And because on a whim, it sounded fun. Fun was something she'd not been privileged to have for so long. She couldn't bear waiting until the wedding for another kiss, and with the way things were going, Ronald being stiffer and more nervous than he first was, she feared that might be the case. Hopefully, this little kiss in the corner would plant a seed in his mind. Apparently his kisses didn't come any other way. They needed planning.

Chapter 25

RONALD HEARD THE DOOR OPEN. He looked out the front window and caught a glimpse of the hem of a skirt, a dark-blue skirt. Dorothy? His heart sped up. Her familiar lively gait confirmed his conjecture. He set his pen down and stared at the end of the partition, awaiting her.

As she rounded the corner, he noticed something in her hands—a dishtowel draped over a plate. Not wanting to be rude by letting his inquisitive instincts take over, he uttered a calm "Good morning, Dorothy." He glanced at the clock on the wall. "Or I should say good afternoon. It's 12:01."

She too glanced at the clock and then focused on him, uttering a soft laugh. "Oh, Ronald, you are so darling."

He hadn't a clue why looking at the clock would prompt her to say such a thing. Nonetheless, he did enjoy her sentiment and smiled. "What brings you by this morning—I mean afternoon?"

"I made something for you." She walked over to his desk and held out what looked to be a very large cookie. "I wanted to somehow express how I feel about you and tell you thank you for making me so happy."

On closer inspection, he noticed the cookie was in the shape of a heart. Crushed walnuts lay sprinkled across the frosting. How did she know he loved walnuts? He'd never told her. "Thank you. It looks delicious," he responded, wishing his words were more eloquent. His focus moved to the upper right-hand side of the heart as his eye noticed the red imprint of a kiss. A flush of warmth spread through his face. Memory of their first kiss and then of her lips brushing the corner of his that time he'd brought her back from the river—and his desire to move his mouth a mere inch to the right to kiss her full on the mouth—sparked a fire inside him. Why hadn't he seized that moment? It was so perfect.

"I do hope you like it." Dorothy placed the plate on his desk, straightening out the cookie so it lay straight up and down. "It's my mother's recipe, the one I gave Sunny to make her cookies with."

"May I?" He motioned to the cookie with his eyes.

"Certainly! That's what I made it for."

He broke off the bottom tip and took a bite of that piece. It had the most delightful combination of salty and sweet. With that and the smell and taste of cinnamon and molasses, he couldn't resist popping the rest of the piece into his mouth. He closed his eyes as he chewed. "This is most excellent. The cookies at Sunny's Place don't hold a candle to this one."

Dorothy beamed, and it made the cookie that much more delicious for him.

"I'm so glad you like it," she said. "I hoped you would."

"I do."

She stared at the floor. "Ronald?"

"Yes."

"Tomorrow night, for our evening together . . ." She raised her eyes to meet his. "I think it would be good if we discussed the wedding. You've mentioned nothing of its details . . . and I'd kind of like to know what we're doing if that's all right."

"Yes, certainly," he said hesitantly. There wasn't much to discuss. They would go to the town hall, just the two of them; there was no need for a long list of guests to watch them make their vows and complicate the day. It had all been planned out three months ago. He had already arranged for the justice of the peace to perform the marriage of June tenth at 10:00 a.m. Because the plan was in place, he didn't have to give it another thought. That's the way he liked things.

"Wonderful." She ran a finger down the back of his hand. "Oh, and by the way, Sunny has a new dish she's having George try out tonight: hearty lamb stew. You might want to come by tonight and give it a go." Her fingers wrapped around his hand and squeezed. "It would really be nice to see you a little more—our strolls to and from Sunny's don't hardly seem like enough. And if business is slow, I'm sure Sunny won't mind if I sit by you and well . . . talk . . . and whatever." She squeezed his hand again.

Ronald gulped. "I will be there." He looked forward to it, even though he disliked lamb stew.

"Wonderful. I should be going now, so you can get back to what you're doing." She let go of his hand and reached up to his mouth. Tapping a single finger against his lips, she said, "This is where that cookie is meant to go—not stay there on that plate just to look at. All right?"

His voice scraped out the word "Yes."

As Dorothy walked out of the office, he feared his heart would take a full hour to calm down to where he could work. He chose to throw logic to the wind and basked in thoughts of her affection. The feeling was so new, so raw, and invigorating. No woman had ever made him feel like this before. Who was he kidding? No woman had ever given him the time of day before. Dorothy was an answer to prayer.

♠

Ronald recombed his hair, fixing the part so it looked perfectly straight. He reexamined the work of his razor, feeling his face for any possible trace of stubble. He'd thought this out all day long—tonight, right before he took Dorothy home, he would kiss her. It would be a simple kiss, very appropriate for a delicate woman in her situation. He bristled at the thought of the men in her past life. She would not be taken advantage of ever again.

He glanced at the clock. He had a full half hour before he was scheduled to pick up Dorothy. He hated feeling rushed, so he scurried down the stairs to make sure the kitchen and parlor were still clean from when Logan had tidied up this afternoon. If all was in order, he'd merely sit on the sofa until it was time to leave so he would arrive at the hotel precisely at 5:30.

He stepped into the kitchen and walked around, dragging his finger across the tabletop to recheck Logan's work, not that he really had to. Logan had done a fairly good job—for a fourteen-year-old boy.

It would look even better when Dorothy was here to manage the household. With the information he'd gleaned from the law school library, Logan's future should no longer be an issue. The orderly path his life was falling into made Ronald smile. He looked again in the pantry to make sure Dorothy would have all the supplies she needed to cook supper. His smile widened as he recalled Dorothy's words of the past evening.

It had been busy at Sunny's Place, and she'd had no extra time for him, but their walk home made up for everything. "Ronald," she had said as she squeezed his hand the way that sent him over the hill in delight. "Don't you think it would be prudent if I were to cook us supper tomorrow night rather than going to Sunny's?"

"Yes," he agreed, loving her thinking.

She made her logic all the better by adding, "Plus, it will be cozier and easier to talk if we're alone."

He had willingly gone along with her—it would help him accomplish the most important activity on his list: the kiss. His plan had also included a walk down to the river for thirty minutes before they ate. Then after they dined, they would engage in an hour of looking at stars while on the porch swing, with the alternate activity of playing rummy on his kitchen table in case of inclement weather. Then he'd kiss her and walk her home. Yes, he could easily combine both of their ideas. He'd take things a step further and ask Logan to stay away for the evening. He ran up the stairs to let Logan know.

On his way down the stairs, a quick glance at the kitchen clock read 5:15. He'd better get going. He straightened one of the kitchen chairs so as to make it match the distance the other three sat back from the table, then he shot into the entry hall and out the front door. The sun warmed his face; it was staying up longer with May drawing to an end.

As he turned onto Yampa Avenue, he surveyed the hustle and bustle of this western town he'd called home for almost four years now. He knew nearly everyone on the street—except for a man in an expensive leather jacket who stepped out of the hotel. Originally, he had planned on giving this "wild adventure," as his mother had called it, four years. She'd viewed it as senseless as his dream to go on safari. If he couldn't make a go of it, he'd promised her he'd come back home to Chicago. The four years would be up in July. He liked it here, helping unfortunate people stand against the ruthless or rich who took advantage of them. This "adventure" had not been senseless. The town needed him. Soon he'd have a good woman by his side and, in time, a family.

He would be staying.

The hotel appeared empty when he walked inside. He looked around and then called out, "Excuse me, Campbell, are you available?"

After a long moment of silence, Campbell's wife, Mary, poked her head out from behind the kitchen door at the back of the dining room.

"Oh, hello, Ronald. Sorry." Mary stepped into the dining room that sat off to the right of the lobby. She had a young child in tow. "Campbell's under the weather, so I'm minding the front desk. Unfortunately, you caught me at suppertime. I'm feeding my brood. Can you wait for just a second?"

Ronald pulled out his pocket watch. It was 5:30 on the mark. How long would Mary's "second" take? "I suppose," he said. "I have merely come to pick up Miss Bednar."

"Well, in that case—"

A child yelled, and Mary pushed the kitchen door open. "I'm comin'," she hollered through the door. Over her shoulder, she said to Ronald, "Just head on up the stairs and knock on her door yourself."

"I shall do that." Ronald tipped his hat to Mary's back and turned toward the staircase.

Still feeling a tad uncomfortable with this, he tiptoed up the steps to her room and knocked. He straightened his back and took a deep breath while he waited for the door to open.

"Tell Ronald I'll be just a minute."

"It is me, Ronald."

"Oh okay, Ronald. I'll be just a minute. I'm not quite ready."

It was more like five minutes before the door opened and Dorothy stepped out into the hall with a shawl and basket in hand. She looked stunning, and her hair smelled of lilac this time as she moved past him and headed down the stairs in front of him. As she passed the empty front desk, he caught up to her, took the basket from her, and hurried past her to the door so he could open it for her.

"Thank you, Ronald. You are always so sweet."

"I'm just doing what any gentleman would do."

"You forget; I haven't been surrounded by *gentle*men. Until now." She slipped her arm around his as they walked outside.

By the time they made it to the corner of Yampa Avenue and Fifth Street, a breeze had kicked up. It held a bit of a chill. She pulled on her shawl.

"Are you warm enough?" he asked.

"This wrap is warmer than it looks."

"Unfortunately, it looks as if a walk down to the river or an hour on the porch swing may not be possible tonight." He tried to keep the disappointment from his voice. "Would a game of rummy at the kitchen table be amenable to you? That is, after we eat of course."

"But you said we could talk?" She sounded a trifle upset.

"Yes, of course. How could I have forgotten?" He twisted his mouth to one side at his untruth. He hadn't forgotten; he just couldn't see how a conversation—without looking at stars or planning next year's flower gardens—could fill an entire hour.

"Good because I ran into Lavender Decker yesterday and this, uh-hum," she cleared her throat, "acquaintance of yours named Kate. Anyway, they made me realize that we've got absolutely nothing planned for our wedding."

"That is not true. I've had the entire thing planned out for months." He held the gate open for Dorothy to walk through the picket fence.

"Aren't you referring to your marriage with Wilhelmina Cooper?"

"Uh . . ." He felt his face flush with warmth despite the breeze.

"Tell you what." Dorothy stood on the front porch, waiting for him to open the front door. "Why not save this discussion until after dinner. I don't care to talk about important matters while having to cut up a chicken."

Dorothy walked straight into the kitchen, removed her shawl, and put on the apron he'd set out for her. She motioned for him to set down the basket and immediately assigned him the task of peeling the potatoes. Then she pulled the chicken from the brown paper an old client of his had wrapped around a good frying hen and given him in trade for some legal work.

"Now you scrub those carrots." She pointed with her knife to a bunch of carrots still with their shriveled last year's tops attached. "Say, where'd you get such nice carrots this time of year?"

"One of my clients." He carried the carrots to the sink. "The same one who gave me the chicken. She and her husband still owe me for some work I did for them last year. They just pay me with farm goods when I need it or when they can."

"Like that lovely young widow, Nettie Harris, who brings you eggs?"

"How did you know about—" Ronald cut his words short, sensing what he thought was a bit of jealousy on Dorothy's part. Not only was it unfounded, it was ridiculous. Could she really still be feeling insecure? "Never mind," he said. "I'll hurry and scrub these carrots for you."

He pumped some water into the sink, chopped off the tops, and cleaned the carrots.

Dorothy walked up beside him, nodding her approval at his work. "Thank you for doing that. I think I've got everything else under control now." She gave him a playful push. "You go into the parlor and read the newspaper or your legal books or whatever it is you do for enjoyment in the evenings. I'll call you when supper's all ready."

He shuffled down the hall into the living room, reluctant to leave the kitchen. What he did in the evening for enjoyment was to think about her. Here was his chance to be in her presence, and he was consigned again to merely think of her.

"It won't take much longer, I promise," she hollered as if she'd read his mind.

An hour later, he finally pulled his chair up to the table. "This looks delicious," he said as his eyes took in the delectable spread of food, china, and fancy tablecloth. "Where, may I ask, did you get the nice dishes? And this tablecloth?" he added as he fingered the fine linen.

"Sunny lent them to me." She sat down in the chair adjacent to his at the table. "I wanted this meal to be special for you."

He reached past the golden fried chicken on the pink floral plater and took her hand. "It would be special if you were to feed me a pickle and a slice of cheese."

"See, that's why I adore you, Ronald. You make me feel like I'm worth my weight in gold."

"You are." He felt her squeeze his hand. He'd gladly tell her that over and over again if only he could get her to totally believe it.

"Would you like to say grace or should I?" She looked to him for an answer.

"I'll be glad to do it, but first, I must inquire as to something."

"All right." She seemed hesitant.

"Given the circumstances under which you have been subjugated to over half of your life, how is it you still have a connection to God and make such beautiful fried chicken?"

"My mother." She pinched her lips together as if to suppress an emotion. "She taught me about both." She paused, then looked away and continued. "And I clung to her every word when things got tough. Especially the part where she taught me that God doesn't make junk and that I'm important to Him. Even though I make mistakes."

"That's beautiful." Ronald's throat tightened. This woman kept surprising him.

He offered grace on their bounteous supper and allowed her to dish up his meal as he gazed at her every movement. He could definitely get used to this setting as an everyday fixture in his life.

As he lifted a bite of chicken to his mouth, Dorothy said, "I must admit, it's been a while since I've made this. I hope it's done to your liking."

He placed the chicken in his mouth and chewed. It had a delectable mix of salt and spice. "Yes, it is, very much so."

After they finished their meal, he helped her with the dishes—to which she acted surprised. Then she took off her apron, grabbed Ronald by the hand, and led him toward the living room. "Okay, now it's time to talk."

As he walked down the hall a step behind her, worry rallied in his gut. This constant reference to this "need to talk" concerned him.

She padded across the living room rug, sat on the sofa, and patted the cushion next to her. "Come. Sit."

He walked over and sat on the cushion next to hers. "What would you like to discuss?"

"Isn't it obvious?" She held out her hands.

"Um, no."

"Our wedding date is two weeks from today, and we have nothing planned."

"I beg to differ. As previously mentioned, I had arranged everything with the justice of the peace months ago. We are booked not only in his schedule but for the town hall as well. What else is there?" He held *his* hands out, wondering what he had possibly left out.

"For one thing . . ." Dorothy stared at her hands as they lay folded in her lap. "I have nothing suitable to wear." She pinched the fabric of her skirt. "This is my best skirt—and it's not even mine. Miss Cooper did give me a pale yellow dress; that might be deemed suitable, but it has a nasty tear in its skirt, and I don't know if it could be fixed in time—or at all."

"I see," Ronald responded, seeing now that he'd not thought of every angle. To him, he saw no logic in spending money on a fancy white dress that would only be worn once. "Apparently, a new wedding dress is something a woman finds needful for her wedding?"

She chewed on her lip. "Well, it would be nice. And it wouldn't have to be new. That lady doctor, Kate, said I could borrow hers. I'm more than fine with that. But it might need some alterations. That takes time too. And what about guests? Have you invited everyone on your list?"

"What list?"

"Your guest list. I imagine it would be large—everyone in town seems to know and revere you. As for me, well, Sunny, Lavender, Mary, and Kate are really the only ones on my list. May I invite them if you haven't already?"

Ronald's tongue felt like dead weight. "I um . . . hadn't planned on inviting any guests. I figured a few people might come—if they wanted to. But truthfully, I'd always envisioned it would be only the two of us and the justice of the peace."

"Even recently?" She looked at him with a touch of sadness in her eyes. "Or was that how you originally planned it when you first sent away for the original mail-order bride?"

"The latter," he admitted.

"I see." She scooted closer to him. "Could we not make this our own wedding, Ronald? I care for you, and I feel as though you share my sentiment."

"Oh I do," he said without hesitation.

"June tenth is so close. That's not enough time to do a proper wedding. Could we not push the date into July or August?"

"Oh no, I—I don't like the feel of that at all," he said without forethought.

"Funny, I haven't pictured you as one who does things by 'feel.' Perhaps we do need more time to get to know each other better. It might be wise postponing our wedding until July or August."

Ronald's insides twisted into a knot. Having her in his kitchen this evening, making supper, playfully pushing him into the living room, and filling his home with her smile and his heart with her charm . . . no, he couldn't bear to wait that long. "No, please, I prefer not to wait until July or August to be wed."

Her eyes widened and a grin formed on her lips. "I have an even better idea! A compromise. It just came to me. Do you want to hear it?" She grabbed his hand, and her face lit up.

Ronald let her grasp pull his body closer. "Yes, I believe I would."

"Let's get married tomorrow!" She jerked his hand toward her and cradled it like a doll. "I was wrong—I, too, find July or August longer than I care to wait. So if you don't want all the fancy frills of a wedding, I respect that, and I can forgo them . . . if we got married tomorrow. We've already established that we care for each other, we get along, and marriage is what we both want. And if I'm not going to have a church ceremony, wear a wedding dress, or invite guests, why wait? I'll even tell Sunny first thing in the morning that I'm quitting." She relaxed her hold on his hand and gazed at him with eyes that seemed to beg. "Can I at least invite Sunny?"

Ronald partially loved the idea. But his logical part, the part that preferred to keep his life orderly and made him feel safe, did not. "By all means, invite Sunny—and anyone else you would like, as long as they will all fit into the town hall—but . . . I fear I just don't feel comfortable getting wed tomorrow. I much prefer staying with the June tenth date. Ten is such a nice, round number. Twenty-seven is not."

"What do you mean? May twenty-seventh is a lovely sounding number." Her smile spread from cheek to cheek, tearing down his resolve.

"I have no idea if the justice of the peace will be available. I'm sure he has his day scheduled already."

"Well, I'm sure he could squeeze us in somewhere."

"I have not yet obtained the marriage license. That is on my schedule for Monday, the thirty-first."

"How hard would it be to change that and do that first thing in the morning?"

"Uh, not too hard but . . ."

"But what?" She chewed on her lip in that endearing way that he'd grown to adore.

He couldn't answer; he knew his feeble excuses were just that: feeble. There was no viable reason as to why they couldn't get married tomorrow. His heart certainly liked the idea. But his fetish for order and the distress of approaching the justice of the peace to disrupt his schedule begged him to keep the date where it was. He shrugged his shoulders in response.

"It's all right, Ronald. If you want to keep the June tenth date, I understand. I don't mind doing that for you—you've done so much for me." She leaned against him, moving her face close as her eyes focused on his. "I can certainly wait fourteen more days seeing as I've waited all my life for this moment—a moment I doubted would ever come."

He soaked up her gaze. *Kiss her.* He resisted the idea; his original intent was to do that right before he walked her back to the hotel. *Kiss her.*

"Dorothy, may I kiss you?" The words came on their own. She smiled as if amused. He was serious. Even though he hadn't thought out his last sentence, he did not care to retract it.

"Oh my dear, sweet, Ronald." She cupped his jaw in her hands. "You don't need to ask permission. Just kiss me!" She pulled his face toward hers.

Their lips met, and every worry slipped from his thoughts. In a flash, Dorothy consumed him. His mouth yearned to stay and enjoy that kiss a little longer, but decorum required he refrain. He drew away. In that unyielding moment, he felt her fingers run through his hair, latch on, and pull his head back into place. He willingly succumbed.

Their kiss felt endless yet much too brief.

Dorothy let go of his hair and settled into the sofa, snuggling up to his arm and shoulder. "I love you, Ronald."

He leaned his head against hers, hoping that would be a sufficient response. Though he felt he loved her, he wasn't a hundred percent sure that he did. And as such, it wouldn't be accurate for him to declare his love. It certainly didn't make sense that he could feel this way after knowing her such a short time.

"You make me happy; you make me feel safe." She turned her head and met his eye. "Thank you."

"You are welcome," he said softly, feeling the exact same way. Maybe he should marry her tomorrow. He *could* make the necessary arrangements.

"I can't wait to make this beautiful home mine too. I've already got some ideas." She pointed to the gray-green draperies covering the two front windows. "Those are much too drab for such a lovely house. May I change them to a pale but cheerful yellow?" Her eyes held excitement.

"You may do whatever you wish to this house."

"It's okay—I can wait until the tenth. There are so many things I'd love to do to make it *our* home, and I can spend the next two weeks planning out ideas."

Chapter 26

DOROTHY AWOKE TO RAYS OF sunshine pouring through the hotel's window and onto her bed. "Good morning," she uttered to the flecks of dust dancing in the streams of light. "Hopefully you got more sleep than I did." She'd replayed last evening over and over in her mind through the course of the night. Her favorite part was when Ronald asked, "May I kiss you" in his business-like voice. And then when *she* kissed him—really kissed him, not that customary kiss they started out with—he melted into her like sweet ice cream in summer. Yet he hadn't said anything when she'd declared her love for him. Was he too shy to say "I love you" in return? Or too unsure?

She crawled out of bed and brushed such thoughts out of her way. It was a lovely day, and it was going to stay that way. After splashing water on her face and toweling it dry, she stepped over to the wardrobe to choose which of her three outfits she should wear. The pale yellow dress called to her, it being the most cheerful. She folded it and tucked in into a nook at the bottom of the wardrobe so she wouldn't be tempted to wear it until it was mended. The task being beyond her skills to be done right, she'd take it to Mary when she gave her Kate's wedding dress to alter.

Mary was busy at the front desk checking someone in when Dorothy came downstairs. It appeared Campbell must still be ill. Dorothy gave a quick wave to Mary, stepped outside, and headed to the mercantile.

Lavender stood behind the front counter when she entered. "Good morning, Lavender." She waved. "I need for you to tell me where I can get a hold of Kate, the woman you introduced to me the other day."

"You don't need to explain none to me who Kate is." Lavender flicked her hand. "You sick or something?"

"I'm fine, more than fine. I merely wanted to ask if she'd still be willing to lend me her wedding dress."

"Land of Goshen!" Lavender slapped the counter. "So you talked Ronald into havin' a normal church weddin' then? When's it goin' to be? July? August?"

"It's still going to be June tenth and in city hall," Dorothy said, grateful that it was just going to happen at all. "Ronald has his heart set on that. I merely thought I'd liven it up a bit and wear a real wedding dress if possible. Oh and invite a few guests. Would you be willing to come?"

"Willing? Of course, child. I'll be there with bells on my toes. I'll bring Sam too. Oh, would it be all right if we invited my daughter Rosie and her fiancé, the marshal? They're good friends of Ronald's, and I'm sure they'd want to be there."

"I suppose," Dorothy said, a bit overwhelmed. Why would all these people want to come to her wedding? *It's Ronald's wedding too.* "Ah, yes. As long as there's room in the town hall."

Lavender wrinkled her brow. "Oooh, yeah, the town hall. I'll bring some of my delphiniums to spruce it up, if that's okay with you."

"That would be lovely. Thank you."

"And what about a weddin' cake?"

"I wasn't planning on anything fancy."

"Then I won't make a fancy one, but you gotta have a cake."

"You want to make us a wedding cake?" Dorothy felt numb, ready to pinch herself to see if she was actually awake and not dreaming.

"You bet your bottom dollar I am."

"I'm not a betting woman." That life was behind Dorothy and would stay there.

"You know what I mean." Lavender wagged a finger at her. "Anyway, I'd better point you to Kate before I talk the whole day away. You'll want to get that dress taken care of pronto."

As Lavender described where to find Kate, Dorothy's mind wandered here and there, thinking there could be others of Ronald's friends who might like to come. They might just have a regular wedding after all.

"Say, Lavender," Dorothy said as she turned to leave. "Could you possibly tell the people you know, who are friends with Ronald, about the wedding and invite them to come if they'd like? I think it would be a pleasant surprise for him."

"Sure thing." Lavender removed her apron and hung it on a nail behind the counter.

Dorothy spent the remainder of her time before work arranging things for their wedding. When Ronald came by to escort her to Sunny's Place, it was with great difficulty that she kept the events of the day to herself. Though she was excited about their wedding, the extra frills would not likely hold Ronald's interest. He wanted a simple ceremony. Suddenly it made sense to her. If he couldn't yet tell her he loved her, why have all the frills of a real wedding? True, he might know her, maybe even care for her more than he would for a typical mail-order bride, but this was still a marriage of utility to Ronald—she was like his accidental bride—a mere step up from a mail-order one.

"You look lovely," Ronald said as they strolled toward Sunny's Place.

"I feel rather a mess. I've been running here and there all day long." She tried to smooth out a wrinkle in the skirt of her red dress with one hand as she held onto her coat with the other. She was working the saloon tonight, and it would be chilly walking home at night in that skimpy dress, so she wanted her coat. "But thank you all the same," she added, at least appreciating his kindness.

"You are most welcome, and you always look lovely to me."

A breeze accompanied them to Sunny's, blowing her hair even farther from its haphazard knot. Would Ronald think she looked lovely now? She didn't dare ask.

At 9:00 sharp, Ronald returned to walk her home. A handful of men sat at the bar, laughing with Dorothy.

Sunny walked into the saloon from the restaurant, spied Ronald leaning against the wall by the side door, and approached Dorothy. "Honey, you let me take care of things."

"Are you certain?"

"Absolutely. The restaurant's empty. Now head on home while you got yourself an escort." Sunny motioned Dorothy to the door. "And give him a kiss good night while you're at it. I always thought our dear Ronald rather adorable in his own drab way."

When they stepped outside Dorothy did up her coat's middle button, glad she'd brought it. She hadn't needed her coat when she'd walked to work, but the spring nights could be cool in Craig, and this one was no exception. They walked in silence except for the swish of the breeze and the occasional clomp of horse hooves in the dried mud of Yampa Avenue. Ronald opened the door to the hotel and motioned for her to enter before him.

A single coal oil lamp burned inside the hotel, shedding its yellow glow across the empty front desk where it sat. The dining room appeared as a chasm of darkness to the right of the empty lobby. They had only shadows for spectators. "It looks like we're all alone," Dorothy said.

"Yes." Ronald looked around. "Unfortunately, Campbell must still be under the weather."

"True. Mary doesn't care to tend the desk this late. She always says, 'If folks don't check in by eight at night, they're not the kind of folks I want staying here anyway.'"

Ronald stepped closer. "Good night, Dorothy." He reached his hand around her waist and pulled her to him. His movement came across as awkward at first, but by the time his other hand slipped around her, his movements felt smooth, like he was at ease with the process. He lowered his mouth toward hers and kissed her.

It tingled her down to her toes just as it had last night. Only this kiss was better—he'd braved it without asking. Maybe he did love her, and he just couldn't say it.

He ended the kiss and leaned away slightly. "Perhaps I've been wrong?" he said.

"Whatever do you mean?"

"I should have married you today."

"Oh, Ronald, that is so sweet."

"I hadn't meant to be sweet, only truthful. I may regret giving in to my silly fetish for planning. You've been good for me, Dorothy. You've helped me see value in spontaneity. Perhaps we should wed tomorrow."

"No, no, let's stick to your—our original plan." She had things all set now for the tenth. "It's not *that* far away."

"You are right." Ronald gave her a quick kiss on the cheek. "Tomorrow I shall stop by at 3:00 as usual. Until then . . ." He tipped his hat and slipped out the door.

Dorothy remained fixed in her spot for several minutes, staring at the door where Ronald had left and thinking about her day. She finally turned the lamp way down for Mary's frugal sake and headed slowly up the stairs. She walked toward her room and then stopped cold. It appeared as if light seeped out from beneath her door. *Impossible.* She must be imagining it. She was certain she'd not left a lamp burning when she'd left in the middle of the day.

She shook her head, took her key from her purse, and opened the door. The lamp was lit! Though glowing ever so slightly, it cast enough light to see that her room was empty. She let out a sigh of relief and stepped inside. The door began to close behind her without even so much as a nudge from her.

She turned. Stanley Jones stood there with his back pressed to the wall by the door. The door continued to close until it snapped shut. The figure of another man became visible, his hand still pushing the door until it closed.

"Good evening, little sister."

Chapter 27

RONALD STRODE OUT OF THE hotel and gazed at the night sky. Vivid pinpricks of light shone through the obsidian heavens at the silhouetted horizon. Directly above the masses of celestial bodies at the heart of the Milky Way appeared a soft blanket of light patterned as with brush strokes of infinite shades of white. He wished Dorothy could witness this piece of natural artwork. He slowed his steps, feeling the urge to hurry back into the hotel and summon her to come and share the view with him.

On second thought, he resumed his brisk pace down Yampa Avenue. A pair of horses caught his attention as he crossed Sixth Street. Why would someone tie their horses to that hitching post? It was in front of the gunsmith shop that had closed hours ago. Maybe the owners were at the Buckhorn Saloon a block down. No, that made little sense.

He shook off the uncomfortable feeling of the illogical choice of those riders and hurried toward home. The sooner he got to bed, the sooner tomorrow would come. And the next day and the next . . . until June tenth arrived.

The next morning, Ronald arose and cooked himself a bowl of mush as soon as he was ready for the office. Logan was nowhere to be seen, only his dirtied bowl. It sat unwashed at the bottom of the sink, telling Ronald the boy had left extra early this morning, most likely putting in a long day at the livery stable again. It also told him he needed to procure Logan's inheritance as soon as possible. He now had cases to back up his arguments. The next step would be to contact Judge McConnell.

Midmorning, the door to Ronald's office opened louder than usual, banging against the wall before creaking closed.

"Hey, Ron, I need to talk to you."

"Come," Ronald hollered over the partition. "My ears are open."

The sound of Logan's feet could be heard coming down the corridor. He emerged from behind the partition and dropped into the chair next to Ronald. "Am I invited to your wedding too?"

"What do you mean by 'too?'"

"I mean everybody I talk to in town is plannin' on comin'. They done got invited by Lavender Decker, I think. I was kind of hopin' I'd get a personal invite. I like Lavender and all, but I'd value it a lot more if it came from you and I knew that it was real if you know what I mean."

"I'm sorry," Ronald said. "I do not know what you mean. In fact, I am rather confused. I have invited no one to our wedding. I do not wish to inconvenience anyone by making them feel obligated to attend a ceremony that has no bearing on them."

"I'm talkin' about a weddin'." Logan scratched his forehead. "What are you talkin' about?"

"My wedding. It is to be a simple exchange of vows sealed with the proper legal authority in the town hall Thursday, the tenth of June, at ten in the morning. Nothing more, nothing less."

"What about Miss Dorothy's wedding?"

Ronald wrinkled his brow. Why was Logan having such difficulty understanding such a simple principle? "It will be hers as well."

"No, Ron, I'm going to have to disagree with you there. I think you were right with that other thing you said."

"What thing was that?"

"When you said, 'my wedding.' What you just described ain't Miss Dorothy's weddin'. No girl in her right mind would want to get married in Craig's town hall with those jail cells sittin' right out in the open for decoration. Heck, what if they've got a criminal in one of those cells? Even I wouldn't want him for a weddin' guest."

Logan may as well have hit him up the side of the head with a brick. "You are absolutely correct," Ronald muttered. "How could I have been so obtuse? What am I going to do?"

"Well, I'd head over to the church right now and talk to Pastor Brown, see if he and the new church are available for that Thursday. Then I'd start inviting folks yourself." Logan pointed to his chest. "You can start with me."

"Yes. Logan, if you wish to come, you are invited." Ronald stood from his desk chair. "I'm afraid I can't stay and chat any longer. I had better walk over and speak with the pastor right now."

"Oh wait. I forgot to tell you the reason I came over in the first place."

Ronald gave him a sideways glance. Wasn't this enough?

"Yesterday I was in Hayden, and I ran into Judge McConnell. He was there visitin' his son. They were down fishin' on the river when I ran into them."

"You came to tell me that?" Ronald tapped his foot on the floor. He wanted to get over to the church as soon as possible.

"No." Logan smiled. "I got to chattin' with him and was tellin' him how you're my good friend and all. When he found out, he was all excited and proceeded to tell me that he had some good news for you. He wouldn't tell me none what it was, only that it concerned some case you've been working on and been talkin' to him about."

"This could be good," Ronald said as he massaged his chin.

"But the judge did ask me to give you a message."

"Yes?" Ronald grabbed his hat from off the coat tree.

"He said to tell you to come over to Hayden if you get a chance so he can talk to you. From what I gathered, he's stoppin' there on his way home from Denver as part of a vacation and won't be back in his office for another couple of weeks. So you'll probably want to head over there if you think this is important."

"I shall do that first thing after I speak with the pastor." He motioned to Logan to accompany him to the door. "I have a favor to ask you. Could you be so kind as to escort Dorothy to and from Sunny's this afternoon and evening in case I don't get back in time from Hayden? Do tell her, however, that I shall be back tomorrow to escort her."

"Is she goin' to keep workin' at Sunny's after you two are married?"

"Thankfully, no," Ronald mumbled under his breath. "And thank you for walking Dorothy to and from work. A lovely woman like her can never be too safe in a cow town." He didn't wish to go into details about Vincent, so he hoped that explanation was sufficient. Heavens, he didn't even want to think of the possibility of Vincent showing up in town, looking for Dorothy.

"Nope. Glad to do it." Logan stepped out of the door in front of Ronald. He waved. "I got some more errands to run for folks. See you around." He untied his horse from the hitching post and mounted up.

Ronald hurried to his house, packed his saddle bags, and headed to his small stable out back.

Ronald grabbed his saddle from its spot on the shelf where he stored it. "How you doing, Mehitable?" He patted her nose as he saddled her. She nuzzled his arm. "I do apologize; I've been a might preoccupied as of late. But things are going to change soon. We're going to have a family, you and I. Dorothy will love you and our children will too. And I think I will build you a window in this place so you can enjoy my sons and daughters too as they play."

He saddled Mehitable in a most efficient fashion, enjoying the good amount of satisfaction that wrought. He led her out of the stable, mounted her, and rode off.

The doors to the church were locked when he got there. He spotted a small frame home behind the church. It looked new, most likely built at the same time as the church. Guilt weighed down his chest. He would have known whether or not that was the pastor's house if he'd been a churchgoing man. He used to be before he came out West and he had family to accompany him to Sunday services.

He'd have a family soon—at least the beginnings of one. *Dorothy.* He picked up his pace and marched toward the house behind the church, determined a proper church wedding would be put into place before he left for Hayden. The steps of the white frame house felt solid under his feet as he took them two at a time. He knocked the second he made it to the door. Mrs. Brown opened the door. Her hair, the same dull brown color of hair as Ronald's was haphazardly piled up on her head, and her brow appeared furrowed in a perpetual scowl.

"Yes?" she said, drawing out the word.

"Is this where the pastor lives?"

"Well, of course it is. Why else would someone build themself a house in the backyard of the church?" She just stood there.

"Is he in?" Ronald asked, though he felt his first question implied as much.

"Yeah."

"May I speak with him?"

"Yeah." She left Ronald out on the porch as she stepped into a back room.

Ronald peered into the house as he waited. Lace curtains hung from a side window, a lace cloth covered a dining table, and lace doilies decorated the two end tables on each side of a blue sofa with a definite feminine flair. The room certainly looked more inviting than his welcome had been and its accoutrements more delicate than their mistress.

Dorothy. She would never treat any of Ronald's clients with such brusque manners—even despite her hard life. The desire to please her with a memorable ceremony grew even stronger.

Pastor Brown, a tall, slender man, emerged from an interior door and sauntered toward Ronald. He wore his white collar of the clergy. "Good morning. May I help you?" he said in a cheerful voice.

"Good morning to you." Ronald extended his hand and shook the pastor's. "My name is Ronald Smith and—"

"Yes, I know who you are. I've heard nothing but positive things about you from my parishioners. It's good to meet you face to face. I hope your visit this morning is to tell me of your plans to join our congregation."

"Uh, well, no. On second thought, yes. I do plan on coming with my soon-to-be wife. And speaking of Dorothy, I have a favor to ask of you."

"Is she one of those shy, bashful females who finds it hard to attend church?"

"No." *No, that would be me.* "I have made a grave error in my judgment, and I am hoping you can help me justify it before it is too late."

"So, you are coming here as part of your confessional then."

"No, well, maybe." Ronald tugged at his collar. "I arranged to hold our wedding in the town hall, thinking nothing wrong with that, but I have since come to realize that perhaps that wasn't the best choice—at least not for my bride."

"I see," the pastor said as he rubbed the wisp of beard on his chin. "So, you are coming here to rectify your bad decision and procure the chapel and my services to give your sweetheart the wedding she deserves?"

"That is precisely correct."

"Let me get my calendar." Pastor Brown ran into the back room and returned with a bound calendar. He opened the booklet to the beginning of July. "Okay, so which day are you looking to hold your wedding?"

"June tenth at ten in the morning."

The pastor's forehead wrinkled upward, and he thumbed backward in the pages. He stopped turning and stared at the page. "That's less than two weeks away. I wouldn't call this very good planning."

But it was good planning—Ronald had been planning this date and time ever since he responded to that ad in the magazine six and a half months ago. "Are you available that day and time?"

The pastor shook his head. "I am sorry. I'm not."

Ronald's thoughts scrambled to readjust. Perhaps he could have the justice of the peace come over to the church and perform the ceremony. "What about the chapel? Is it still available?"

"No. I've already got a wedding scheduled that day in the morning. The Caldwell family—homesteaders living out there west of the Circle J—it's their daughter. She's marrying a man from Hayden. They've scheduled the chapel for well into the afternoon. Both have lots of family, from what I hear. You could have an evening wedding."

Ronald felt sick. He swallowed a wad of disappointment lodged in his throat and mustered some words. "Thank you anyway, Pastor Brown, for your time," he said and walked away.

As the door to the house swung closed, Ronald turned on his heel and ran back up the steps. "Wait!"

The door opened back up. "Yes?" the pastor said.

"Could you put us down for the evening of the tenth and the morning of the eleventh of June at 10:00 a.m.?"

Pastor Brown raised an eyebrow. "Both?"

"Temporarily," Ronald said. "Only until I have had a chance to discuss a suitable, alternate time with my fiancée. Right now, I've got business out of town, but I'll be back. Rather, my fiancée and I shall be back," he corrected himself. No longer would he be doing all the planning on his own.

Chapter 28

By the time he located the McConnell home, he'd traipsed around the grazing land on the outskirts of Hayden, finally finding the two-story brick house the local storekeeper had described. He knocked on the door while gazing at the sky. The sun dipped toward the west.

The door opened and a ratty-haired woman with a toddler on her hip stared at Ronald. "Howdy. What can I do for you, mister?"

"Is this the McConnell residence?"

"Yep."

"I was told Judge McConnell is here visiting family. May I speak with him?"

"Yep." She stood there, unmoving.

Ronald glanced through the doorway to each side of her, hoping to catch a glimpse of the judge, hoping he'd come to Ronald's rescue and get this woman to expand her vocabulary. "Well then, I would like to do so."

The woman turned and yelled over her shoulder. "Hey, Grandma, where's Grandpa?"

"He went fishing with the boys," a mature female voice said from inside the house.

The woman remained in the doorway. "He's gone fishin'."

Ronald gathered this young woman to be the judge's daughter-in-law, knowing the judge had only one son. He also gathered she could use some lessons on etiquette. He mustered some fortitude and braved a forward persona. "I have traveled some distance to see the judge, being summoned to come here by the man himself. I would appreciate it very much if you could tell me where exactly I might find the judge before the sun sets." Ronald held onto the doorframe, hardly believing he'd rambled on as such to a woman.

Dorothy. She'd helped him learn to open up to women.

"Please, ma'am, I'll be glad to go down to the river and find him myself if you'd just be so kind as to point me in the right direction."

A young man about Ronald's age walked up behind the woman and nudged her to one side. "Move aside, dear. I'll show him the way down to the river." The man with a large nose the exact replica of Judge McConnell's stepped outside and motioned for Ronald to follow him.

"I'm Jim," the young man said as he traipsed through the barnyard. "You must be Ronald Smith. My pa said you might be coming by."

The sun dipped low in the western sky as Jim led him through a grove of trees. They emerged at the river's edge. Judge McConnell sat on a gray rock that matched his hair, threading a worm—that looked the same color—onto a young boy's hook. He looked up from his task. Their eyes met.

"Ah, Ronald, my boy. It appears you got Logan's message. Though I hadn't expected such a quick response."

"My friend Logan mentioned you wanted to talk to me about his case. I have information I've gleaned as well. I'd love to talk with you."

The judge held up his hand as if to stop Ronald from speaking further. "Not here. Let's go back to the ranch house to talk. It's my grandsons' suppertime." He patted his ample middle. "And mine."

"Is there really a need to do that?" Ronald glanced at the evening sun. If he were to leave right now, he could make it back to Craig by twilight.

"Yep, I don't want discuss such matters on an empty stomach." The judge placed his hand on Ronald's shoulder.

"You're more than welcome to come join us for supper," Jim said. "My wife makes a scrumptious meat pie, and we're having that tonight. I do hope you're planning on spending the night here in Hayden."

Ronald had hoped not to do so. "Yes, I presume I am. Though I haven't checked into the local boarding house as of yet."

"Now don't go and do that." The judge looked to his son and received a nod. "We'll set you up a cot in the back room. No sense paying ole Mrs. Simpson for a room when there's no need to."

"That's right," Jim said.

After a noisy supper, sitting at the table with five children under eight years old, Ronald was anxious to leave the dining room and talk with Judge McConnell one-on-one. Still, he had enjoyed the meal. It had turned out much more endurable than he had anticipated, mingling with strangers. The judge motioned for Ronald to leave the table with him, and together they walked into a large parlor replete with lace curtains and doilies similar to the pastor's house.

The judge picked up a folder that had been sitting on the piano and settled onto the dark-blue sofa.

Ronald sat in a green armchair adjacent to him. "Logan mentioned you had some good news for me."

"A few weeks ago, you asked me a question that I couldn't answer, and I wanted to rectify that. I was heading into Denver anyway and to the court-house. I was glad to research the matter for you." He covered his mouth somewhat and leaned toward Ronald. "Personally, I think the boy deserves it."

Ronald instantly knew to whom the judge referred. It appeared as if everyone in the area thought Logan deserved to have Benedict's old will abrogated. Ronald pulled out the notebook he'd brought with him and sat at the edge of his chair. "I'm ready when you are."

"You won't be needing that notebook. I took all the notes you need." Judge McConnell pulled a couple sheets of paper from his folder and held them out to Ronald. "Don't worry. I was very thorough. And I found not only one case similar to yours but two. In each one," he wagged the papers as a smile lifted one corner of his mouth, "the handwritten will found in the deceased's property was accepted as long as the majority of his children signed an affidavit that they are in agreement."

Ronald took possession of the papers. "This is wonderful. Added to the cases I found at the University of Chicago, I think there will be no problem getting Logan his inheritance. I would like you to get the appeal process underway if you would, Judge." Two out of three children was a majority. There would be Susannah and Logan. He no longer needed Stanley's sworn statement that Benedict's signature was authentic.

"Sure thing."

Ronald glanced at the clock on the dark wooden mantelpiece. The night was no longer young. A second glance to the side observed the darkening sky outside. This interchange had taken all of five minutes. He could have been almost to Craig by now if only the judge and his family had been more efficient and less chatty. He tucked the papers into his notebook.

Ronald stood, ready to be shown his cot in the back room. He looked around the parlor, not caring if his nervousness displayed itself. Hopefully Judge McConnell would deduce that Ronald was uncomfortable asking for his room early and then voice what Ronald wanted to hear: "Are you ready to be shown your room now?"

"Ah, sit down, young man," he said instead. "The night's early. How about a game of cards? You play poker? Rummy? Pinochle?"

"No, I can't say that I have much call to play cards."

"That's too bad. It's about time we fix that, isn't it." Judge McConnell leaned toward the doorway. "Hey, Jim, go back into the dining room and bring Katie or Grandma with you. We need two more people so we can play pinochle."

Mr. and Mrs. McConnell joined Ronald and the judge around the dining room table. After the first two hands, Ronald discovered that he liked the card game. "This is rather enjoyable," he spoke his thoughts aloud.

"You act as though you've never learned to have fun," Katie McConnell said.

"Uh, well, now I wouldn't exactly say that." Ronald picked up the new hand Jim had dealt to him. "I've had my share of fun in my day."

"I've seen your version of it," the judge said. "I've been in the courtroom and joined you in the occasional walk about town enough to know that your definition of fun is about as accurate as a blind man with one of those fancy new scopes on his rifle."

When Katie finally announced she'd better head up to bed, Ronald and the other two men stood up as well. Judge McConnell walked Ronald to the back of the house, placing a hand on his shoulder when they stopped by the door to the back room. "I think you were actually enjoying yourself in there."

"I believe I was," Ronald responded.

The next morning, Ronald got up with the sun. He kept Mehitable at a comfortable pace for both of them.

As he approached the southwest end of Craig, he noticed a horse and its rider galloping toward him. He kept Mehitable at the same brisk pace and didn't succumb to the urge to rush to meet this person, who for some reason appeared to be focusing in on him.

The horse became familiar before the rider. "Logan," he hollered and kicked his heels into Mehitable. They both pulled their horses to a stop as they met up. Ronald could see trouble in Logan's eyes. "Is something the matter?"

"Thank heavens I found you," Logan said as he panted. "It's Dorothy."

"Dorothy?" Ronald's chest tightened.

"Yes. Yesterday when I went to escort her to work, she wasn't there. I assumed she must have left early and walked herself. When I went to walk her home last night, she wasn't there either. And Sunny said she never came in to work. Campbell and Mary, they ain't seen her neither, not hide nor hair of her since Thursday evenin'—since before you talked to her last."

Since I talked to her and crushed her dreams of a proper wedding.

Chapter 29

"VINCE—"

Dorothy struggled to breathe as her brother's hand clamped hard against her mouth and nose. Panic seized her. She fought to be free. Now both Vincent's and Stanley's arms enveloped her.

"Stop fighting me. I'm only doing this for your welfare," Vincent whispered in her ear. "Now be a good girl and promise to be quiet, and I'll take my hand away from your mouth." He moved his fingers slightly, allowing a trace of air to reach her nostrils.

The stench of grime and horse sweat flowed in with a much needed breath. She didn't move, still trying to process the gush of fear flooding her body. It threatened to carry her back to the way things were. Before she came to Craig.

"Smart girl." Vincent loosened his grip, and Stanley stepped away. "Now, get your things, little sister. We're going."

She stood still as an emptied glass, assessing the situation. This couldn't be happening. She couldn't *let* this happen—she'd finally broken free from her prison.

"No." The moment she stated her defiance, fear felt like it might cripple her. She knew the façade of her courage could begin to crumble. "I don't want to leave Craig," she forced her plea out through trembling lips. "I have a good life ahead of me here. Please don't make me leave." Why had she begged? It never helped. But she could think of nothing else. "You don't have to take care of me any longer. I promise I'm all right on my own."

"Yeah, you're good at looking out for yourself, aren't you?" Vincent said in his fake suave tone. Yet the bitterness in his eyes was clearly visible despite the weak glow of the room's single lamp. "Running out on me in our last town, leaving me to deal with the law on my own." He raised his hand in his usual fashion that usually led to a blow.

Dorothy instinctively shielded her face. "I'm sorry. I'm really, really sorry."

Vincent lowered his hand. He smiled, flashing his nice set of teeth. "You're lucky, little sister."

"I am?"

"Yes," he said in a singsong manner. "The law in that town was as crooked as you. I was able to pay 'em off. They let me go." He cleared his throat. "But now you owe me," he said in his normal, deep voice. "So you see, I can't let you go even if you can take care of yourself," he burst out with a laugh. "You gotta help me win back all that money I done shelled out to get *me* outta jail. Understand?"

Dorothy shook her head. "I can't leave. I like it here in Craig. I even have a job—I found it all on my own."

"Who'd hire you?"

"I work—" Dorothy wrapped her coat tightly across her red dress. A sinking feeling pulled her down as she realized where this could lead.

"She works in the town's best saloon." Stanley stepped from the shadows, where he'd stayed until now. "Tell her to show you what's she's wearing."

Vincent nodded at Dorothy. "Go ahead."

Reluctantly, she opened her coat.

Vincent stroked his chin with his thumb and forefinger. "Oh really now." An unsettling expression darkened his face as he paused in thought. "Yeah, this town could work." He bobbed his head up and down. "Especially since you're already settled into the job."

"No, Vincent," Dorothy cried out. "I have a fiancé. For goodness' sake, I'm getting married in two weeks!"

"She has a way with her customers," Stanley added, wearing a wicked grin. "People seem to trust her."

"Yes, yes," Vincent murmured. "I think we could set up shop real easy here in this town."

"But I could never—not here, not to my friends!"

"I say you could."

"But I promised Ronald I'd not work after we're married. He's a lawyer, so we don't need the money. It could never work." She scrambled for any and all reasons.

"Then maybe you shouldn't get married." Vincent said it more as a demand than a suggestion. "I'm sure I could convince your *duped* fiancé that he has in fact been *duped* by you. You know you're no good, that you're lying through your teeth. You'd have to be lying to convince a fellow like him that you're good enough to be his wife."

"But, but . . . you don't even know Ronald."

"Don't matter. That Ronald fellow deserves better than you, and you know it." Vincent stared at her. "I'm sure you can convince him of that fact." He cleared his throat. "Do it quick so we can get set up in our old routine, you hear?"

Dorothy felt as though her throat was on fire. She could never work their nefarious scheme in Craig. *Never!* And the only way she could prevent Vincent from going through with that nightmare would be to leave town with him.

The very thought felt as though it tore her heart from her chest. But it would be the best thing for everyone. After all, Vincent was right about one thing; she wasn't good enough to be Ronald's wife.

Dorothy held her breath momentarily to smother her pain the best she could. It might be her only option now, but she'd make sure she had more options down the road. She'd play Vincent like he'd taught her to play all those men they had cheated out of their money. She put on her actress face and used her sugary voice. "Vincent, you'd never make any money in this town. People's pockets are shallow, and you'd always be looking over your shoulder. The marshal's a good friend of the owner of the Sunny Saloon. And he's not crooked. It's best we leave this place." She stifled a sob as she stepped toward the wardrobe. "Hold on. I'll grab my belongings."

"She's right," Stanley said. "People here got no money, 'cept me. And I done learned my lesson." He glared at Vincent.

"I'll get your things." Vincent ripped the handbag from her grasp and motioned for her to stay put. He walked over to the wardrobe, grabbed the traveling bag and stuffed in her handbag, then her nightgown, blouses, and skirts he'd pulled from the hangers. "Is this all you got?" he mumbled. "Fool girl, see, you can't take care of—"

Stanley held his finger up to his lips. "Quiet! Someone's comin'."

Vincent froze.

Quiet footsteps padded up the stairs. A timid knock rapped on the door. "Miss Dorothy?" It was Nyda, the oldest of the Tucker girls. "Are you all right?"

Vincent shot Dorothy a warning glare. "Send her away," he whispered with venom shrouding his voice.

"Yes, I'm fine—just reading a book. Go back to bed, Caroline." Dorothy hoped she'd confused the girl sufficiently to get her thinking. But why? What kind of help could the young girl muster to get Dorothy out of this mess now?

"Okay, if you're sure."

"Yep."

Nyda's footsteps padded down the hallway, and soon the stairs produced their familiar creak.

After a minute or so, Vincent shot Stanley a sideways glance and motioned to the door with a jut of his chin. "Let's get out of here. Make sure the coast is clear." He threw Dorothy's bag to Stanley and shuffled her toward the door. "Walk softly and don't make a noise." His hot breath sent chills from her ear to her toes as his grip shot pain through her arm.

The single lamp still glowed on the front desk, its glow casting shadows against the far wall of her struggle down the stairs. She prayed Campbell or Mary would come to turn off the light any second now. In the same breath, she prayed they would stay put in their bedroom behind the kitchen.

At the bottom of the stairs, Stanley moved in front of them and poked his head out the door. "It's clear," he whispered.

Vincent pulled Dorothy outside and then down the sidewalk. They turned the first corner. Now in the cover of darkness, Vincent pulled her faster, causing her to stumble. She also felt his anger as if it had come through his clenched hand into her body like a bolt of lightning. Any normal brother would be happy for his sister's upcoming marriage and would be grateful she no longer needed a guardian. Vincent only wanted her for the money she helped him cheat out of people, and he was dragging her back into that life.

They approached a pair of horses tied to a hitching post. "Climb up there," Vincent growled. He pointed to the horse closest to Dorothy.

With her tight, red satin dress, she struggled to mount. Vincent pushed her up on top of the horse and climbed into the saddle behind her. A second later, they took off. She grabbed onto the saddle horn to keep from falling. Vincent didn't even try to hold on to her, and she preferred he didn't.

The cold night air poured through her open coat. She wanted to button it all the way up to her neck but dared not let go of the saddle.

Neither did she dare take her eyes off the road ahead once they left the light of the town behind them. The moon shown only half-full and the rutted trail soon blurred into the darkness surrounding them. Stanley led the way. She felt Vincent's hold on the reins relax, and he basically let his horse free to follow Stanley's.

Free. She wanted to be free. More than anything. She had miraculously escaped her prison once, but she dared not hope for such good fortune a second time. Vincent would be more overbearing now than ever. And what of Ronald? She tried not to think about him. Leaving him behind was best for everyone.

Except for her.

But she didn't count.

It felt like forever, but Dorothy knew it was more like an hour when she spotted two squares of light in the distance. The lights grew brighter as they closed in on what appeared to be a large ranch house. They dismounted. Vincent shoved Dorothy's bag into her hands and pushed her toward the house as they followed Stanley.

They entered through what she guessed to be a back door. They walked through a cramped area, then the light grew somewhat stronger, and she spotted a lamp hanging from the ceiling of a large kitchen. Dorothy could make out the features of a stove and sink, wishing Stanley would turn up the lamp—obviously, this was his house.

Instead, Stanley inserted a key into a door at the back of the kitchen and opened it. "You can put her in here." He pointed to a doorway of pure darkness. "She won't go anywhere. It's the larder—no windows or nothin'."

"That'll work." Vincent shoved Dorothy into the darkness.

"No! I'm not going to run away, I promise." The door closed quickly behind her. Then came the click of the lock. And the panic.

Dorothy grappled the walls to get her bearings. The complete lack of light engulfed her in such fear that she felt she might suffocate from its intensity. Shelves upon shelves of cans and bags of beans or flour or something else she couldn't discern filled both walls. She crouched down and ran her hand across the floor. Her fingers detected coolness and a measure of softness. The musty smell confirmed her guess: hard-packed dirt. She lowered herself onto the floor, and using her bag as a pillow, she cinched her coat around herself and lay down.

Muffled voices sounded through the door. She sat up and strained her ears to listen, to possibly catch any tidbit of information that might help her.

"Where am I going to sleep?" It was Vincent's voice.

"That's not my concern." Stanley's voice held an edge of bitterness.

"But—"

"And I want you out of here first thing in the mornin'. The way I see it, I've more than paid what I owed you. A bed don't come with it." The screech of chair legs dragged across the floor. "Here, use this."

Boot steps clomped her way. They sounded lighter than Vincent's gait. Was Stanley having second thoughts? Was he coming to let her out of the larder and then offer her a kitchen chair to sleep on too? She stared at the door, awaiting his arrival, when she perceived a pinprick of light. She looked closer and realized a minuscule glow of light poured through the keyhole. Why that small measure of light brought her comfort, she didn't understand. But she held on to it nonetheless.

The door opened. A silhouette filled the doorway. She assumed it was Stanley's by the shape of the hat. He held on to something. It lacked a distinct shape, and she couldn't even guess what it might be. A split second later, he threw it at her. Her initial reaction was to jump out of the way—but to where? The larder was not more than six feet across. The thing hit her. Soft folds of cotton engulfed her. A blanket. Why had Stanley thrown her a blanket? Had Vincent requested one for her? Or was Stanley feeling sorry for her? Or was it merely an act of belligerence aimed at Vincent?

She placed the blanket on the cold dirt floor and lay down on it, trying not to think about the latter. She had to hold on to the positive. Maybe her brother did care about her in a small sort of way. And though it made no sense to do so, she grabbed on to the slim hope that Ronald would come looking for her too.

She found herself unable to hold on to that hope for very long. Her past wouldn't let her.

She plumped her traveling-bag-pillow and tried to get comfortable. Sleep refused to come. It was probably close to midnight by now. That meant Thursday was almost over. The Thursday after next she was supposed to get married. Tears gathered in her eyes. She knew the wedding would not take place as planned, and that would upset Ronald—he so hated having his schedule disrupted.

Chapter 30

EVERYTHING BLURRED AND SEEMED TO fall away around Ronald. Even Mehitable didn't exist beneath him; his whole world had shattered at Logan's announcement. "Dorothy? Gone? Impossible." But it wasn't impossible. He very well could have given her rightful cause to leave. He knew so very little about women. How could he have been so careless as to not research their needs more? Surely some page in one of those books of his—if only he'd kept reading—would have told him that females expect a church wedding with a fancy dress and other such superfluous frills. If only he could have been forewarned, he would have prepared. Those were such little things, things he would have gladly done for Dorothy.

On the other hand, his darn books had only made matters worse. If he hadn't been so dead set on organization, lists, and schedules, he would have jumped on her suggestion to get married immediately. He raked his hand through his hair—he certainly had much on his *list* of self-improvements.

"I've got to find her." He reached out to Logan.

Logan swept his arm in a wide arc toward town. "Well, come on; I'll help you look some more."

Ronald maneuvered Mehitable alongside Logan. "Where have you looked so far?"

"The hotel of course. It was the first place."

"Are you sure she didn't leave some sort of clue as to where she was going?"

"Nope. Campbell checked her room. The bed was all made up, and her belongings were gone."

"And the Tuckers were told nothing of her leaving?"

"Nope. Though Campbell admits he's been under the weather and hasn't been at the desk like he should."

"Where else have you checked?"

"Deckers' store."

"Besides the Deckers' and the Tuckers', where else have you looked? Who else have you spoken with?"

Logan hunched his shoulders. "Almost everywhere and everyone I could think of."

"Then I'll just have to retrace your steps a second time. No offense meant, but sometimes clues can be overlooked the first go around."

"No offense taken. Heck, I know a second set of eyes and ears is always good." Logan grinned and looked down toward his feet. "And legs. Especially if mine are the first set. I admit I didn't look none too much upstairs places."

"So you didn't look in Kate's office?"

"Nope."

"You know she has a spare room up there with a bed."

"I forgot about that."

"Did you look in Dorothy's hotel room?"

"Nope, I didn't. Campbell done said she was gone and that was good enough for me."

"Not for me." Ronald kicked his heels into Mehitable and sped forward.

Logan caught up. "You goin' to Doc Kate's?" he yelled.

Ronald barely heard him over the gallop of hooves. He nodded, not wanting to attempt more conversation, only to get to town as soon as possible and begin his own investigation.

As Ronald rode the remaining stretch of road to town, he felt as though he and Mehitable crawled despite the trees and sagebrush flying by. Possibility after possibility of Dorothy's whereabouts ran through his mind, each unacceptable, especially the one that sat in his gut like coal tar: Vincent had found her and had taken her away. The very thought made his body writhe in agony. He clung to the hope, though extremely painful, that she had left because of him and his thoughtlessness. And if that was the case, she very well could be holing up in the doctor's spare room; Kate would be the kind to take Dorothy in.

He and Logan slowed their horses when they reached the edge of town. Clomping up Yampa Avenue at a respectable gait felt like torture. Ronald moved ahead of Logan, arriving at Hoy's Saddle Shop first. He dismounted, not bothering to wrap his reins around the hitching post, and flew up the stairs on the outside of the shop to Kate's office on the second floor.

"I'll stay down here," Logan called out from atop his horse.

Ronald reached the landing at the top of the stairs and saw the open sign hanging on the door. "Good." He blew out a breath of relief, knowing she wasn't in every day. He opened the door and walked in.

Kate stood at a cabinet with her back to Ronald. She turned around, and her brow wrinkled in concern. "Ronald, what's wrong?"

"I am coming to inquire about my fiancée, Dorothy Bednar. By chance are you letting her stay in your back room?"

"No, no, I'm not. Why do you ask?" Her eyes widened.

"She is missing," Ronald said. "I was hoping she was merely looking for another place to stay and that she'd asked to borrow your spare room."

"I'm sorry. I haven't seen her since last Tuesday in the mercantile. By the way, do you know if she has decided to take me up on my offer?"

"What offer?"

"To borrow my wedding dress. Lavender and I were convincing her that a few extra frills might go a long way in making her wedding day even more memorable." Kate held her hand up to her mouth momentarily. "Not that your wedding would not have been just fine as you'd planned."

"It would not have been," Ronald stated. "If you do happen to see her, would you please let her know I am looking for her?"

"Oh." Kate's face wore an expression Ronald read easily enough—she wondered what had happened to the "storybook" romance. Though as illogical as anything he could imagine, he wondered the same thing.

"Thank you for your time, Kate. Good day." He lifted his hat and stepped outside.

"No luck?" Logan asked as he reached the bottom.

Ronald shook his head and mounted his horse.

"Where we goin' next?"

"The hotel."

Three blocks down Yampa Avenue, they dismounted and tied their horses to the hitching post in front of the Craig Hotel. Logan limped inside, a pace behind. Ronald went to the desk where Campbell stood busy with a customer. He waited as patiently as possible while Campbell described the breakfast schedule to a middle-aged man. Tapping the toe of his shoe on the floor appeased his nerves only so long. He leaned toward the desk. "Excuse me, Campbell. Might I have your permission to search Dorothy's old room? I'd like to see if she might have left some clue as to her disappearance that has been overlooked."

"Sure. You know where it is. It's empty, but it's still yours through next week. If'n you'd like a refund, I'd be glad to work something out." Campbell handed him a key and waved him toward the stairs.

"I'm not worried about that right now." Ronald shot toward the stairs.

Logan followed close behind. "I'm comin' too."

Ronald stepped into the room first. A pastel quilt lay neatly spread across the bed with pillows at the head, fluffed and untouched. He stopped and stared—what had he expected? Two nights had passed since he'd accompanied Dorothy home. He couldn't expect Mary to leave this room untouched.

Logan ran into his back. "Whoa, did you find somethin'?"

"No."

"What is it you're lookin' for exactly?"

"I admit I don't really know. A clue I suppose, something to give me hint as to why Dorothy left without a word to anyone." Ronald stepped farther into the room.

He knelt and looked under the bed while Logan removed the cushion from the armchair. Ronald moved over to the table holding a porcelain pitcher and bowl. He looked under the bowl and then under the cloth covering the table. Logan hobbled to the wardrobe. Ronald glanced over as Logan opened the double doors. As expected, no clothing hung from the hangers dangling inside the piece of furniture.

"I found somethin', I think," Logan said. Ronald hurried over as he lifted a pale yellow article of clothing from off the floor of the wardrobe. "Is this somethin' you'd consider a clue?"

"Definitely." Ronald recognized it as Dorothy's yellow dress, the one that brought out the green shades in her eyes and her brown hair so nicely. "The fact that she left it behind speaks volumes."

Lifting an eyebrow, Logan gave him a sideways glance. "How?"

Ronald picked up the dress. Its fabric reminded him vividly of Dorothy with its scent of lavender and feel of softness. He swallowed hard. "The way I see it, this means one of two things: either she left it behind because she knew it was my favorite dress on her and she didn't want to keep it around to remind her of me and my selfishness or—"

"That's ridiculous, Ron. She'd never do that any more than you'd be selfish. What's the other choice?"

Ronald liked the second choice even less, so much so he had a hard time spitting it out. "That . . . that she didn't leave on her own accord. She didn't have time to pack her things properly—because someone took her."

"You mean like kidnappin' her?"

"Not exactly but close enough." Ronald's chest tightened. If it was Vincent who took her, he was technically still her guardian. Legally, the despicable man possibly had a leg to stand on—at least until Dorothy turned twenty-one or was married. Unfortunately, he didn't know when that was, for he'd never even bothered to ask her as to her birthday. What a cold, insensitive man he was. Though he deserved to no longer enjoy the affections of Miss Dorothy Bednar, Vincent Bednar deserved her company even less. Dorothy deserved to be free of the both of them. "We've got to find her." Ronald kept hold of the dress and ran from the room.

He flattened his back against the wall on the way down to allow the new guest to climb the stairs with suitcase in hand and then rushed to the desk. "I know you've probably already told Logan all you know about Dorothy," he said to Campbell, "but please tell it again to me. Did you see her leave? Was she with someone? It's very important that I know."

"Like I told the boy . . ." Campbell scratched his head as he motioned to Logan descending the stairs. "Neither me nor Mary saw her leave. Mary just went up there yesterday morning to clean her room, and it was empty. That's all I can tell you, honest."

"Can you tell me if the bed was made?" He had a suspicion he wanted to pursue.

"I couldn't, but Mary could." Campbell put his hand to the side of his mouth and yelled, "Hey, Mary, come on out here. Ronald wants to ask you some questions about Miss Bednar's room."

Mary scurried from the kitchen. A second after her, the door swung open, and the oldest Tucker girl followed after her mother. She stood by her mother's side as Mary spoke to Ronald.

"I can't imagine I got much to say that hasn't already been said. But I'll be glad to spill it out again if it'll help. I really did take a liking to Miss Bednar. I hope everything is all right."

Campbell pointed up the stairs. "He wants to know if Miss Dorothy's bed was made when you went up there Friday morning."

"Why, yes, it was. In fact, it had not been slept in."

"How can you be sure?" Ronald's fear kept growing. "What if she'd merely risen early and made the bed up herself?"

"Because I always lay a little sprig of lilac or lavender on the pillow when I make my beds up, and it was still there."

"What about the rest of the room?" Ronald asked. "Did it look the same?"

"Oh no, it was quite messy." Mary brought her hand to the side of her head. "No. No, that's not what I'd call it. Dorothy was never messy, but I did find it strange that the chair was sitting crooked and one of the wardrobe doors was left hanging open. I glanced in and saw nothing was hanging inside, so I closed it and hurried over to straighten out the chair. Little things like that bother me. Sorry."

"No need to be sorry," Ronald said, thinking how he too was sorry for letting little things bother him. "You've been a big help and confirmed some of my suspicions. Thank you." He tipped his hat, ready to leave. He noticed the Tucker girl tug on Mary's arm so as to lower her mother's ear down to whisper something.

Mary straightened back up and looked at Ronald. "Nyda says she saw Miss Dorothy Thursday night after you left her. And something else too. But she's not sure that's what you're looking for."

"Let's hear it." Ronald moved his attention to the girl.

Nyda ducked her head. "Sorry, but I was listening in the kitchen. I really liked Miss Dorothy; she always ate breakfast in the kitchen with us, not out in the dining room like most of the guests."

"I'm glad you liked her. I did too." Ronald lifted Nyda's chin so her eyes would meet his. "Please tell me what you know. It could very well help her."

"It was late Thursday night. I was hungry, so I sneaked out of my bed to grab a slice of bread. Then I heard some noise upstairs. I swore I heard Miss Dorothy scream, so I went upstairs to see if she was okay. When I knocked on her door, she took a while to answer. Then she sounded funny, like people do when they're lying to you. I asked her if she was okay. She told me she was, but I don't know if I believe her now. She must have not felt too good 'cause she called me Caroline. I didn't think too much of it at the time, so I went downstairs to the kitchen to finish eating my bread. Right before I went back to bed, I heard someone coming down the stairs. Actually, it sounded like more than one someone. So I peeked at them through the door. I hardly opened it at all."

"Was it Dorothy?" Ronald worked to keep his voice steady.

"Yes, her and two men. I couldn't see them that good. It was dark, but I swore both of the men looked like Mr. Jones."

"My brother?" Logan interjected.

Ronald had almost forgotten Logan was there. "Yes, was it Stanley Jones they looked like?"

"Yeah." Nyda looked at the floor once again. "That's why I didn't say nothing before now. I didn't want people to think I was funny in the head. I mean I swore I was seeing double—one Stanley in front of her and another Stanley behind her, walking out of the hotel."

Ronald reached out and hugged the little girl. "Thank you. And you weren't seeing double, I assure you. I know exactly who you saw." He tipped his hat at Mary and Campbell. "Thank you for your trouble." Then he turned to Logan. "I'm heading out to the Circle J. You can come if you want, but I'll understand if you don't."

"I'll come."

♠

Chapter 31

"I'll take the horses over to the corral," Logan said. "You go see if Stanley's home. I'll join you in a bit."

Ronald trudged onto the ranch house porch. He'd sworn he would never set foot on the Circle J Ranch again. But here he was. He lifted his hand and knocked.

The door opened and the sour-faced housekeeper glared at Ronald. "What do you want?"

"May I speak with Mr. Jones please?"

"Well, ain't you the lucky one. Wish I could say the same for me—he's here again." She opened the door and allowed Ronald to step inside.

"Thank you." Ronald followed her down the tiled entryway and into the great room.

Stanley rose from an overstuffed chair and approached Ronald. They met on the edge of the large room's circular rug. "Well, if it ain't Craig's lousy thorn-in-my-side lawyer. I'm not signin' nothing, so you may as well turn around and go home if that's why you're here."

Ronald took a deep breath to calm his stomach. "This has nothing to do with your father's will. It has to do with Miss Dorothy Bednar."

"You want me to sign something to appeal her father's will?" He laughed. "Sure, why not?"

"Her father passed away ten years ago," Ronald said, clenching his jaw. "I have a witness that saw you and," he took a chance here, "Vincent Bednar walking out of the hotel together last Thursday night." He was about to ask, "Is that true?" but refrained. "Where is she? Tell me, or I'll have you thrown in jail for kidnapping."

In all the time Ronald had known Stanley Jones, this was the first time he'd spotted fear in the man's arrogant demeanor. "You can't do nothin' to me."

"Come on, Stanley." The words fell from Ronald's mouth, sounding almost foreign to him. "Just tell me where she is if you know. I promise to keep the law out of this if you do."

Stanley straightened his back. "Okay, fine, I will—on one condition."

"What is that?"

"You leave my pa's will alone. It's fine the way it is. You hear me?"

"Do not worry. I will not bother you with signing another affidavit. The appeal process is underway without needing your signature."

"Why, you good-for-nothin—" Stanley threw a right punch.

Ronald ducked. "Sorry, it is out of my hands now."

"You're a smart fellow, as slick a lawyer as they come. I'm sure you could finagle things somehow to get it stopped."

"Like I said, it is out of my hands." Ronald backed away and held out his hands in a gesture of truce. "This was not what I came here to discuss. It is the matter of Dorothy Bednar for which I have come here. Do not make me bring in the marshal to get you to talk."

"Tell you what." Stanley twisted one end of his mustache. "You do some fancy lawyering and get that appeal stopped, and I'll tell you what you want to know. It's that simple."

"But that will take time. Dorothy could be well out of the state by the time I could arrange that." Why was he saying this? He couldn't back down on the matter of Logan's rightful inheritance. But neither could he let Vincent take Dorothy back into a life of crime and misery.

The front door creaked open, and a gust of air flowed into the great room.

"I know I'm takin' a risk here, but I'm willin' to take your word as a guarantee." Stanley lifted one corner of his mouth in an unsettling smile.

Two dilemmas fought with each other in Ronald's mind as he pictured the two people who meant the most to him, one of which he heard approaching through the entryway. He pictured Logan's continual smile before he saw the boy round the corner, knowing how the boy loved working in the livery stable for two bits a day, delivering mail to folks around town for the sheer joy of helping people. Then he pictured Dorothy's sweet smile and remembered her sincere gratitude for her new life here in Craig.

What should he do? He couldn't give up the fight for Logan's rightful inheritance. Yet he couldn't let Dorothy go back to her brother. He paced to the other side of the room, blowing his cheeks out like he was going to explode. Releasing the pent-up air, he turned to Stanley. "Can you give me some time to think about this?"

Logan stepped into the room. "What do you need time to think about?" He looked at Ronald.

"Ron-Ron here is in a dilemma. I might say you are too, little brother." Stanley jutted his chin out. "You see, I have some information he wants concernin' his gal. You two's gotta make a decision. That information comes at a cost."

"Why, you know Ron ain't got that much money. Folks pay him with eggs and potatoes half the time. Me—I got nothin'."

"I told him to leave Pa's old will alone, quit with all that appeal nonsense. Then I'd be glad to tell him what he wants to know."

Logan turned to Ronald. "The way I see it, this ain't much of a decision. Dorothy's way more important. Heck, I already done told you I was doin' fine without my pa's money."

"But I have discovered we no longer needed Stanley's signature to appeal the will, only Susannah's and yours."

"Well, I'm goin' to make your decision easier." Logan folded his arms across his chest. "As soon as I'm done here, I'll go find Judge McConnell myself and scratch my name off that paper you had me sign."

"But—"

Stanley cut Ronald off. "I always knew you had a good head on your shoulders, boy," he said, wrapping his arm around Logan.

Logan weaseled out from underneath Stanley's arm.

Ronald bristled at the artificial expression of affection—Stanley didn't care about Logan. Then he froze. Were his intentions that much different? Was he really fighting for Logan? Or was he only trying to fulfill what he, Ronald Smith, attorney at law, thought was logical and proper?

Ronald exhaled deeply. "Okay, Stanley, I give you my word I will do everything in my power to stop the appeal of your father's will."

"Good decision," Logan said.

"Shake on it?" Stanley held out his hand.

Ronald accepted his hand, shook it, and promptly pulled his own hand behind his back, then clasped both of his hands together. "All right, Stanley, let's start with how you know Vincent Bednar, and then most importantly, tell me where he and Dorothy are right now."

"I don't really know the man all that much." Stanley's mouth turned down. "I just happened to owe him something."

"May I ask, did you by chance play poker with this fellow, Vincent?"

"Yeah, what of it?"

"Did you lose a lot of money to him?"

"Depends on what you consider a lot. It wasn't all that much because he lost a couple hundred dollars to me first."

"Let me guess." Ronald leaned against the wall. "You owed him a considerable sum and he made a bargain with you to let you out of your debt if you helped him get his 'wife' back. Am I right?"

"Somethin' like that." Stanley's back stiffened. "Then I found out she weren't his wife but his sister."

"I'm sorry to have to tell you this, Stanley, but you've been taken. Vincent Bednar is a card shark. He cheats at poker, and that's how he beat you and thus conned you into helping him. How much did you owe him?"

"Couple thousand dollars." Stanley pounded the wall next to Ronald. "The dirty rotten scum!" He turned to Ronald. "How come you know so much about him? And why should I trust you?"

"You forget—Dorothy and I were about to be wed. She has told me everything. She ran away from him because he was forcing her to help him cheat. But I'm sure he had other means to accomplish his crimes without her. And I daresay I would rather trust her word than Vincent's."

"Wow," Logan said, eyes wide, obviously taking in more information than he'd bargained for. He took a moment, as if regaining his bearings, then said, "I know I would."

"I always felt there was something off about the maggot."

Ronald cleared his throat. "So, you will tell me where I might find the two of them?"

"You gotta believe me on this one, Ron-Ron, because I ain't beholdin' to that maggot one bit. I don't know where they are."

"But you helped Vincent take Dorothy from the hotel Thursday night," Logan cut in. "Nyda Tucker saw you and Vincent comin' down the stairs."

"Yeah, I did. And they stayed at my house that night. But the next mornin', I kicked the two of them out at dawn and told Vince I done paid my debt and more. He said something about headin' east by way of Denver, but that's all I can tell you. Honest."

Ronald bolted toward the door.

"Where you going?" Stanley called out.

"To Denver."

"One more thing," Stanley said, and Ronald turned around. "Just so you know, she went willingly."

Ronald stepped outside, wondering if the bad news would ever stop coming.

Chapter 32

THE STAIRS CREAKED WORSE THAN the bed Dorothy had slept in last night. But this flea-infested, two-bit hotel in Denver was a whole lot better than her previous night spent with Vincent in a livery stable outside of a town called Steamboat Springs. Vincent kept hold of her elbow as they continued down the steps and into the dismal lobby with its dust an inch thick and the curtains hanging in the front window the same shade of gray as the walls.

"Are we getting on a stage?" Dorothy asked, hoping they wouldn't have to continue on horseback. The first leg of their trip had been horrible. But pain of the saddle had been nothing compared to all the other things paining her. Two days on the road with Vincent constantly at her side and reality finally sinking in still hadn't numbed her sufficiently to accept her lot in life once again.

"No, little sis, I'm going to be nice to you." Vincent squeezed her arm to where it hurt. "We're taking the train like you did that night you so inconsiderately left me holding the bag back in Missouri. Again, how you ever managed to buy a ticket and hoodwink a man, a rich attorney no less, to take you on as a mail-order bride I'll never understand. But I do know that such skills didn't come on your own. What you learned you learned from me, and I deserve to be the recipient of such cunning. Understood?"

"Yes," Dorothy mumbled, determined more than ever to make Vincent the recipient of her acquired cunning.

She could do this. She *would* do this.

But it wouldn't be on the fly like most everything she did. While on horseback, on her way here, she'd planned this out, step by step the way Ronald approached problems.

The first step needed to be tackled now. She couldn't move any farther east. "Vincent," she spoke up, mustering courage and using her saloon girl voice, "I say we save the money we'd spend on train tickets and stay in Denver for a while to work some saloons here."

"Meh," Vincent grunted. "We're going to the train station. I'll decide what we're doing."

"Fine. At least let go of my arm." Dorothy jerked it from his grasp. "Haven't you determined by now that I'm coming along peaceably? Besides, keeping your hands to yourself will be best to keep appearances."

"Fine," Vincent grumbled.

Dorothy stayed close by Vincent as they walked side by side with her smiling a fake cheerfulness to all whom they passed on the way to the train station. By the time they made it to the ticket booth, Vincent seemed to have loosened his shoulders a bit and wasn't side-glancing her every other minute. "Wait here." He motioned with his eyes for her to stay put. "I'll go see about our tickets, see where's the cheapest place for us to go. I'll let that determine our next town."

"All right," Dorothy said, being supportive, letting him feel in control while hoping her words had sunk in. She motioned for him to step up to the ticket booth.

Vincent had stood at the window for barely a half minute before he stepped away. He walked back over to her. "The cheapest tickets would get us nowhere but some two-bit town that'd be worse than that hole you call Craig. I say we stay here in Denver."

"If that's what you want, that's what we'll do," Dorothy said, her heart leaping at her mini victory. For the first time since Vincent's hand smothered her yell she felt something inside her other than darkness.

Chapter 33

Ronald climbed out of the saddle, secured Mehitable to the hitching post, and waddled toward the rundown hotel, his legs struggling to adjust. He gazed at the weathered clapboards covering the hotel. They certainly could use a new coat of the green paint, the existing one having peeled mostly away. He could afford better, but from myriad inquiries on the road, he'd learned this particular hotel on the south side of Denver was commonly used by travelers on a tight budget. Plus, it was located across the street from the stagecoach line and a half block from the train station. If there was a chance to glean information about a particular traveler, this would be the place.

The lobby smelled of whiskey and cheap cigars, most likely from the saloon attached to the side of the hotel. Ronald breathed through his mouth and approached the front desk, hoping the smell didn't reach up to his room.

"What can I do you for?" the man behind the desk asked. He sported a bushy gray mustache that extended from one ear to the other.

"I'd like a room," Ronald said, wondering why the man would ask such an obvious question. To ask how many rooms or how long one would like to rent a room would make more sense.

"How long you plan to stay for?" The man scratched his bushy mustache.

Okay, that question was logical. "It depends," Ronald said, wishing his answer was more logical.

"Depends on what?"

"I'm trying to find my fiancée."

"So you're hopin' the girl of your dreams will waltz right in here and you won't have to do nothing more about it?" The man laughed and shook his head. "Sorry, mister, as much as I think my hotel is right dandy, I think you're lookin' in the wrong place."

Ronald felt a flush of warmth move down his face. "Let me rephrase: my fiancée has gone missing, and I have reason to believe she has been brought to Denver against her will. My hope is to find her and bring her back home where she belongs."

"Well, that makes a whole lot more sense. It still doesn't tell me how long you want your room for."

"I shall book it for two days, and then I'll go from there." Ronald pulled out his billfold. "Have you by chance seen a beautiful woman come through here?"

"Mister, I've seen lots of beautiful women. You gotta be more specific than that."

"She has dark-brown hair the color of golden coffee, bucolic green eyes, and lips so soft and pink they look like a rose," Ronald said, aching with each word. He pulled a photograph of Stanley from his wallet. Logan had given it to him before leaving Craig for this very purpose. He held up the photograph for the attendant to see. He wished he had one of Dorothy. "The man she is with looks like this."

The man scratched his extensive mustache as he gazed at the picture. "You know, I believe there was a man that came in here a day ago that looked a lot like this fellow. And as I think of it now, there was a pretty young thing with him."

"That has got to be them." Ronald reached out, ready to grab the man by his lapels in excitement. He refrained before his hands got too far. "Did they give you their names?"

Of course they didn't—and even if they had, the man had no business giving them to Ronald. In that moment, he realized he hadn't thought this out at all. He'd spent three days straight in the saddle, living off beef jerky and sleeping on the cold ground in a flimsy bedroll. The journey had taken its toll. "Please, I realize you're not at liberty to share such information about your guests, but if you could give me anything, even but a hint or two concerning them, I'd be much obliged."

"Aw, stop your blubbering. I've got no problem telling you what I know."

"Thank you, sir." Ronald reached his hand to shake the man's. The man took a step back, and Ronald retracted his arm and shoved his hand into his pocket.

"Don't go thankin' me yet. I don't have much to tell you, only that I saw the two of them. They registered in the book under Mr. and Mrs. Smith— that's always a red flag to me." He winked, making his bushy mustache wiggle.

"Are they still here?" Ronald hoped his name in the book hadn't raised any suspicions with the man as warmth flushed his face.

"They checked out first thing this morning."

"Did they say where they were headed?"

"Not to me."

"Of course they wouldn't."

"Sorry, mister, but that's all I got for you. You still want a room for two nights?"

"No, just one night." Ronald would have liked to not stay at all and immediately continue his search. To have gotten this close and go away empty-handed nearly crushed him with distress. But his sore legs could not take another minute in the saddle, and the darkness quickly gathering outside would be foolish to venture out in. "Are you sure there is not something you've overlooked? Even the most miniscule thing might be helpful."

The man scratched a thick head of hair that matched his mustache. "It's not much, but now that I think of it, I remember him mentioning the word *train* to the girl."

"Wonderful! Thank you so much."

As Ronald climbed a creaky set of steps up to his room, he realized the hotel attendant's new information wasn't as "wonderful" as he'd first thought. The railway system in the West was not as simple as it used to be once it headed out of this city. Vincent could essentially be taking Dorothy to anywhere east of Denver.

Tomorrow Ronald would head to Omaha, then maybe to St. Louis. After that . . . he wasn't sure. He doubted even the best of planning could help him search for a needle in a haystack, but he had to try.

♠

Chapter 34

Six months later

DOROTHY AWOKE TO POUNDING AT her door. It took her a moment to shake off the grogginess. It was Vincent's knock. He never came to her place this early in the morning. This wasn't good.

"Dorothy, open the door." Vincent's voice came through with obvious impatience.

She climbed out of bed and put on her dressing gown. "Coming." She took her time, walking past a set of drawers, a small table, and one chair that, along with her straw mattress, constituted the sum of the furniture in her place. It was good to make Vincent wait. Ever since they'd left Craig last May, she'd learned that the less she bowed and scraped to her brother the more confidence she had in herself. And the more confidence she had, the more she could work her plans. She just hoped he wasn't onto her. She chewed on her lip and opened the door.

"Finally," Vincent growled and stepped inside. "I'm headed to the station. I want to catch the ten o'clock train to Omaha."

"Really?" Dorothy said in a submissive-sounding voice, but inside, she dreaded what this meant. His leaving right now could be just as disastrous as him figuring out her newest scheme.

"I think they might be onto us here in Denver, so I say it's time to move on."

She breathed deep and braved a modification to his idea. "One more day won't matter. I think it would be good to wait." For the past six months, she'd played her perfect sister role. That had allowed her to sneak in carefully placed suggestions, which Vincent usually fell for. If he'd come to her with this plan for Omaha just a month earlier, she would have been elated—it was exactly what she'd been working toward with her original plan. She would have convinced him to scout out a new town without her. The moment after he would have left, she would have walked away from this life. She was, after all, twenty-one now and no longer his ward. But she had a better plan now, one based on real information, not lies her brother had fed her concerning his guardianship. Vincent leaving town at this moment would ruin everything.

"Why wait?" Vincent wrinkled his brow.

"I get paid tonight," she said with a straight face. It was a flat-out lie. After tonight, she was done with them. There'd been more than enough lies pouring from her mouth these past six months and in her short time with Ronald Smith before that. But they'd been a means to an end.

"All right, one more night. You just make sure it's a productive one, you hear?"

"Oh, I'll make sure." She figured if all went as planned, it would be very productive—for everyone but Vincent. He really wasn't as sharp as she used to think he was. Not even close. "Do you have any idea how long it will take to go to Omaha and get things set up?" she asked to keep him thinking she was on his side.

Vincent inched toward the door. "I'm guessing at least a good week." He stepped out of her place and shut the door.

Dorothy locked the door behind him and then walked calmly over to the room's single window—just in case Vincent still had his spare key and decided to poke his head back in. She peered outside onto the street below. When she spotted Vincent's back and determined he was in fact heading away from her, then and only then did she dare dash to her tiny dresser. She threw open the bottom drawer and pulled out her white blouse and blue skirt. She hurriedly changed, grateful for Wilhelmina's respectable outfit. It and her brown skirt and cream-colored blouse had enabled her to sneak out during the day. She'd gotten to know a handful of good people while Vincent slept off the whiskey of the previous night's card game, all the while assuming she was sleeping too.

Dorothy brushed out her hair, thinking with fondness of two particular women. They were likely the only ones she'd have time to say a proper good-bye to, given all she had to do.

She twisted her hair, piled it on her head, and pinned it into place while looking into the handkerchief-sized mirror that hung above the dresser. Once her hair looked presentable, she looked around her apartment. She would not miss this place at all, though it had felt less of a prison than any past place she'd lived while working with Vincent. Having a goal to work toward certainly helped. *Dear sweet Ronald, you are to thank for that.* She smiled at the memory of Ronald's numerous checklists and well laid plans. Her time with him had taught her much. She grabbed her coat from its hook and walked out onto the landing. She shut the door and hurried down the stairs, not looking back.

She approached the clerk.

He stood behind the counter, dusting out the mail cubby holes of the rundown hotel that let its room out one month at a time. He pulled his attention from his task and looked at Dorothy. "Ah, Miss Conner. Good to see you so bright and early this morning."

"Thank you, Mr. Willis." She placed her hand on the counter. "I will be checking out first thing tomorrow morning. I believe my room has been paid in full up through this week. Am I not correct?"

"Yes, you are."

"I would appreciate any refund you might care to give me for the remaining five nights I have paid for." Dorothy thought how that extra dollar or so would be helpful while she got resettled. "I realize that wasn't part of our agreement when I moved in, but I'm just saying that it would be helpful. Moving to another city costs money."

"Sure, Miss Conner, I can do that for you."

Dorothy cringed inside at his use of her false name. She breathed out a sigh as he counted two dollars into her hand. She was determined this was the last time she'd ever go by a name other than Dorothy Bednar. "Thank you so much, Mr. Willis." She inclined her head as a token of thanks, pulled on her coat, and walked out.

She glanced at the clock built into the brick above the door of the bank. It read 9:50. The library would be open in ten minutes. She'd head there first. It was a good five blocks away. She'd stumbled upon it by accident one afternoon while walking out her frustrations concerning Vincent. The image of Ronald's law books neatly lining the shelves behind his desk had come to mind that day, and she'd wondered at that time if there was some information inside that library that she could use against Vincent. She'd found that and more: someone to teach her to read them.

Her friend Lila, the librarian, was unlocking the front door of the library when she arrived.

"Good morning, Dorothy." Lila opened the door and motioned for her to step inside. "What brings you around so early in the day?" she asked, looking Dorothy in the eye. "Oh, gracious be, I can see it in your eyes. You're going through with it, aren't you?"

"Yes!" Dorothy grasped the hand Lila held out for her.

"When?"

"Tonight."

"So soon?" Lila blinked several times. "Last we spoke I got the impression it was several days away at the very least."

"My brother, unfortunately, has got the itch to leave sooner than I'd anticipated. My only chance is tonight, whether we're ready for it or not."

"Have you arranged things with Chief Holmes yet?"

"I'm going there next." Dorothy took in a deep breath. She'd confessed to the chief weeks ago but still had two weeks left of cleaning the jail to pay off her sentence. "You were on the way. I stopped here first to say goodbye and thank you again for all your instruction. And giving me the encouragement and books I needed." She reached out and pulled Lila into an embrace. "You and your brother helped me see that I have a right to a better life. Will you give him my thanks again?"

"You are most welcome, dear." Lila returned the hug. "And I'll certainly tell him."

Every time Dorothy had met with Lila's brother, one of Denver's best attorneys—who'd donated his time no less—the man reminded her of Ronald. This always pained Dorothy inwardly. She'd rather not see him again now that her plea of guilty to aiding a criminal had been made and a lesser sentence given in exchange for her helping to catch Vincent in the act. She'd wished many times it had been Ronald who was assisting her with all the legal matters, but she knew that was not realistic. Hoping Ronald would still be there and willing to give her another chance if she returned was not realistic either. Widow Nettie Harris was a fine catch. Or he likely had moved back to Chicago.

Dorothy released Lila and petitioned with her eyes. "Right now I could use some more words of encouragement. Do you think the chief would let me off for good behavior? I certainly don't want to be working at the jail if Vincent's in there." Neither did she want to skip out on her responsibility if things fell apart and Vincent forced her to leave with him tomorrow.

"I imagine he would." Lila smiled. "My brother admitted the chief has a soft spot for you."

"Thanks. You always lift my spirits. Well, I'd better be going." Dorothy backed away. "I wish we could chat longer, reminisce on those times I thought I'd shocked you with my stories. I appreciate how you took them all in stride." She wiped away the tears gratitude had prompted from her eyes. "Thanks. Goodbye, Lila."

"Goodbye, Dorothy." Lila waved, and Dorothy slipped out the door.

Dorothy hurried along to the police station, all the way hoping Chief Holmes and the officer he'd chosen would be ready enough to enact their plan tonight. When she got there, she walked inside and up to the main desk. "Is Chief Holmes in?" she asked.

The officer behind the desk brushed a crumb off his blue uniform, catching a finger on one of its gold buttons. "Sorry, but he is out for the rest of the day. Is there something I can help you with?"

Dorothy winced and dropped into a chair adjacent to the desk. "No, no you can't." Only the police chief, and an officer she didn't know yet, knew about this case. "Do you know where I might find him?"

"No. Sorry, miss." The officer leaned his head slightly to one side. "I'm sure there is someone else here in the station who can help you if you could just tell me what's troubling you."

"The chief was helping me with something, and in return, I was to help him. There's another officer involved, but I have yet to meet him, and I don't know his name. But it's important to let either the chief or this officer know that we need to act tonight, or it is all for naught. I wish I could tell you more, but I can't."

"I think you did just fine. Hold on." The officer slipped down a hallway that held a row of offices. He returned several minutes later followed by another officer.

Dorothy startled when she saw the other officer. "You? You were at—"

"Yes," he responded. "I'm Officer Spencer, by the way. We'll talk back here." He motioned for her to follow him.

Her worn-out shoes clapped against the tile floor down the long hallway as she followed the man she'd seen last night at her saloon. Only he hadn't been wearing the blue uniform and rounded, narrow-brimmed hat last night. He'd worn a white shirt, a thin black tie looped in an impeccably neat bow, and a black cowboy hat. Once seated in a small office, and the man shut the door, she let out her feelings. "You weren't there by accident last night, were you?"

"Nope, but I tried to make it appear as such, finding myself involved in a poker game when I'd had no intent at all to play. Was I convincing?"

"Yes, very." Dorothy nodded. "Though you never played with Vincent."

"That was on purpose. I was observing. I made sure he saw me though."

Dorothy nodded. "So I take it Chief Holmes has told you all about me?"

"Enough."

"And about what needs to be done?"

"Yes."

"That's good because it has to happen tonight."

"Tonight?" Officer Spencer blew out a breath. "I presume you have a good reason for this bothersome change of plans? I barely learned of this undercover assignment yesterday. More preparation would be prudent."

"My brother is nervous. He wants to move on to another city. I convinced him to stay one more night, but I doubt I could get him to stay any longer."

"I see." Officer Spencer twisted one end of his long mustache. "We have much to discuss then if we are to move on this tonight."

An hour later, Dorothy left the station feeling overwhelmed. It would take every ounce of her acting skills, if not more, to perform what she and Officer Spencer had lain out.

On her way back to her place, she stopped by the corner bakery to bid her friend Susan goodbye.

"I'm sad to see you go but happy at the same time," Susan said after Dorothy explained the reason for her visit.

"Thank you again for allowing me to work for you here and there," Dorothy said as Susan gave her a hug. "I could have never managed to save enough to move on without you."

"Oh pish." Susan let go of Dorothy and flicked her wrist. "It was you doing me and my husband a favor. Your cookies have done our bakery good. We'll forever be indebted to you for that recipe."

Dorothy said her final farewell and hurried back to her apartment. She needed to eat something and then bathe and do herself up just right so as to lend any bit of extra confidence she could muster.

The sun had set, and the evening air held a chill as she walked to what looked like her last night of work at this Denver saloon. If circumstances didn't lend themselves to revealing Vincent's cheating, he would be on that train to Omaha first thing in the morning. Dorothy refused to be on that train with him. She might have to fall back on her original plan—a plan she'd prefer not to follow. In that plan, she would convince Vincent to go on to Omaha without her. It would be easier to set things up without her. Then the moment he left, she would run. But he would undoubtedly know where she'd run to. This was the big flaw in her old plan. Her turning twenty-one meant nothing to Vincent. He'd find her and try to pull her back into her old life or ruin her new life in his attempts.

"Evening," the bartender said to Dorothy as she walked in.

"Good evening, Slim." Dorothy returned the greeting and walked into the back room to hang up her coat.

As she set to the tasks of her job, it felt as though less drinks needed serving, empty spots at the bar abounded, and not a single poker table held a game. If business didn't pick up, she feared Vincent would walk in, have a drink, decide tonight was not a good night to work their act, and walk out. He would have given Dorothy her extra night, and he'd leave Denver tomorrow.

The evening wore on. Dorothy's eyes kept skirting toward the swinging doors. Each time they swung in, she welcomed the new customers with extra attention. "Let me get you a drink," she offered before they even reached the bar. "Why don't you have a seat rather than standing at the bar." She'd pat the back of a chair set around one of the poker tables. "Would you like me to give you a deck of cards so you can play a little solitaire while you wait?"

Three of the five poker tables now held paying customers, some merely drinking and chewing the fat with the man sitting next to them. One table actually engaged in a game of poker.

The front doors swung open, and Dorothy instinctively looked over. Vincent strutted in. She steeled her nerves and invited him to sit at a table so as to not appear to treat him any differently. He sent her a glance that communicated volumes: he didn't like the numbers. A fuller saloon would have been his preference as much as Dorothy's.

"I guess I'll sit," he mumbled and lowered into a chair. "Whiskey," he said to Dorothy and then turned his attention to the three men at the table, picking up the deck of cards she'd left there earlier.

Dorothy headed to the bar and noticed the doors swing open. Officer Spencer strolled in. He wore a blue shirt this time. His tie was as neat as before, his black cowboy hat spotless and his pants pressed. If she hadn't known him, she would have sized him up as a man with money and willing to gamble it. She let out a sigh of relief.

She didn't have to bother guiding him to a chair. Vincent did that for her.

"Sir," Vincent called out. He held up a hand and motioned for Officer Spencer to come his way. "We need one more for a decent game of poker. You care to join us?"

Officer Spencer appeared surprised. "Oh, all right. Don't mind if I do."

When Dorothy returned with Vincent's drink, the cards had been dealt, and another man in overalls had joined them. The table had five players, each looking eerily similar to the men sitting around that table in Missouri when Vincent had been caught last time. Officer Spencer and the man in the overalls ordered beers. Sauntering around the table on her way to the bar, she caught a glimpse at everyone's hands. She hurried back with the drinks and then lingered, giving out signals, some to Vincent, some to Officer Spencer.

By the time Vincent's table was done with their third game, Dorothy breathed easier. Vincent had won only one of the hands. He was playing it safe before he went for the cards up his sleeve, which he was bound to do this next game. She could see it in his eyes. With the sweep of her hand, she gave the signal to Officer Spencer—moving an imaginary strand of hair out of her eyes. It was his turn to deal. It was now or never.

Officer Spencer picked up the cards and shuffled. If Dorothy hadn't watched Vincent practice all these years, she would have never even suspected the officer was stacking the deck. He did it with a finesse her brother had never had. That's probably why Vincent preferred to hide cards up his sleeves instead.

Dorothy strolled around the table. "Does anyone care for some pretzels?" she said as she glanced at their cards. Vincent had two kings—clubs and diamonds—a nine, a two, and a five. She was amazed that Officer Spencer had actually managed to deal that. A sense of thrill mingled in with her jitter of nerves. She hid them both behind her fake smile. No one responded to her request, and Slim the bartender didn't appear to need her, so she kept strolling. She gave signals to Vincent about everyone's hands except Officer Spencer's. He kept his hand pulled together as he threw in his first chip. After he asked for two cards, he placed them facedown on the table and threw in another chip.

Vincent gave her a sideways glance as he threw in his chip to stay in the game, his signal for her to give him Officer Spencer's hand. She tugged on her earlobe, telling him she couldn't see his cards. Vincent heaved his shoulders, apparently believing her this time.

Relieved, she let *her* shoulders relax. True, she couldn't see Officer Spencer's cards, but she knew what they were: a straight flush—nine, ten, jack, queen, king—all in spades. She could hardly believe that Officer Spencer had liked her idea of how to trap Vincent. But then again, her way had been tested.

"I'll take three cards," Vincent said.

Officer Spencer dealt him three cards as Dorothy strolled by, catching a glimpse of three more worthless low cards.

Vincent "accidently" knocked his empty whiskey glass off the table. Bending down, he caught it on the way to the floor. He sat back up and patted the top of the glass. "No harm done," he said to no one in particular. He then threw in a chip. "I'll meet you and raise," he said and then fanned out his hands sufficiently for Dorothy to see. Four kings and a seven of hearts.

"Let me take this out of your way." Dorothy reached for the empty whiskey glass, grateful for an excuse to get herself away from that table. Just like last April in that Missouri saloon, she didn't care to be present when Vincent and Officer Spencer kept raising the ante and then showed their cards. She hurried the glass to the bar and then turned her attention to the table with the other poker game going.

"Can anyone here use another drink or some pretzels?" she asked the other table of men.

"I'll take a beer."

"Me too."

Thank you, thank you, thank you. Dorothy scurried to the bar, not daring to look in Vincent's direction. She didn't care if he was mad at her. He would not be at her apartment later on to express his anger. Hopefully. "Two beers, Slim." As she waited for the bartender to fill the mugs, she maneuvered herself such that she could see Officer Spencer's face but not Vincent's.

"I'll meet your two and raise two," Officer Spencer said straight-faced and calm.

She delivered the beers to the other table and then hurried toward the back room, passing Slim at the bar on her way. "I've got to go to the privy," she said, feeling like she was reliving a bad dream. Only this time, she didn't run outside but stayed in the back room and peered around the doorframe.

All the players at Vincent's table had folded except him and Officer Spencer.

Vincent looked around the room, probably looking for her. After a moment or two, he said, "I raise." He tossed in two chips.

"I'll meet you," Officer Spencer slid two chips into the hefty pile, "and I call."

This is it. Dorothy bit on her lip. She didn't look through the doorway, only listened.

"Four kings," came Vincent's voice.

"Impossible," Officer Spencer said, "because I have a straight flush, king high. I say your king of spades came out of your sleeve because one certainly didn't come out of mine. What do you have to say for yourself?"

Dorothy could hear a chair topple over. She braved a look.

Vincent was on his feet. "I've nothing to say. How about you explain?"

"Fine, I say we let these other gentlemen pat us down and look in both our sleeves."

Vincent raised his fists in front of his face. "Don't you lay a finger on me."

"Sounds like you've got something to hide," the man in the overalls said.

"Yeah," the man at the table next to Vincent agreed. He stood and tugged on the sleeve of Vincent's jacket while ducking a punch from Vincent's other hand. Cards fluttered to the ground.

Officer Spencer stood, pulled out his badge, and flashed it in Vincent's face. "I'm with the Denver City Police Department, and you, Mr. Vincent Bednar, are under arrest."

"What? I never gave you my name." Vincent jerked his head from side to side, looking desperately around the room. Then he tried to run. The man in the overalls tackled him. "I'm not alone in this. Dorothy! Get that good-for-nothing saloon girl out here. If I'm going to jail, then so is she. She's as guilty as the day is long."

"She's the one who put the police department onto you, Mr. Bednar." Officer Spencer clamped a set of handcuffs on Vincent.

"What? She's lying to you, playing you like a fiddle." A string of profanity then shot from Vincent's mouth.

Officer Spencer dragged him toward the door. "I will be the judge of that." He laughed. "Actually, the police department already has. And if a judge agrees with us, your days of cheating and abuse are over, Mr. Bednar."

Chapter 35

RONALD SHOVED AN ADDITIONAL PAIR of socks into his suitcase. "One can never have too many spare stockings," he said to Bill.

Bill moved to his side and smoothed out a shirt disrupted by the socks. "You were always the neat one, making me look like a slob, but here I am fixing your packing job. You really have changed, haven't you?"

"At least somewhat." Ronald closed his suitcase. "I would not have told you so if I had not. Good heavens, six months ago when I came for a visit, it about killed me to take three weeks off. Now you've got me taking off an entire two months to go on a safari." He shook his head. "I still can't believe I'm actually going."

"Well, big brother, you are." Bill scratched his clean-shaven upper lip.

It was about the only feature on Bill's face that didn't look like Ronald's.

"I have to admit," Bill continued, "I was rather surprised when you agreed to come so easily. I came out here fully expecting to have a fight on my hands, you know, in getting you to come with me to Africa. Even though I am paying for it."

"Well, you didn't." Ronald snapped the latches shut on his suitcase. "I suppose I am ready for a vacation, for a diversion."

"Why is that?" Bill pushed the suitcase out of the way, sat down on the edge of Ron's bed, and looked him in the eye. "For the past four days you've been showing me around Craig, Colorado, and I've been loving it—except for one thing. I've been quietly waiting for you to open up as to the reason for all this 'change' you talk about in yourself. But you haven't. What's eating at you, Ron? Your letters are another thing that have changed. They've been so infrequent. Mother's worried about you, and frankly, I am too."

"I'd rather not talk about what's in the past, only what lies ahead." Ronald let out a quick breath, determined to keep his thoughts on the thrill of his upcoming trip. Mulling over mistakes made six months ago accomplished nothing.

"It's a gal, isn't it?" Bill asked. "You finally ventured past that old maid—what was her name? Oh yes, Wilhelmina Cooper. Good for you. Ah, but she's broken your heart. I can see it in your eyes." Bill gave him a pat on the back. "Don't worry. This trip will be just what you need to get over her."

Ronald pulled his suitcase off the bed and set it by the door so it would be ready for their departure first thing in the morning. "Come now. Let's go get us some supper. I am famished," he said, purposely changing the subject. "By the way, I hope you don't mind if we engage in some entertainment same as last night."

Bill stood and followed Ronald out of the bedroom. "Playing poker with a bunch of farmers down at the local saloon is hardly my idea of entertainment. It's merely a diversion, a sharpening of one's analytical skills."

"No wonder I enjoy it so."

"Is that why we're doing it again tonight?" Bill flicked a hand at him. "I come out West to pay my big brother a visit, and what does he want to do? Play card games rather than take me to see the sights of the Wild West."

"First of all, for the past four days I have shown you everything of interest there is to be seen around Craig. It's not that wild anymore. It is 1897. A new century is almost upon us. Second of all, I'm doing it for Sunny, the owner of the place. I had my fill of poker last night, but today she stopped by my office while I was there tying up some loose ends, and she asked me to come by tonight. She said the same fellows would be there and that they wanted to play a few more hands and buy me a drink as a proper send-off for my adventure in Africa."

Bill climbed down the stairs behind Ronald. "All right, I'll play some poker if you answer my question."

"We've really nothing else to do this evening, so we may as well pass the time dining out and then engaging in an enjoyable game or two of cards."

"I didn't mean the question of why we're playing poker again tonight." Bill punched him in the arm as they reached the bottom of the stairs. "I meant about it being a gal. That's the only explanation as to why you're so bothered."

Logan walked in the front door as they moved into the entry. Logan took off his hat and tossed it onto the rack of hooks. "Howdy, Ron. Howdy, Bill. You fellas headed out for a bite to eat, I'm guessin'?"

"That is correct," Ronald said. "We're dining at Sunny's tonight. Don't wait up; we are going to play a few rounds of cards after we eat. But we'll for sure say a proper goodbye to you tomorrow morning before we leave."

"I'll cook you two up a nice breakfast before you go." Logan smiled. "We're goin' to miss you around here, Ronald."

"Thank you. That is most kind." Ronald grabbed his hat from the rack. As he placed his hat on his head, a wave of regret resurfaced. He thought about the nice clothing and easy life Logan could be living right now if only Ronald had not given his word to Stanley. The fact that it had all been for naught made it even more painful. If only Susannah and Logan had fought for the appeal on their own. But they hadn't.

Once out on the porch, Bill grabbed him by the arm and prevented him from descending the stairs. "Enough stalling. I'm not ten, and you aren't the mighty big brother anymore. I'm not going to back down. Tell me about this gal. She obviously got under your skin."

Ronald heaved a sigh, figuring he'd eventually have to talk about it, so he may as well get it over with before they got to Sunny's. "Yes, there was a 'gal' as you put it. But I would like to think of her as a woman, a beautiful woman, in more ways than the mere obvious. And yes, my heart has been bruised."

"We'll have plenty of time to talk in the stage tomorrow morning. Now that my suspicions have been substantiated, I'm willing to wait." Bill gave Ronald a slap on the shoulder.

By the time they reached Sunny's place, the sun was setting. Ronald disliked how the days grew shorter as winter approached. But like other things he disliked, he faced the situation and adjusted accordingly, albeit rather recalcitrant, like he had been with Benedict's will and four months earlier when his search for Dorothy had hit a dead end, and he'd been forced to do the logical thing: give it up.

Bill ordered the chicken and dumplings from a somewhat distracted Sunny—she kept looking at the clock on the wall. Ronald ordered the roast beef. He smiled ever so slightly, remembering how that had been Dorothy's favorite. That was all he had now of Dorothy: memories. And a large, empty spot in his heart that he was unable to fill. He'd worked around it, however, carrying on at a somewhat lethargic pace. He was glad Bill had come. And maybe Bill was right; getting out of Craig and going on safari would be good for him. And when they returned, maybe he *would* move back to Chicago like he'd planned to four years ago—if he didn't have a wife and a forthcoming family to keep him here in Craig.

A new waitress served them their food. Ronald would have preferred Sunny; this new gal wasn't as careful—just like the other three Sunny had gone through since Dorothy had left. "Sunny is busy I take it?" Ronald asked as the young girl, who couldn't have been more than sixteen, placed his roast beef dinner on the table in front of him, letting some of the gravy spill onto the tablecloth.

"Yeah." The girl plopped Bill's chicken and dumplings onto the table. "An old friend of hers just got into town on the stage. Sunny's helping her get settled in upstairs, I guess."

Ronald nodded his thanks to the waitress and dug into his food—who knew when he'd have his next decent meal. "Promise me I'm not going to regret this trip," he said to Bill. "Perhaps I should just follow you as far as Chicago, stop there, and visit Mother for a few days and then return to Craig." Long enough to pack up and move.

"I promise you'll not regret it." Bill ate a full dumpling before saying, "Come on, tell me you've had time to use a rifle while sitting behind your desk. Just because you live out West, it doesn't sound like you've been acting much like a cowboy. Nothing like smothering a heartache by making it pump up a storm while tracking down a wild animal or two." He pointed to Ronald's freshly laundered shirt. "It'll do you good to roll around in some dirt."

"I can enjoy my trip to Africa just fine without rolling around in the dirt, thank you."

They finished their meals. Ronald left the new girl a sizeable tip despite all the gravy on the tablecloth, and they ventured over to the saloon section of the building. There, at the same table as last night, sat Marshal Hank Walker, Stewart Hoy, and Sam Decker. A pile of cards rested in the middle of the table, untouched, like it was waiting for Ronald and Bill to get there before being shuffled. Two empty chairs leaned against the table.

"Ah, there you are," Stewart spoke up, sweeping his arm in the air. "It's time we get started. Daylight's done already burnt out."

Ronald righted and slid into one of the empty chairs next to Bill. His back to the restaurant, and his eyes looked through the front window out onto a dark Yampa Avenue. Stewart started dealing, and Sam scooted a pile of chips into place in front of each of them. Last night, they had deemed the chips worth a penny apiece. "Playing for high stakes again tonight?" Ronald asked.

Sam scratched his graying mustache. "Yep. And the man with the most chips at the end of the night gets his cookie free and clear. The rest of us pitch in an actual penny apiece to pay for it."

"High stakes all right," Bill said with a laugh.

Ronald smiled. "They'd be even higher if only those cookies came with a—" *ruby red kiss in the corner.* "Never mind," he said. "Let's get started."

Bill cleared his throat. "I'm afraid we can't play as long as we did last night—"

"'Cause you're leaving for Africa in the mornin'," Sam finished for him.

"Chicago first," Ronald corrected Sam as he picked up his cards to see his hand. They were junk. Tossing a three of diamonds and a nine and two of clubs onto the table, he kept his queen of spades and king of hearts. "I'll take three," he said to Lucas.

"I'll take two," Bill said along with Sam and Hank.

While Ronald waited for his new cards to be dealt, he sensed someone walk up behind him. Everyone seemed intent on receiving their cards, so he thought nothing of it. Soon though he saw a female hand with slender fingers reach over his shoulder and point to his cards.

A whisper sounded in his ear. "That ain't no pair—two wrongs don't make a right. But then again, maybe the queen of spades and a king of hearts can lead to something good."

Ronald's heart leaped in his chest. *That voice!* He spun around in his chair. "Dorothy!" His face, mere inches from hers, caught her eyes as she straightened back up. He jumped to his feet. Latching onto her arms, he pulled her to where he could gaze into them. "You're here. I can't believe you are actually here! Sorry, that was not at all a logical statement. Of course you are here. I can see you standing in front of me yet—"

"Shh." She placed her finger on his lips. "I need to apologize." She ran her finger along his lips, causing a most delectable sensation. "I have much to explain and would love to do so."

"Dorothy? Is this *the* Dorothy?" Bill's voice interrupted Ronald's euphoria. "And is she the . . ."

Ronald turned toward his brother. "Yes. And where are my manners?" He held out his trembling hand in front of Dorothy. "Bill, I'd like to introduce you to Miss Dorothy Bednar." He looked into her eyes. "And, Dorothy, this is my brother, William."

"Pleased to meet you, William." Dorothy held out her hand.

Bill kissed the top of her fingers after he'd lifted them to his mouth. "Nice to meet you. Months ago, my brother told me about you. But not nearly enough."

Dorothy pulled her hands in and clasped them together in front of her. "So, Ronald, may I speak with you for a moment? Privately?" Her voice sounded unsteady yet hopeful.

"Certainly." Ronald placed a hand on the small of her back and led her a few feet away to a somewhat quiet corner of the saloon.

Dorothy gently bit her lip. "Ronald . . . are you—I mean is it possible . . . that you are still unmarried?"

"Yes, still unmarried," Ronald said, gulping down a spot of nerves.

She inched closer to him. With her body mere inches from his, she tilted her head back and gazed into his eyes. "Ronald, I only left because I had to—for your sake. You don't understand my brother like I do. I also left for my sake. I know that now. I could have never been shed of Vincent until I learned to face him first. I've done that now, thanks to you."

"Me?" Ronald's head felt as if it were in a daze.

She seemed to hesitate, then asked, "Dare I hope you still have feelings for me?" Her voice was but a wisp, though it sounded as if declared by trumpets. She ducked her head. "I still care for you." She raised it back up, stood on her tiptoes, and brought her lips near his ear. Brushing them against his lobe, she whispered, "Stronger now than ever since I have been apart from you all these months." She lowered from off her toes and looked him in the eyes. "I came to Craig this time as Dorothy Bednar. No taking anyone else's place. No lies, no secrets. I'll understand if you say no, but Mr. Ronald Smith, will you give me another chance as your mail-order bride?"

Ronald wrapped hands around her waist, pulling her against him. "Absolutely. I will give you another chance so long as you give me one," he said louder than he had intended. He brushed his poor manners aside, not caring a single whit, lowered his mouth onto hers, and kissed her full on the lips.

Bill's laughter sounded in the background along with a catcall or two. Ronald ignored the noise and kissed Dorothy again.

"Hey, what about Africa?" Bill's voice teased.

Ronald reluctantly ended his kiss and held Dorothy at arm's length. "Dear me," he muttered, realizing his predicament. "My brother and I are leaving for Africa tomorrow. We'll be gone for two months. Our tickets are purchased. Everything is set in place. Yet you stand before me. I don't care to leave now."

"I'll be here when you return," Dorothy said. "Sunny said I could have my old job back. Just knowing you still care for me is enough to help me wait. It is much more than I had dared hope for."

Ronald didn't want her to have to wait. He didn't want to wait.

An irrational idea emerged in his head. He latched onto it despite how it went against his nature. "Dorothy, come with me to Africa."

"Africa?" Dorothy's voice warbled. "Wouldn't that take time to arrange?"

"She can take my place," Bill offered. He had turned his chair and was obviously listening in on their conversation. "Mother would more than compensate me for the ocean liner ticket." He wore a coy grin. "And I'm sure I can take another train if there's not room on yours to Chicago."

Ronald gazed at his brother. Then he turned to Dorothy. "Dorothy, it can be our honeymoon," he said with an unfamiliar burst of exhilaration. Not one ounce of premeditation was in this plan, but he loved it, and it kept coming. "We can get married in Chicago in the cathedral down the street from my parents' home. Mother without a doubt will pull together a grand wedding within the week's time before we need to leave for Africa." He glanced around the saloon and into Sunny's Place, seeing the faces of friends gazing his way. These were all Dorothy's friends too. "Or we could have Mother leave immediately and attend our wedding ceremony here in Craig if you wish."

"I know she'd come," Bill said.

Dorothy took hold of his hands. "Are you asking me to be your mail-order bride once again?"

"No, I am asking you to be my wife, to become Mrs. Ronald Smith."

"Oh, Ronald, yes. And this time, I can rightfully change my name," she said and smiled.

Dorothy's Oatmeal Raisin Cookies

Cookie:

> 1 cup butter
> ¾ cup sugar
> 2 tbsp. molasses
> 2 eggs
> 1 tsp. vanilla extract

Cream above ingredients together, then add:

> 1 ⅔ cup flour
> ½ tsp. baking powder
> ½ tsp. baking soda
> ½ tsp. salt
> ½ tsp. ground cinnamon

Mix together until smooth, then add:

> 2 cups oatmeal
> ¾ cup raisins

Mix together, then drop 2 tbsp. for a smaller cookie or 4 tbsp. for a larger cookie onto a greased baking sheet. Bake in a 350-degree oven for 10 minutes for small cookies or 13 minutes for large cookies. Cool. Drizzle with glaze and chopped walnuts if desired.

Glaze:

> ¼ cup butter
> ⅓ cup milk
> ¾ cup sugar

Place above ingredients in a small saucepan, bring to a boil, stirring often, and cook to a soft ball stage. Remove from heat and whip with a whisk or beaters until thickened (2 to 3 minutes) and glaze is of spreading consistency. If the glaze becomes too thick, stir in additional milk, 1 tsp. at a time, until thinned to desired consistency. Using a spoon or a piping bag, drizzle glaze onto cookies in a zigzag pattern.

Makes 30 small cookies or 15 large cookies. Recipe can be easily doubled.

About the Author

CAROLYN TWEDE FRANK LIVES IN the Rocky Mountains and has always enjoyed old black-and-white movies, especially ones depicting the American frontier and those spiced up with a bit of romance. *His Accidental Bride* is Carolyn's fourth historical romance novel set in the Old West. Carolyn is not new to the genre of historical fiction. Some of her earlier works include *The Hitler Dilemma* and *Trapped in East Germany*. When Carolyn is not writing, she enjoys gardening, sewing, renovating houses, and playing with her grandkids. She also loves taking road trips in the western United States with her husband, scoping out interesting tidbits of history to weave into her next novel.